"You asked me if I could help you see what lies ahead of you. I did as you asked. I was with you and you with me; watching, perceiving, trying to understand." Rising and walking forward, she lifted a paw and placed it on his bare thigh.

"You are doomed to unremitting misery, your quest to failure, the rest of your life to cold emptiness. Unless you end this now. Go home, back to your village and back to your family. Before it is too late. Before you die." Her paw slipped off his leg.

Ehomba looked away, feeling the warmth of the fire against his back, and considered the dog's words . . .

⚔ ⚔ ⚔ ⚔

PRAISE FOR
CARNIVORES OF LIGHT AND DARKNESS
The first volume in the Journeys of the Catechist
by Alan Dean Foster

"The effect of this book is that of tales within tales, like those of Sinbad and his many voyages. . . . This is Foster at his best, thoughtful and fun."
—*Booklist*

"This odd and engaging fantasy has an apparently African setting, but . . . owes far more to Grimm's fairy tales. . . . It's a wondrous journey."
—*Locus*

P9-DVI-846

more . . .

INTO THE
THINKING
KINGDOMS

Also by Alan Dean Foster

The Journeys of the Catechist Series:

Carnivores of Light and Darkness
Into the Thinking Kingdoms
A Triumph of Souls

The Dig
The I Inside

ALAN DEAN FOSTER

JOURNEYS OF THE CATECHIST · BOOK 2

INTO THE THINKING KINGDOMS

ASPECT®

WARNER BOOKS

A Time Warner Company

WARNER BOOKS EDITION

Cover design by Don Puckey
Cover illustration by Keith Parkinson

Warner Books, Inc.
1271 Avenue of the Americas
New York, NY 10020

Visit our Web site at
www.twbookmark.com

 A Time Warner Company

Printed in the United States of America

Originally published in hardcover by Warner Books
First Paperback Printing: February 2000

10 9 8 7 6 5 4 3 2

For my niece, Alexandra Rachel Carroll

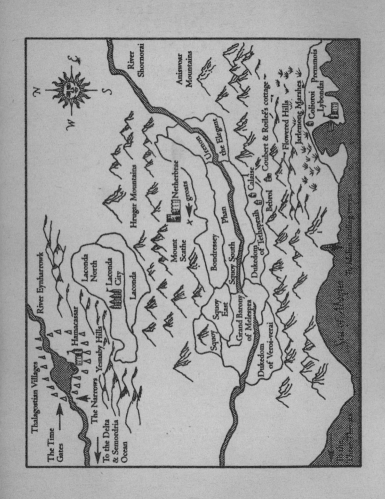

INTO THE THINKING KINGDOMS

I

The most powerful man in the world couldn't sleep.

At least Hymneth the Possessed thought of himself as the most powerful man in the world, and since those few who might have contemplated disputing him were no longer alive, he felt comfortable with having appropriated the title to himself. And if not the most powerful man, then he was certainly the most powerful mage. Granted that there might be a handful of imprudent individuals foolhardy enough to stand before him as men and women, there were none who dared confront him in the realm of the arcane and necromantic. There *he* was the Master of masters, and all who dabbled in the black arts must pay him homage, or suffer his whims at their peril.

Yet despite the knowing of this, and the sum of all his knowing, he could not sleep.

Rising from his bed, a graven cathedral to Morpheus that had taken the ten finest wood-carvers in the land six years to render from select pieces of cobal, redwood, cherry, walnut, and purpleheart, Hymneth walked slowly to the vaulted window that looked out upon his kingdom. The rich and populous reach of Ehl-Larimar stretched out before him, from the rolling green hills at the base of his mountaintop fortress retreat to the distant, sun-washed shores of the boundless ocean called Aurel. Every home and farm, every shop and industry within that field of view acknowledged *him* as supreme over all other earthly authorities. He tried to submerge his soul in the warmth and security of that understanding, to let it wash over and burnish him like a shower of liquid pleasure. But he could not.

He couldn't shake the accursed dream that had kept him awake.

Worse than the loss of sleep was his inability to recall the details. Nebulous, hazy images of other beings had tormented his rest. Awake, he found that he was unable to remember them with any degree of resolution. His inability to identify them meant it was impossible to deal with their condition or take steps to prevent their return. He was convinced that some of the likenesses had been human, others not. Why they should disturb him so he could not say. Unable to distinguish them from any other wraiths, he could not formulate a means for dealing with them directly. The situation was more than merely irritating. Priding himself as he did on the precision with which he conducted all his dealings, the persisting inexactitude of the dream was disquieting.

He would go out, he decided. Out among his people. Receiving their obeisance, grandly deigning to acknowledge their fealty, always made him feel better. Walking to the center of the grandiose but impeccably decorated bedroom, he stood in the center of the floor, raised his arms, and recited one of several thousand small yet potent litanies he knew by heart.

Light materialized that was solid, as opposed to the feeble sunbeams that entered through the tall window. Taking the form of small yellow fingers that were detached from hands, it set about dressing him. He preferred light to the hands of human servitors. The feathery touch of commandeered glow would not pinch him, or forget to do up a button, or scratch against his neck. It would never choose the wrong undergarments or lose track of a valuable pin or necklace. And light would never try to stick a poisoned dagger into his back, twisting it fiercely, slicing through nerve and muscle until rich red Hymneth blood gushed forth over the polished tile of the floor, staining the bedposts and ruining the invaluable rugs fashioned from the flayed coats of rare, dead animals.

So what if the digits of congealed yellow light reminded his attendants not of agile, proficient fingers but coveys of sallow, diseased worms writhing and twisting as they coiled and probed about his person? Servants' flights of torpid imagination did not concern him.

While the silken undergarments caressed his body, the luxurious outer raiment transformed him into a figure of magnificence fit to do sartorial battle with the emperor birds-of-paradise. The horned helmet of chased steel and the red-and-purple cloak contributed mightily to the plenary image of irresistible power and majesty. Seven feet tall fully dressed, he was ready to go out among his people and seek the balm of their benison.

The pair of griffins who lived out their lives chained to the outside of his bedroom door snapped to attention as he emerged, their topaz cat eyes flashing. He paused a moment to pet first one, then the other. Watchdogs of his slumber, they would rip to pieces anyone he did not escort or beckon into the inner sanctum in person. They could not be bribed or frightened away, and it would take a small army to overpower them. As he departed, they settled back down on their haunches, seemingly returning to rest but in reality preternaturally alert and awake as always.

Peregriff was waiting for him in the antechamber, seated

at his desk. After a quick glance at the two pig-sized black clouds that trailed behind the sorcerer, he rose from behind his scrolls and papers.

"Good morning, Lord."

"No it is not." Hymneth halted on the other side of the desk. "I have not been sleeping well."

"I am sorry to hear that, Lord." Behind the ruddy cheeks and neatly trimmed white beard, the eyes of the old soldier were blue damascened steel. Nearly six and a half feet tall and two hundred and twenty pounds of still solid muscle, Peregriff could take up the saber and deal with a dozen men half his age. Only Hymneth he feared, knowing that the Possessed could take his life with a few well-chosen words and the flick of one chain-mailed wrist. So the ex-general served, and made himself be content.

"Strange dreams, Peregriff. Indistinct oddities and peculiar perturbations."

"Perhaps a sleeping potion, Lord?"

Hymneth shook his head peevishily. "I've tried that. This particular dream is not amenable to the usual elixirs. Something convoluted is going on." Straightening, he took a deep breath and, as he exhaled, the air in the room shuddered. "I'm going out today. See to the preparations."

The soldier of soldiers nodded once. "Immediately, Lord." He turned to comply.

"Oh, and Peregriff?"

"Yes, Lord?"

"How do you sleep lately?"

The soldier considered carefully before replying. "Reasonably well, Lord."

"I prefer that you did not. My misery might benefit from company."

"Certainly, Lord. I will begin by not sleeping well tonight."

Behind the helmet, Hymneth smiled contentedly. "Good. I can always count on you to make me feel better, Peregriff."

"That is my service, Lord." The soldier departed to make ready his master's means for going out among his people.

Hymneth took pleasure in a leisurely descent from the heights of the fortress, using the stairs. Sometimes he would descend on a pillar of fire, or a chute of polished silver. It was good to keep in practice. But the body also needed exercise, he knew.

As he descended, he passed many hallways and side passages. Attendants and servants and guards stopped whatever they were doing to acknowledge his presence. Most smiled; a few did not. Serveral noted the presence of the noisome, coagulated black vapors that tagged along at their master's heels, and they trembled. Passing one particular portal that led to a separate tower, he paused to look upward. The *woman* was up there, secluded in the small paradise he had made for her. A word from her would have seen him on his way exalted. That was not to be, he knew. Not yet. But he had measureless reserves of confidence, and more patience than even those closest to him suspected. The words would come, and the smiles, and the embraces. All in good time, of which he had a fullness.

He could have forced her. A few words, a pinch of powders, a few drops of potion in her evening wine and her resistance would be forgotten, as frail and fractured as certain tortured tracts of land to the east. But that would be a subjugation, not a triumph. Having everything, he wanted more. Mere bodies equally magnificent he could acquire with gold or spell. A heart was a much more difficult thing to win. He sought a covenant, not a conquest.

With a last look of longing at the portal, he resumed his descent. Passing through the grand hall with its imposing pendent banners of purple and crimson, its mounted heads of sabertooths and dragons, arctic bears and tropical thylacines, he turned left just before the imposing entryway and made his way to the smaller door that was nearer the stables.

Outside, the sun was shining brightly, as it usually was in Ehl-Larimar. Several stable attendants were concluding their grooming of his chariot team: four matched red stallions with golden manes. The chariot itself was large enough to accommodate his cumbersome frame in addition to that of a charioteer. Peregriff was waiting on the platform, reins in hand. He had donned his gilded armor and looked quite splendid in his own right, though he was both overshone and overshadowed by the towering figure of the caped necromancer.

The scarlet stallions bucked restlessly in harness, eager for a run. Hymneth found that he was feeling better already. He climbed into the chariot alongside his master of house and horse.

"Let's go, Peregriff. We will do the population the honor of viewing my magnificence. I feel—I feel like bestowing a boon or two today. I may not even kill anyone."

"Your magnanimity is truly legendary, Lord." The old soldier chucked the reins. "Gi'up!"

Snorting and whinnying, the team broke forward, speeding down the curved roadway that led up to and fronted the fortress. Through the massive portico in the outer wall they raced, sending dust and gravel flying from their hooves. These were inlaid with cut spessartine and pyrope. Catching the sunlight, the faceted insets gave the team the appearance of running on burning embers.

Down the mountainside they flew, Peregriff using the whip only to direct them, Hymneth the Possessed exhilarating in the wild ride. Down through the foothills, through groves of orange and olive and almond, past small country shops and farmhouses, and into the outskirts of the sprawling country metropolis of wondrous, unrivaled Ehl-Larimar.

Looking back, he found that he could see the fortress

clearly. It dominated the crest of the highest moutain overlooking the fertile lands below. But the direction in which
they were traveling prohibited him from seeing one part of
the fortress complex, one particular tower. In that obscured
spire languished the only unfulfilled part of himself, the single absent element of his perfection. It bothered him that he
could not see it as the chariot raced onward.

Inability to sleep, inadequate angle of vision. Two bad
things in one morning. Troubled but willing to be refreshed,
he turned away from the receding view of his sanctuary and
back toward the wild rush of flying manes and approaching
streets.

Manipulating the team masterfully, Peregriff shouted to
his liege. "Where would you like to go, Lord?"

"Toward the ocean, I think." The warlock brooded on the
possibilities. "It always does me good to visit the shore. The
ocean is the only thing in my kingdom that's almost as powerful as me."

Without a word, the soldier cracked the long whip over
the team. Instantly, they swerved to their right, taking a different road and nearly running down a flock of domesticated
moas in the process. Mindful of the increased pace, the twin
ebon miasmas that always trailed behind the necromancer
clung closer to his heels. When a brightly hued sparrow took
momentary refuge from the wind on the back of the chariot,
they promptly pounced on the intruder. Moments later, only
a few feathers emerged from one of the silken, inky black
clouds to indicate that the sparrow had ever been.

They sped past farmers riding wagons laden with goods
intended for market, raced around slow, big-wheeled curts
piled high with firewood or rough-milled lumber. Iron workers peered out from beneath the soot and spark of their
smithies while nursing mothers took time to glance up from
their infants and nod as forcefully as they were able.

Through the sprawling municipality they flew, the chariot

a blazing vision of carmine magnificence illuminating the lives of wealthy and indigent alike, until at last they arrived at the harbor. Hymneth directed his charioteer to head out onto one of the major breakwaters whose rocky surface had been rendered smooth through the application of coralline cement. Fishermen repairing nets and young boys and girls helping with the gutting of catch scrambled their way clear of the approaching, twinkling hooves. Buckets and baskets of smelly sustenance rolled wildly as they were kicked aside. In the chariot's wake, their relieved owners scrambled to recover the piscine fruits of their labors.

Within the harbor, tall-masted clippers and squat merchantmen vied for quay space with svelte coastal river traders and poky, utilitarian barges. Activity never ceased where the rest of Ehl-Larimar met the sea. Gulls, cormorants, and diving dragonets harried stoic pelicans, jabbing and poking at the swollen jaw pouches of the latter in hopes of stealing their catch. Except for the inescapable stink of fish, Hymneth always enjoyed visiting the far end of the long stone breakwater. It allowed him to look back at a significant part of his kingdom.

There the great city spread southward, terminating finally in the gigantic wall of Motops. Two thousand years ago it had been raised by the peoples of the central valleys and plains to protect them from the bloodthirsty incursions of the barbarians who dwelled in the far south. Ehl-Larimar had long since spread southward beyond its stony shadow, but the wall remained, too massive to ignore, too labor-intensive to tear down.

Northward the city marched into increasingly higher hills, fragrant with oak and cedar, lush with vineyards and citrus groves. To the east the soaring ramparts of the Curridgian Mountains separated the city from the rest of the kingdom, a natural barrier to invaders as well as ancient commerce.

Under his rule the kingdom had prospered. Distant dominions paid Ehl-Larimar homage, ever fearful of incurring the wrath of its liege and master. And now, after years of searching and inquiry, the most beautiful woman in the world was his. Well, not quite yet his, he self-confessed. But he was supremely confident that time would break down her resistance, and worthy entreaty overcome her distaste.

Unlike the commercially oriented, who employed boats and crews to ply the fecund waters offshore beyond Ehl-Larimar's fringing reefs, solitary fisherfolk often settled themselves along the breakwater and at its terminus, casting their lines into the blue-green sea in hopes of reeling in the evening's supper or, failing that, some low-cost recreation. A number were doing so even as he stood watching from the chariot. All had risen at his approach and genuflected to acknowledge his arrival. All—save one.

A lesser ruler would have ignored the oversight. A weaker man would have dismissed it. Hymneth the Possessed was neither.

Alighting from the chariot, he bade his general remain behind to maintain control of the still feisty stallions. Trailing purple and splendor, his regal cape flowing behind him, he strode over to the north side of the breakwater to confront the neglectful. Peregriff waited and watched, his face impassive.

Other fisherfolk edged away from his approach, clutching their children close to them as they tried their best to make their individual withdrawals inconspicuous. The last thing any of them wanted to do was attract his attention. That was natural, he knew. It was understandable that simple folk such as they should be intimidated and even a little frightened by the grandeur of his presence. He preferred it that way. It made the business of day-to-day governing much simpler.

Which was why he was taking the time to query the one

individual among them who had not responded to his arrival with an appropriate gesture of obeisance.

The stubble-cheeked man was clad in long coveralls of some tough, rough-sewn cotton fabric. His long-sleeved shirt was greasy at the wrists with fish blood and oil. He sat on a portion of the breakwater facing the sea, long pole in hand, two small metal buckets at his side. One held bait, the other fish. The bait bucket was the fuller of the two. By his side sat a tousle-haired boy of perhaps six, simply dressed and holding a smaller pole. He kept sneaking looks at the commanding figure that now towered silently behind him and his father. The expressionless fisherman ignored them both.

"I see by your pails that the fish are as disrespectful of you as you are of me."

The man did not flinch. "'Tis a slow morning, and we had a late start."

No honorific, the necromancer mused. No title, no "Good morning, Lord." By his slow yet skillful manipulation of the pole, Hymneth determined that the fellow was not blind. His reply had already marked him as not deaf.

"You know me."

The man gave the rod a little twitch, the better to jog the bait for the benefit of any watching fish. "Everyone knows who you are."

Still no praise, no proper acknowledgment! What was happening here? It made no sense. Hymneth was fully aware that others were watching. Surreptitiously, covertly as they could manage, but watching still. He would not have turned and walked away had he, fisherman, and child been on the far side of the moon, but the presence of others made it imperative that he not do so.

"You do not properly acknowledge me."

The man seemed to bend a little lower over his pole, but his voice remained strong. "I would prefer to be given a choice in who I acknowledge. Without any such choice, the actual execution of it seems superfluous."

An educated bumpkin, Hymneth reflected. All the more important then, to add to the body of his edification. "You might be more careful in your choice of metaphors. The use of certain words might inspire others, such as myself, to employ them in another context."

For the first time, the fisherman looked up and back. He did not flinch at the sight of the horned helmet, or the glowing eyes that glowered down at him. "I'm not afraid of you, Hymneth the Possessed. A man can only live so long anyway, and there are too many times when I find myself thinking that it would be better to die in a state of freedom than to continue to exist without it."

"Without freedom?" The wizard waved effusively. "Here you sit on these public stones, on this beautiful day, with your son at your side, engaging in a pursuit that most of your fellow citizens would consider a veritable vacation, and you complain of a lack of freedom?"

"You know what I'm talking about." The fellow's tone was positively surly, Hymneth decided appraisingly. "Ultimately, nothing can be done without your approval, or that of your appointed lackeys like the stone-faced old soldier who waits silently in your chariot. You rule ultimately, tolerating no dissent, no discussion. Throughout the length and breadth of all Ehl-Larimar nothing can be done without your knowledge. You spy on everyone, or have it done for you."

"Knowledge is a necessary prerequisite of good governance, my man."

"Ignoring the will of the people is not." Again the pole was jiggled, the long, thin wisp of a line punctuating the surface with small black twitches.

"It's a dangerous thing for people to have too much will." Stepping closer, Hymneth knelt directly behind the man so that he could feel the warm breath of the Possessed on his own dirty, exposed neck. "It makes them restless, and upsets everyone's digestion. Much better simply to live and enjoy each day as it comes, and leave the matter of willing to another."

"Like you." Still the man did not flinch, or pull away. "Go ahead—do your worst. It can't be any worse than the rest of my luck this morning."

"My worst? You really do think ill of me, don't you? If you were more worldly, my man, you'd know that I'm not such a bad sort, as absolute rulers go. I have no intention of doing anything to you." The front of the helmet turned slightly to the right. "Fine boy you have there." Reaching out a mailed hand, Hymneth ruffled the child's hair. The expression on the face of the six-year-old was of one torn between uncertain admiration and absolute terror.

For the first time, the fisherman's granite resolution appeared to falter ever so slightly. "Leave the boy alone. Deal with me if you must."

"Deal with you? But my man, I *am* dealing with you." Reaching into a pocket, the necromancer removed a small stoppered glass vial. It was half full of an oily black liquid. "I will not trouble you with the name of this elixir. I *will* tell you that if I were to sprinkle a couple of drops of it onto this fine stalwart young lad's hip, it would shrivel up his legs like the last overlooked stalks of summer wheat. They would become brittle, like the stems of dried flowers. Walking would cause the bones to splinter and shatter, causing excruciating pain no doctor or country alchemist could treat. Then they would heal, slowly and agonizingly, until the next time he took a wrong step, and then they would break again. And again and again, over and over, the pain as bad or worse with each new fracture, healing and breaking, breaking and healing, no matter how careful the young fellow strove to be, until by adulthood, if he survived the pain that long, both legs had become a mass of deformed, misshapen bony freaks useless for walking or any other purpose except the giving of agony."

His helmeted face was very close to the fisherman's ear now, and his commanding voice had dropped to a whisper. The man's face was twitching now, and several tears rolled down his stubbled cheek.

"Don't do that. Please don't do that."

"Ah." Within the helmet, a smile creased the steel shrouded face of Hymneth the Possessed. "Please don't do that—what?"

"Please . . ." The fisherman's head fell forward and his eyes squeezed tight shut. "Please don't do that—Lord."

"Good. Very good." Reaching over, the warlock ran a mail-enclosed forefinger along the young boy's cheek. The little lad was quivering now, manfully not crying but obviously wanting to, shivering at the touch of the cold metal. "That wasn't so difficult, was it? I'm leaving you now. Remember this encounter with pride. It's not every day that Hymneth the Possessed stoops to converse with one of his people. And be sure to respect my departure appropriately." The silky voice darkened ever so slightly. "You don't want me to come back and talk to you again."

Straightening to his full, commanding height, he returned to the chariot and stepped aboard. "Let's go, Peregriff. For some reason the ocean doesn't hold its usual cheer for me this morning."

"It's the woman, Lord. The Visioness. She preys on your thoughts. But her misgivings will pass."

"I know. But it's hard to be patient."

Peregriff ventured an old soldier's smile. "The time spent in extended contemplation will make the eventual resolution all the more agreeable, Lord."

"Yes. Yes, that's true." The sorcerer put a hand on the older man's arm. "You always know the right thing to say to comfort me, Peregriff."

The white-maned head dipped deferentially. "I try, Lord."

"Back to the fortress! We'll have a good meal, and deal with the turgid matters of state. Let's away from the stench of this place, and these people."

"Yes, Lord." Peregriff rattled the reins and the magnificent mounts responded, turning the chariot neatly in the limited space available. As it turned, Hymneth glanced in the direction of the breakwater's edge. The people there were standing, poles set aside, hats in hand and heads bowed reverentially. The head of one particular man was set especially low, as was that of his son. Both were trembling slightly. Seeing this, Hymneth let his gaze linger on them for longer than was necessary, even though he knew it was petty of him to find enjoyment in such trivial exercises of power.

Then Peregriff chucked the reins forcefully, shouted a command, and the chariot leaped forward, racing down the breakwater back toward the harbor, the city, and the stern cliffs of the Curridgians. Food awaited, and drink, and contemplation of the as yet unattained comeliness of his special guest.

Something darted out in front of the chariot, scrambling frantically to avoid the pounding, approaching hooves of the scarlet stallions. A black cat, skittering across the chariot's path.

"Look out," the necromancer yelled, "don't hit it!"

Even though it brought them dangerously close to the edge of the breakwater, Peregriff obediently and expertly utilized the reins to angle the galloping chargers slightly to the right. Spared, the unprepossessing cat vanished into the rocks. Looking back sharply, Hymneth tried to locate it, but could not.

Having guided the striding stallions back to the middle of the breakwater, his chief attendant was looking at him uncertainly. "Lord, it was only a mangy stray cat. No loss if it were killed."

"No—no loss." Hymneth found himself frowning. What had that singular moment been about? For just an instant, something had burrowed into and infected his state of mind, causing him to act in a manner not only unbecoming but atypical. Whom had he been panicked for—the cat, or himself? It was very peculiar.

Two inexplicable incidents in little more than as many minutes. First the fisherman, then the cat. It was turning out to be an idiosyncratic morning. One that, for reasons unknown and despite Peregriff's best efforts to cheer him, saw him finally reach the fortress still unsettled in mind and more ill at ease than he had been in years.

II

As a conduit for goods from the interior and imports from the exotic south and east, Lybondai provided refuge on a daily basis to a goodly number of extraordinary sights. But even in a port city as worldly and cosmopolitan as the pearl of the southern coast, the somber sight of a jet-black, five-hundred-pound cat with the legs of an overmuscled feline sprinter and the teeth and mane of a fully mature lion padding through the harborfront marketplace succeeded in turning heads.

"What makes you think they're all staring at you?" Drawing himself up to his full, if limited, height, Simna ibn Sind strode along importantly over the well-worn diamond-shaped paving stones.

Ahlitah the black litah snorted softly.

"There are a thousand and one humans milling around us and I can scent thousands more. There are cats, too, the largest of which would provide me with less than an afternoon snack. You don't need a kingdom to rule and pay you homage, Simna. You do that tirelessly yourself."

Glancing upward, the swordsman saw two young women

leaning out of a window to follow their progress. When he grinned and waved up at them, they drew back within the painted walls, giggling and covering their mouths.

"There, you see! They were looking at me."

"No," the big cat replied, "They were laughing at you. Me, they were looking at. Rather admiringly, if I do say so."

"Be silent, the both of you." Etjole Ehomba cast a disapproving look back at his garrulous companions. "We will try making inquiries at this harbor pilot's shack first, and if we have no luck there we will move on to the ships themselves."

Hope segued quickly into disappointment. At least the harbor pilots were understanding of their request and sympathetic to their situation. But they were no more encouraging than the ship mates and masters. Among the latter, the kindest were those who brusquely ordered the visitors off their ships. Sadly, they were outnumbered by colleagues who laughed openly in the faces of the supplicants. These were fewer than they might have been, for those who caught sight of Ahlitah lurking behind the two humans wisely decided it might be impolitic to make fun of the inquiry, no matter how outrageous its content.

The last captain to whom they presented the request Ehomba mistook for one of the lesser mates. He was a strapping redhead, freckled of face and taut of sinew, with a broad chest on which curly hairs posed like tiny frozen flames and a mustache that would have been the envy of an emperor tamarin. But when questioned, his bluff good humor and kindly nature proved no substitute for reality.

Letting go of the line he had been holding, the young shipmaster rested hands on hips as he confronted Ehomba. As he preferred to do at such moments, Simna remained in the background. By now the swordsman was thoroughly bored with the endlessly negative responses to their inquiries, which had taken most of the day, and predictive of the response they were likely to receive. In this the young Captain did not disappoint him.

"Take passage across the Semordria? Are ye daft?" A soft growl caused him to glance behind the tall, dark southerner to see the slit-eyed mass of muscle and claw lying supine on the deck behind him. He immediately softened his tone, if not his opinion. "No one sails across the Semordria. At least no ship that I be aware of."

"Are you afraid?" Simna piped up. It was late, and he no longer much cared if he happened to offend some local mariner stinking of fish oil and barnacle scrapings.

The young Captain bristled but, perhaps mindful of the lolling but very much alert Ahlitah, swallowed his instinctive response like a spoonful of sour medicine. "I fear only what is unknown, and no one knows the reaches of the Semordria. Some say that the stories of lands far to the west are nothing more than that: the imaginative ramblings of besotted seamen and inventive minstrels. From the crews of the few ships that venture out one of the Three Throats of the Aboqua to sail up and down the legendary western coasts come tales of creatures monstrous enough to swallow whole ships, and of underwater terrors most foul." He turned back to his work.

"I command this ship at the behest of my two uncles. They have given it unto my care, and as such I have responsibilities to discharge to them. Even if I were so inclined, or sufficiently crazy, I would not contemplate such an undertaking. Best you not do so, either."

"I can understand what you say about a responsibility to others." Ehomba spoke quietly, having heard the same narrative from the captains of more than two dozen other vessels. "I am traveling under similar conditions." His gaze drifted southward. Toward home, and as importantly, toward the grave of a noble man of far distant shores whose dying request had implored the herdsman to save a mysterious woman he had called the Visioness Themaryl.

Pulling hard on the line, the Captain spoke without turning to look at them. "Then you'd best get it through your head that the Semordria is not for crossing. Leastwise, not by any ship or captain or crew that sails the Aboqua." And that was the last he would say on the subject.

"Now what?" Simna stretched as they descended the boarding ramp to the wooden quay.

"We find a place to sleep." Already Ehomba was scanning the inns and taverns that fronted the main harbor. "Tomorrow we try once more."

"Hoy, not again!"

A grim-faced Ehomba whirled on his friend. "What would you have me do, Simna? We cannot walk across the Semordria. Nor can we fly."

"Pour drink enough down me, bruther, and I'll show you who can fly!" The swordsman's tone was belligerent.

"Gentlemen, gentlemen—there's no need to argue between yourselves. Not when I'm here to help you."

They turned together, tall herdsman and stocky easterner. His attention having been diverted by a barrel full of bait fish, Ahlitah ignored it all. The three fishermen who had been making use of the barrel lifted their poles from the water and silently and with wide eyes edged out of the cat's way.

Ehomba studied the stranger. "Who are you, that you want to help those you do not know?"

The man stepped forward. "My name is Haramos bin Grue. I was passing by this very spot when I chanced to overhear your conversation with the captain of this ignoble vessel. Of course he refused your request." The stranger eyed the nearby craft dubiously. "I wouldn't trust that bass barge to convey my ass safely from one side of the harbor to the other, much less across the great Semordria." He winked meaningfully. "You need a proper ship, crewed by men who are used to making such a crossing. Not fair-weather amateur sailors such as these." He swung an arm wide, dismissing the entire harbor and every boat docked or riding at anchor with a single wave.

Ehomba considered the individual who was so casual in impugning the professional capabilities of everyone he and his companions had sounded out that day. Pushy, to be sure, but did he know what he was talking about or was he merely being boastful?

It was impossible to tell simply by looking at him. A stump of a man, several inches shorter than Simna ibn Sind but without the swordsman's incident-inspired musculature, bin Grue was nonetheless a solid specimen, from his short arms to the profound gut that, interestingly, did not quiver when he walked. A tart-smelling cigar protruded from one corner of his mouth, around which his very white, very even teeth were clamped as if on a loose coin. His eyes were deep set and his cheeks bantamweight duplicates of his belly. A fringe of wavy white hair crowned his large head, which protruded above the halo of fluff like a whale shoving its snout through old pack ice. Virtually nonexistent, his neck was a ring of squat muscle on which the impressive head sat and swiveled like a fire-throwing turret on a Vendesian warship. He did not speak words so much as saw them up into individual syllables, spitting out one after another like hunks of rough lumber awaiting the attention of some absent master carver.

For all the man's affability and fine clothing, complete to high-strapped sandals, long pants, and puff-sleeved overshirt cut in a wide V down to the middle of his chest, Ehomba was uncertain as to his motives. Still, there was no harm in learning what he might have to offer.

"You know where we might find such a ship?"

"I certainly do. Not here, in this backass dimple on the

Premmoisian coast. To find *real* sailors, you need to go north." His eyes glittered with a recollection that might have been his—or bought, or borrowed. "For a ship to take you across the Semordria, you need to go to Hamacassar."

Ehomba glanced over at Simna, who shrugged. "Never heard of the place."

"The journey is long and difficult. Few know of Hamacassar, and even fewer have visited there."

"But you have." Ehomba was watching the shorter man closely.

"No." Not in the least embarrassed by this admission, bin Grue masticated his fuming cigar as he met the herdsman's unblinking stare. "Did you expect me to lie and say that I had?"

"Let's just say that we wouldn't have been shocked." Simna watched the stranger closely, wishing to find promise in that broad face while at the same time warily searching for snakes. Behind him, Ahlitah was making a mess of the bait barrel and its contents. The barrel's owners stood a goodly distance away, looking on helplessly.

"I won't say that I never lie. I'm a businessman, and sometimes it's a necessary constituent of my vocation. But I'm not lying to you now." Pulling the cigar from his thick lips, he flicked the ash at its tip aside, heedless of where it might land, and replaced it between his teeth, clamping down with a bite of iron that threatened to sever the slowly smoking brown stalk.

"I can fix it so you make it safely to Hamacassar. From there on, you're on your own."

"Not up to the journey yourself?" Simna was toying idly with the hilt of his sword.

"Not me, no. My business is here. Only fools and idiots would attempt such a journey."

"I see." The swordsman's fingers danced faster over the

sword hilt. "And I ask, by Glespthin, which, in your opinion, are we?"

Bin Grue was not in the least intimidated by Simna's suggestive behavior. "Supply your own definitions. That's not my job. You want to get across the Semordria? Take my advice and head northwest to Hamacassar. You won't find a ship here, that's for sure."

"We would be glad to accept any advice you can give," Ehomba assured him politely.

The smile that appeared briefly on the trader's face was as terse as his manner of speech. "Good! But not here. My guidance is for my friends and my customers, not for passing noseybodies."

"And again I say," Simna murmured, "which are we?"

"Both, I hope." With a grunt that would have done a warthog proud, the trader pivoted and beckoned for them to follow.

Simna had more to say, but with Ehomba already striding along in the other man's wake, he held his questions. Time enough to quiz this brusque barterer before they found themselves in too deep with someone who might turn out to be all talk and no substance. Simna was ready to give the man credit for one thing, though: virtuous or prevaricator, he was one tough son of a bitch. Throughout the course of the conversation he hadn't flinched once, not even when the swordsman had shown signs of readiness to draw his weapon and put an end to the discussion on an abrupt note.

Looking over his shoulder, he called out to the third member of their party. "Pull your snout out of that rank keg, cat, and catch up!"

Mouth full of bait fish, Ahlitah looked over at him and growled. Though it was directed at Simna and not them, two of the three fishermen took the imposing rumble as a sign to make a precipitous entry into the turgid water of the harbor, while the third dropped to his knees and prayed. Ignoring them, the massive black cat trotted off in pursuit of his two-legged companions, occasionally pausing briefly to shake first one paw and then another in a vain attempt to flick away the fishy water that clung to his toes.

As their new guide led them deeper and deeper into the maze of tightly packed buildings that crowded the water-front, Simna ibn Sind stayed close to his tall, solemn-visaged companion.

"Where's this fat fixer leading us? I don't like narrow alleys and empty walkways and dead-end closes even when I know their names." He eyed uneasily the high stone walls that pressed close on all sides.

"A good question." Ehomba raised his voice. "Where *are* you taking us, Haramos bin Grue?"

The trader looked back and grinned. Ehomba was adept at interpreting expressions, and bin Grue's seemed genuine enough, if tight. He smiled like a man having difficulty moving his bowels.

"You look tired, and hungry. I thought we'd discuss our business over some food and drink." He turned to his left, into a constricted close, and halted. "Be of good cheer. We're here."

They found themselves waiting while their guide pushed repeatedly on a shuttered door. It was a bland slab of wood, devoid of ornamentation, wholly utilitarian and in no way suggestive that gustatory delights might lie beyond. Dust spilled from around the eaves and it groaned in protest as it was forced inward.

Simna whispered tautly. "Doesn't look like a real popular place. In fact, it doesn't look like any sort of place at all."

"Perhaps the dreary exterior is a camouflage of some sort." Ehomba remained hopeful. "The inside may be a revelation."

It was, but not in the sense the herdsman hoped. Trailing bin Grue, they found themselves in a large, dusty warehouse. The center of the high-ceilinged structure was empty, its floor of pegged, heavily scored wood planks. A rotting pile of hoary crates occupied a far corner while several still intact casks boasting unimaginably aged contents were stacked against the opposite wall. Sunlight fought with varying degrees of success to penetrate the cracked veneer of grime and sea salt that partially opaqued the narrow, oblong upper windows. Responding to their entry, a small, distant shape sprang for cover. Ahlitah leaped after the rat, which, used to dodging and doing occasional battle with stray house cats, expired of heart failure at the sight of the pouncing black-maned behemoth. Settling himself down in a patch of feeble sunlight, the master of the open veldt crunched contentedly on the obscure but zestful morsel.

Simna kept one hand on the hilt of his sword. The warehouse was quiet, deserted, and isolated—the perfect place for an ambush. Ehomba was his usual serene self, too slopping over with inner contentment to realize when he was in grave danger, the swordsman was convinced.

"I'm looking for grog and all I see is rat piss," he snapped at their guide. "Where's this fine tavern you promised us?" He was all but ready to draw his sword and put an end to the bold but perjuring jabberer.

"Right here." Reaching into a pocket of his billowing shirt, the trader withdrew a small box. Both Ehomba and Simna came closer for a better look. The box was fashioned of some light-colored wood, perhaps lignum vitae. All six sides were inscribed with cryptic symbols whose meanings were a mystery to the two travelers.

Grimacing suggestively, bin Grue moved to the center of the open floor, held the box carefully at eye height, and dropped it. Perhaps he also mumbled some words, or spat softly on the wood, or did something unseen with his hands. The box fell, bounced once, twice—and suddenly righted itself, shivering like a rabbit transfixed by the gaze of a hungry quoll.

Retreating from the quivering cube, bin Grue advised his companions to do the same. "Give it room to breathe," he told them. Without understanding what was happening, they both stepped back. Even Ahlitah looked up from the remnants of his rat, the tiny bit of remaining skeleton gleaming whitely from between his enormous front paws.

The box popped open, its sides unfolding smoothly. These in turn unfolded again, multiplying with astonishing, accelerating speed. Light shot upward from the newly hatched sides, which melded together to form a floor. As the travelers watched in amazement and bin Grue stood with hands on hips nodding approvingly, the expanding box sides threw up other shapes. A bar rose from nothingness, complete to back wall decorated with mirrors and lascivious paintings. Tables appeared, and jars and jugs and mugs and tankards atop them. There was bright light that bounded from mirrors, and music from a trio of musicians only one of whom was human, and laughter, and shouting. Most remarkably of all, patrons appeared, arising out of the exponentially multiplying box sides. They took shape and form, hands lifting drinks and food to mouths. Some were drunk, some convivial, a few argumentative. Most laughed and guffawed as if they were having the categorical good time.

A final box side unfolded a large cockroach, which immediately scurried for cover beneath the bar. Bin Grue frowned at it. "Been meaning to get rid of that. There's such a thing as too much atmosphere." Striding purposefully to an empty table, he bade them join him.

More than a little dazed, they did so. Simna had removed his hand from the vicinity of his sword hilt. He continued to regard the trader warily, but with new respect. "So you're not just some wandering merchant. You're a powerful wizard. Well, don't get any ideas." He gestured at Ehomba. "So's my lean and lanky friend here."

"Is he?" Bin Grue grunted speculatively. "Well, he needn't worry about me trying to cast any spells while he's around. I'm no sorcerer, swordsman. Just a trader of goods and services, like I told you."

"But the box, all this . . . ?" Simna stared admiringly at the busy tavern that now filled the formerly empty warehouse.

The trader nodded. "Fine piece of work, isn't it? Hard to find this kind of craftsmanship anymore these days. I told you that I'm no wizard, and I meant it. But I do business with anyone and everyone. My specialty is the rare and exotic. Inventory sometimes brings me in contact with those who practice magic." He peered steadfastly at Ehomba. "If you're truly a sorcerer, as your friend claims, then you'll know that even the greatest of necromancers can't always conjure up what they need. That's where someone like myself steps in." He indicated a small stain on the floor. A square stain, the color of polished lignum vitae. "I acquired the tavern box from an elderly witch woman of Tarsis. She offered me three models: ordinary, with additional gold, or the deluxe. I chose the deluxe."

"What was the difference?" a curious Ehomba asked.

Sitting forward in his chair, bin Grue hefted a tankard that, miraculously, was already full. When he drank, it was full bore and without delicacy. Beer dribbled from his heavy lips and he was quick to wipe the errant droplets away. In his drinking habits as with his manner of speaking he was foursquare and blunt, but no slob.

"The ordinary boxes contain only the tavern. No accessories." He took another swallow. "I like the atmosphere the patrons add."

Simna was watching people eat and drink and make

merry all around them. "Are they real? Or only phantasms? Could I put my hand through one of them?"

Bin Grue chuckled. "Can you put your hand through the chair you're sitting on? I wouldn't try it. An ignominious fate, to be thrown out of a nonexistent tavern by artificial habitués." His eyes gleamed and his voice darkened slightly. "Besides, if you get in a fight with any of them you're liable to find yourself sucked down into the box when it shrinks back in upon itself. The spell only holds for a finite amount of time."

"Then we had better get down to talking." Sampling the liquid in the tall metal goblet before him, Ehomba found it to his taste. He sipped courteously.

Simna labored under no such restraint. Slugging down the contents of his tankard, he called for more. The tavern maid who refilled his drinking container topped it off with a saucy smile, and did not object when he drew her close for a kiss.

"Hoy, this is my kind of necromancy!" With drink in hand, the swordsman saluted their host approvingly.

"But you must be hungry as well." Turning, bin Grue clapped his hands. From an unseen kitchen in an unimaginable fragment of the plenum, a quartet of waiters appeared, marching deliberately toward the table carrying platters piled high with all manner of well-sauced and piquant foodstuffs. The last one was stacked high with long slabs of raw meat. This was set before an approving Ahlitah, who fell to devouring them with unrestrained feline gusto.

"Eat!" their host admonished them as he chomped down enthusiastically on a leg of broasted unicorn.

"I've got to hand it to you." Simna's words were muffled by the meat in his mouth. "I've seen travelers use magic to conjure up food. But a whole tavern, complete to back kitchen and bar and celebrating customers?" He waved an unidentifiable drumstick in his friend's direction. "What I wouldn't have given to have had that little box with us when we were crossing the desert!"

"A remarkable piece of enchantment." Ehomba made the confession even as he continued to put away copious quantities of food.

They ate and drank for what seemed like hours, until even the redoubtable Simna ibn Sind could eat no more. As he slumped in his chair, his engorged belly gave him the appearance of a pregnant jackal. Proportionately distended, the great black feline lay on his side on the floor, sound asleep.

Only Ehomba, to bin Grue's unalloyed amazement, continued to eat, steadily and without obvious harm to his digestion.

"Where do you put it?" the wide-eyed trader wondered. "Your stomach is only a little enlarged."

Around a mouthful of steamed vegetables, the herdsman replied contentedly. "Growing up in a dry, poor country, one learns never to turn down food when it is offered, and trains the body to accept quite a lot on those rare occasions when large quantities are present."

"Don't believe a word of it—oohhhhh." Moaning, Simna tried to encompass his immensely augmented gut with both hands, and failed. He became briefly alert when Ehomba removed a small vial from his pack. "There, you see! It's only through the use of sorcery that he's able to eat like this! Tell him, bruther. Tell him what alchemy of reduction is contained in that tiny container you've been secretly sipping from."

"I will." So saying, Ehomba tilted the vial over the top of his overflowing plate. Small white particles fell from its perforated stopper. "Sea salt. Not only does it remind me of home, but I always like a bit of extra seasoning on my food."

Disappointed by this revelation that was not, Simna groaned and fell back in his chair. A hand came down to rest gently on his shoulder. Looking up, he saw the smiling face and other components of the sultry barmaid who had been attending to their liquid requirements.

"Dance with a lonely lady, soldier?"

"Dance?" Simna mumbled. "Dance—sure." Struggling to his feet, he did his best to sweep her up in his arms as they staggered together out onto the small empty section of floor opposite the tooting musicians. It was difficult to tell who was holding up whom. As the trader had promised, the swordsman found to his wonder and delight that his hands did not go through her.

And all the while, to the heavyset merchant's protracted incredulity, Ehomba continued to eat. "I have never seen three men consume as much as you," bin Grue marveled openly. "I am also mindful of something your friend said earlier. Are you truly a sorcerer?"

"Not at all. A simple herder of cattle and sheep, from the far south. Nothing more. Tell me now, Haramos bin Grue— how are you going to help us reach this far-distant Hamacassar?"

"It will be difficult for you, but not impossible. First you must . . . Etjole Ehomba, are you feeling unwell?"

It was not so much that the herdsman was feeling unwell as he was unsteady. Though he did not feel in the least filled up, and still retained much of his extraordinary appetite, he found that his vision had begun to blur. The laughter of the preboxed tavern patrons seemed to reverberate in his ears instead of simply sounding, and the light from the mirrors behind the bar to grow hazy. Outlines became indistinct, and even the formidable bin Grue acquired a certain fuzziness around the edges of his blocky, smooth-domed skull. He was speaking, talking to the herdsman, but his words had suddenly become as indistinct as his face, on which individual features now seemed to float freely, nose switching places with mouth, lips reinforcing eyebrows.

Ehomba's gaze fell to his elegant, slim goblet. The liquor

within was light in color and afire with small bubbles that tickled the palate. Perhaps it was the bubbles, a new experience for him. Active and intriguing, they could also serve to divert a man's attention from the actual taste of the nectar. It struck him suddenly that there was something in the current flagon of wine that could not trace its ancestry to any honorable grape.

Striving to look up, he found that he could not even lift his head. The trader had been nothing if not subtle. His blunt and forthright manner had fooled the herdsman into believing their host was not one to exercise patience in any matter. It was to his credit, then, that he had managed to disguise this component of his personality so successfully. Having plied them with ample food and fine drink of inestimable purity, he had similarly bided his time.

Ehomba tried to mumble something, but his lips and tongue were working no better than his eyes. As darkness began to descend, shutting out the bright lights of the mirrors and the now mocking laughter of the reconstituted tavern patrons, he thought he saw bin Grue rise and beckon. Not to his guests, or to any of the discorporal crowd, but to a number of large and ready men who were entering through the single, dusty doorway that opened onto the obscure close beyond.

Then his vision blanked altogether, leaving only his digestion functioning actively, and his stomach the only organ still capable of making noise.

III

It was still light out when sensibility returned to him. Having been gifted with an impressive headache, he found himself sitting up on the dry, bare floor of the deserted warehouse. Of preboxed, unfolded tavern and jovial customers there was no sign. Nor was the owner of the remarkable cube anywhere to be seen. That was hardly an unexpected development, the herdsman mused dourly.

Rising, he staggered slightly until he could confirm his balance. His belongings lay nearby, undisturbed by intruders real or imagined. No doubt one such as Haramos bin Grue regarded such poor possessions as unworthy of his attention, more bother than they would be worth in the marketplace. Or perhaps his avaricious nature had been wholly engaged with more promising matters.

Ahlitah was gone. There was no sign of the big cat, not on the floor where he had been lying nor back among the few crates and corners. Standing in silence, alone in a shaft of sunlight, Ehomba concentrated hard on recovering fragments of memory like scavenged tatters of old rags.

The men whom he recalled entering the warehouse just

before he had blacked out had been carrying something between them. What was it? Shutting his eyes tightly, he
fought to remember. Snakes? No—ropes. Ropes and chains.
Not to rig a ship, he decided. Ehomba had never seen a cat
like Ahlitah until he had rescued it from the angry spiraling
wind. Half lion, half cheetah, his four-legged companion
was unique. Haramos bin Grue was a self-confessed dealer
in the unique.

Realizing where the cat must be, the herdsman went in
search of his one other traveling companion.

He found him in a far corner, immobilized in the midst of
an attempt to carry out an impossible act of physical con-
gress with a beer keg. Half awake, half boiled, he was mumbling under his breath, a besotted smile on his face.

"Ah, Melinda, sweet Melinda. Melinda of the
succulent . . ."

Ehomba kicked the keg hard. It rolled over, sending its
human companion tumbling. Finding himself suddenly on
his back, Simna ibn Sind blinked and tried to stand. One
hand fumbled for the sword slung at his side. The fingers
kept missing, grabbing at empty air.

"What—? Who dares—? Oh, by Gwasik—my head!"

"Get up." Reaching down, Ehomba extended a hand.
Glum-faced and thoroughly abashed, the swordsman accepted the offer.

"Not so hard!" he shouted. "Don't pull so hard!"

Standing behind him, Ehomba held his friend erect with
both arms under those of his companion's. It took a moment
or two before the stocky swordsman shook himself free.
"I'm all right, Etjole. I'm okay." He brushed repeatedly at
his eyes, as if by so doing he could wipe away the film of in-
distinctness that lingered there. "By Ghophot—we were
drugged!"

"Very effectively, too." The herdsman was looking toward the door. It hung dangling from one hinge, ready to

break free at the slightest touch. Doped or not, Ahlitah had evidently not been taken without a fight. "They have stolen away with our friend."

"What, the cat? Who's taken him?" Simna stumbled slightly but did not fall.

"Our friend Haramos bin Grue. Our would-be guide. With the aid of others, whom he had waiting until the proper moment. But he did not lie to us. He never said anything about abducting our companion." He regarded the nearly demolished door thoughtfully. "The black litah would be worth a great deal to a collector of rare animals. Visitors to the village have mentioned that in larger, more prosperous towns such individuals are not uncommon. I imagine there would be many such in a city as large and sophisticated as Lybondai."

"Well, let's go!" Trying to draw his sword, Simna staggered in the general direction of the doorway. "Let's get after them!"

Reaching out, Ehomba put a hand on his friend's shoulder to restrain him. "Why should we do that?" he declared softly.

Simna gazed blankly up at his stolid, unassuming companion. As always, there was not the slightest suggestion of artifice in the herdsman's tone or expression. "What do you mean, 'why should we do that'? The cat is our friend, our ally. He's saved us more than once."

The herdsman barely nodded. "It was his choice, a burden he decided to take on himself. If we three were starving, he would eat first you and then me."

"Under similar circumstances, I'd eat him, though I'm not very fond of cat. Too stringy. But this situation isn't that situation."

"He is an acquaintance. I like him. But not enough to risk my life and the failure of my journey to burrow into a den of thieves to rescue him. Maybe you do not understand, Simna, but he would."

"Would he, now? Would that we could ask him that question to his flat, furry face. Stay if you must—I'm going after him." The swordsman turned and stumbled, albeit gallantly, toward the doorway.

"What about your pledge to me?"

Simna peered back over his shoulder. "It will be fulfilled—after I've rescued Ahlitah."

"You will fail."

"Has that been written? Who are you to interpret the pages of Fate before they've been turned? Do you think no one is capable of heroics except in your company?"

"Look at you! You can barely walk." Was that an inkling of hesitation in the herdsman's voice? Simna continued to weave an uncertain path toward the door.

"I'm better with a sword falling down drunk than any three warriors stone-cold sober." He paused at the dangling door, frowning. "Didn't this used to have a knob?"

"It does not matter." With a sigh, Ehomba moved to rejoin his companion. "Give it a push and it will most likely fall off that last hinge."

"Oh." Simna did so and was rewarded with a crash as the creaking barrier fell to the floor. "So maybe there are certain pages of Fate you *can* decipher."

"Fate had nothing to do with it." The herdsman strode past him. "Right now I can see straight and you cannot. Come on."

"Right!" Simna ibn Sind drew himself up. "Uh—where are we going?"

"To try and free the cat, if he has indeed been taken by the venal bin Grue. I do not mind leaving him behind, and I do not mind leaving you behind, but if you get yourself killed on account of my reluctance, I would have to carry that with me forever. My soul bears enough encumbrances without having to pile your stupid death on top of them."

"Ah, you don't fool me, Etjole Ehomba." A wide grin split the swordsman's face. "You were just looking for an excuse, a rationalization, to go after the litah."

The herdsman did not reply. He was already out the door and heading for the waterfront.

Despite his boasts of commercial achievement, or perhaps because of them, they were unable to find anyone who had heard of Haramos bin Grue. Repeated questioning of touts, travelers, seamen and servants, merchants and mongers produced blank stares, or bemused head shakes, or indifference. Sometimes the latter was mixed with contempt for the questioners. Ehomba's simple garb and Simna's unindentured status sank them beneath the notice of the city's privileged and elite. Those who replied to their polite inquiries were usually not in a position to know, and those who might be often did not condescend to respond.

"This isn't getting us anywhere." Simna was still determined, but discouragement was settling into his voice like a bad cold.

"Maybe we are going about it wrong." Ehomba was gazing out to sea, a distant look in his eyes as he stared unblinkingly at the southern horizon. A ship corrupted his vision and he blinked. "Perhaps instead of asking individuals on the street, we should seek out one who can look by other means."

"A seer?" Simna eyed his friend uncertainly. "But aren't you a seer, long bruther? Can't you do the far-looking?"

"If I could, do you think I would be discussing the matter now? When will you accept, Simna, that I am nothing more than what I say?"

"When prodigious abnormalities stop occurring in your company. But I accept that you cannot seer." The swordsman turned to drink in the surging mass of humanity and other creatures who filled the waterfront with unceasing activity. "If these insipid folk cannot tell us where to find bin Grue, then maybe they can tell us where to find someone who can."

They were directed to a tiny shopfront set in a stone building lined with narrow shuttered doorways, like vertical shingles. There was no name above the portal, which was embellished with many words written in scripts alien to Ehomba. The more worldly Simna recognized bits of two different languages, and by combining those words he knew from each, he was able to divine some meaning, like reconstituting juice from concentrate.

"'Moleshohn the All-Knowing,'" he translated for his companion. "'Comprehender of Worlds and Provider of Sage Mandates.'" He sniffed. "Let's see what he has to offer."

"How will we compensate him for his services?" Ehomba wondered.

The swordsman sighed. "After paying for our passage across the Aboqua I still have some Chlengguu gold left. More than enough to satisfy some substandard waterfront wise man, anyway."

The door was not latched, and a small bell rang as they entered. The unpretentious front room contained a dusty clutter of incunabula, a table piled high with old books of dubious extraction, and a great deal of spoiling food and stale clothing. It did not look promising.

The individual who emerged from a back room popped out to greet them like a badger winkling its way free of a too-small burrow. Moleshohn the All-Knowing's appearance reflected far more prosperity than did his environment. Short and slim, he had a narrow face, bright ferret-eyes, a goatee that appeared to have been grafted onto his pointed chin from a much larger man, flowing gray hair, and more rapid hand movements than a professional shuffler of cards.

The air in the modest room was stagnant until he entered. His ceaseless, highly animated waving stirred both it and innumerable dust particles into torpid motion.

"Welcome, welcome, progenitors of a thousand benevolences! What can I do for you?" He did not so much sit as throw himself into the chair behind the table. Ehomba thought the worried wood would collapse from the impact, but the seat and back held. "You need a cheating lover found?" The seer smirked knowingly at Simna. "You seek gainful employment in Lybondai? You want to know the best inn, or where to find the sauciest wenches? The nature of mankind troubles you, or you have acquired some small but embarrassing disease that requires treatment?"

"We have lost something." Ehomba did not take a seat. Given a choice, herdsmen often preferred to stand. There was only one other chair in the room anyway, and Simna had already requisitioned it.

"Do say, do say." As he spoke, Moleshohn was rapidly tapping the tips of his fingers against one another.

"To digress for just a second," a curious Simna responded, "but what *is* the nature of mankind?"

"Confused, my friend." The seer extended an open palm. "That will be one half a gold Xarus, please."

"We are not through." Ehomba frowned at his companion, who shrugged helplessly.

"I always wanted to know that."

"I am no oracle, Simna, and I could have answered that question for you." Looking back at their host, the herdsman explained their purpose and their need.

"I see, I see." Moleshohn's fingers tapped a lot faster now that he had something of substance to consider. "Very large, is it, with the legs of a different sort of great feline altogether?"

Ehomba nodded. "That, and it can speak the general language of men."

"A remarkable animal, to be sure, to be sure. And you say it was taken from you, abducted, by this Haramos bin Grue?"

"He's a slick bastard," Simna informed the seer. "But this all happened only yesterday, so we don't think he can have gone far. Not with Ahlitah as unwilling freight."

"I would think both would still be in the city." Ehomba seemed mildly indifferent to the proceedings, but Simna knew his friend better. "It would take time to find the proper buyer for something like the litah. Nor would a trader as clever as bin Grue accept the first offer to come along. He will seek to get the best price for his acquisition."

"Gentlemen, gentlemen, you are in luck." The diminutive diviner was beaming. "You have come to the right man. Not only am I familiar with the name of Haramos bin Grue, but for a small fee I can have this feline re-abducted and returned to you! Your lives will not be put at risk. There are many men of daring and greed in this city who can be induced to participate in such an enterprise for a pittance. If you will but wait here, relaxing with my books and objects of interest, I will arrange for everything." He rose from his seat. "Your purloined friend shall be returned to you this very night!"

"As Gouyoustos is my witness," declared Simna, "I applaud your initiative, All-Knowing One!" His expression darkened slightly and his voice fell. "What exactly will this 'enterprise' cost us?"

The All-Knowing named a figure, which struck the swordsman as pretty much all-draining. But if the seer could deliver on his promise, it would save them both danger and difficulty. Moleshohn sealed the pact by assenting to accept half payment now, so that he could hire the necessary individuals, and the rest upon safe return of Ahlitah.

It was agreed. They would remain in the cramped but

cozy shop until their host returned with their four-legged friend.

"You are not afraid of this bin Grue?" Ehomba put the question to Moleshohn as he was about to depart.

"I know his reputation. Because of . . . certain goods that he deals in, he is known to be more than a mere trader." The oracle winked twice. "But I am the All-Knowing, and as such, I know how to deal with men like him. Do not fear for me, Cosigner of a Solemn Bargain. I can take care of myself." He opened the door, his fingers rapping excitably on the jamb. "I will be back before the turn of midnight with your companion, and for the rest of my money." He shut the door resoundingly behind him. Moleshohn the All-Knowing did everything resoundingly.

The two travelers were left to their own resources, perusing their host's collections by the soft light of well-fueled oil lamps. Somewhat to Simna's surprise, Ehomba revealed that he could read, though his learning was restricted to only the general language of men. Simna could boast of a knowledge of many tongues, though his fluency was frequently restricted to those words not usually to be found in the scholarly tomes of which their host was fond.

In this manner they passed a fair many hours, during which time the sun surrendered the day to the moon, and the noise of the waterfront, though never passing away completely, was much reduced from that of the busy day.

"I wonder if it is after midnight." Ehomba looked up from the book of many pictures he was perusing. "It feels so."

"There's a clock on that shelf over there." Simna pointed. "Can't you see by its face that it's after midnight?"

"A clock?" Closing the book, Ehomba rose to have a look at the strange device. "So that is what this is. I wondered."

Simna gaped at him. "You mean you've never seen a clock before?"

"No, never." Standing before the shelf, Ehomba gazed in

fascination at the softly ticking mechanism. "What is a 'clock'?"

"A device for the telling of time." The swordsman studied his friend in disbelief. "It's a peculiar sort of sorcerer you are, that doesn't know the functioning of a clock. How do you tell time?"

"By the sun and the stars." The herdsman was leaning toward the shelf, his nose nearly touching the carved wooden hands that told the hour and the minute. "This is a wonderful thing."

"Hoy, sure." A disappointed Simna found himself wondering if, perhaps, just perhaps, in spite of all they had seen and survived, Etjole Ehomba was in truth little more than what he claimed to be: a humble herder of food animals.

There was a noise at the door and both men turned to regard it expectantly. "Moleshohn!" Simna blurted. "About time. We were beginning to get a trifle concerned about—"

The door burst inward, thrown aside by a brace of Khorog. They were a large, beefy folk, with warty, unkind faces, who were much in demand in the municipalities and kingdoms of the Aboqua's northern shore as mercenaries and bodyguards. They could also, it was abundantly and immediately evident, be employed for less noble purposes. Clad in light chain armor with heavy solid shoulder- and breastplates, they wielded weapons of little refinement, weighty war axes and ponderous maces being the manglers of choice.

Simna had his sword out and had leaped atop the table in a trice. "No wonder Moleshohn the Deceiver wasn't afraid of bin Grue! He's sold us out!" As he flailed madly with his sword, using his superior position to slow the first rush of assailants and keep them momentarily at bay, he shouted frantically. "Do something, bruther! Slaughter them where they stand! They'll be too many through that door and all over us in a moment!"

In the surprise and confusion of the initial assault, Ehomba reached behind his back to grab for the sword of sky metal. Instead, his hand wrapped around his long spear. With no time in which to adjust for the mistake and with grunting, murderous Khorog swarming through the open door, he was forced to thrust with the weapon at hand instead of the one of choice. This despite knowing that the consequences could be as deadly for the spear holder as for those on the receiving end of its inherent inimical qualities.

He knew that the cramped chamber was too small to contain the spirit of the spearpoint, but he had no time in which to consider another action. The grunting, homicidal Khorog were right on top of them. What burst forth from the tooth that tipped the end of his spear expanded not simply to dominate the room, but to fill it.

"Out the back way, quickly!" He could only shout and hope that the swordsman could respond rapidly enough as the dead spirit of the tyrannosaur ballooned to occupy the entire room. The massive, switching tail barely missed him as he grabbed for his backpack and dove through the rear portal.

Those Khorog who were not crushed instantly beneath the weight of the reconstituted carnivore suffocated themselves as they tried to squeeze back through the narrow front door. More were slain, devoured by the rampaging demon as, seeking space to move about and breathe, it burst through the storefront and the outer wall of the building. Its terrible roars and bellows resounded across the waterfront, sending hitherto placid pedestrians running for their lives or plunging into the harbor to escape. Surviving Khorog scattered in all directions, throwing down their cumbersome weapons in their haste to flee. The tyrannosaur's spirit pursued them, snapping at would-be assassins and blameless citizens alike.

Simna had just avoided being stepped on and smashed to

a pulp. Only his familiarity with his friend's unexpected stratagems had enabled him to react with a minimum of shock and flee before it was too late. Now he let himself be led, following the herdsman as they stumbled out into the alley behind the shop and hurried back toward the harbor-front.

"Wait a minute!" he yelled breathlessly, "why are we going this way? The monster you let loose is out there!"

"I know." Ehomba's tone was as equable as ever, but the swordsman thought he might have detected just a hint of suppressed passion. "But I am hoping there may also be a smaller one slinking about."

Sure enough, they found Moleshohn lying in a small pinnace tied to the main quay, cowering beneath loose canvas as he sought to hide from both the raging prehistoric spirit and the surviving angry Khorog. When the canvas was pulled back to expose his startled face, the All-Knowing appeared something less than omnipotent.

Simna shoved the point of his sword against the seer's throat until he was forced to lean back over the side of the small sailing craft. Eyes wide, their erstwhile host found himself hanging inches from the dark water. Both hands clung to the rail to keep him from tumbling over into the depths, the fingers tapping out a panicked ostinato on the smooth wood.

Teeth clenched, Simna ibn Sind pushed harder with the sword. "I'll give you a choice, oracle. That's more than you gave us. Tell us where to find Haramos bin Grue, and I'll only cut your face instead of your throat!"

"I don't—" the failed prophet began, but Ehomba, looming behind the tense swordsman, silenced the incipient protest with his eyes.

"You betrayed us to him. I should have at least suspected, but I am used to dealings among the people of my country, where souls and manhood are not bartered for gold. Being the All-Knowing, you knew where he was, and what he would pay to be rid of us. Being the All-Knowing, you know that I speak the truth when I tell you that if you do not reveal his whereabouts to us within your next heart's breath, it will be your last."

Simna's sword drew blood from the slim, wrinkled throat.

"Yes, yes, I'll tell you, I'll tell you!" So loudly and hard were the smaller man's fingertips rapping nervously on the gunwale of the pinnace that they had begun to bleed. "He—he has a place of business on Zintois Street. The house is behind. Are you going to kill me?"

Simna grinned wolfishly. "You mean you're the All-Knowing and you don't have the answer to that? Maybe you should change your title to the Maybe-Guessing."

Leaning forward, Ehomba put a hand on the swordsman's shoulder. "Let it go, Simna. If we are going to make the effort to free Ahlitah, we should hurry."

Breathing hard, his friend hesitated. "There is the small matter of the money we paid. In good faith for information, not betrayal." Palm up, he extended a demanding hand.

A trembling Moleshohn fumbled with a hidden pocket. Straightening, he passed the swordsman a fistful of coin. Counting it while Ehomba waited impatiently, Simna had a few choice final words for their betrayer. "If you're lying to us, or have given us the wrong address, we'll find you. My friend is a great sorcerer, a *true* sorcerer. Not a cheap storefront fake like yourself!"

Moleshohn managed to summon a sufficient reserve of inner strength to protest feebly, "I am not cheap!" before the swordsman fetched him a solid blow to the forehead with the hilt of his sword. The All-Knowing became the Wholly Unconscious and fell back onto the floor of the boat. Tossing the canvas over the body, Simna followed Ehomba back onto the quay. His blade made short work of the hawser that secured the pinnace to the dock. Nodding with satisfaction, he watched as the little boat began to drift slowly out into the harbor.

"When he wakes beneath that heavy cover, maybe he'll think he's dead. A good fright is the least the old scoundrel deserves."

"Come." In the distance, the sounds of destruction and screaming were beginning to fade. The spirit of the tooth could only stalk the earth for a finite amount of time. Meanwhile, a few small fires had erupted in the wake of the two-legged monster's rampage. These would keep the locals occupied for a while, and the few surviving Khorog were in no condition to respond to questions. Content that they faced no pursuit, the two travelers hurried from the scene of confusion.

Zintois Street was situated away from the waterfront and deeper within the city proper. Neatly paved with cobblestones, it wound its way up a small hill, providing those fortunate enough to have their businesses located near the crest with a pleasant view of the harbor and the surrounding city. The storefronts here were large and impressive, bespeaking a wider commercial success than what had been achieved by the lowlier waterfront merchants.

The house of Haramos bin Grue clung like a he-crab to its mate, rising behind and above the street-facing offices. A high stone wall encircled and protected the compound. Its parapet was lined with large shards of broken glass, as beautiful as they were deadly, spiked into the rounded mortar. On the walls and within the compound, as well as on the dark street itself, all was quiet.

"I see no signs of life." Ehomba frowned slightly. "Do not the wealthy folk of these foreign lands set someone to keep watch over their homes and possessions?"

Crouching as he ran, Simna was edging along the wall toward the front door. "If someone is powerful enough, or ruthless enough, their reputation can act as adequate protection. It's cheaper, and can be just as effective. That seems to be the case with our friend bin Grue."

Stretching to his full height, Ehomba tried to see over the wall. "I would expect the merchant to keep a property as valuable and difficult to manage as the litah somewhere in the back of his establishment, out of sight and hearing of random visitors."

Simna nodded agreement. "I don't like going in through the front door, but it might prove the easiest way. If ordinary thieves are afraid to enter, it may be protected by nothing more than a simple lock."

The herdsman looked down at his friend. "Are there such things as simple locks?"

Simna grinned knowingly. "To someone who has made the aquaintance of many, yes."

True to his word, the swordsman made short work of the keyed entrance while Ehomba kept watch on the street. No one was abroad in the much-esteemed neighborhood at that late hour save a few stray cats. Two of these lingered to enjoy Ehomba's earnest attention, waltzing back and forth beneath his soothing palm as he stroked their backs and smoothed out their tails as if they were candle wicks.

"Will you stop that?" whispered Simna urgently as he finished with the lock.

"Why?" Ehomba wondered innocently. "I cannot help you in your work. I *can* help these cats."

"Well, you're wasting your energy. They'll never be able to help *you*."

Rising, the herdsman moved closer to the door. "You do not know that, my friend. You never know when something you meet may be able to do you a service. Better to show respect to all Nature's creations."

"I'll remind you of that if we ever find ourselves lost in a cloud of mosquitoes." At his gentle but firm push, the door gave inward, squeaking slightly. "There. We're in."

Ehomba followed him through the doorway. "Do you usually find yourself breaking into other people's property?"

"No. Usually I find myself breaking out." Simna squinted as they advanced inward. "Shit!" He jerked back sharply, then relaxed. Something small and fast skittered away into the shadows. "Just a rat."

There was barely enough light to allow them to find their way between high desks and wooden cabinets. A back door led to a small storeroom that was piled high with exotic goods. It smelled wonderfully of fragrant spices and packages of incense, of fine silks and cloths brought from the far corners of the world. There were jars of aromatic liquids and wooden crates bound with hammered brass and copper. Clearly Haramos bin Grue was no dealer in baskets of fish or wagonloads of vegetables. If his tastes reflected his clientele, he would be likely to have powerful friends.

All the more reason, Ehomba knew, to conclude their business and depart as quickly as possible.

They found the big cat at the very back of the inner storeroom, slumped on his side in a cage walled with steel bars that crisscrossed in a herringbone pattern. In the dim light Simna tiptoed forward to whisper urgently at the sleeping feline.

"Ahlitah! It's Etjole and Simna, come to rescue you. Get up, cat! This is no time to nap."

Silent as a shadow, Ehomba peered past him. "He is not sleeping. He has been drugged. It is what I would do if I had to try and keep something like a black litah under control."

Searching for a way in, the swordsman located a half-height door at one end of the cage. It was secured with the largest padlock he had ever seen, a veritable iron monster the size of a melon. Its dimensions did not trouble him. The fact that it took three keys to unlock it did.

"Can you solve it?" Ehomba had never seen such a thing. The Naumkib had no need of such devices.

"I don't know." Simna had his face pressed right up against the heavy appliance, trying to peer within. "The biggest problem is that the multiple locks are most likely sequenced. If I solve the wrong set of tumblers first, it could cause the others to freeze up. Then we'll never get it open."

"You have to try. Which one feels like the first?"

Employing the same small knife he had used to pick the lock on the front door, the swordsman sweated over the three keyholes, trying to decide where to begin.

"Trust your instincts," Ehomba advised him.

"I would, if I were dealing with three women instead of three locks. Metal gives you no clues." Taking a deep breath, he prepared to ease the tip of the small blade into the middle keyhole. "Might as well try here as anywhere else."

"A good choice. Your friend is right, swordsman. You have excellent instincts."

Whirling, they found themselves confronted by a wide-awake Haramos bin Grue. The trader was standing before an open portal where none had appeared to exist. He had gained entrance to the storeroom via a secret door set in a blank wall, a not uncommon conceit of suspicious merchants. In one hand he held a small lamp that threw a halo of light around him. That their nocturnal visit had caught him by surprise was proven by the fact that he stood there in his elegant one-piece sleeping gown. The fingers of his left hand were curled tightly around some small object. On his right shoulder, chittering away as madly as any pet parrot, was the scruffy, naked-tailed rat Simna had nearly tripped over in the outer offices.

As Simna continued to fumble with the lock, a solemn-faced Ehomba turned to step between him and the trader. Oblivious to the strained confrontation, the black litah slept on.

"We have come for our friend," the herdsman explained quietly.

"Have you now?" Bin Grue was not smiling. "In the middle of the night, by breaking into my rooms?"

"A thief has no claim on the protection of the law."

Now the merchant did smile, a slight parting of the lips that was devoid of humor. "I thought you were an expert on cow dung. Now I see that you are secretly a philosopher."

"What I am does not matter. Unlock the enclosure and let our companion go."

"The exceptional cat is my property. I already have three potential buyers bidding against one another for the rights to it. Their agitation as they frantically drive up the price is wonderful to behold. Naturally you must understand I could not give him back to you now." He gestured with the lamp, making the only source of real light in the room dance according to his whim. "Why so much concern over the fate of a mere animal? So it speaks the language of men. A good horse is more valuable, and I have yet to encounter one that can speak even a single word."

"Do not be so quick to judge value until you have talked to the horse," the herdsman replied calmly. "I was not so concerned for the litah as you think. In fact, as my friend can attest, I would have left him to his fate but for one thing."

Bin Grue was listening intently. "What one thing?"

In the uneasy shadows Ehomba's dark eyes might have glittered ever so slightly with a light that was not a reflection of the trader's lamp. "You tried to have us killed."

Bin Grue did his best to shrug off the accusation. "That was Moleshohn's doing."

"Some men are easier to take the measure of than others. The All-Knowing would not have taken that step without your direction, or at least your approval."

"I deny having given it, and having denied it, I offer my apology if you insist on believing otherwise." He smiled broadly, encouragingly. "Come now, herdsman. Why should we let something that reeks mightily and sprays indiscriminately come between us? Allow me to bribe you. I will cut you a fair piece of the action. Why not? There will be plenty to satisfy all. Consent with me, and I promise that you both will leave Lybondai with new clothing, sturdy mounts, and money in your pockets. What say you?"

"I say—that these clothes suit me fine, and that I will not shake the hand of one who acceded in trying to have me murdered." Behind him, Simna's fingers flew over iron as the agitated swordsman tried to work faster. But the bloated padlock was proving as obstinate as a teenage daughter refused permission to attend the annual Fair of Crisola the Procreant.

On the trader's shoulder, the watchrat crouched low, digging its tiny claws into the material of bin Grue's sleeping gown. The merchant's smile vanished. "I'm sorry to hear that, lover of sheep dags. It means that I will be forced to finish what the helpful but lamentably ineffectual Moleshohn was unable to do." Extending his left arm, he opened his fingers to show what he was holding.

Ehomba eyed it emotionlessly. Behind him, Simna ibn Sind looked up from his so far futile efforts. His eyes widened slightly, then narrowed. Initially wary, he quickly now found himself more perplexed than fearful.

It was another box.

IV

"What are you going to do with that?" The swordsman's tone reflected his uncertainty and confusion. "Tavern us to death?"

A second thin, humorless smile split the trader's no-nonsense visage. His jaws worked redundantly, grinding on an invisible cigar. "Did you think I had only one box, night thief? I have a box full of boxes. Not all are home to the benign." Casually, as if utterly indifferent to the consequences of his action, he tossed the box in their direction. Ehomba took a step back as it struck the floor between them.

And began, exactly as the portable tavern bin Grue had brought to light previously before them, to unfold.

No mirrors flashed the light of delectation from behind a bar attended by indulgent countermen. No lithe-limbed maids danced between tables bearing pitchers and goblets of imported libations. There was no cadre of good-natured celebrants to welcome the travelers into their company.

That did not mean that the box was empty.

As the box continued to open and its unfolding sides to multiply, a towering figure rose from its center. It wore heavy iron armor and had shoulders like a buffalo. The massive skull hung low on the chest, and mordant eyes blazed deep within the cold-forged helmet. A spike-studded club rested on one shoulder, and its thighs were as big around as Simna ibn Sind's entire body.

"Brorunous the Destroyer." Bin Grue announced the apparition's arrival with a contented grunt.

A second figure emerged from the softly pulsing, inch-high platform generated by the ever-expanding box. Eight feet tall and thin as a whip, it leaned forward so that its elongated arms touched the floor. Resembling a cross between a spider monkey and an assortment of cutthroats Simna had once known, it held a pair of throwing knives in each hand and drooled like an idiot. A demented, homicidal idiot.

Bin Grue spoke again. "Yoloth-tott, Cardinal Assassin to Emperor Cing the Third of Umur."

Other figures began to appear, massive of limb, effusive of arms, and maniacal of mien. They crowded together in the defiled space limned by the ichorous phosphorescence that spilled from the dilating box. Haramos bin Grue had a name for each one, though he did not call them out as if reciting a register of old friends. His tone was unimpassioned and impersonal, the same he might have used to itemize any inventory.

The result was a pageant of perversion, a bringing together of slavering, marching evil not to be found at any one time in any one place anywhere in the world.

"Behold," he proclaimed flatly when the final apparition had been called forth and the box had unfolded its last. "No greater aggregation of murderers, butchers, and psychopaths is to be found anywhere. All gathered together for your consideration. They act only at the bidding of the master of the box that contains them, and I can tell you from previous experience that their extended suppression in a much-confined space does nothing to improve their already misanthropic temperament. At such times when they are freed from that confinement, as they are now, they're eager to express their sentiments."

Simna ibn Sind had drawn his sword. No coward, he was ready to stand and fight. But, looking at the awful assemblage of accumulated annihilation arrayed before them, he could not help but be less than sanguine about their prospects.

Still, there was something the cold-blooded merchant did not know.

"The sky-metal sword!" he whispered tensely to his tall, phlegmatic companion. "Use the sword! Draw down the wind from the heavens and blow these hard-featured horrors away!"

"In so confined a space that could be dangerous to all of us." Ehomba eyed the assembled grinning, grunting, expectant specters thoughtfully. His unruffled demeanor was beginning to unnerve the trader.

"Look upon the fate that has unfolded before you, herdsman. I have but to give the word and they will rend you from head to foot. They'll rip out your organs and feast on them raw. Have you no fear? Or are you too ignorant to know when death is staring you in the face?"

Ignoring the conglomeration of anticipative vileness, Ehomba reached slowly over his back. Not for either of the two swords slung there, but for something small concealed within his pack. Nor did he thrust forward his walking stick–spear with the dark, enchanted fossil tooth that was lashed to its tip. While the merchant watched curiously to see what he was about and Simna ibn Sind hovered anxiously by his side, the herdsman uncurled his fingers to reveal . . .

"A piece of string?" Ibn Sind's lower jaw dropped.

Ehomba nodded once. "Yes. Though my people would say twine, and not string."

Haramos bin Grue sighed regretfully. "It all makes sense now. You have the fearlessness of the mad. Only the completely crazy can be truly brave, because they really never comprehend the dangers before them." He started to turn away. "That won't stop me from having you killed, of course." He proceeded to wave his hand in a certain way, and finished by snapping his fingers three times.

Spriest of all the cunning executioners, the mass murderer Lohem En-Qaun leaped forward, all four eyes ablaze, eager to be the first to draw blood. Matching the leaping wraith's agility, Simna raised his sword preparatory to fending off the attack. As he did so, Ehomba brought his right arm down and up, flinging his short length of twine at the bounding assailant.

A light enveloped the strand, an eerie radiance that seemed to course along its individual fibers. It was not a fiery glow, not in any way especially dazzling or brilliant. The thin cord simply metamorphosed into a kind of coruscating brownness that transcended its lowly origins.

Like a snake emerging from its hole, it lengthened and grew. It whipped around Lohem En-Qaun and snapped all four of his arms to his sides, pinning them to multiple ribs and freezing the would-be slayer in his tracks. Bin Grue gaped, but wore the mask of disbelief for only a moment. He was a hardened man, was the merchant, and in his time had seen much that had toughened him against surprise.

"Kill them." Raising a hand that did not shake, he pointed straight at the two intruders. "Kill them now!"

Unintimidated by their compeer's consternation, the rest of the murderous throng rushed forward—only to be met by the darting, writhing, sinuous length of twine. It caught the ankles of Brorunous the Destroyer and brought the hulking body crashing to the floor, as if binding a mountain. Singing through the night air, loops of glowing strands enveloped and secured Yoloth the Assassin, preventing him from wielding so much as a single knife or throwing star. It fettered the hands and constrained the claws and locked the feet and shuttered the jaws of a dozen of the most vile, proficient killers who had ever lived, and bound them all up together in a single howling, raving mass of impotent destruction.

And then, having done this, it looped and twisted and coiled and curled until it had squeezed them right back down into a strangely imprinted and inscribed box small enough to fit in the palm of a man's hand. Around the box was fitted, snugly and with no room to slip a querulous finger beneath, the original length of string Etjole Ehomba had removed from his pack. No insult was intended, no dry humor contrived, but the little bow with which the binding was finished was far more suggestive than any knot could have been.

Haramos bin Grue was gone. Having finally acknowledged the reality of what he was seeing, he had fled through the back door before the graceful compacting of his terrors could be completed. Simna approached the box and, with gathering boldness, picked it up. Marveling at the simple, six-sided wonder, he rolled it over in his fingers, glanced sharply back at his friend.

"Is it harmless now?"

Ehomba had walked over to the sturdy cage and was gazing at the black, furry mass within. Ahlitah had slept through it all. "So long as you're careful not to loosen the bow." Swinging his pack around, he began to search its depths.

Keeping his fingers well away from the simple twine that secured the box, the swordsman looked around until he found a tall amphora full of fine olive oil. Removing the lid, he dropped the box inside and watched as it slowly sank out of sight in the viscous, aromatic liquid. It would not be among the first places the merchant would think to search.

Satisfied, he replaced the cover and moved to rejoin his friend.

As he did so, he kept glancing worriedly at the rear door through which the trader had disappeared. "I know bin Grue's type. He won't give up something this important to him, even in the face of superior sorcery. We've got to get out of here."

Ehomba glared at him and the swordsman was taken aback. The herdsman rarely showed much emotion. "You talked me into this. We are not leaving here without what we came for."

"By Gittam's eyelashes, that's fine with me, Etjole—but we'd best hurry." He indicated the massive padlock. "I can try my hand at that again, but the risk remains the same. Or is there some alchemy you can use on it?"

"I know no alchemy."

"Right," the swordsman retorted sardonically. "You only know twine."

"That was not my doing. In the village there is a man called Akanauk. He is—simple. Here." He tapped the side of his head. "The Naumkib are a tolerant folk, and he is left to himself, to be himself. When he needs food, it is given to him. Sleeping in a house makes him cry out in the night and wake the children, so some of us built him a platform high up in one of the village's few trees. He climbs up there at night and there he lies and gurgles happily, like a baby.

"Akanauk does not farm, or help in the watching of the herds, or gather shellfish on the shore." As he studied the cage and its single heavily drugged occupant, Ehomba again touched finger to temple. "He does not have the ability to do so. What he does is sit by himself and make things. Simple things. A necklace of colored beach pebbles like those I carry with me in my pocket, or a crown of mint leaves, or armlets of woven palm frond, or lengths of strong cord."

Still watching the back door, Simna indicated that he understood. "So the village simpleton gave you a piece of his homemade string and you took it just to please him, and to remind you of home."

"No," the herdsman replied blandly. "I took it because a traveler never knows when he might need a piece of cord to tie something up."

"Gellsteng knows it's so. Now, use your wizardry to pick this lock so we can get out of here. Even as we speak, that slug bin Grue may be raising arms against us."

"I cannot do anything with that lock. I do not have your skill with such things. And I am no wizard, Simna. You should know that by now."

"Hoy, the evidence is all around me." His gaze narrowed as his friend revealed a small bottle cupped in one hand. It was very tiny. Even when full, the swordsman estimated it could hold no more than a few drops.

The sound of running feet, striking distant stone like gathering rain, made him turn sharply. "If you're going to do anything, you'd better do it quickly. They're coming."

Kneeling by the side of the cage, Ehomba put an arm between the bars and held the little bottle as close to the anesthetized Ahlitah's head as possible. Laying his spear carefully by his side, he reached through the close-set bars with his other hand.

"You might want to step back a little," he advised his companion.

Sword once more in hand, Simna was trying to watch the back door and the cage at the same time. "Why?" he asked pointedly. "Is some djinn going to burst from the phial? Are you going to use a special acid to dissolve away the bars?"

"Nothing like that." The herdsman carefully loosened the bottle's minuscule stopper. When it was almost free, he placed the thumb of his left hand against it and removed his right hand from the cage. This he used for the prosaic and decidedly unsorceral purpose of pinching his nostrils together.

Feet came pounding down unseen steps and the voices of alert, angry men could be heard shouting. "Hurry!" the swordsman admonished his companion. Even as he sounded a final warning he was backing away. Not from the door, nor from the cage, but from that tiny, undistinguished phial of cheap trade glass. Anything that made Etjole Ehomba want to hold his nose suggested strongly that others in the vicinity should be prepared to beat a hasty retreat.

As the back door was flung wide to reveal the stocky figure of Haramos bin Grue backed by a bevy of armed servants and soldiers, the herdsman's thumb flicked the loosened stopper free. Simna saw nothing, but most perfumes are invisible to the eye. What wafted from the interior of the tiny bottle, however, must have been somewhat stronger than attar of roses or essence of myrrh.

As bin Grue's disciples poured in, Ahlitah's nostrils flared wide enough to accommodate a pair of ripened mangoes. Startlingly yellow eyes burst open, a snort louder and higher than that of a breaching whale rolled through the storeroom, and the big cat leaped straight up until its black-maned head banged against the top of the cage. Startled by this sight, the first men into the chamber were brought up short.

The trader harried them onward. "It's only a cat safely secured in a cage. Where is your manhood? Get them!" He thrust an accusing hand at the pair of intruders.

With an invigorated roar that must have been heard aboard sailing ships well out to sea, the black litah whirled within the trap, parted its mighty jaws, and bit down on both latch and attached padlock. Caught within that single massive bite, the lock exploded, sending bits of tumbler and spring and pin flying in multiple directions. As Simna warded off blows from two assailants simultaneously and Ehomba blocked a lance thrust with his spear, the litah

pressed its huge skull against the door of its cage and
snapped it open.

"Get them, quickly—kill them both!" bin Grue was
shouting with mounting concern.

His servitors were no longer listening. No amount of
guaranteed remuneration or personal loyalty could compel
any man to face the raging quarter-ton Ahlitah. Freed from
its stoned slumber, the cat was not only ablaze with a desire
for revenge, he was hungry.

Bin Grue was courageous and even fearless, but he was
not stupid. Beating a retreat back through the doorway, he
vowed to regain possession of the emancipated feline and
extract a measure of retribution from its liberators. Between
the energized roars of the litah and the screams of men trying to get out of its way, the merchant's audacious affiances
went unheard.

The storeroom emptied in less than a minute. The litah
would have settled down to eat, but Ehomba was at its side,
fingers tugging on the thick mane. "We need to leave. The
man who abducted you is no coward. He will try again."

"Let him," snapped Ahlitah, one massive forepaw resting
on the back of an unfortunate fighter who had been too slow
in fleeing. "I'll deal with any humans who come back."

"We don't want trouble with the city authorities." Breathing hard and still watching the back door, Simna stood on
the cat's other side. "If I were bin Grue, that would be my
next step. Try to inveigle the local law into helping by
telling them that there's a dangerous, crazed animal on the
loose in a populated area. A threat to the general citizenry."

"I'm no threat to anyone but that muck master."

"You know that, and I know that, and Etjole knows it too,
but it's been my experience that nervous humans tend to
throw arrows and other sharp objects at large carnivores
long before they'll sit down to discuss events calmly and rationally with them."

"Simna is right." Straightening, Ehomba prepared to depart, spear in hand. He had restoppered the diminutive phial and replaced it in his pack. "We need to go."

Still the furious predator hesitated. Then it turned and, with a parting snarl, followed the two men toward the front doorway. But not before pausing several times along the way to spray the interior of the storeroom with essence of large male cat, thereby ruining for good a succession of exceptionally rare and valuable commodities.

No one was waiting for them out in the street and there was no confrontation as they raced not back toward the waterfront, but in the general direction of the rolling, heavily forested hills that marked the landlocked side of the city.

"Bin Grue's people probably haven't stopped running." Simna jogged effortlessly alongside his taller friend.

Ehomba ran with the supple, relaxed lope of one used to covering long, lonely distances by himself. "If we are lucky. What you told Ahlitah makes sense to me, too, but I think it may take the merchant some time to convince the authorities that there is real urgency to the matter." The herdsman glanced at the sky. "It is still several hours to sunrise. At this hour he may have trouble finding anyone to listen to him, sympathetic *or* skeptical."

Simna nodded agreement. "Tell me, bruther—if it wasn't sorcery, what *did* you use to rouse our four-legged friend from his trance? I've never seen anything, man or beast, released so quickly from the bonds of heavy sedation."

"It was a potion made for me by old Meruba. To wake a man unconscious from injury, so that he may have a chance to walk away from a place of danger."

"Ah," commented the swordsman knowingly. "Some kind of smelling salts."

The herdsman looked down at him. "No salts, my friend. In the sheltered river valleys of my country there is an animal we call the oris. It is the size of a mature, healthy pig, has four short horns and long black fur that it drags upon the ground. Three red stripes run from its head along its back and down to the tip of its tail. The female defends itself against those like Ahlitah that eat meat by spraying from glands above its hind parts a scent that is God's own musk. This is the same stink it uses to attract males of its kind, but it will also attract any other warm-blooded male animal in the vicinity. It can only hope that a male of its own kind reaches it first. When employed as a defense, it works by altering the intention of any male meat-eater that threatens attack, and by confusing any female predator."

"I see." Simna grinned as he ran. "So the perfume of this oris is irresistible to any male, and you roused our four-legged friend by letting him have a whiff of the stuff." He found himself eyeing the herdsman's pack. "When we again find ourselves in more accommodating surroundings, I might ask you to let me have a quick sniff. Just out of curiosity's sake, you understand," he added hastily.

"You do not want to do that."

"Why not?" The swordsman nodded in the direction of the black litah, who was leading the way through darkened city streets. "He handled it without trouble."

"The capacity of his nose is many times yours, or ours. But that is not the problem."

"Hoy? Then what is?"

"Meruba's bottle holds only a couple of drops, but they are not drops of oris musk. They are drops concentrated from musk taken from the glands of fifty oris."

"Oh." Simna frowned uncertainly. "That's bad?"

Ehomba looked down at him. As usual, the herdsman was not smiling. "If need be, you will attack yourself."

Simna ibn Sind considered this. He contemplated it from several angles, eventually coming to the conclusion that he fervently disliked every one of them.

"That's nasty," he finally confessed to his friend.

"Indeed it is."

Again the swordsman indicated the big cat, pacing along in front of them. "Greater capacity or not, our swarthy friend seems to be managing the aftereffects with no difficulty."

"So far," Ehomba agreed. "Still, with oris musk one can never be too careful." He met Simna's eye as they ran, racing to reach the outskirts of sleepy Lybondai before sunrise. "Why do you think I am making sure to run *behind* the litah?"

V

Everywhere they paused for breath they asked if anyone had news of one Haramos bin Grue, but the people who lived on the outskirts of the great port city had little to do with sailors and traders and those who haunted the waterfront. These craftsfolk survived beneath the notice of the wealthier merchants and traders who dominated the commerce of the south coast of Premmois. At least the wily merchant had not lied about Hamacassar: those they questioned confirmed that it was indeed a real place, and the port most likely to harbor ships and men willing to dare a crossing of the vast Semordria.

In the hilly suburb of Colioroi they did find several local greengrocers who had heard of bin Grue. He was known to them only by reputation, as an influential trafficker in specialty goods whose wealth placed him somewhere in the upper third of the merchant class, but who was by no means as celebrated or affluent or powerful as the famed Bouleshias family or Vinmar the Profuse.

Given the choice, Ahlitah would have scoured the city in search of the man who had briefly reduced him to the status of merchandise. "He not only stole my freedom, he pocketed my dignity and put a price on it." Yellow eyes gleamed as the big cat's words were subsumed in snarl. "I want to eat him. I want to hear his bones break between my teeth and feel the warm flow of his blood running down my throat."

"Maybe another time." Marking step and hour with his walking stick–spear, Ehomba led the way along the narrow road that wound through the low forested hills. With each stride the milling masses of Lybondai fell farther behind, and distant, fabled Hamacassar came a step nearer. "First I must fulfill my obligation."

The black cat paced him, the top of its mane even with the tall herdsman's face. "What of my dignity?"

It was always a shock when Ehomba lost his composure. Usually soft-spoken to the point of occasional inaudibility, it was doubly startling on those rare occasions when he did raise his voice. He whirled sharply on the litah.

"To Hell with your dignity! I am unlucky enough to be beholden to a dead man. That is a real thing, not an abstraction of self." He tapped his sternum. "Do you think you are the only one with such worries? The only creature with personal concerns?" Making a grand gesture with his free hand, he took in the sloping seacoast valley behind them and the glistening blue sea against which it snuggled like a sleeping dog by its master's side.

"My wife, my mate, lies uncounted leagues to the south, and my two children, and my friends, and none of them know at this moment if I live or am food for worms. That is a real thing, too. I would just as soon not be here as fervently as you!" Aware that he was shouting, he lowered his voice. "When we reached the southern shore of the Aboqua I was happy, because I thought we could find a ship in the trading towns of the Maliin to carry us across the Semordria. When we reached this place I was happy, because I thought the same thing." His attention shifted back to the path ahead.

"Now I find that we must once again travel an uncertain distance overland to this place called Hamacassar before that will be possible. And who knows what we will find when we get there? More frightened seamen, more reluctant captains? Will we have to cross the river where this city lies and keep marching, keep walking, because in spite of what we have been told its ships, too, will not dare the ocean reaches? I do not want to have to walk across the top of the world."

They strode on in silence for a while, ignoring the stares of farmers tending to their crops or children with sticks herding pigs and fowl, armadillos and small hoofed things with fluttering trunks and feathery tails.

Having initiated the silence, it was Ahlitah who broke it. "You have a mate and cubs. I have nothing but my dignity. So it is more important to me than to you."

Ehomba pondered the feline reply, then nodded slowly. "You are right. I was being selfish. Forgive me."

"Not necessary," rumbled the big cat. "The impulse to selfishness is a natural impulse, one we are all heir to." The great black-maned head turned to look at him. "I wish you would lose your temper more often. It would make you more catlike."

"I am not sure I want to be more catlike. I—" The herdsman broke off. On his other side and slightly behind him, Simna ibn Sind was struggling to suppress his laughter. "What are you sniggering about?"

"You. You're discussing philosophy with a cat." The swordsman was grinning broadly.

Ehomba did not smile back. "What could be more natural? Cats are by their very nature deeply philosophical."

The litah nodded agreement. "When we're not sleeping or killing something."

"You mistake babble for profundity." Raising an arm, Simna pointed. "Better to concentrate on how we're going to get through that."

Just ahead, the hills gave way to broad, flat marshland of interminable width. It extended as far to east and west as they could see. On the northern horizon, a second range of hills lifted rounded knolls toward the sky, but they were quite distant.

Rushes and reeds rose in profusion from the marsh, and throngs of songbirds darted from tree to occasional tree like clouds of iridescent midges. Wading birds stalked subsurface prey while flightless, toothed cousins darted and dove through the murky water. Water dragonets with webbed feet and vestigial wings competed for food with their feathered relatives. Ehomba could see miniature jets of flame spurt from hidden hunting sites as the leathery blue and green predators brought down large insect prey.

That there was plenty of that to go around he did not doubt. The nearer they drew to the water's edge, the more they found themselves executing the informal marshland salute, which consisted of waving a hand back and forth in front of their faces with ever-increasing frequency. Against the irritating insects Ahlitah could only blink rapidly and attempt to defend his rear with rapid switches of his tufted tail.

Simna was first to the water. He knelt and stirred it with a hand. Decaying vegetation bunched up against the shore, its steady decomposition creating a rich soup for those small creatures that dwelled within. Rising, he shook drops from his fingers.

"It's shallow here, but that doesn't mean we can count on walking all the way across." He nodded toward the distant hills, partially obscured behind a rose-hued pastel haze. "Better to paddle."

"Another boat." Ehomba sighed. "It seems we are always to be looking for boats."

They found one with surprising ease, but in addition to paddles, storage lockers, rudder, and a small anchor, it came equipped with an admonition. The orangutan who rented it to them wore a tattered shirt, short pants, and a rag of a mariner's cap. As he advised them, he was continually reigniting the small-bowled, long-stemmed pipe that was clamped between his substantial lips.

"This is a one-way trip for us." A reluctant Simna was counting out some of the last of his Chlengguu gold. "How will we get your boat back to you?"

"Oh, I ain't worried about that, I ain't." In the haze-diffused sunlight, the blond in the reddish gold hair gleamed more golden than usual. "You'll be bringin' it back yourselves, you see." He sat in the rocking chair on the porch outside his small wooden shack and bobbed contentedly back and forth.

Swordsman and herdsman exchanged a look. Indifferent to matters of commerce, the black litah sat by the water's edge and amused himself catching shallow-loving minnows with casual flicks of one paw.

"Why would we be doing that?" Simna asked him straightforwardly.

Removing the attenuated pipe from his mouth, the orang gestured at the marsh with a long finger. "Because you'll never get across, that's why. You can try, but sooner or later you'll have to turn back."

Simna bristled at the ape's conviction but held his temper. "You don't know us, friend. I am an adventurer and swordsman of some note, my tall friend here is an eminent wizard, and that cat that plays so quietly by your little pier can, when roused, be terrible to behold. We have come a long way through many difficulties. No reed-choked, smelly slough is going to stop us."

"It won't be the fen that turns you back," the orang informed him. "It'll be the horses."

"Horses?" Ehomba made a face. "What is a horse?"

"By Gleronto's green gaze!" Simna gaped at his friend. "You don't know what a horse is?"

Ehomba eyed him impassively. "I have never seen one."

The swordsman did not try to disguise his disbelief. "Tall at the shoulder, like a big antelope. Leaner than a buffalo. Like a zebra, only without stripes."

"Ah! That I can envision." Confident once more, the headsman turned his attention back to their host. "Why should a few horses keep us from crossing the marsh?"

The old ape squinted, staring past them at the concealing reeds and enshrouding bullrushes. "Because they're mad, that's why."

"Mad?" Turning his head to his right, Simna spat, just missing the porch. "What are they mad at?"

With his softly smoking pipe, the orang made stabbing gestures at the swordsman. "Not angry-mad. Insane-mad. Crazy as loons. Deranged, the whole great gallumphing lot of 'em." He stuck the pipe back in his mouth and puffed a little harder. "Always been that way, always will be. They're why nobody can get across the marsh. Have to follow the coast for weeks in either direction to get around, it, but can't get across. Horses. Lunatics on four legs. And a couple of 'em have eight." He nodded meaningfully, seconding his own wisdom.

"That's impossible." Simna found himself starting to wonder about their hirsute host's sanity.

"It's more than impossible, no-lips. It's crazy." The orange-haired ape fluttered an indifferent hand at the endless reach of rush and reed. "But you three go on. You'll see. You've got my little flat-bottom there. Paddle and pole to your hearts' content. Who knows? Maybe you'll get lucky. Maybe you'll be the first to make it across. But me, I don't think so. Them horses are thorough, and they've got big ears."

For the moment, Ehomba chose to accept the old man of the forest's narrative as truth. As a youth he had learned not to disparage even the most outrageous tale, lest it turn out, to his embarrassment and detriment, to be true. As they had already learned on their journey, the world was full to overflowing with the unexpected. Perhaps it was even home to insane horses.

"I do not understand. Sane or otherwise, why should a herd of horses care whether anyone crosses this marshland or not?"

Thick lips concaved in a simian smile. "Why ask me? I'm only a semiretired fisherman. If you want to know, ask the horses."

"We will." Rising from his crouch, Ehomba turned and stepped off the porch. "Let us go, Simna."

"Hoy." Favoring the ape with a last look of skepticism, the swordsman pivoted to follow his friend.

The boat wasn't much, but the edge of the marsh was not the grand harbor of Lybondai. It was all they had been able to find. There had been other fisherfolk, with other boats, but none willing to rent their craft to the travelers. Without exception all had declined sans an explanation. Now the reason for their reluctance was clear. They were afraid of losing their craft to the horses.

With its flat, sturdy bottom and simple low wooden sides, the boat more nearly resembled a loose plank with seats. There was a rudder, which helped them to locate the stern, and the prow was undercut to allow the occupants to propel it over obstructing water plants. There were no paddles, only poles.

"Shallow all the way across, then." Simna hefted one of the tough, unyielding wooden shafts.

"So it would seem." Ehomba had selected a slightly longer rod and was similarly sampling its heft.

"Sadly," declared Ahlitah as he hopped lithely into the unlovely craft, "I have no hands, and can therefore not help." Curling up in the center of the floor, he promptly went to sleep.

"Cats." Shaking his head, the swordsman eyed the litah with digust. "First cats and now, it would seem, maybe horses." Placing one end of his pole in the water, he strained as he and Ehomba shoved hard against the sodden shore. "I don't like animals that much. Except when they're well done, and served up in a proper sauce."

"Then you and the litah have something in common," the herdsman pointed out. "He feels the same way about people."

The marshland might have been a paradise if not for the mosquitoes and black flies and no-see-ums. To his companions' surprise, Simna voiced little in the way of complaint. When a curious Ehomba finally inquired as to the reason for his uncharacteristic stoicism, the swordsman explained that based on the insect life they had encounterd on shore, he had expected it to be much worse out in the middle of the slough.

"Birds and frogs." Ehomba's pole rose and dipped steadily, rhythmically, as he ignored the rushes and reeds that brushed against his arms and torso. "They keep the population of small biting things down." He watched as a pair of lilac-breasted rollers went bulleting through the bushes off to their left. "If not for such as them, we would have no blood left by the time we reached the other side of this quagmire."

Simna nodded, then frowned as he glanced down at the litah dozing peacefully in the middle of the boat. "For once I envy you your black fur."

A single tawny eye popped open halfway. "Don't. It's hot, and I still get bitten on both ends if not in between."

Ehomba tilted back his head to watch a flock of a hundred or more turquoise flamingos glide past overhead, their coloration rendering them almost invisible against the sky. Unlike much of what he was seeing and hearing, they were a familiar bird. They acquired their brilliant sky hue, he knew, as a consequence of eating the bright blue shrimp that thrived in warm, shallow lakes.

Disturbed by their passing, a covey of will-o'-the-wisps broke cover and drifted off in all directions, their ghostly white phosphorescence difficult to track in the bright light of day. A herd of sitatunga went splashing past, their splayed feet allowing the downsized antelope to walk on a surface of lily pads, flowering hyacinth, and other water plants. Capybara gamboled in the tall grass, and the guttural honking of hippos, like a convocation of fat men enjoying a good joke, reverberated in the distance.

Yellow-and-gray-spotted coats dripping, giant ground sloths shuffled lugubriously through the water, their long prehensile tongues curling around and snapping off the succulent buds of flowering plants. Web-footed wombats competed for living space with families of pink-nosed nutria. The marshland was a fertile and thriving place, catalyzed with life large and small.

But no horses, mentally unbalanced or otherwise. Not yet.

"Maybe old Red-hair was right *and* wrong." Simna poled a little faster, forcing Ehomba to increase his own efforts to keep up. "Maybe there are a few crazy horses living in here, but they can't be everywhere at once. In a swamp this big they could easily overlook us." He paused briefly to wipe perspiration from his brow. The interior of the marshland was not particularly hot, but the humidity was as bad as one would expect.

"It is possible." The herdsman was scanning their immediate surroundings. All around the boat there was motion, and noise, and small splashings, but no sign of the equine impediment the ape had warned them against. "If this morass is as extensive as he said, then we certainly have a chance to slip across unnoticed. It is not as if we represent the forerunners of a noisy, invading army."

"That's right." The farther they traveled without confrontation, the more confident Simna allowed himself to feel. "There's just the three of us in this little boat. It has no profile to speak of, and neither do we."

"We will try to find some land to camp on tonight. If not, we will have to sleep in the boat."

Simna grimaced. "Better a hard dry bed than a soft wet one. I know—in my time I've had to sleep in both."

It was not exactly a rocky pinnacle thrusting its head above the surrounding reeds, but the accumulation of dirt had small trees with trunks of real wood growing from it and soil dry enough to suit the swordsman. Ehomba was especially appreciative of the discovery. The damp climate was harder on him than on his companions, since of them all he hailed from the driest country. But he was a very adaptable man, and rarely gave voice to his complaints.

As was to be expected, all manner of marsh dwellers sought out the unique opportunities created by dry land, whose highest point rose less than a foot above the water. Birds nested in every one of the small-boled trees, and water-loving lizards and terrapins came ashore to lay their eggs. Boomerang-headed diplocauls kept their young close to shore for protection while on the far side of the little island juvenile black caimans and phytosaurs slumbered on, indifferent to their bipedal mammalian visitors.

Night brought with it a cacophony of insect and amphibian songs, far fewer mosquitoes than feared, and still no horses.

"There are meat-eaters here." Simna lay on his back on the sandy soil, listening to the nocturnal symphony and watching the stars through the clouds that had begun to gather above the marsh. "We haven't seen any really big ones, but with this much game there would have to be some around."

"You'd think so." Nearby, the black litah dug his bloodied muzzle deep into the still warm belly of the young water buffalo he had killed. Its eyes were closed, its fins stilled. "Easy meat."

"That is one thing about Ahlitah." Ehomba rested nearby, his hands forming a pillow beneath his braided blond hair.

"He sleeps lightly and would wake us if any danger came near."

"Hoy, I'm not worried about being trampled in my sleep. Bitten maybe, but not trampled." Simna turned away from his friend, onto his side, struggling to find the most comfortable position. "I'm even beginning to think that our only concern here might be the tall tales of one crazy old ape, instead of crazy horses."

"He did not seem to me to be mad. A little senile perhaps, but not mad."

"I don't care, so long as we make it safely through this stinking slough." A sharp report punctuated the smaller man's words as he slapped at a marauding hungry bug. His swordsman's instincts and reactions served him well: His clothes were already covered with the splattered trophies of his many mini conquests.

Their slumber was not disturbed, and they slept better than they had any right to expect. Save for the unavoidable bites of night-flying insects that prudently waited until Simna was unconscious before striking, they emerged unscathed from their fine rest.

Rising last, the swordsman stretched and yawned. For sheer degree of fetidness, his untreated morning breath matched any odor rising from the surrounding bog. That was soon mended by a leisurely breakfast of dried meat, fruit, and tepid tea.

Throughout the meal Ehomba repeatedly scanned the reed-wracked horizons, occasionally urging his friends to hurry. Ahlitah was naturally slow to wake, while Simna was clearly relishing the opportunity to dine on dry land.

"Those wise old women and men of your tribe seem to have filled your pack with all manner of useful potions and powders." The swordsman gestured with a strip of dried beef. "Didn't they give you anything to make you relax?"

Ehomba's black eyes tried to penetrate the froth of surrounding vegetation. "I do not think any such elixir exists. If it did, I promise you I would take it." He glanced back at his friend. "I know I worry too much, Simna. And when I am not worrying about things I should be worrying about, I find myself worrying about things I should not be worrying about."

"Hoy now, that makes you a bit of a worrier, wouldn't you say?" The swordsman tore off a strip of dark brown, white-edged, fibrous protein.

"Yes," the herdsman agreed. "Or perhaps I am just exceedingly conscientious."

"I know another word for that." His friend gestured with the remaining piece of jerked meat. "It's 'fool.'"

"That may be." Ehomba did not dispute the other man's definition. "Certainly it is one reason why I am here, patiently tolerating your prattle and the grunts of that cat, instead of at home lying with my wife and listening to the laughter of my children."

Simna's words rattled around a mouthful of meat that required more mastication than most. "Just confirms what I said. Geeprax knows it's true." A look of mild curiosity swept down his face as he folded the last of the jerky into his mouth. "What's up? You see something?" Immediately he rose to peer anxiously in the direction in which his tall companion was staring.

"No." The litah spoke without looking up from its kill. But it began to eat a little faster. "Heard something."

"The cat is right." Wishing he were taller still, Ehomba was straining to see off to the west. Nothing unusual crossed his field of vision. But several large wading birds tucked their long legs beneath them and unfurled imposing wings as they took to the saturated sky. "I cannot see anything, but I can hear it."

Simna had always believed he possessed senses far sharper than those of the average man, and in this he was in fact correct. But as he had learned over the past weeks, he was blind and deaf when compared to both his human and fe-line companions. It was all that time spent herding cattle, Ehomba had explained to him. Alone in the wilderness, one's senses naturally sharpened. Simna had listened to the expla-nation, and had nodded understanding, because it made sense. But it did not explain everything. Nothing that he had heard or seen since they had first met quite explained every-thing about Etjole Ehomba.

With a grunt of contentment, the satiated Ahlitah rose from the neatly butchered remnants of his kill and began to clean himself, massive paws taking the place of towels, saliva sub-stituting for soap and water. Ignoring him, Ehomba contin-ued to stare stolidly westward.

"I still don't hear anything." Simna strained to listen, knowing that with his shorter stature there was no way he would see something before the beanpole of a herdsman did. "By Gyiemot, what are you two hearing, anyway?"

"Splashing," Ehomba informed him quietly.

"Splashing? In an endless marsh? Now there's a revela-tion. I certainly wouldn't have expected to hear anything like that." As usual, his sarcasm had no effect on the southerner.

"Feet," Ehomba told him somberly. "Many feet."

The swordsman tensed slightly. Looking around, he made certain he knew the location of his sword, removed and set aside during the night. "Hoy. Feet. How many feet?"

The fine-featured herdsman glanced down at him, his voice unchanged. Sometimes Simna found himself wonder-ing if it would change if its master suddenly found himself confronted with the end of the world. He decided that it would not.

"Thousands."

Nodding somberly, Simna ibn Sind turned and bent to pick up his sword.

VI

The pulsing, living wave came at them out of the west, inclining slightly to the north of the island. For a brief moment Ehomba and Simna thought it might pass them in its inexorable surge eastward. Then it began to turn, to curl in their direction, and they knew it was they that the wave sought, and that it would not rush on past.

Its leading edge was uneven, not the regular, predictable curl of a sea wave but a broken, churning froth. The reason behind the raggedness soon became apparent. It was not a wave at all, but water thrown up from beneath thousands of hooves. The horses were driving the water before them, the flying spume like panicked insects fleeing a fire.

The two men and one cat stood their ground. It was an easy decision to make because they had no other choice. The island on which they had spent the night was the only ground on which to stand, and despite their most vigorous poling, the sturdy but unhydrodynamic flat-bottomed boat would have been hard pressed to outrun a determined turtle, much less a stampeding herd. So they stood and watched, and waited.

Potential for trampling aside, it was a magnificent sight. For Ehomba, who had never before seen a horse, the beauty and grace of the massed animals was a revelation. He had not expected that such a variety of size and color might be found within a single fundamental body type. Simna's description had been accurate—within its limitations. These horses *were* much like zebras, but whereas the herdsman knew only three different kinds of zebras, the vast herd thundering toward them exhibited as many varieties as could be conjured from a drawn-out dream.

Simna was equally impressed, but for different reasons. "I've never seen so many kinds. Most of them are unknown to me."

Ehomba looked over at his friend as they stood side by side on the sodden shore, their sandaled feet sinking slightly into the mushy sand. "I thought you said that you knew this animal."

"A few breeds and colors, yes, but I've never seen anything like this." He indicated the approaching mob. "I have a feeling no one's ever seen anything like this—not the barbarians of the Coh Plateau, who practically live on horseback, or the cavalry masters of the Murengo Kings, who account the residents of their gilded stables their most precious possessions. A man with a good rope, experience, and strong tack could take some prizes here."

"I think you speak of capture and domestication in the wrong place." Ahlitah had finally risen from his drowsing to consider the approaching herd. "These grazers stink of wildness."

Simna sniffed. "You see them as just food."

"No. Not these." The big cat's eyes narrowed as he assessed the onrushing torrent of strong legs and long necks. "Ordinarily, in the midst of such a dense gathering I could make a quick and easy kill and settle down to eat, but these grass-eaters smell of panic and desperation. Crazed grazers don't act normally. They'd be likely to turn on me and trample. Give me sane prey any day."

"Then they *are* mad." Ehomba leaned on his spear and contemplated the massed ranks of animals, which had finally begun to slow as they neared the little island. "I wonder why? They look healthy enough."

"Look at their eyes," Ahlitah advised. "They should be set forward, and staring. Too many roll, as if they're loose in their sockets." Stretching front and then back, he drew himself up to his full height. "Crazy or not, I don't think they'll rush me. No one wants to be the first to die. Stay close, and watch out for their front hooves."

Splashing through the shallows, the front ranks of the equine regiment approached the island and its three occupants. Round, piercing eyes stared, but not all were focused on the intruders. Just as the litah professed, many spun wildly and uncontrollably, staring at nothing, gazing at everything, enfolding visions that were denied to the tense but curious travelers. Several stallions sniffed of the boat where it had been pulled up on shore and tied by a single small line to a tree. One bite of heavy teeth could sever the cord. Or the weight of massed bodies could trample the craft to splinters, marooning them on the island. If the herd chose to do so, Ehomba knew, nothing could prevent them.

Simna's thoughts were exploring similar territory. "Whatever they do, don't try to stop them. They're obviously on edge and unbalanced enough as it is. We don't want to do anything to set them off."

"I do not set anyone off," the herdsman replied quietly. "It is not in my nature. But with the insane, who knows what may be considered a provocation?"

"Steady," Ahlitah advised them. "I've confronted panicked herds before. It's important to hold your ground. Flee, and they'll run you over."

An uneasy silence settled over the standoff, enveloping

visitors and herd alike. Even the waterbirds and insects in the immediate vicinity of the island were subdued. Perspiration glistened on the faces of the two men while the litah fought down the urge to pant. Meanwhile, the horses watched quietly. A few lowered their mouths to sample the water plants near their feet that had not been trampled into the mud. Others shook their heads and necks, tossing manes and sending water flying. Neighbors pawed uncertainly at the shallows.

Straining, Ehomba tried to see over their backs, to ascertain the size of the herd. He could not. Graceful necks and elegant heads stretched as far as he could see in all directions. Certainly there were thousands of them. How many thousands he could not have said. If something startled them, if they all chose to rush forward in a frenzy, he and his friends would go down beneath those pounding hooves as helplessly and fatally as mice.

Simna was whispering names at him. Breeds and types in unanticipated profusion. Palomino and bay, chestnut and grizzle, calico and sorrel, roan and dapple-gray rainbowed alongside pintos and Appaloosas. Massive Percherons and shires shaded diminutive but tough ponies while tarpans snorted at the hindquarters of wild-eyed mustangs, and Thoroughbreds held themselves aloof and proud.

There were breeds so exotic and strange even the well-traveled Simna had not a clue to their origins. Despite their outlandish appearance, under the skin every one of them was all horse. There were unicorns pure of color and mottled, with horns ranging in hue from metallic gold to deep green. Eight-legged sleipnirs jostled for space with black mares whose eyes were absent of pupil. Mesohippuses pushed against anchitheriums as hipparions and hippidons nuzzled one another nervously.

"Surely there are not so many kinds in the country you come from," Ehomba whispered to his friend.

The swordsman was overwhelmed by the diversity spread out before him. "Etjole, I don't think there are so many kinds in *any* country. Or maybe in all countries. I think we are seeing not only all the horses that are, but all that ever were. For some reason they have been trapped here, and gone mad."

"You know, Simna, I do not think they look deranged so much as they do frustrated."

"It won't matter if something spooks them and they bolt in our direction. Their frustration will kill us as surely as any insanity." He spared a glance for the sky. Except for a few wandering streaks of white, it was cloudless. No danger to the herd from thunder, then.

But the animals, magnificent and alert, would not leave.

"Let's try something," the swordsman suggested.

Ehomba indicated his willingness. "You know these animals better than I."

"I wonder." Turning, Simna started across the island, careful to make no sudden movements. Along the way, he picked up his sword and pack. Ehomba duplicated his actions while Ahlitah trailed along behind.

The herdsman glanced back. "They are not following."

"No. Now, let's see what happens if we turn north." He proceeded to do so.

The percussive sloshing of water behind them heralded movement on the part of the herd. When the travelers reached the eastern edge of the island and found themselves once more facing the distant, haze-obscured hills, they found that the herd had shifted its position just enough to block their way once again.

Having verified what they had been told, Simna was nodding to himself. "The ape was right. They won't let anyone pass. We can go east or west, or back, but not across the bog."

"We have to cross the marshlands." Ehomba watched the

horses watching him. "I have been too long away from home already and we do not know how far it is to this Hamacassar. I do not want to spend months bypassing this place, especially when we are halfway across already."

Simna grooved the wet sand with his foot. "Maybe you should ask them why they won't let anyone through."

The herdsman nodded once. "Yes. Maybe I should." He started forward.

"Hoy! I didn't mean that literally, long bruther."

Swordsman and Ahlitah tensed as the tall southerner strode forward until he was standing ankle deep in the warm water. Among those animals nearest him, one or two glanced sharply in his direction. Most ignored him, or continued to roll their eyes.

"*Can* he talk to them?" The black litah's claws dug into the moist, unfeeling earth.

"I don't see how. Before today he claimed he'd never even seen one." Simna stared at his friend's back. "But I've learned not to underestimate our cattle-loving companion. He seems simple—until he does something extraordinary." The swordsman gestured at the pack that rode high on narrow shoulders. "Maybe some village elder made him a potion that lets him talk to other beasts."

But Ehomba did not reach for his pack. Instead, he stood straight and tall in the shallow water, one hand firmly clutching his spear. Properly wielded, Simna knew that spear could spread panic and terror. Such a reaction would be counterproductive with all of them standing exposed in the path of an unstoppable stampede.

Raising his left hand, palm facing the herd, Ehomba spoke in clear, curious tones in the language of men. "We were told you would not let anyone cross the marshland. We were told that this is because you are deranged. I see wildness before me, and great beauty, but no madness. Only frustration, and its cousin, concealed rage."

At the piercing tones of the herdsman's voice several of the horses stirred nervously, and Simna made ready to run even though there was nowhere to run to. But the herd's composure held. There was, however, no response to Ehomba's words.

Anyone else would have turned and left, defeated by the massed silence. Not Ehomba. Already he carried too many unanswered questions in his head. It was stuffed full, so much so that he felt he could not abide another addition. So in the face of imminent death, he tried again.

"If you will not let us pass, then at least tell us why. I believe you are not mad. I would like to leave knowing that you are also not stupid."

Again there was no response. Not of the verbal kind. But a new class of horse stepped forward, shouldering its way between a sturdy Morgan and a deerlike eohippus. Its coat was a gleaming metallic white, its outrageous belly-length mane like thin strips of hammered silver. In the muted sunlight it looked more like the effort of a master lapidary than a living creature, something forged and drawn and pounded out and sculpted. It was alive, though.

"I am an Argentus." It spoke in the dulcet tones of a cultured soprano. "A breed that is not yet." Eyes sweet and sorrowful focused on the entranced Simna.

What a mount that would make, the swordsman was thinking, on which to canter into frolicsome Sabad or Vyorala-on-the-Baque! Delighted maidens would spill from their windows like wine. Regretfully, he knew the spectacular courser was not for riding. As the equine itself had proclaimed, it did not yet exist. Somehow he was not surprised. Not so extraordinary, he mused, to find the impossible among the demented. He was moved to comment.

"Horses cannot talk," he declared conclusively, defying the evidence of his senses.

The directness and acumen of the animal's stare was disconcerting. Simna was left with the uneasy feeling that not only was this creature intelligent, it was more intelligent than himself.

"These my cousins cannot." The great wealth of mane flowed like silver wine as the speaker gestured with his perfect head. "But I am from tomorrow, where many animals can. So I must speak for all. You were right, man. Here are representatives of all the horses that are, all that ever were—and all that will be. To a certain point in time, anyway." Displaying common cause with its diverse kin, it pawed at the water and the mud underfoot with hooves like solid silver. "I know of none that come after me."

Etjole Ehomba was too focused to be dazzled, too uncomplicated to be awed, either by sight or by confession. "Why will you not let anyone cross the marshland?"

"Because we are angry. Not insane, as other humans who come and affront us claim. Not maddened. We act, just as you see, from frustration." Again the magnificent head shook, sending waves of silver rippling sinuously. "In our running, which is what we do best, each of us has come to find him- or herself trapped in this place. Whether it is something in the heavy, humid air, or in the lukewarm waters, or something else, I do not know. I know only that, run hard and fast as we might, we cannot break free of the grip of this fey fen. It holds us here, turning us individually or as a herd, whenever we try to run free.

"We are in no danger." It glanced briefly and unafraid at the watching, unblinking Ahlitah. "There are predators, but we hold together and none no matter how hungry will chance an attack on so great a gathering. There is more than enough to eat, plentiful in variety and nourishment." It smiled slightly, the one facial cast horses with their expressive lips can effect even better than humans. "And of course, there is plenty of water. But we cannot escape the marshes. Past and present and future, we are all trapped here.

"In our collective anger and frustration, we long ago vowed that for so long as we cannot cross out from this place, none shall cross through. It is a way of expressing our solidarity, our herd-self. Our horseness. You, too, will have to turn around and go back."

"Be reasonable." Feeling a little less endangered, a little bolder, Simna waded out into the water to stand beside his friend. "We mean you no harm, and we're not responsible for your situation here."

"I would be reasonable," declared the Argentus earnestly, "but before I can be reasonable I must be horse. Solidarity is the essence of the herd."

"All of you have at one time or another passed this way, and all of you became trapped here. You say that what you do best is run, yet you cannot run free of this dank, clinging slough." Ehomba's chin rested in his free hand. Watching him, Simna was certain he could actually hear the herdsman think. "It must be wearying to have to run always in water. Perhaps if you had a better, firmer surface you could run easier, run faster." Looking up from his meditation, he locked eyes with the empathetic Argentus. "You might even find a way to run out of this marsh."

"Unfounded speculation is the progenitor of disappointment," the horse that not yet was murmured dolefully.

"I agree, but without speculation there is no consequence."

Simna's spirits soared as he saw Ehomba silently swing his unprepossessing pack off his shoulders. "Now tell me, Sorcerer-not, what wonder are you intending to pluck from that raggedy bag? A rainbow bridge to span the marshland? A roll of string that will uncoil to become a road?" He looked on eagerly. Feigning disinterest, Ahlitah could not keep himself from similarly glancing over to see what the unassuming herdsman was up to.

"I command nothing like that." As he searched the pack's

interior, Ehomba gave his hopeful friend a disapproving look. "You expect too much of a few simple villagers."

"If I do," Simna responded without taking his eyes off the paradoxical pack, "it's because I have seen firsthand what the efforts of a few simple villagers have wrought."

"Then you may be disappointed." The herdsman finally withdrew his hand from the depths of the pack. "All I have is this." He held up a tiny, yellow-brown, five-armed starfish no more than a couple of inches across.

Simna's expression darkened uncertainly. "It looks like a starfish."

"That is what it is. A memory from the shores of my home. The little sack of pebbles in my pocket I packed myself, but before I left I did not see everything my family and friends packed for me. I came across this many days ago."

"It's—a starfish." Leaning forward, Simna sniffed slightly. "Still smells of tidepool and surge." He was quite baffled. "Of what use is it except to remind you of the ocean? Are you going to wave it beneath that stallion's nose in the hopes it will drive him mad for salt water, and he will break free of whatever mysterious bond holds him here and lead the entire herd to the shores of the nearest sea?"

"What a wild notion." Ehomba contemplated the tiny, slim-limbed echinoderm. Its splayed arms did not cover his palm. "Something like that is quite impossible. I am surprised, Simna. I thought you were a rational person and not one to give consideration to such bizarre fancies."

"Hoy! Me? Now *I'm* the one with the bizarre fancies?" Mightily affronted, he stabbed an accusing finger at the inconsequential sand dweller. "Then what do you propose to do with that scrap of insignificant sea life? Give it to the tomorrow horse to eat in hopes it will make him think of the sea?"

"Now you are being truly silly," Ehomba chided him. "Starfish are not edible." Whereupon he turned to his left, drew back his arm, and hurled the tiny five-armed invertebrate as far as he could.

A mystified Simna watched it fly, its minuscule arms spinning around the central knot of its hard, dry body. Ahlitah tracked it too, and the Argentus traced its path through the oppressive humidity with an air of superior detachment. The starfish descended in a smooth arc and struck the sluggish water with a tiny plop. It promptly sank out of sight.

Simna stared. Ahlitah stared. The Argentus looked away. And then, it looked back.

Something was happening to the marsh where the starfish had vanished.

A cool boiling began to roil the surface. In the absence of geothermal activity, something else was causing the fen water to bubble and froth. The herd stirred and a flurry of whinnies punctuated the air like a chorus of woodwinds embarking on some mad composer's allegro equus.

Simna edged closer to the nearest tree. Slight of diameter as it was, it still offered the best protection on the island. "Watch out, bruther. If they break and panic . . ."

But there was no stampede. A shriller, sharper neighing rose above the mixed chorale. Responding to the recognizably superior among themselves, the herd looked to the Argentus for direction. It trotted back and forth between the front ranks and the island shore, calming its nervous precursors. Together with the travelers, the massed animals held their ground, and watched, and listened.

The frothing, fermenting water where the starfish had sunk turned cloudy, then dark with mud. The seething subsurface disturbance began to spread, not in widening concentric circles as might have been expected, but in perfectly straight lines. Five of them, shooting outward from an effervescent nexus, each aligning itself with an arm of the no-longer-visible starfish. As the streaks of bubbling mud rushed away from their source, they expanded until each was five, ten, then twenty feet wide. One raced right past the island, passing between the herd and the sand.

As quickly as it had begun, the boiling and bubbling began to recede. It left behind a residue of uplifted muck and marsh bottom. With the recession of activity, this began to congeal and solidify, leaving behind a wide, solid pathway. Five of them, each corresponding to an arm of the starfish. They rose only an inch or two above the surface of the water. Ehomba hoped it would be enough.

"You have been running too long in water." He indicated the improbable dirt roads. "Try running on that. You might even see a way to run back to where you belong."

Tentatively, the Argentus stepped up onto the raised causeway. Ehomba held his breath, but the stiffened mud did not collapse beneath the horse's weight, did not slump and separate back into a slurry of soil and water. Experimentally, the Argentus turned a slow circle. It pawed at the surface with a front hoof. When finally it turned back to face the travelers, Ehomba could see that it was crying silently.

"I did not know horses could cry," he observed.

"I can talk. Why should I not be able to cry? I don't know how to thank you. We don't know how to thank you."

"Do not give thanks yet," Ehomba warned it. "You are still here, in the middle of these marshes. First see if the paths let you go free. When you are no longer here, then you can thank me." The herdsman smiled. "However far away you may be, I will hear you."

"I believe that you will." Turning, the Argentus reared back on its hind legs and pawed the air, a sharply whinnying shaft of silver standing on hooves like bullion, mane shining in the hazy sunshine. Thousands of ears pricked forward to listen. Once more the herd began to stir, but it was a different furor than before, the agitation that arises from expectation instead of apprehension.

Hesitantly at first, then with increasing boldness, small

groups began to break away from the main body. The paints and the heavy horses led the way down one of the five temporary roads. Trotting soon gave way to an energetic canter, and then to a joyous, exuberant, massed gallop. The thunder of thousands of hooves shook the marsh, making the waterlogged surface of the island tremble with the rumble of the herd's departure.

Hipparions and eohippuses led the hairier dawn horses off in another direction, choosing a different road, as indeed they must. Their run led them not only out of the imprisoning marshes, but out of the present context. In this world some of them would remain, but in all others they would find themselves running back through time as well as meadow and field.

Eight-legged sleipnirs and narwhal-horned unicorns churned newly made dust from still a third path. Winged horses shadowed their run, gliding low and easy above the path to freedom. All manner and variety of imaginary and imagined siblings filled out this most remarkable gathering of all. There were horses with glowing red eyes and fire breathing from their nostrils, horses with armored skin, and horses the size of hippos. Several of these supported the merhorses, who with their webbed front feet and piscine hind ends could not gallop in company with their cousins.

Two more roads still lay open and unused. Trotting forward, the Argentus came right up to the travelers. The thunder raised by the partitioned herd in its flight to freedom was already beginning to fade. A silvery muzzle nuzzled Ehomba's face and neck. Even so close, Simna was unable to tell if the animal's skin was fashioned of flesh or the most finely wrought silver imaginable.

Ehomba put a hand on the horse's snout and rubbed gently. Zebras responded to a similar touch and the Argentus was no different. Superior it might be, perhaps even more intelligent than the humans, but it reacted with a pleased snuffle and snort nonetheless.

Then it backed off, turned, and climbed up onto one of the two roads not yet taken. With a last flurry of flashing mane and sterling tail, it trotted off down the empty roadway—alone.

Birdsong returned hesitantly to the marsh, then in full avian cry. The hidden mutterings and querulous cheeps of the bog again filled the now still air. From a nearby copse of high reeds a covey of green herons unfolded grandly into the sky. The marshland was returning to normal.

In the distance in several directions, the dust raised by thousands of departing hooves was beginning to settle. The edges of the roads were already starting to crumble, the momentarily consolidated marsh bottom slowly ebbing under the patient infusion of water from beneath and both sides. Shouldering his pack, Ehomba started forward.

"Hurry up. We need to make use of the road while it is still walkable."

Uncertain in mind but knowing better than to linger when the herdsman said to move, Simna grabbed his own pack and splashed through the shallows after his friend. Ahlitah followed at a leisurely pace.

The swordsman glanced back at the island. "What about the boat?"

Ehomba had crossed the road the Argentus had taken. That path was not for them. It led to the future, and he had business in the present. He splashed energetically through the shallows toward the next road. Simna trailed behind, working to catch up. The litah kept pace effortlessly, save for when it paused to shake water from one submerged foot or the other.

"If we hurry and make time before the road comes apart completely, we will not need the boat," Ehomba informed his companion. "It means that we may have to run for a while, but we should be able to get out of these lowlands before evening." As he climbed up onto the second roadbed he glanced back in the direction of the island. "I hope the old ape finds his boat. As soon as people discover that the way through the marshland is no longer blocked by mad horses, they will begin exploring. I have a feeling he will be among the first to do so." He started northward along the dry, flat surface. "I do not feel bad about not returning it. More important matters draw us onward, and in any case, you overpaid him significantly."

"I thought you didn't pay attention to such things." Simna trotted along fluidly next to his friend, marsh water trailing down his lower legs to drain out between his toes. As they ran, both sides of the road continued to crumble slowly but steadily into the turbid water. Ahlitah would run on ahead, then sit down to lick and dry his feet as the two humans passed him, then rise up and pass them in turn once again. He persevered with this procedure until his feet and lower legs were once more dry enough to pacify his vanity.

"Five roads arose from the five arms of the starfish," Simna was murmuring aloud. "One for the horses of now, one for the horses of the imagination, one for those that live both in the past and the present, and one for the horses of the future."

"And this fifth road, not for horses, but for us," Ehomba finished for him.

The swordsman nodded. "What if you had been carrying only a four-armed starfish?"

Ehomba glanced down at him as he ran. "Then we would be back in that unadorned, slow boat, leaning hard on poles and hoping that the herd left nothing behind that would keep us from traveling in this direction. But this is better."

"Yes," agreed Simna, running easily along the center of the disintegrating roadway, "this is better. Tell me something—how does a nonsorcerer raise five roads from the middle of a waterlogged marsh with the aid only of a dried-out starfish?"

"It was not I." Ehomba shifted his grip on his spear, making sure to carry it parallel to the ground.

"Hoy, I know that. It's never you." The swordsman smiled sardonically.

"Meruba gave me the starfish. She knows more about the little bays that dimple our coast than anyone else in the village. Many are the days I have seen her wading farther out than even bold fishermen would dare go. She always seemed to know just where to put her feet. She told me that if ever I found myself lost in water with no place certain to stand, to use the starfish and it would help me."

Simna saw that the failing roadbed led toward the nearest of the low, rounded hills that comprised the northern reaches of the Jarlemone Marshes. He hoped the solid dirt underfoot would last until they reached it. The rate of erosion seemed to be increasing.

"What magic do you think trapped all those horses here in the first place?" Simna asked him.

"Who can say? It might have been no more than confusion. Confusion is a great constrictor, ensnaring people as well as animals in its grasp. Once let loose, it feeds upon itself, growing stronger with each uncertainty that it accrues to its bloating body. It makes a tough, invisible barrier that once raised is hard to break through." He shrugged. "Or it might have been a curse, though who could curse creatures so beautiful? Or an act of Nature."

"Not any Nature I know." Simna's sandals pad-padded rhythmically against the crumbling but still supportive surface underfoot.

"There are many Natures, Simna. Most people look at the world and see only one, the one that affects them at that particular moment. But there are many. To see them one has to look deeper. You should spend more time in the country and less in town. Then you would get to see the many Natures."

"I have enough trouble coping with the one, hoy. And I happen to like towns and cities. They have taverns, and inns, and comradeship, and indoor plumbing, and screens to keep out annoying flying things." He looked over at his friend, loping along lithe as an antelope beside him. "Not everyone is enamored of a life of standing on one leg in the wilderness acting as servant to a bunch of dumb cattle."

Ehomba smiled gently. "The Naumkib serve the cattle and the cattle serve us. As do the sheep, and the chickens and pigs. We are happy with the arrangement. It is enough for us."

"A thousand blessings on you and your simple village and simple people and simple lifestyle. Me, I aspire to something more than that."

"I hope you find it, Simna. You are a good person, and I hope that you do."

"Oh, I'll find it, all right! All I have to do is stick to you like a tick on a dog until we get to the treasure. You really don't think I believe all this twaddle about devoted cattle-herding and wanting to live always in houses made of rock and whalebone and thatch, do you?"

"I thought once that you might. You have shown me many times how wrong I was to think that."

"By Ghocuun, that's right! So don't think to slough me off like an old shirt with tales of how much you delight in cleaning up daggy sheep or sick cows. You're a man, just as I am, and you want what all men do."

"And what would that be, Simna?"

"Wealth and power, of course. The treasure of Damura-sese, if it is to be had. Whatever treasure you seek if the lost city really is nothing more than a legend."

"Of course. Do not worry, Simna. I will not try to discourage you. You are too perceptive for me."

"Hoy, that's for sure." Confident in his insight, the swordsman kept a stride or two ahead of the tall southerner, just to show that he could do so whenever he wished.

The hills were drawing near, but beneath their feet the roadway was crumbling ever more rapidly as the marsh sought to reclaim that which had been temporarily raised up from its murky depths. From a width of twenty feet and more the causeway had shrunk to a path less than a yard wide. Down this the travelers ran in single file, increasing their pace. Simna led the way, followed by Ehomba, with Ahlitah effortlessly bringing up the rear. From a yard in width the path shrank by a third, and then a half, until it seemed only a matter of time until they found themselves leaping from one last dry mound to the next.

But they never had to wade. Before the last of the road ceased to exist completely they were standing on dry, grassy land that sloped gently upwards. Turning to look back as they caught their breath, they saw the last stretches of starfish road dissipate, dissolving back into the surrounding waters like a bar of chocolate left too long out in the sun. Exhausted from their run, they settled down on the welcoming green grass and sought in their packs for something to eat.

Before them, the Jarlemone Marshes spread out in all directions, flat and reed-choked, bustling with life both above and below the still waters—but empty of horse.

"This would be a fine place to make a home," Ehomba commented conversationally. "Good grazing for animals, enough of a rise to provide a view yet not subject to landslips, plenty of birds to catch and fish to net."

Simna was biting into a dried apple. "Wait until the people of Lybondai find out that the crazy horses are gone and they can cross the marshland at will. I give this place six months until it looks just like the city suburbs."

The herdsman frowned. "An unpretty picture. The grass will be gone with the quiet."

The swordsman waved the apple at his friend. "Not everyone is like the Naumkib, Etjole. Not everyone finds delight in emptiness and solitude. Most people like to be around other people. When they're not, they get nervous, and lonely."

Resting his chin on his crossed arms, the tall southerner leaned forward. "How strange. When I am around large groups of people, I find myself more lonely than ever. But when I am out in the open spaces, with the wind and the trees and the streams and the rocks for company, I am not lonely at all."

"But you miss your family," Simna reminded him.

"Yes. I miss my family." Rising abruptly, he picked up his pack. "And while very pleasant, sitting here is not bringing me any closer to them."

"Hoy, wait a minute!" Simna scrambled to gather up his own belongings. "I haven't finished my apple yet!"

A short distance away, the litah snorted softly. He had caught a fish and was using his claws to dismember it delicately. Now he was forced to swallow his catch whole. That was fine for his stomach, but not for his attitude. He would have enjoyed lingering over the tasty prize. But the taller human was on the move again. The cat would be glad when Ehomba finished what he had started. This vow of feline fealty was taking them ever farther from the litah's beloved veldt.

Still, a promise was a promise. With a sigh, he rose from the edge of the marsh and padded off after the retreating humans, growling resignedly under his breath.

VII

The War of the Flowers

No one knew exactly when the battle for the valley had begun. The origins of the conflict were lost in the mists of time, flowers being very interested in mist but considerably less so in chronology.

Blessed with growing conditions that were only rarely less than perfect, the blossoming plants had thrived on the hilltops and hillsides. For reasons unknown, the soil that so willingly nourished florescence proved inhospitable to the larger woody plants. Trees and bushes never became established. Most of the errant seeds that were dropped by birds or bats or dragonites never germinated. Those that did quickly found themselves shouldered aside by the vigorous perennials. Blossoms and leaves expanded in the sun, stealing the light and suffocating any hopeful treelets before they could reach the status of sapling. Layers of accumulated ancient nutrients and just the right amount of vital trace minerals ensured perpetual flowering, and every year rain fell when and where necessary: enough to slake but not to wash soil from tender roots.

Damaging hail and wind were unknown. The climate varied lazily between balmy and temperate, never searing hot or killing cold. There were no frosts and no droughts. Grazing animals did not visit the hills, and those insects that were not overtly beneficial were tolerated. These never swarmed in damaging numbers, never achieved the status of a plague. Bees and wasps, birds and beetles and bats took their turn attending to the matter of pollination. And the flowers throve, layering the gentle hills with exorbitant splashes of stunning color, as if some Titan of aesthetic bent had taken a giant's brush and palette to the rolling terrain.

In all this kingdom of flowers only one tract did not bloom. In its very center lay a broad, shallow valley where so much moisture accumulated that the soil became a veritable sponge, too loose and uncompacted to support normal root growth. Long ago the little valley had become a bog, which is a swamp without attitude. In its waterlogged reaches grew ferns and liverworts, but none of the noble blooms. A patrician rose would not have been caught out with blight in such surroundings, and gladioli and snapdragon recoiled from the stench of decomposing vegetation and insects. So tenancy of the valley was left to the flowers' poor cousins, the epiworts and fungi.

Centuries passed, and the flowers were content. On the beneficent hills nothing changed. The summer rains came and were replaced by the winter rains. The sun shifted its arc across the sky but was never less than accommodating. Blossoms opened and closed, petals fell and were replaced, and the empire of color was not challenged.

But while the hills stayed untouched and inviolate, change began to come to the valley. Imperceptible at first, it did not attract notice until the ferns began to die. Soon even the tough fungi started to disappear, vanishing from the shady places and decaying hollows as if abducted. Perhaps some sort of subterranean drain had opened beneath the valley, siphoning off the surplus water that had for so long accumulated there. Or maybe subtle earth movements had compacted the saturated soil so that it no longer held unnecessary rainfall as effortlessly.

The valley was drying up. No, not up—out. It was becoming exactly like the hills that surrounded it. With one exception: Because of all the plant matter that over the centuries had decayed and accumulated in the soggy depression, the soil that resulted was incredibly rich, improbably productive, supremely nourishing. Forever restricted to their ancestral ranges by untenable sandy soils marking their far boundaries, the many varieties of flowering plants that blanketed the hills suddenly found themselves presented with a new phenomenon—room for expansion. This they proceeded to do, sending out shoots and roots and dropping seed at an accelerated rate.

In doing so, they eventually and inevitably bumped up against other flowers from other hillsides attempting to assert their right to the recently reclaimed land. Something new had arrived in the land of the flowers. Something foreign and hitherto unknown.

Competition.

No species needed to move into the valley to survive. No variety or hybrid was in danger of extinction. But the attractions of the enriched soil and open space would not be ignored. Like drugs, they drew every plant in the vicinity forward. New flowers expanded in ecstasy under the stimulus of untapped nutrients and brazen sunshine. And then, they began to crowd one another.

In the past this could not happen. Every flower knew its ancestral space and kept to it, every root acknowledged the primacy of its neighbor. But the novelty of newly opened land had not come with rules. Roots made contact, recoiled uncertainly, and then thrust outward afresh, seeing no reason why they should not. Rootlets began to push against one another, and then to twist, and to attempt to strangle. Above the surface, stems fought to be the first to put forth leaves to catch the life-giving sunlight, and then to blossom and attract insects.

Strife led to adaptation. Flowers grew faster, stronger, taller. Roots became more active, more prehensile, as they did battle for control beneath the surface. Alliances were struck among species. Bold but defenseless camas and fuchsia sought the protection of thorned roses. Verbena and tulip huddled close to poisonous oleander.

Continuous and unrelenting competition led to rapid mutation as first one variety and then another fought for dominance of the fertile valley. Not to be outdone or intimidated by the roses, rhododendron grew thorns of its own. Poppies sprouted tendrils that curled like snakes, coiling around the stems of other flowers and tightening until they cut through the defenseless plant matter. Zinnias developed the ability to raise up on their roots and move, albeit slowly, across the surface, avoiding the skirmishing roots below. Peonies and gladioli seeped caustic liquids from their petals to burn any competing flower that grew too near.

Larkspurs and marigolds put forth leaves with knifelike edges that twitched like green Samurai if another plant came close. Hibiscus and frangipani and other tropicals tried to dominate the senses of pollinating insects by escalating their emissions, thereby denying those life-continuing services to less aromatic growths. Rafflesia flailed at sprouting stems with already massive red and green leaves. Across the length and breadth of the valley the conflict raged, for the most part invisible, insensible, and so slowly that anyone passing through would not have seen or thought anything amiss. This did not matter, since no one was ever present to observe and decide if what was happening in the valley constituted normality or an aberration.

That is, until the three travelers arrived.

They paused for a long time at the top of the southernmost hill. Standing there, they gazed endlessly northward, as if there was something unique or unusual about the sight. As if the millions of flowers spread out before them in blazing profusion were something remarkable and not simply the product of centuries of placid, steady growth.

A silent rush spread throughout the hills as this unprecedented arrival was noted. From the flowers immediately proximate to the visitors there was an initial exhalation of apprehension. This vanished the instant it became apparent that the visitors were not grazers and that young shoots and new blossoms were in no danger of being consumed.

As the visitors resumed their northward march, a number of plants were stepped upon. This was inevitable, given that the flowers grew so closely together that there was no open space between them. But most were resilient enough to spring back, and those that were not provided gaps in which new seedlings would be able to germinate. The flowers did not complain. They bloomed, and tracked the progress of the wonderfully mobile visitors.

Despite the glaring differences between them, the travelers excited no feelings of animosity among the plants. Just like flowers, the three were of different color, shape, and size, showing that normal variation existed even among alien intruders. Similarly, they were crowned by rounded, blossomlike structures atop long stems, and a pair of attenuated forms like leaves protruded from these stems. Only their roots were unusual, giving them more motility than even the most mobile flowers. But taken as a whole, they were not so very different at all.

And they were moving straight for the valley that had long ago become a silent zone of horticultural conflict.

There they paused again. The sun was setting and, like all other growing things, they clearly needed to reduce their activity to coincide with the absence of sunlight. Prior to clos-

ing their petals and curling up their leaf-extensions for the
night, they utilized wonderfully flexible stem-parts to remove objects from their dorsal sides. From within these they
withdrew small bits of dead plant and animal matter, which
they proceeded to ingest. The flowers were neither surprised
nor appalled. There had long been pitcher plants and flytraps
within their midst. In their method of taking nourishment the
visitors were being nothing less than plantlike.

Strenuous competition had given a number of the flowers
in the valley the ability to function after dark. They did this
by storing extra fuel during the day for use after sunset. As
soon as the visitors had gone quiescent, just like any normal
plant during nighttime, these growths began to stir.

Tendrils of modified columbine and amaryllis twitched,
arose, and slowly crept forward. They made contact with the
motionless visitor shapes and delicately began to explore
their trunks, feeling of roots and blossom-caps with the
feathery extensions at their tips. One slumbering form raised
a leaf-stem and with astonishing speed slapped at the tendril
tip that was traveling gently across its bloom. The runner recoiled, bruised but otherwise undamaged.

The mass of the visitors was astonishing. They seemed to
be almost as dense as trees, which the flowers knew from
legend, before they had come to dominate the surrounding
hills completely. Like plants, the now recumbent stems were
composed mostly of water. Colorwise, they were for the
most part undistinguished, a sure sign of primitiveness.

Then the probing tendrils made a shocking discovery.
There was no indication anywhere within the stout bodies of
the presence of chlorophyll! Among those flowers not entirely enveloped in the torpor of night a hasty reassessment
was deemed in order. If not plants, what could the visitors
be? Superficially, they were nothing like fungi. But fungi
could assume many peculiar forms. And if not flower, fungi,

or tree, then what? They were much too cumbersome to be insects, or birds.

It was proposed that they might be some monstrous exotic variety of wingless bat. While they seemed to have more in common with plants than bats, there were undeniable similarities. Bats had dense bodies, and were warm to the touch. That was fine for two of the creatures, but the third was completely different, not only from the average flower, but from its companions. It was a great puzzlement.

Identification and classification could wait. As the columbine and amaryllis withdrew their probing tentacles in opposite directions, all sides knew what had to be done. With the coming of the dawn, each would attempt to persuade the visitors to ally themselves with one faction or another. There could be no neutrality in the battle for control of the valley. If they were plants, or even distant relations, they would understand. Understanding, they would be able to make decisions.

And while each of the several blocs desired to make allies of the travelers, none were overwhelmed with concern. Except for their exceptional mobility and unusual mass, none of the three appeared to have any especially useful ability to contribute to the conflict. They boasted no thorns, exhibited no cutting leaves, gave no indication of containing potentially useful toxins. Their large but narrow stems could not steal the shade from a significant number of blossoms, and their drab coloration was hardly a threat to draw pollinators away from even the most unprepossessing common daisy.

Still, in the fight for the valley any ally was welcome. The travelers' exceptional motility held the most promise, though what use a bloc of confederated flowers could make of it remained to be seen. Further evaluation would have to await the return of the sun.

Like any blossoming growth, the visitors' stems strengthened and their leaves unfolded as the first light appeared over the horizon. Extending their leaf pedicels to their fullest extent, the travelers straightened from their resting positions and became fully vertical to greet the sun. One even held its ground for long moments, its bloom fully opened to take in the life-giving light. This action only reaffirmed the visitors' kinship to the brilliant fields of color that surrounded them. Of one thing the flowers were now certain: Whatever they might be, the travelers were no fungi.

But they were too mobile, too free-ranging to be flowers. Some strange combination of batlike creature and plant, perhaps. As the flowers warmed and strengthened under the effects of the rising sun, they considered how best to proceed.

It was the phlox that moved first. Coiled tendrils extended, hesitantly at first, then with increasing determination, to curl around the lower limbs of two of the visitors. At first the newcomers simply shrugged them off, but as the several became dozens and the dozens became hundreds, they reacted more vigorously, emitting loud sounds on frequencies very different from those of bats.

When they backed away, tearing at the clutching tendrils, the orchids saw their chance. In their multitudinous variety, orchids had acquired a great command of chemistry. Operating on the theory that the desirable visitors had more in common with bats than flowers, they generated in one concerted push a single vast exhalation of nectar. The sticky, sweet liquid coated the startled visitors, rendering them flush with stimulation, but they did not react gratefully. Instead of throwing themselves into alliance with the orchids and their collaborators, they began wiping at themselves with their leaves. It was much the sort of reaction a plant might have, since one growth had no need of another's nectar. Perhaps they were not so batlike after all.

The azaleas and honeysuckle continued to hold to that theory. To their way of thinking, the orchids' analysis was correct but not their execution. Considering the mobility of the travelers, more aggressive action was in order. So they gathered themselves and put forth not nectar, but scent. Always strong smelling, they modified their bouquet based on what they knew of the senses of bats and batlike creatures.

The unified emission had the desired effect. Engulfed by the cloud of fragrance, all three of the travelers began to move more slowly. Two of them started to sway unsteadily, and one collapsed. The flowers on which it fell struggled to support it. Working together, they began to move the motionless form up and away from the contested area of the dried bog, hundreds of stems and thousands of petals toiling to shift the considerable weight.

Alarmed, competing verbena and marigolds tried to hold the remaining travelers back, to drag them to their side. Sharpened leaves were thrust forth, threatening to cut at the visitors' stems if they attempted to follow their captured companion. Other leaves covered with tiny, siliceous needles loaded with concentrated alkaloid poisons attempted to set up a barrier between the two larger visitors and the one being slowly but steadily carried uphill by triumphant morning glory and primrose. In the center of the disputed terrain, poisonous poinsettia battled numbing opium poppies for primacy.

That was when the tallest, but by no means the largest, of the three travelers proved once and for all that it and its companions were not flowers. After first steadying its larger companion, it removed a separate stem from its back and attached it to one of its pedicels. As the traveler rotated, this extended pedicel began to swing in great arcs, even though there was no wind. Its augmented, elongated leaf edge was sharper than any thorn.

Flowers went flying as the silvery leaf slashed through stems. Cutting a path through hopeful friend and convicted antagonist growths alike, showing no preference for one blossom over another, the traveler slashed and hacked indiscriminately until it had reached its companion. Advancing on its long, motile double stems, it traveled far faster than the victorious blooms could move the motionless body of the downed visitor.

The astonishingly durable leaf cut a path all around the recumbent individual. Then the taller visitor bent double and, in a display of strength and agility no flower could match, lifted the motionless one up onto its shoulders. Turning, it began to retrace its steps. Hopeful growths tried to trap its stems with their own while tendrils and strong roots sought to ensnare it and bring it down, but that single sharp leaf kept swinging and slashing. Against its irresistible edge not even the toughest root could endure.

Continuing to mow down all before it, the traveler crossed the contested area and rejoined the third member of the group. Though still swaying unsteadily on multiple stems, this largest of the three continued to stand against the combined efforts of every blossom in its immediate vicinity. When the recharged azaleas and honeysuckle tried their vaporous attack a second time, the visitors placed the tips of their leaves over the front part of their blooms, with the result that the effect of the previously overpowering effluvia was not repeated.

Together, the three began to make their way northward across the hills. Millions of alerted flowers waited to contest their passage, but there was little they could do against the devastating power of the silver leaf. In addition, the largest member of the party was now once more fully alert and sensible. It swung its own leaf-ends back and forth, tearing great gouges out of the earth, shredding blossoms and leaves, stems and roots, with equal indifference.

In the immediate vicinity of their flight the devastation was shocking. Whole communities of blooms were destroyed. But the demise of a few thousand flowers was as nothing to the ocean of color that covered the hills. It would take only one growing season for the despoiled route to be fully regenerated, and new seeds would welcome the gift of open space in which to germinate.

Eventually, each family of flowers gave up the idea of enlisting the travelers in the fight for control of the dried bogland. Instead of trying to restrain the visitors, they inclined their stems out of the way, allowing the remarkable but dangerous specimens free and unfettered passage through the hills. As the ripple of understanding passed through endless fields of brilliant color, a path opened before the travelers. At first they were reluctant to put up their murderous leaves and continued to hack and cut at every blossom within reach. But their suspicion soon ebbed, and they marched on without doing any more damage, increasing their pace as they did so.

Behind them, in the expansive hollow once occupied by the bog, violets wrestled with hollyhocks, and periwinkles took sly cuts at the stems of forceful daffodils. The war for the new soil went on, the adventure of the intruders already forgotten. Once, a small would-be sapling sprang from the dirt to reach for the sun. It might have been a sycamore, or perhaps a poplar. No one would ever know, because a knot of active foxglove and buttercup sprang upon it and smothered it. Deprived of light, it withered and died.

No tree was permitted to grow on the lush, fecund hills. No mushroom poked its cap above the surface, no toadstool had a chance to spread its spores across the fertile soil. From hill to dale, crest to crevice, there were only the flowers. They throve madly, creating a canvas of color unmatched anywhere, and waited for the next visitors. Perhaps others would be more amenable to persuasion, or more flowerlike in their aspect.

It was truly the most beautiful place imaginable. But for one not a flower, a chancy place to linger and smell the roses.

VIII

They did not stop until that evening, when they had ascended to heights where only a few wildflowers grew. Unlike the millions that covered the hills from which they had fled, these were most emphatically nonaggressive.

Ehomba laid Simna down at the base of a large tree with far-spreading limbs and deeply grooved bark so dark it was almost black. A small stream meandered nearby, heading for the flower hills and the distant sea. In another tree a pair of crows argued for the sheer raucous delight of hearing themselves caw.

Ahlitah stood nearby, shaking his head as he stumbled nowhere in particular on unsteady legs, trying to shake off the effects of the insidious perfume. He had handled the effects better than the swordsman, but if Ehomba had not apprised him of what was happening and helped to hurry him out of the hills, he too would surely have succumbed to the second cloud of invisible perfume.

Simna must have taken the brunt of the first discharge, Ehomba felt. A blissful look had come over the swordsman's face and he had gone down as if beneath the half dozen houris he spoke of so frequently and fondly. Then the flowers, the impossible, unreal, fantastic flowers, had actually picked him up and started to carry him off to some unimaginable destination of their own. The herdsman had drawn the sky-metal sword and gone grimly to work, trying not to think of the beauty he was destroying as he cut a path to liberate his friend. The blossoms he was shredding were not indifferent, he had told himself. Their agenda was not friendly. The intervention of active thorns and sharp-edged leaves and other inimical vegetation had been proof enough of that. His lower legs were covered with scratches and small puncture wounds.

The litah had fared better. Unable to penetrate his fur, small, sharp objects caused him no difficulty. Unsteady as he was, he had still been able to clear away large patches of flowers with great swings of his huge paws. Now he tottered about in circles, shaking his head, his great mane tossing violently as he fought to clear the effects of the concentrated fragrance from his senses.

Electing to conserve the safe town water that filled the carrying bag in his pack, Ehomba walked to the stream and returned with a double handful of cool liquid. He let it trickle slowly through his long fingers, directly over the swordsman's face. Simna blinked, sputtered, and sat up. Or tried to. Ehomba had to help him. Woozy as a sailor in from a long voyage and just concluding a three-day drunk, the swordsman wiped at his face and tried to focus on the figure crouching concernedly before him.

"Etjole? What happened?" Simna looked around as if seeing the grass-covered hills, the grove of trees, and his friends for the first time. To his left, the big cat fell over on its side, growled irritably, and climbed to its feet again. "What's wrong with kitty?"

"The same thing that is wrong with you, only to a lesser extent."

"Wrong with me?" The swordsman looked puzzled. He started to stand, immediately listed severely to starboard, and promptly sat down again. "Hoy!" Placing a hand on either side of his head, he sat very still while rubbing his temples. "I remember smelling something so sweet and wonderful it can't be described." He looked up suddenly. "The flowers!"

"Yes, the flowers." Ehomba looked back toward the south, toward the resplendent hills from which they had fled. "For some reason they wanted to keep us there. I cannot imagine why. Who can know how a flower thinks?" He turned back to his friend. "They tried to hold us back with little vines and roots and sharp leaves. When that did not work, they tried to smother us with delight. I caught very little of the perfume. Ahlitah received more. You were all but suffocated." He held a hand up before the other man's face. "How many fingers am I holding up?"

"Five. That's four too many." The swordsman coughed lightly. "First horses and now flowers. Give me the reeking warrens of a city with its cutthroats and thieves and honest, straightforward assassins any day. Those I know how to deal with. But flowers?" Lowering his palms from the sides of his head, he took several deep breaths. "I'll never again be able to feel the same way about picking a bouquet for a favorite lady."

"I am glad that you are feeling better."

"So am I, though I don't ever before remember being knocked unconscious quite so pleasantly." He rose, only slightly shaky. Nearby, the litah was exercising and testing its recovered reflexes by leaping high in playful attempts to knock the agitated crows out of their tree.

"By Glelaraith, wait a minute. If I was unconscious and the cat indisposed, how did I get out of those hills?"

"I carried you." Ehomba was scanning the northern horizon. Ahead, the terrain continued to climb, but gently. No ragged escarpments, no jagged peaks appeared to block their way northward.

The swordsman's gaze narrowed. "The aroma didn't affect you?"

"I told you—you and Ahlitah received a stronger dose than I did. Besides, my sense of smell is much weaker than either of yours." Looking back down, he smiled. "Many years of herding cattle and sheep, of living close to them every day, have dulled my nose to anything very distilled."

"Hoy—the preserving power of heavy stink." With a grunt, Simna straightened his pack on his back. "I'm used to my assailants smelling like six-month-old bed linen, not attar of camellia."

"In a new and strange land one must be prepared to deal with anything." Ehomba started northward. The grass was low and patchy, the ground firm and supportive. Able to hike in any direction they preferred, they did not need to follow a particular path. Behind them, the litah gave up its game of leap and strike, conceding victory to the exhausted crows. "Old forms may no longer be valid. Seeming friends may be masked by lies, and conspicuous enemies nothing more than upright individuals in disguise."

Having shaken off the last lingering effects of the potent perfume, the swordsman strode along strongly beside him. "Hoy, that's not a problem a man has in a dark alley."

Ehomba took in their clean, bracing environs with a sweep of his free hand. "I would rather find myself in surroundings like this facing adversaries unknown than in some crowded, noisy city where one has to deal with people all the time."

"Then we make a good team, long bruther. I'll take care of the people, and you deal with the flowers. And damned if I don't think I'll have the easier time of it."

They slept that night in a grove of smaller trees, welcoming in their silence and lack of activity. They were indisputably trees and nothing more, as was the grass that grew thickly at their bases and the occasional weed flower that added a dab of color to the campsite. The stars shone unblinkingly overhead in a cool, pellucid sky, and they enjoyed the best night's sleep they had had since before embarking on their crossing of the Aboqua.

At least Simna ibn Sind and Ahlitah did. Ehomba found his slumber unexpectedly disturbed.

She was very tall, the vision was, though not so tall as the herdsman. Her skin had the texture of new ivory and the sheen of the finest silk. Large eyes of sapphire blue framed by high cheekbones gazed down at him, and her hair was a talus of black diamonds. Beneath a gown of crimson lace she was naked, and her body was as supplely inviting as a down-filled bed on a cold winter's night.

Her lips parted, and the very act of separation was an invitation to passion. They moved, but no sounds emerged. Yet in the absence of words he felt that she was calling out to him, her arms spread wide in supplication. With her eyes and her posture, her limbs and the striking shape beneath the gown, he was convinced that she was promising him anything, anything, if he would but redeem her from her current plight.

Discomfited by her consummate union of lubricity and innocent appeal, he stirred uneasily in his sleep, tossing about on the cushioning grass. Her hands reached out to him, the long, lissome fingers drawing down his cheek to her lips, then his neck, his chest. She smiled enticingly, and it was as if the stars themselves had invited him to waltz in their hot and august company. He felt himself embraced, and the heat rose in his body like steam trapped within a kettle.

Then he became aware of another, a horned presence looming ominously above the both of them. It too was incapable of speech, though much was conveyed by glaring eyes and clenching teeth. Eyes downcast, the vision of the Visioness pulled back from him, drawn away by an awful unseen strength. In her place threatened the helmeted figure. It blotted out the light, and what it did not obscure, a pair of keening dark clouds that crept along at its heels enveloped and devoured.

"Etjole. Etjole!"

The hideous figure was shaking him now, thrusting him violently back and forth, and he was helpless to stop it. Shaking and—no, it was not the horned and helmeted one. That was a beast inhabiting his dream. The hands on his shoulders were solid, and real, and belonged entirely to the realm of wakefulness.

He opened his eyes to find a concerned Simna gazing down at him. It was still night, still dark out. Unable to stay long in one place, the stars had moved. But the grove of trees was unchanged, undisturbed by hideous intrusion. Nearby, the great humped mass of the black litah lay on its side, snoring softly.

The swordsman sat back on his heels. "Hoy, I don't know what dream you were having, but don't share it with me."

Ehomba raised up on one elbow and considered his memories. "The first part was good. I am ashamed to admit it, but it was good."

"Ah!" In the darkness the worldly swordsman grinned knowingly. "A woman, then. Your wife?"

Ehomba did not meet his gaze. "No. It was not Mirhanja."

A gratified Simna slapped one knee to punctuate his satisfaction. "By Geuvar, you are human, then. Tell me what she was like." His voice dripped eagerness.

Ehomba eyed him distastefully. "I would rather not. I am not happy with my reaction."

"It was only a dream, bruther!" The swordsman was chuckling at his stolid companion's obvious discomfiture. "Wedded or not, a man cannot be acclaimed guilty for enjoying his sleep. A dream is not a prosecutable offense—no matter what women think."

"It is not that. It was not just any woman, Simna. It was her."

"Hoy—then there was significance to it." The swordsman's smile was replaced by a look of grave concern. "What did you learn from it?"

"Nothing, except that she may somehow know that we are coming to try and help her. That, and the realization that she is more ravishing than even the image we saw above the fire that night on the veldt."

"So beautiful," Simna murmured, a far-off look in his eye. "Too beautiful for simple mortals like you and I, methinks." His grin returned, its lubriciousness muted. "That doesn't mean we can't look, at least in dreams. But that wasn't her you were seeing there at the last. You were moaning and rolling about."

"Hymneth the Possessed. It had to be, I think." Ehomba had lain back down, staring up at the stars, his head resting on the cup formed by his linked fingers. "As before, his face was hidden. I wonder if he is hideous to look upon in person."

"With luck we'll never find out." Returning to his own bedroll, the swordsman slipped back beneath the blanket. Having climbed beyond the hills into the gentle mountains, they were now high above sea level, and along with fresh air and quilted silence the night brought with it a creeping chill.

Ehomba lay still for a long time, listening to the quick, sharp calls of nocturnal birds and the muffled voices of inquiring insects. He was both eager and afraid of returning to the dream. But when he finally drifted off, it was into that restful and rejuvenating region where nothing stirred—not even the vaporous images of imagination.

The next day they continued to ascend, but at such a gentle incline and over such accommodating gradients that the increasing altitude imposed no burden on them and did not slow their progress. They saw small herds of moose and si-vatherium, camelops and wapiti. Ahlitah made a fine swift kill of a young bull bison, and they feasted luxuriantly.

Small tarns glittered like pendants of peridot and aqua-marine at the foot of pure white snowpacks, casting reflections that shone like inverse cameos among the bare gray granites. At this altitude trees were stunted, whipped and twisted like taffy by relentless winter winds. Diminutive wildflowers burst forth in knots of blue and lavender, corn red and old butter yellow. None of them attempted to trip, seduce, or otherwise restrain the impassive hikers in their midst. Small rodents and marsupials dove for cover among the rock piles whenever the marchers approached, and Ahli-tah amused himself by stalking them, pouncing, and then magnanimously letting the less-than-bite-size snacks scamper free.

They had already begun to descend from the heights when they encountered the sheep. Simna pronounced them to be quite ordinary sheep, but to the man from the far south they were strikingly different from the animals he had grown up with. Their fleece was thick and billowy where that of the Naumkib's herds tended to be straight and stringy. Their narrowing faces were black or dirty white instead of brown and yellow. And their feet were smaller, to the point of being dainty. These were coddled animals, he decided, not one of which would survive for a week in the wilds of the dry country inland from the village. Yet they remained, indisputably, sheep.

At the strangers' approach they showed they were not as helpless as they looked. Amid much distraught baaing and bleating, they hastened to form a circle; lambs in the middle, ewes facing determinedly outward, young rams spacing themselves efficiently along the outermost rim.

One old ram, obviously the herd dominant and leader.

INTO THE THINKING KINGDOMS 113

lowered his head and pawed angrily at the ground. Bleating furiously, he took several challenging pronks in the direction of the newcomers. At this point Ahlitah, who had been dawdling behind his human companions, trotted forward to rejoin them. Espying and taking nonchalant note of the ram's challenge, he vouchsafed to give forth a midrange snarl, whereupon the suddenly paralyzed ram froze at the end of an advancing pronk, stood tottering on all fours for an instant or two, and proceeded to keel over onto one side in a dead faint, all four legs locked sideways and straight, parallel to the ground.

"Easy meat," the litah commented idly as they strolled past the trembling herd.

"Mind your manners," Ehomba chided his four-legged companion. "You cannot be hungry. Not after that half an animal you just devoured."

"You're right; I'm not hungry. But I've run too many hot mornings in pursuit of prey that eventually escaped ever to ignore something that looks like roast on a stick." The maned head gestured scornfully in the direction of the herd, and thin, hoofed legs quaked at the casual nod. "These things are domesticated. They are become the vassals of human appetite."

"You can say that again. I love mutton." Simna was eyeing several plump members of the herd more covetously than the big cat.

Ehomba sighed. Belying his stocky frame, the swordsman's appetites were outsized in every way. "If not the shepherd, we may encounter the landholder. Perhaps we can bargain for some chops, if you must have some."

Walking on, they stumbled not on the landowner but upon his dwelling, a modest and unprepossessing structure of stone walls and thatched roof. There was a well out front, and a small garden fenced to keep out the wild vermin as well as sheep and goats. Smoke rose unhurriedly from the stone chimney, and flowering wisteria vined its way up the walls and around the door and the single window. Several young lambs grazed in a stone paddock back of the main building. At the travelers' approach, an old dog lifted its head to check them out. Broad bands of white streaked her long black fur. Apparently satisfied, it laid its lower jaw back down on its paws. It did not bark, not even at the sight and smell of the litah.

"Quiet, tidy little place," Simna declared grudgingly. "Simple lodgings for simple folk."

"Even simple folk may have useful information to give." Tilting back his head, the herdsman squinted at the sky. "And there are clouds gathering. If we are polite, and pleasant, perhaps the owner will let us stay the night." Trying to see inside, Ehomba bent low and shaded his eyes with one hand. "When traveling in a strange land, any known direction is welcome." Advancing on the half-open swinging door, the lower half of which was latched, he raised his voice. Impressively, the dog continued to disregard them.

"Hello! Is anyone at home? We see your smoke."

"It's not my smoke, no. It belongs to the fire. But you may come in anyhow, all of you."

Ehomba led the way into the cottage, which was very neat and clean. Among the Naumkib, it would have been accounted a palace. Sturdy chairs surrounded a table. Both were decorated with carvings and fine scrollwork. An iron pot hung from a swing-out cooking bar in the large fireplace, and there was a sink with a hand pump on the far side of the room. Facing a stone fireplace off to the right were larger, upholstered chairs and a sitting couch. Bookshelves filled with well-thumbed tomes lined the walls, and hanging oil-filled lamps were in place to provide light throughout the evening hours. To the left, a door led to rooms unseen, and a short ladder leaning against one wall hinted at the presence of a copious attic. The cottage's lone occupant was working at the sink, wet up to his elbows. He turned to smile at them as they entered.

"Mind your head, stranger. I don't get many visitors, and few your size. Now, I'll be with you in a moment. I'm just finishing up these dishes."

The owner was plainly dressed in ankle-length pants and matching shirt of dark brown. Both were devoid of decoration. The simple elegance and efficiency of the furnishings suggested that they had not been made by the cottage's occupant, but were the product of other craftsmen and had been bought and brought to this place by wagon or other means of transport. If true, it meant that the owner's isolation was deceptive. He was here by choice rather than out of necessity, and had the resources to pay for more than basic needs.

Not that there was any overt reference to wealth to be seen anywhere within the cottage, unless one so considered the many books. But even a poor man could accumulate a decent library through careful purchasing, especially if it was accomplished over a matter of decades. And their diminutive host certainly had, if not obvious wealth, many years to his credit. His beard and hair were entirely gray, full but neatly trimmed, and despite the blush in his pale cheeks he was clearly an individual of considerable maturity.

"Just have a seat, over there, by the fire," he instructed them as he ran a rag across the face of a ceramic plate. "I should have attended to these earlier, but there were new lambs in need of docking, and I thought it better to take care of them first."

"Yes," Ehomba agreed. He watched Simna flop like a rag doll into one of the big overstuffed chairs and then carefully imitated the swordsman's actions. He was not used to such comfort. In the village, beds were stuffed but chairs were straight-backed and hard. "Better to see to that as quickly as possible or they are liable to become fly-blown."

Putting the plate in a drying rack, the owner turned in surprise. "You are a sheep man, then?"

Simna rolled his eyes. "Oh no." Near his feet, Ahlitah wound three times around himself before, satisfied, he lay down in front of the fire.

"Sheep, yes, and cattle. Mostly cattle."

"I have never been a man for cattle." Taking an intricately carved pipe from its stand, the homeowner ambled over to the stone hearth. Selecting a narrow taper from a small box affixed to the rockwork, he stuck it into the flames until it acquired one of its own, then touched the flickering tip to the bowl of the pipe. While he drew on the contents, he spoke around each puff. "Too rambunctious for me, and a bit much for one man to handle. Even with Roileé to help."

"Roileé?" The herdsman searched the room for signs of another resident.

"My dog." The owner smiled delightfully around the stem of his pipe. "She's getting on, and she's lost a step or two, but she's still the best sheepdog in these mountains. I am Lamidy Coubert, and I think you are not from the Thinking Kingdoms."

"How can you tell?" Simna chuckled softly.

Coubert laughed along with the swordsman. Removing the pipe from his mouth, he gestured with its bowl. "Well for one thing, no one I have heard of, not even lords and noblemen, travels with a house cat of quite such imposing dimensions. Much less one that speaks." Seeing Ehomba's expression, he added, "I heard all three of you talking outside as you approached the cottage. And your manner of dress, my friend, is also strikingly new to me." He frowned slightly as he turned to Simna. "Your attire I can almost place."

"You live alone here, Lamidy Coubert?" Ehomba asked him.

"Yes. Except for Roileé, of course."

"Yet you allow us, three strangers, freely into your home. Two well armed, and the third a meat-eater of great size and strength. And you are not afraid?"

Coubert coughed lightly, checked his pipe. "If your intentions were malicious I could not have stopped you. So I might as well greet you." His smile returned. "Besides, I have lived a long time now by myself. Here on the edge of civilization I get few visitors. So I try to treasure those I do."

"I hate to disillusion you, old man, but this isn't the edge of civilization. South of here lies the port of Lybondai and a host of other coastal cities." Simna's throat was calling for refreshment but he decided to hold off a while longer to see if their host offered before he made the request. "And beyond that, the sea of Aboqua, and the cities and cultures of the south. Myself, I'm from far to the east, and I can tell you, we're goddamn civilized out that way."

"I am sure." The oldster was courteously contrite. "I meant no insult. It is simply the view that is generally held in the Thinking Kingdoms, and therefore one with which I am familiar, though I do not hold to it myself." He gestured expansively. "Obviously, you three are as civilized as any people."

"Two." On the thick oval carpet before the crackling fireplace, Ahlitah spoke without lifting his head from his paws.

"Yes, well."

"Where are the Thinking Kingdoms?" Ehomba inquired softly. Beyond the door and window, evening was stealing stealthily over the land. The muffled baaing of sheep was interrupted by the occasional booming of muted thunder. He could not tell which way the gathering storm was moving. With each strobing flash of unseen lightning the walls of the cottage seemed to grow stronger, and to tighten around them all like a finely made, heavy coat. A chill entered via the still open upper half of the double door. Feeling it, Coubert moved to shut the remaining barrier against the rising wind.

"The Thinking Kingdoms are all the lands to the north of here," their host explained as he returned to stand near the fireplace, slightly to one side of the sputtering, popping blaze itself. "There is Bondressey, and the Dukedom of Veroi-verai. Farther to the north one may enter the Grand Barony of Melespra, which is bordered by Squoy East and Squoy South. East of the Grand Barony lies the river port of Urenon the Elegant, and downstream from it the province of Phan that is ruled by the enlightened Count Tyrahnar Cresthelmare.

"Those are only a few of the most notable kingdoms immediately to the north of here. There are many more, to east and west and to the north of Phan."

"And all these tribes—these kingdoms," Ehomba corrected himself. "They are at peace? I ask because we must travel farther north still."

"There are always disputes and altercations, bickerings and controversies." Coubert turned philosophical. "It is the nature of sovereigns to debate. But war is rare in the Thinking Kingdoms. Each ruler prides himself on his or her intelligence and learning. Altercations are most likely to be settled through reasoned discussion, sometimes by greatly respected teams of logicians."

Simna indicated the pack and sword he had removed and placed near his feet. "Everybody's different, Gulyulo says. Where I come from, we talk a lot while we're arguing, but it's usually loud, unreasoning, and in words of one syllable."

"I can believe that." Coubert turned back to Ehomba. "And you, my tall friend? How are disputations settled in your country?"

"The Naumkib are too small and too few to enjoy the luxury of infighting. We are too busy surviving to waste time and energy on individual quarrels."

"Yet despite this claimed pacifity you carry not one but

three large and unusual weapons," the observant sheep-herder pointed out sagely.

"It was thought I should be as well equipped as possible for this journey. Not every creature, much less every human, that one meets in strange lands is ready or willing to sit down and peacefully work out disagreements."

"Hoy, you can say that again! Especially the ones that want to eat you." Simna started to curl his legs up on the chair beneath his backside, then thought better of it. Not that he was shy, but his feet had not been washed in days, and though he would never admit to it, he was slightly intimidated by the unexpected tidiness of their surroundings.

"Whither are you bound, then?" their host inquired. "To which of the Thinking Kingdoms?" Reflected firelight danced in his pale green eyes.

"To none of them, based on what you have told us." Ehomba felt himself growing sleepy. It had been a long day's march, the welcoming warmth of the fire was seeping inexorably into his tired muscles, and the plushness of the couch on which his lanky frame reposed was intoxicating. "We have to cross the Semordria, and to do that we have learned that we must go to Hamacassar to find a ship."

"Hamacassar!" For the first time since their arrival, the little man looked startled. "So far! And yet just a prelude to a greater journey still. I am impressed. You are great travelers."

"You bet your chin hairs we are." Simna nodded in the herdsman's direction. "And my friend there, he's a grand and powerful wizard. He claims to be doing this only to help some lady, but I know he's really after a great treasure." Looking smug, the swordsman crossed his arms over his chest and compromised with his legs by laying them across a small serving table.

The sheepherder nodded slowly as he digested this information before turning back to Ehomba. "Is what your friend says true? Are you a wizard?"

"Not only not a wizard," the southerner protested, "but not grand or powerful, either. I was well prepared for this journey by the good people of my village, that is all." He threw Simna a dirty look, but the swordsman ignored him. "Some people get an idea into their heads and no matter what you do, you cannot get it away from them. They bury it as deeply as a dog does a favorite bit of offal."

"Oh, don't I know that!" Puffing on his pipe, Lamidy Coubert chuckled under his breath. "A person's mind is a hard thing to change, it is. Living up here by myself like this, I'm often the butt of jokes from the people of Cailase village, where I buy those things I can't make myself. Or I am looked upon with suspicion and uncertainty by those few visitors who do manage to make it this far into the mountains." He manifested a kindly grin. "But after they meet me, their concerns usually disappear quite rapidly. I'm not what even the most fearful would call a threatening figure." He gestured with one hand at the surrounding room.

"As you can see, I don't even keep any weapons here."

Ehomba nodded, then eyed the old man with interest. "Where I live there are many predators. They are very fond of sheep as well as cattle. We have to watch over our herds every minute, or the meat-eaters would take the chance to snatch a lamb or calf. So we need our weapons. You have no predators here?"

"Oh yes, of course. Dire wolves and pumas, small smilodons and the occasional hungry griffin. But Roileé generally keeps them off, and if they're persistent, whether out of deep hunger or ignorance or real stubbornness, I can usually make enough noise and fuss to drive them away."

"That old dog would face down a griffin?" Simna was disbelieving. "She hardly looks steady enough to make it to the nearest ridge top."

"Roileé may have lost a step or two, but she still has her bark, and she can still bite. I haven't lost a lamb to a predator in twelve years."

The swordsman grunted. "Hoy, it just goes to show. Appearances can be deceiving for people, I guess it can be the same for dogs." He scrunched deeper into the obliging back of the chair. "I don't suppose you've got anything to drink? We've been a long time walking with nothing but water to sustain us."

"Of course, of course!" For the second time Coubert looked startled. "My manners—I am getting old." Thunder rumbled in the distance, and not as far off as before. The storm was definitely moving in the direction of the solidly built little cottage.

From an ice-chilled cabinet their elderly host brought out wine, and from a chest small metal goblets. Simna was disappointed in the limited capacity of the drinking utensils, but relaxed after their host set the bottle on the table and did not comment when refills were poured.

"You must tell me." Coubert had taken a seat on the hearth just to the left of the fire. "What are the sheep like in your country? Are they the same as mine, or very different?"

Emitting a soft moan of despair, Simna poured himself a third glass of the excellent spirits and tried to shutter his ears as well as his mouth. Ehomba took up the question energetically, and the two men embarked on a discussion of sheep and sheep-raising, with an occasional aside to accommodate the dissimilar nature of cattle, that required the addition of several logs to the fire. Despite the steady cannonade of approaching heavy weather, Ahlitah was already submerged deep in cat sleep. With his abnormally long legs fully extended to front and rear, his paws nearly touched opposite walls of the cottage. With the assistance of more wine, Simna ibn Sind soon followed the imposing feline into similar latitudes of slumber.

Coubert's hospitality extended to his offering his guest the only bed. Ehomba would not hear of it.

"Besides," he told the oldster, "it has been my experience that the beds of more civilized people are too soft for me, and I would probably not sleep well in it. Better for me to remain here with my friends." He pushed down on the cushion that was supporting him. "If this couch is also too soft, I assure you I will be very comfortable here on the floor, beside your excellent fire." He glanced significantly upwards. "I think that tonight a strong roof will be the most important aid to sleep."

"I think you're right, my friend." With a kindly smile, their host tapped the bowl of his pipe against the stone mantel, knocking the contents into the fireplace. "Actually, it's been pretty dry hereabouts lately. We could use a good rain." Thunder echoed through the surrounding vales in counterpoint to his comment. "From the sound of it, we're about to have some. I hope you sleep well, Etjole."

"Thank you, Lamidy."

After the old man had retired to the room behind the kitchen, closing the door gently behind him, Ehomba struggled to negotiate with the couch for reconciliation of his long frame. It took some twisting and turning, and his legs still dangled off the far end, but the final position he settled on was not an impossible one, and he felt he would be able to sleep. The soothing fire was a great help, and the profundo purring of the black litah a suitable if not entirely exact substitution for the soothing susurration of the small waves that curled and broke rhythmically on the shore beneath the village.

He awoke to the peal of thunder and the flash of lightning. It revealed a world transformed into brief glimpses of stark black and white. Color returned only when the shocked purple faded from his sight, allowing him to see once again by the light of the dying fire. Ahlitah now reposed on his back with all four legs in the air, his massive skull lolling to one side, leaving him looking for all the world like a contented, spoiled tabby. That was one thing about cats, Ehomba knew: No matter how much they were scaled up in size, they all retained their essential, inherent catness.

Simna lay slumped in the chair, quite unconscious and smelling strongly of the fruit of the vine. The earth could have opened beneath the cottage and the swordsman would have slept until he hit bottom.

A second rumble rattled the room, leaving the herdsman more awake than ever. Rain tiptoed on the thatch and spilled in a succession of channeled bells off the roof to strike the compacted ground outside. Sleeping in the awkward position had left him with a cramp in his thighs. Grimacing, he swung his legs off the arm of the couch and onto the floor. He would walk off the cramp and then try to go back to sleep in a different position.

In the dwindling firelight he paced back and forth between the couch and the kitchen, feeling the sensation return to his legs. It was on one such turn that he happened to glance out a window precisely when distant lightning flared. What he saw, or thought he saw, momentarily frozen in the stark dazzle, gave him pause.

An uncertain frown on his face, he walked to the door and unlatched the top half. Cool, wet wind greeted him and blowing rain assailed his bare skin. He blinked it away, trying to penetrate the darkness. His eyes were sharp, his night vision acute, but he was no owl. Another flash of light, a boom of thunder close at hand, and his eyes finally confirmed what he had seen through the window a moment before. There could be no question about it.

Yapping and barking excitedly with the strength of a much younger animal, darting back and forth with impossible swiftness, leaping higher into the air than any impala, Lamidy Coubert's dog was herding the lightning.

IX

Wonderment writ large on his face, Ehomba stood in the half-open doorway, watching the implausible. It was enthralling to see the little long-haired dog cut off a bolt before it struck the ground, turning it with a stentorian yelp, cutting back and forth in front of the shimmering flash until it was penned back among the rocks with several others. They hovered there, flickering wildly, apparently unable to decide whether to strike the ground beneath them or recoil back up into the clouds. Like cornered livestock, they were waiting for directions from the supernal sheepdog.

A fresh bolt attempted to slash at one of the garden fence posts. Anticipating its arrival, the dog flashed through the air faster than even Ehomba's trained eye could follow. With a clashing of its jaws it snapped at the descending tip of the thunderbolt, sending it whipping sideways to slam harmlessly into an open, empty patch of ground.

Tongue lolling, eyes bright and alert, the dog stood stolidly next to the garden awaiting the next lashing from the heavens. Then something made her turn, and she saw Ehomba standing in the doorway, staring. Sneezing once, she shook her head dog-style and trotted over to the pen of boulders to yap boisterously at the lightning trapped within. With a great concerted crash and roll the cornered bolts were sucked back up into the roiling clouds from whence they had come, to crackle and threaten no more.

Satisfied, the old dog pivoted and came loping back toward the house. Halting beneath the overhanging lip of the thatched roof, she shook violently, sending water flying in every direction. Her long fur fluffed out, but only partway. It would take more than a shake or two to dry out that thick mop of black and white. Slurping up her tongue, she considered the tall stranger watching her from the other side of the door.

"Well," she exclaimed in words of perfect inflection, "are you going to let me in so I can dry off, or do you mean to make me stand out here until I catch my death of cold?"

"No." Taking a step back, Ehomba opened the lower half of the door. "I would not want that."

She trotted past him and headed straight for the fire. Seeing that the somnolent Ahlitah occupied nearly all of the space before the glowing embers, she sighed and managed to find an unoccupied bit of floor between the big cat's mountainous shoulder muscles and the hearth. There she lay down, breathing easily, and closed her eyes in a picture of fine canine contentment.

Ehomba shut and latched both the upper and lower halves of the door against the wind and rain before walking over to sit down on the hearth opposite the sheepdog. "I have seen dogs work cattle, and I have seen them work antelope. I have even seen them work camels. But never before have I seen one work lightning."

Roileé wiped at her left eye with one paw before replying. "Lamidy has always been a good man, kind and caring. But he is getting old faster than I, and he cannot play as easily or as often as he used to. When I get bored, I have to find ways to entertain myself." She nodded in the direction of the door. "Herding the lightning keeps my reflexes sharp."

"I would think that any dog that can herd lightning could handle even a large flock of sheep on one leg."

"Tut! Lightning is fast; sheep are tricky and, when they want to be, deliberately deceptive. As a herdsman yourself, you should know that."

"I spend most of my time with cattle. Cattle are not tricky."

"No, you are right. Cattle are quite predictable."

"And while we are talking," Ehomba suggested, "I would be very interested to know how it is that you came to be able to talk."

Roileé shook her head and began licking the damp backs of her paws. "Many animals can talk. They just choose not to do so in the presence of humans, who think it a unique faculty of their own. Your striking feline companion talks. He does not want to, though. It is a curse to him."

"A curse?"

"Yes. All he wants to do is kill, and eat, and sleep, and make love, and lie in the sun in a quiet place. That is why he keeps his talking brief. It is not because he is rude; only impatient with an ability he would just as soon not have."

"You assume much in a very short time."

"I assume nothing, Etjole Ehomba. I know."

"Even a dog that can speak does not know everything."

"That is true." The long muzzle bobbed in a canine nod. "But I know a great deal. More than most dogs. You see, I am a witch."

"Ah, now I understand." Ehomba nodded solemnly. "You are a woman who has, through some hex or misfortune, been turned into a dog."

"No, you do *not* understand. It is nothing like that. I was born a dog, I have always been a dog, and I will die a dog. I have never been, nor would I ever want to be, human. Some dogs do nothing all their lives but proffer companionship. Others work. I am a sheepdog. But I am also a witch, taught by witches when I was a puppy." She nodded in the direction of the bedroom door. "For many years I have kept company with Lamidy, I could have done worse. He is a kind and un derstanding man who knows what I am and is untroubled by the knowledge. It is good for a dog to have a human around. Good for the soul, and to have someone to change a water dish."

"Well, witch Roileé, it is good to know you."

"And I you." Limpid, intelligent dog eyes met his. "You are an unusual man, Etjole Ehomba."

The tall southerner shrugged. "Just a simple herdsman."

"Herdsman perhaps. Simple, I am not so sure. Where are you bound?"

He told her, as he had told people before her, and when he was through she was whimpering querulously.

"It all sounds very noble and self-sacrificing."

"Not at all," he argued. "It is what any virtuous man would do."

"You impute to your fellow humans a greater dignity than they deserve. I like you, Etjole Ehomba. I would help you if I could, but I am bound by the oath that binds together dog and man to remain here with my Lamidy."

"Maybe you can help anyway." Ehomba considered whether he wanted to make the request. And, more significantly, whether he wanted it fulfilled. In the end, he decided that knowledge of a woeful kind was an improvement over no knowledge at all. All enlightenment was good. Or at least, so claimed Asab and the other people of importance. "Can you tell me what lies ahead for my friends and me? We know little of the lands that await us."

The dog exhaled sharply. "Why should I know anything about that?"

"I did not say that you did," the herdsman replied quietly.

On the other side of the cat-a-mountain, Simna made gargling pig noises in his sleep. Behind Ehomba, the withering fire continued to cast warmth from its bones. "I asked if you could find out."

Canine eyes searched his fine, honest face. "You are an interesting man, Etjole Ehomba. I can herd the lightning, but I think maybe you could shear it."

He smiled. "Even if such a thing were possible, which it is not, what would one do with clippings from the lightning?"

"I don't know. Feed it to a machine, perhaps." Coming to a decision, she rose, stretched her front feet out before her and thrust her hips high in the air, yawned, and beckoned for him to follow.

She stopped in the cozy room's farthest corner, facing a two-foot-high handmade wooden box with a forward-slanting lid. On the front of the lid someone had used a large-bladed knife to engrave a pair of crossed bones with a dog heart above and singular paw print below. "Open it."

For the barest instant, Ehomba hesitated. His mother and father and aunts and uncles and the elders of the village had often told the children stories of warlocks and witches, of sorcerers and sorceresses who could turn themselves into eagles, or frogs, into oryx or into great saber-toothed cats. He had grown up hearing tales of necromancers who could become like trees to listen silently and spy on people, and of others capable of turning themselves into barracuda to bite off the legs of unwary gatherers of shellfish. There were rumors of hermits who at night became blood-supping bats, and of scarecrowlike women who could become wind. Others were said to be able to slip out of their skins, much as one would shed a shirt or kilt. Some grew long fangs and claws and their eyes were said to be like small glowing moons of fire.

But he had never heard of a witch among the animals

themselves, who had not at some time been human. He told
her so.

"Do you think only humans have their conjurers and
seers? Animals have their own magic, which we share but
rarely with your kind. Most of it you would not understand.
Some of it would not even seem like magic to you. We see
things differently, hear things differently, taste and smell and
feel things differently. Why should our alchemy also not be
different?" Eyes the color of molten amber stared back up at
him. "If you want my help, Etjole Ehomba, you must open
the box."

Still he hesitated. A backward glance showed that his companions slept on. There was no sign of movement from the
direction of the cottage's single bedroom. "Does Coubert
know?"

"Of course he knows." Her muzzle brushed the back of his
hand, her wet nose momentarily damp against his dry skin.
"No one can live with a witch and not know what she is.
Human or dog, cat or mouse, we are all the same. Some
things you cannot hide forever even from the ones you love."

"And he has no magic powers of his own?"

"None whatsoever," she assured him. "But he is good to
me. I have clean water every day, and I do not have to kill my
own food." For the barest instant, her eyes blazed with something that ran deeper than dogness. "We are comfortable
here, the two of us, and if a right woman or strong husky
were to come along, neither of us would resent the other's
pairing. We complement one another in too many ways." She
gestured with her black nose. "The box."

His long, strong fingers continued to hover over the lid.
"What is in it?"

"Dog magic."

Lifting the cover and resting it back against the wall, he
peered inside. No crystal globe or golden tuning fork greeted
his gaze. No bottles of powdered arcanity or pin-pierced

dolls stared back up at him. There was not much at all in the bin, and what there was would not have intrigued a disgruntled thief for more than a second.

Some old bones, more than a little rancid and well chewed; a long strip of thick old leather, also heavily gnawed; a ball of solid rubber from which most of the color and design had long since been eroded; a stick of some highly polished pale yellow wood covered with bite marks; and a few pieces of aromatic root tugged from a reluctant earth comprised the bin's entire contents.

"My treasures," murmured Roileé. "Take them out and lay them before the fire."

Ehomba did so, taking a seat on the hearth when he had finished. As he looked on, the dog witch used her paws to align them in a particular way: bones here, stick crossed there, ball in position, leather strip curled just so, roots positioned properly to frame them all. With her nose, she nudged and pushed, making final adjustments. When all was in readiness, she lay down on her belly, tilted back her head, and began to moan and whimper softly. Neither Simna nor Ahlitah moved in their sleep, but from outside the cottage there came distant answering howls as wolves and other canids found their slumber disturbed. Ehomba felt something stir deep inside him, emotions primal and hoary, that spoke fervently of the ancient link between dog and man.

Roileé's soft whimpering and moaning was not constant, but varied in ways he had never before heard from a dog. It was not language as he knew it, but something more basic and yet within its own special parameters equally complex. It bespoke wisdom denied to men, the intimate knowings of creatures that moved on four legs instead of two. It reeked of smells he could never know, and an acuity of hearing beyond the human pale. With these skills and senses other knowings were possible, and Roileé was a master of all these.

Within the incandescent depths of the fire something

snapped, sending a glowing ember flying. It arced over the hearth to land amid the pile of gatherings. A tiny puff of smoke rose where it had settled among the leather and bones. The puff expanded, became a cloud obscuring the bright eyes of the old sheepdog, and then Ehomba too found himself engulfed.

He had always been a fast runner, but now he seemed to flow effortlessly over the ground as fast as a low-flying eagle. Trees and rocks and bushes and flowers flew past him, the flowers at shoulder level, the trees immense impossible towers that seemed to support the sky. Every sense was heightened to a degree he would not have thought possible, so that distant sights and smells and sounds threatened to overwhelm his brain's ability to process them.

A subtle but distinct odor caused him to swerve to his left. Immediately, the musk sharpened, and seconds later a covey of startled quail exploded from the bush in which they had been hiding. He snapped at them, more out of an instinct to play than a desire to kill, for he was not hungry. Advancing on a small stream, he slaked his slight thirst, and was amazed by the distinctiveness of each swallow, at the chill of the water against his throat and the discrete flavors discernible within something seemingly as bland as the water itself.

A distant rumble caused him to lift his head from the stream, water trickling from his muzzle. Turning in the direction of the sound, ears pricked, he listened intently for a moment. When the rumble came again, he trotted eagerly in its direction, ears erect and alert, nose held high.

As he neared the source of the sound, a new smell filled his incredibly sensitive nostrils. It was acrid and distinct and he knew without having to think that he had smelled it before. But so intent was he on tracking the sound that he put off giving a name to it.

A dark shape, sleek and muscular, materialized from a thick copse of brush nearby. Startled by the unexpected appearance, he bristled and bared his teeth. Recognition quickly allayed any concern. Though far larger and stronger, the shape was familiar. Astonished at the incongruity, both parties stared at one another for a long moment. Then they turned together and, without speaking a word between them, sped off side by side, tracking the source of the sound.

It appeared so abruptly neither of them had a chance to change course, or retreat. Looming over the trees before them, it advanced like soup rising to a fast boil. Devoid of color and nasty of countenance, it swamped the trees, turning bark to black and presenting death as a shower of green needles. Ehomba and his companion turned and tried to flee, but it was too late. The dire emptiness swallowed them both. Most of the sharpened senses he had become heir to vanished: the keen sight, the splendid hearing, the acute taste. Only smell remained, and was rapidly overwhelmed. The acrid, dry, lifeless stink of the eromakadi filled his nostrils, seared his throat, and threatened to inundate his lungs, causing them to swell until they burst. . . .

He blinked, and coughed, but not loudly or harshly. He was back in the main room of the cottage. A few flames still leaped hesitantly from the pile of glowing clinkers that was all that remained of the once blazing fire. In his chair, Simna ibn Sind slept the sleep of spirituous stupefaction. But the litah no longer stretched across the floor from wall to wall. He had curled himself into a tight ball of black fur and was twitching and moaning in his sleep.

"It will pass."

Looking down, Ehomba saw that the sheepdog was watching the larger animal. Turning her head, her warm brown eyes met his. "The big cat was in your dream. Sometimes that will happen. Dreams are like smoke. If there happens to be more than one in the same sleep space, sometimes they will merge and flow together. I don't think that was the kind of dream the cat is used to, but when he wakes he may well not remember any of it." The witch eyes stared. "You remember, though."

"Yes, I remember," the herdsman admitted. "But I do not know what it means."

"You asked me if I could help you see what lies ahead of you. I did as you asked. I was with you and you with me, watching, perceiving, trying to understand." Rising and walking forward, she lifted a paw and placed it on his bare thigh.

"You are doomed to unremitting misery, your quest to failure, the rest of your life to cold emptiness. Unless you end this now. Go home, back to your village and back to your family. Before it is too late. Before you die." Her paw slipped off his leg.

Ehomba looked away, feeling the warmth of the fire against his back, and considered the dog's words. They were words he had heard before, in a town far, far to the south, from someone else. Another female, but not a dog. Another seeress, but one who walked on two legs instead of four. They were very different, Roileé and Rael, and yet they had spoken to him the same words. It was not encouraging.

"I cannot go back. Not until I have fulfilled a dying man's promise. I took that upon myself willingly, and no matter how many prophets and diviners repeat to me the same death mantra I will follow this through to its end."

"From what I just saw and felt, its end will be your end." This pronouncement she delivered in a matter-of-fact manner and without emotion.

"That remains to be seen. It is your interpretation, and that of one other. Events will convince me, not divinations."

"I can only do what you asked me to do."

He smiled gently. "I know, and I thank you for that." Automatically, he reached out and patted her on the head. If he had thought about it he might not have done so, but he need not have worried. Instead of upbraiding him for his temerity, she moved nearer and pressed her muzzle and head against his comforting palm.

"There are some things," she explained, "for which even witchcraft cannot substitute. A kind and comforting hand is one."

"I understand." Sitting there on the hearth, he continued to pet her. "There are many times since I left the village that I could have used such a touch myself."

"You are a good man, Etjole Ehomba." Her head pushed insistently against his soothing palm and she panted easily in the reflected heat of the fire. "The world is a poorer place whenever a good man dies."

"Or a good dog," he added graciously.

"Or a good dog."

"Do not worry. I have no intention of dying."

"Then do not disregard what I have just told you. Try to overcome it. Make me out to be a liar."

He grinned. "I will do my best. Now, tell me something I can use. What lies to the north of here, below these mountains? Coubert spoke of many small kingdoms."

"He spoke accurately." She turned her head up to him but did not move away from his hand. "Lamidy is a learned man, but there are many in the towns and cities to the north who could put his erudition to shame. Not all of them are kind and decent," she warned the herdsman. "You may have to match wits with more than one. I have looked inside your mind, but only a little. I don't know if you're up to it."

"I will manage." He spoke reassuringly if not with complete confidence. "I have always managed. Learning does not frighten me."

"That's good. What of your companions?"

Ehomba eyed his sleeping fellow travelers. "The litah is smarter than anyone thinks but prefers not to show it. No one will expect anything more scholarly from a big cat than a roar or loud meow anyway. As for Simna ibn Sind, his smarts are of a kind not to be found in books and scrolls, and a valuable complement to my own poor insight in such areas."

The she-dog sniffed. "I don't know if that will be enough to get you safely through places like Melespra or Phan. When you are uncertain, look to the night sky, to the left of the moon. There is a certain star there that may help to guide you safely through moments of uncertainty."

"What star is that?"

"The dog star, of course," she told him. "It is there if you need it, for serious travelers to follow. That is all I can do for you."

Ehomba nodded appreciatively. "It will have to be enough." Rising, he yawned sleepily. "The dream was as tiring as it was interesting. I think I had better get some rest, or tomorrow my friends will lecture me endlessly on my neglect. You must be tired, too."

The witch dog stretched first her front end, then her rear, and also yawned, her tongue quivering with the effort. "Yes. Magic is always exhausting."

"As must be herding lightning," he reminded her as he sought somehow to compact his lanky frame enough for the couch to accommodate it.

"No." Head snuggled up against tail, she curled up in front of the fire. "That was fun."

In the morning Coubert made breakfast for them, providing eggs and lamb chops and bread, along with a complete haunch of mutton for the grudgingly grateful Ahlitah. When Ehomba protested at this largesse, the sheepherder only smiled.

"I have plenty of food. It must be something in these mountains. The air, or the water, or the forage, but my sheep do better than anyone else's. They grow fatter, and produce thicker wool, and drop more lambs."

"You are fortunate," Ehomba told him even as he glanced

in the direction of a certain dog. But Roileé did not react, busy gnawing methodically on a scrungy femur.

"You'll hit Bebrol first," Coubert was telling them. On the other side of the table, Simna was devouring all that was set before him. "It is the southernmost town in the Dukedom of Tethspraih. A small province, but a proud one. North of Tethspraih lies Phan, an altogether more wealthy and cosmopolitan sort of place. You three will stand out in Tethspraih, but not so much in Phan and the larger kingdoms. If you want to make time you should keep to yourselves as much as possible."

"We always do." His mouth full of mutton, the swordsman had difficulty speaking.

"How far from Phan to Hamacassar?" Ehomba ate delicately but steadily.

Coubert sat back in his chair, fork in one hand, and pondered, his lower lip pushing out past the upper edge of his beard. "Hard for me to say. I've never been that far north. Never even met anyone who has." His smile returned. "You'll be able to get more accurate information in Phan. More tea?"

"No, no thank you." Simna wiped at his greasy lips with the back of his forearm. "Your fount of generosity filled me with enough liquid last night. Now I need to fill my gut with solid stuff to sop it up." He punctuated his confession by shoving a sizable chunk of brown bread into his mouth.

"At least let me top off your supplies. I don't know what resources you have."

Food muffled Simna's grunted response. "Hoy! Spent most of our resources, we have."

"You have been too kind to us already," Ehomba told him, ignoring the swordsman's bugging eyes and frantic semaphoring.

"Please allow me to help. It's my pleasure. I have so much, and your journey is of noble intent." Pushing back his chair, he placed his linen napkin on the table and rose. "Besides, Roileé seems to like you, and over the years I've come to trust her judgment. Strange how sometimes a dog can be more perceptive than a person."

"Passing strange," agreed Ehomba. From her place prone on the floor, the witch dog winked at him. No one else saw it, as was intended.

They departed the cottage with their packs stuffed full of jerked mutton and their water bags filled to overflowing. Though Coubert offered to supply one, Ahlitah refused to wear a pack. It was enough, he growled, that he was compelled to suffer the company of men. To expect him to adopt, however temporarily, their constricting accoutrements was too much. He would remain free physically if not otherwise.

Coubert stood in the doorway of his home and waved until they passed out of sight. His dog sat at his feet, saluting their departure with several joyful yips and barks.

"Nice dog, that one," Simna was moved to comment as he hitched his heavy pack higher on his shoulders. "Getting on in years, but still good company."

"More than you know." As always, Ehomba's gaze was focused forward, scanning the lay of the land ahead of them. "She was a witch."

"Hoy? By Gyerboh, I never would have guessed!" The swordsman looked back the way they had come, but the little cottage had already disappeared from view, swallowed up by rolling boulders and brush and the gentle incline they were now descending. "How could you tell?"

"She told me. And showed me some things. In a dream."

Ahlitah looked around sharply. "So that was not a dream within a dream. Thought it might have been you there with me, but couldn't be sure." The big cat shook its head and the great black mane flowed and rippled. "Don't remember much of it. What were you doing in my dream, man?"

"I thought you were in mine. Not that it matters."

Simna's bewilderment underlined his words. "What the Ghoska are you two babbling about?"

"Nothing. Nothing real." Ehomba stepped over a wandering rivulet, doing his best to avoid crushing the tiny flowers that fought for life on its far side. "It is all gone, like smoke."

The swordsman snorted derisively, a common reaction when Ehomba or the cat spoke of things he did not understand. After a while he exclaimed, "So she was a witch, was she? I've known bitches who thought they were witches, but this is the first one who fully qualifies on both counts."

"She was righteous, and helpful." The herdsman did not tell his friend that Roileé had recapitulated the virulent prediction that had first been read to him in distant Kora Keri.

"A man can't ask any more of a bitch, be she witch or otherwise." Pleased with that proclamation of itinerant swordsman sagacity, Simna took the lead. "It'll be great to be back among civilized society again, where a man can find decent food and drink wherever he turns. And perhaps even a little entertainment." His eyes flashed.

"As you yourself pointed out to Coubert, our assets are much reduced. We need to conserve them for necessities, my friend."

"Hoy, bruther, I can see that you and I need to achieve a consensus on just what constitutes a necessity."

They discussed the matter of their meager remaining resources as they walked. When it came to the laying out of specifics, the litah sided with Simna, the only difference being that while the big cat sympathized with and understood the swordsman's baser needs, he himself had no use for any human medium of exchange, being accustomed as he was to taking what he required when he needed it, and slaughtering the rest.

X

Because the mountains that formed the southern boundary of the Thinking Kingdoms sloped so gently from their heights, the travelers did not encounter the grand, sweeping panorama that might have been expected. Instead, they came upon the first outlying pastures and villages of Tethspraih unexpectedly and without drama.

Unlike the farms they had seen south of Aboqua, these were not patches of forest or desert reclaimed for planting. Neat hedgerows and stone walls demarcated fields that had been planted and harvested for hundreds of years. Venerable irrigation canals carried water to faultlessly straight furrows. There were fields of wheat and rye as well as vegetables and ground-hugging fruits, orchards as tidily pruned as flower beds, vineyards clean enough to sleep in. Sturdier trees hung heavy with nut crops, and melons lined the ridges of water-filled ditches like bumps on a lizard's hide. Flocks of songbirds and small parrots filled the trees with color and the air with song. All were intoxicated with pigment, a golden parrot sporting a bright emerald crest being the most prevalent. A small flock of these opalescent birds performed aerial acrobatics above the heads of the travelers as they advanced, as if greeting them with avian sign language.

Flowers brightened the fronts of even the smallest houses, and the weed-free dirt roads soon gave way to sophisticated stone paving. They passed through small clusters of homes and craft shops that had not quite matured into villages, and then into the first real towns. Wherever they went they excited stares and gossip among the well-dressed populace, due in large part to the inability of even the most supercilious residents to ignore the hulking presence of Ahlitah on their spotless streets. But Ehomba and Simna drew their fair share of stares as well, thanks to their exotic costume and barbaric aspect.

"I don't like being the object of everyone's interest." The swordsman strode along insolently, oblivious to the giggling of the women and the disapproving glares of the men. "This would be a hard place for us to hide—if we needed to hide."

"I fear we will just have to resign ourselves to being conspicuous." The worn butt of Ehomba's spear clacked against the stone of the sidewalk every time he took a stride forward. "This is a much more cosseted country than any we have passed through previously. I do not mind them looking down on us, or thinking we are uncivilized savages, so long as they leave us free to go on our way."

"We don't need food. Our good friend the sheepherder saw to that." The swordsman was peering hopefully at storefronts and into windows of real glass. "But I could use something stronger than tea to drink. It was an easy hike but a long one out of those mountains."

Ehomba sighed resignedly. "You always need something to drink."

His friend shrugged. "Can I help it if I have thin blood?"

"I think a thin constitution is more like it." From his greater height, the southerner searched the street on which they found themselves. "But a tavern is a good place to find information. And that, friend Coubert did not supply in great quantities." Lowering the tip of his spear, he gestured at a likely-looking establishment. Birds nested in the eaves above the entrance, suggesting either that they were inured to noise and violence or that it was a well-behaved place.

The nattily dressed owner took a stance directly opposite the door as soon as he saw what had entered. His disapproving scowl vanished the instant Ahlitah's eye caught his, and he seemed to shrink several inches. While he did not invite them in, neither did he find it expedient to bar their way. Mindful of the fuss their foreign presence had roused, Ehomba and his companions settled themselves in the most isolated booth in the place, thereby relieving the perspiring owner of one major concern, if not exactly endearing themselves to him.

Gold from Simna's rapidly dwindling Chlengguu hoard turned out to be as welcome in Tethspraih as anywhere else, and drink was duly if coolly brought. The tired travelers drank, and watched the comings and goings of patrons, admiring the cut of their fine clothing. Silk and satin were much in evidence, and this was only a modest municipality and not one of the Thinking Kingdom's great cities. Its citizens smelled of wealth and prosperity. And yet, beneath the superficial veneer of general happiness, Ehomba sensed overtones of discontent, of pockets of gloom scattered among the comfortable like measles on a beautiful girl's countenance.

Thoughtfully, he turned back to the mug set before him. Its contents were refined, and warmed his belly. A bright-eyed Simna was already on his second.

"By Goilen-ghosen, Etjole, will you never put away that long face?" The swordsman waved at their impeccable, almost elegant, surroundings. "There's no danger here, no threat. We're not out in the hinterlands of nowhere now, dealing with mad horses and all-consuming black clouds. Can't you relax?"

"I will relax when this journey is done and I am back home with my friends and family."

"Hoy, what a melancholy, brooding traveling companion you are. Might as well be roaming with an undertaker."

"That is not fair," Ehomba protested. "I enjoy a good laugh as much as the next person. And have done so, in your presence."

"Yeah, yeah, so you have. I'm not saying you don't have a sense of humor. It's your general attitude that sours the air around you."

"Then maybe you should point your nose in a different direction!" Seeing that other patrons were staring at them, he lowered his voice. "It is just that when I am not talking, I am always thinking."

Simna was smiling at a distant woman, who was gracefully clad in a flowing dress with fine lace trim. She smiled back, seemed abruptly to remember herself, and turned haughtily away—but not before sneaking another surreptitious glance in the swordsman's direction. He flashed her another grin.

"Then that's your curse, Etjole. Myself, when I'm not talking, I'm not thinking. It's a very restful way to live and lets a man sink into the world instead of having it dumped on his shoulders. You should try it sometime." He took a hearty swallow from the mug before him.

"I have," Ehomba replied disconsolately. "It does not seem to work for me."

Simna nodded understandingly. "Actually, we should both envy him." He gestured with the mug at the black litah. The heavily muscled predator was lying with its spine against the back wall, eyes closed, sound asleep. "Cats now, they not only know how to relax, they've made an art of it."

Abruptly, the laughter and bubbling conversation that

filled the tavern died. Through the main doorway, a knot of men had entered as one. The owner, who had been prepared to challenge Ehomba and his friends, did not even attempt to bar their entry. Instead, he moved hastily aside, bowing his head several times out of fearful respect. As soon as they had identified the intruders, the rest of the apprehensive patrons resumed their conversations, keeping their voices unnaturally low.

The men and women wore uniforms of loose-fitting yellow and white, with high-puffed front-lidded caps and yellow leather boots. They carried rapiers and flintlock pistols, whose function the more worldly Simna had to explain to the astonished Ehomba. He had never encountered firearms before, though itinerant traders who occasionally made forays into Naumkib country spoke of seeing such things in the southern cities of Askaskos and Wallab.

The leader of the intruders was a big, burly individual with a profound mustache and close-cropped red hair. As he led his people deeper into the tavern, Ehomba was surprised to see that two of the uniforms were worn by grim-faced older women.

They finally halted before the travelers' table. Hands rested as inconspicuously as possible close to pistol butts and sword hilts. "You!" the leader declared.

"Us?" Simna responded querulously.

"Yes. You are under arrest and are to come with us immediately."

"Under arrest?" An openly confused Simna frowned. "By Gobula, what for? Who are you?"

Muted laughter rose from the uniformed intruders at this blatant confession of ignorance. Their leader, however, hushed them sternly. He did not smile.

"You are obviously strangers here, so it is not surprising you do not know. We are the Servitors of the Guardians of

Right Thinking, and you are under arrest for improper contemplations."

"Improper contemplations?" Ehomba's face contorted. "What is that?"

"Thinking not in alignment or kind with the approved general mode of thinking decreed for Tethspraih," the mind cop informed him importantly.

"Well," murmured Ehomba, "since we just arrived in your country, there is no way we could know what constitutes approved thinking and what does not, now could we? I have never heard of such a thing."

"Hoy, that's true," Simna concurred self-righteously. "How can you arrest us for violating some ordinance we know nothing about?"

"I am only following orders. I was told to bring you to the rectory." His fingers hovered close to his sword, and those behind him tensed. On the far side of the tavern, two couples departed in haste without paying their bill. The owner, a petrified expression on his face, did not go after them.

Simna's jaw tightened and his own hand started to shift, but Ehomba raised a hand to forestall him. "Of course we will go with you."

The swordsman gaped at him. "We will?"

"We do not want any trouble. And I would like to know who has been reading our thoughts, and how."

"Well, I wouldn't."

"Then stay." Ehomba waked Ahlitah, whose unexpected and suddenly looming presence swiftly wiped the complacent smiles from the faces of the police contingent. After whispering an explanation to the big cat, it nodded once and ambled out from behind the table. The police drew back farther, but at a sign from their leader kept their weapons holstered and sheathed.

"I'm glad you've decided to cooperate." The officer nodded in the big cat's direction and invoked a grateful smile. "Very glad."

"We have just arrived here and we do not want to make any trouble." Ehomba started toward the door. "Let us go to this rectory and see what is wanted of us."

Simna hesitated, growled something nasty under his breath, then picked up his own pack and followed, falling in beside his friend. "You better know what you're doing," he whispered as the police escorted them out onto the street and turned left. "I don't like jails."

The herdsman barely glanced in his companion's direction. He was much more interested in their new surroundings and in the people who were staring back at him than in the swordsman's complaints. The citizens of the Dukedom were wholly human; no other simians here. No intelligent apes and orangs, chimps or bonobos. To his way of thinking it rendered the otherwise imposing town a poorer place.

Striding along importantly in the forefront, the police official led them through the streets, past stores and restaurants, apartments and workshops, until they crossed a neatly paved square to halt outside the towering wooden door of a large stone structure. It was decorated with finely sculpted portraits of men and women holding all manner of articles upon which writing had been incised. There were tablets and scrolls, bare slabs of rock, and thickly bound books. The graven expressions of the statues bespoke ancient wisdom and the accumulation of centuries of knowledge.

Other signatures of learning festooned the building: chemical apparatus and tools whose function was unknown to Ehomba, mathematical signs and symbols, human figures raising bridges and towers and other structures—all indicating a reverence for knowledge and erudition. For the endemic songbirds and parrots the multiplicity of sculptures provided a nesting ground that verged on the paradisiacal.

Simna was openly mystified. "This doesn't have the look or feel of any jail I ever spent time in."

"You are especially knowledgeable in that area?" Ehomba inquired dryly.

"Hoy, sure!" the swordsman replied cheerfully. "Just part of my extensive résumé of experience."

The herdsman grunted as the door was opened wide by an acolyte clad in a simple white robe emblazoned with mathematical symbols. "We may need to draw on it. Though prior to this journey I had spent little time in towns, I am pretty sure that a police escort is not sent forth to escort people anywhere other than to a jail."

It did not look much like a lockup, however. Simna continued to offer unsolicited comments on their surroundings as they were marched inside. There were no cells, no bars, no downcast prisoners shuffling about in irons. The interior was a fair spiritual and aesthetic reflection of the exterior, with uncowled monks busy at desks and laboratory tables, delving deep into books or arguing animatedly about this or that matter of science.

They were taken to a large chamber that was more like a comfortable living room than a theater of interrogation and directed to seat themselves opposite an empty, curved table. A trio of monks, two men and one woman all of serious mien and middle age, marched in. As soon as they took their chairs, the police official stepped forward and saluted by pressing his open palm to his forehead and then pulling it quickly away in a broad, sweeping gesture.

"Here are the ones you sent us to bring, Exalted Savant."

Simna leaned over to whisper to his friend. "Hoy, let me guess. These are the right high and mighty Guardians of Right Thinking. If you ask me, they look a little bent. I like the gold embroidery on those white robes, though."

"You like anything gold," Ehomba snapped.

The swordsman weighed his friend's comment. "Not always. When I was a stripling I remember a certain aunt whose mouth was full of gold teeth. Whenever she bent to kiss me I would cry. I thought her teeth were solid metal, like little gold swords, and that she was going to eat me up."

"Be quiet," the herdsman admonished him, "and maybe we can get out of here without any fuss if we satisfy them as to our purpose in being in their country." Behind him and slightly to his right, Ahlitah sat on his haunches and busied himself cleaning his face, utterly indifferent to however the humans, friends and strangers alike, might elect to proceed.

"Welcome to Tethspraih." The man in the middle folded his hands on the table before him and smiled. His expression was, as best as Ehomba could tell, genuine.

"Funny sort of way you've got of welcoming strangers," Simna retorted promptly. Ehomba gave him a sharp nudge in the ribs.

The woman was instantly concerned. "Were you wounded while being brought here? Are you in pain? Or are you suffering from injuries incurred while coming down from the Aniswoar Mountains?"

"We are unhurt." Ehomba eyed her curiously. "How did you know we came from those mountains? We could as easily have entered your land from the east, or the west."

Simna commented sarcastically. "I know how, long bruther. A little birdie told them."

The monk seated on the left, with a pleasant round face and twinkling eyes, sat a little straighter. "That's right! That's exactly right." Lowering his voice, he murmured to his associates. "They have been talking to citizens."

"No," insisted the man in the middle. "I think he is just perceptive."

"Funny." The woman was staring at Simna. "He doesn't look perceptive."

Ehomba hastened to draw the conversation away from his companion. "We were told that we were brought here because our thinking was 'not in alignment' with the kind of thinking you have decreed for this country. I never heard of such a thing. How can you decree what people can think?"

"Not 'what,'" the woman corrected him. "'How.' It's the way people think that we are concerned with. What they think about is not our concern."

"Absolutely not," added the man on the far end. "That would constitute an inexcusable invasion of privacy."

Ehomba was unconvinced. "And telling people how to think does not?"

"Not at all." The beaming monk in the center unfolded his hands and placed them flat on the table. The subdued light in the chamber made the gold symbols on his robe dance and sparkle. "It leads to a thriving and prosperous society. Wouldn't you agree that what you've seen of Tethspraih is flourishing, that the people are as healthy and attractive as their surroundings?"

"I would," the herdsman conceded. Not only had these people allowed him and Simna to keep their weapons during the interrogation, but the litah had also been permitted to accompany them into this inner sanctum. This suggested great confidence. But in what? The armed servitors who had escorted him and his friends were stationed outside the chamber. Insofar as he could tell, not one of the monks carried so much as a dagger. What could they do to defend themselves if, for example, someone like Simna lost his temper and leaped at them with sword drawn? Sitting behind their table, they appeared quite indifferent to any danger the armed strangers might pose. Ehomba was simultaneously impressed and wary, and curious to know why.

"All right." The swordsman sighed. "Tell us what we have to do to get out of here. If it's a fine, we'll try to come up with the money to pay it."

"Oh no. Fining you would be a useless gesture characteristic of primitive extortionate regimes." The woman was smiling at him once again. "We might as well put a knife to your ribs in the middle of the street. We'd never think of doing such a thing."

"No indeed," the middle monk added. "We are not an agency of punishment, fiduciary or physical."

Simna relaxed a llule. "Hoy, that's good to hear."

"Then what do you want of us?" Unlike his friend, Ehomba did not relax. "Why have we been brought here?"

"Why, so you can be helped, of course." The smiles of the three were brighter than ever.

At this pronouncement the swordsman lost his composure. "What do you mean, 'helped'?"

The monk on the end gazed across at him with infinite compassion. "To think appropriately, of course."

Simna ibn Sind did not like the sound of that. He did not like the sound of it one bit. "Thanks, but I've been thinking for myself for nigh on thirty-one years now, and I'm comfortable with the process just as it is. Set in my ways, you might say."

"Oh, that's all right," the monk assured him. "It's a consideration common to many improper thinkers, and one easily corrected. Don't worry—we'll take care of it for you."

"By Gambrala, do I have to spell it out for you? I don't want 'it' taken care of!"

Ehomba put a calming hand on his companion's shoulder. A by now highly agitated Simna shook it off, but out of consideration for his friend held back the stream of words his tongue was preparing to launch.

"Why do you care how we think?" The herdsman addressed the panel in a voice calm with respect and genuine interest. "We come from other lands and are just passing through your country. With luck we will be beyond the borders of Tethspraih and inside Phan in a few days. Then our way of thinking will no longer concern you."

The woman was shaking her head slowly. "If we allowed

that to happen we would be derelict in our duty to our fellow man. All of us would have to do penance."

"If you treat every visitor this way I'd think you wouldn't have much trade with your neighbors." Simna had calmed down—a little.

"Some of our neighbors are amenable to persuasion," the monk on the end informed them. "With others we have treaties that, regrettably, prohibit us from exposing them to the satisfactions that come with decreed thinking. But we have no such treaty with you."

"And because of that," the man in the center added, "we have a wonderful opportunity to spread right thinking to countries whose names we may not even know! Because when you return to your homelands it will be as disciples for the Tethspraih way of life."

"I got news for you," Simna retorted. "The only way of life I'm a disciple for is the Simna ibn Sind way of life. It's pretty popular in its own right, and while I'm real fond of it myself, I'd no more run around trying to inflict it on someone else than I would try to make them eat my favorite pudding."

"We can fix that." The man on the end wore a big smile that thoroughly belied the implied threat behind his words.

"No one said anything to us about such things when we entered your country," Ehomba told them. "If they had, we would have avoided Tethspraih, and gone around its borders."

"The sheepherder should have told you." The woman shook her head sadly. "What a waste of a fine mind. The majority of his thinking is improper."

When he had first met Lamidy Coubert, Ehomba had been unable to understand why such a gregarious and congenial individual would choose a life of isolation in the high mountains. Now he knew. Perhaps Roileé had helped him to escape. But the average citizen of Tethspraih had no bitch witch to assist him or her in flight. Prosperous and successful they might be, but they were trapped here. Or perhaps, he corrected himself, their bodies were free, and only their minds were ensnared.

"I do not know what you mean by proper or improper thinking," he told them. "I know only that my friend Simna thinks the way he thinks, and I think the way I think, and Ahlitah thinks the way he thinks—and that is how we will continue to think."

"We are not concerned about the great cat," the woman replied. "Such beasts are creatures of instinct and not reason." At these words the litah paused momentarily in cleaning its face, then resumed licking and brushing. It seemed content to let Ehomba deal with the controversy.

"But you and your friend will be brought into the fold. And you will be the happier for it."

"I'm already happy enough," an angry Simna retorted. "And I'll stomp anyone who says different!" His fingers grasped the hilt of his sword.

Despite this openly hostile gesture, none of the three monks behind the table reacted apprehensively. From what Ehomba could see, they did not even tense. Where was their protection? he found himself wondering. How were they able to remain completely unruffled in the face of an implied challenge from an obviously agitated, intemperate personality like Simna?

Despite their intransigent words, he was still hoping to avoid a confrontation. With that in mind, he again tried to divert their attention from the combative swordsman. "I do not understand. How did you know how we were thinking when we entered your country? Something must have told you or you would not have been able to send your servitors, your police, to that tavern to find us."

"Your friend already knows, and explained it." The monk

in the middle sat back slightly in his chair and smiled deprecatingly. "A little bird told us."

Turning toward the door, he snapped his fingers twice. Simna tensed, expecting the armed servitors to enter. Instead, a young white-clad acolyte appeared. His robe was emblazoned with only two golden symbols. In the wire cage he carried, two small golden parrots were chattering and chirping contentedly. Ehomba remembered seeing their like among the flocks of songbirds that had announced their arrival in Tethspraih. And they had been common in the eaves above the tavern, and in the streets of the town, and among the stone sculptures that festooned the rectory.

They looked like ordinary birds, more spectacularly plumaged than some, less active than others. No more, no less.

After placing the cage on the table, the acolyte bowed respectfully to his superiors and backed out the way he had come. As he passed through the door, Ehomba noted that at least some of the armed servitors remained stationed in the hall outside. While impressive, the monks' confidence was evidently not absolute.

The middle speaker placed an affectionate hand on the top of the cage. "These are Spraithian cockatells. They are very good mimics. Most parrots and other members of their related families can listen to human speech and recite it back. Cockatells are able to do the same with thoughts."

"So that's how you spy on your people." Simna's lips were tight. "We saw the damn little shitters everywhere. How can someone's thoughts be their own if there's a bird on every windowsill, in every branch, on the fence post outside each house, soaking up what and how they're thinking? And of course, you people have 'em trained like pigeons, so that after soaking up enough thoughts they come flying back here, where you can milk them of other folks' privacy."

"You make it sound like a forced intrusion," the woman

responded disapprovingly. "No one is harmed, no one senses the cockatells at work, and peace and prosperity reign throughout the land." Reaching into a pocket of her robe, she removed something and stuck it between the bars of the cage. The vivacious, feathered pair immediately descended from the perch where they had been chattering to nibble eagerly at the proffered gift. "In addition, they are playful, attractive birds."

"I didn't see anyone playing with 'em," Simna responded. "And why do I have this gut feeling they're not real popular as pets?"

"Do not blame the birds." Ehomba gently admonished his friend. "It is not their fault they have been put to such a use. I doubt they have any notion of what they are involved in." He watched the pair use their sharp beaks to shell and then spit out the husks of tiny seeds. "As the savants say, they are only mimics. They listen, and repeat, but do not understand."

"You couldn't find better spies," Simna growled. His outrage at the invasion of his innermost privacy was complete, but out of deference to his friend his sword stayed in its scabbard.

"So from what you have learned from some birds you have decided that our manner of thinking is wrong, and that you have the right to change it. Even if we are happy with the way we think and do not want it changed." The herdsman met each of the savants' eyes in turn.

"You will thank us when we are done." The woman was beaming again. "You," she declared, directing her words to the quietly fuming Simna, "will become a much more pleasant and less belligerent person, one who is kind to others and supportive of extended contemplation."

"By Gouzpoul, don't count on it." The swordsman's fingers tightened on the hilt of his weapon.

"And you," she continued as she turned slightly to face

Ehomba, "will become a teacher, devoting your life to the spreading of the way of proper thinking among uncivilized peoples."

"It sounds like an admirable calling," Ehomba told her. "Unfortunately, I already have one. There are cattle to be supervised, and chores to be done. The Naumkib must give over all their waking hours to surviving. I have no time to devote to the profession of wandering teacher. You need to find another."

"You are the first of your people to visit Tethspraih." The monk seated at the other end of the table was speaking forcefully. "As such, you must be the one to carry our teachings to your land. It is a great honor."

"Yes," added the middle savant. "Besides, you have no choice. You do not have to waste time and energy arguing about it because the decision has been made for you." He smiled encouragingly, reassuringly. "That is the job of savants. To make the right choices for others. We prevent many headaches before they happen."

"Then why are you giving me one now?" Simna ibn Sind had listened to just about enough. Avoiding Ehomba's attempt to restrain him, the swordsman took a bold step forward and drew his blade. Sensing his thoughts, the pair of cockatells stopped eating and fell back to the far side of their cage. They remained huddled together there, their shimmering golden feathers quivering slightly as they were forced to listen to and absorb the blast of unfettered aggression from the swordsman's mind.

Showing that they were indeed human, the savants reacted to Simna's provocation by losing their seemingly everlasting smiles. But no one leaped from their chair or tried to flee. Nor did anyone raise a warning cry to the servitors stationed outside.

Instead, the monk in the center reached quickly beneath the table and brought out a most curious-looking device.

The length of a man's arm, it had a handle and a long tubular body that was fluted and flared at the end like an open flower. One finger curled around a small curve of metal set into the underside of the apparatus. Attached to the top was a small bottle or canister. This was fashioned of an opaque substance and Ehomba could not see what it contained.

Resting the wooden handle against his shoulder, the savant pointed the flowerlike end of the device directly at Simna. Exposed blade hanging at his side, the swordsman's gaze narrowed as he stared down the barrel of the awkward contrivance. Not knowing what it did, he was unsure how to deal with the threat its wielder's posture implicitly implied.

"Simna," the herdsman told his friend warningly, "that's enough! Stay where you are!"

The monk at the far end of the table spoke somberly. "It does not matter. Advance or retreat, the end will be the same." His smile returned, though in muted form. "And you will be the better for it."

"The better for it?" Simna glared furiously at the man, utterly frustrated by the unshakable composure of the smugly complacent trio seated behind the table. "I'll be the better for *this*!" Raising the shining blade over his head, he took another step forward. Ehomba shouted a warning and Ahlitah crouched, instantly alert.

The monk aiming the device did not hesitate as he pulled the trigger and fired.

XI

The litah snarled warningly but held his ground. Ehomba instinctively drew back. As for Simna, he ducked sharply, frowned, and then straightened anew. To all outward appearances he was entirely unharmed.

The cloud of powder that puffed from the muzzle of the strange device was primarily pink with deeper overtones of cerise. It enveloped the swordsman for the briefest of moments before dissipating in the still air of the chamber. Simna sniffed once, twice, and then laughed out loud.

"A decent little fragrance. Delicate, not too strong. Reminds me of a girl I spent some time with in a town on the western edge of the Abrangian Steppes."

"Good." The monk lowered the contraption but did not set it aside. "I'm glad it brings back fond memories for you."

"Very fond." Simna grinned wolfishly at the savant. "Fonder than you'll ever know."

"That may very well be true. You are obviously a man of extensive appetites. Mine, I am not ashamed to confess, are more modest. In that respect I envy you, though I cannot say that my envy translates into admiration." He indicated the swordsman's upraised weapon. His two associates were watching closely. "What, may I ask, were you planning to do with that impressive-looking piece of steel?"

Simna looked down at the sword in his hand. "This? Why I was going to . . . I was going to . . ."

His words trailed away along with his anger. He stared stupidly at the weapon, as if he had once known its purpose but had forgotten, like someone who finds a long-lost piece of clothing in an old drawer and cannot remember how it is to be worn. Slowly, he lowered the blade. His expression brightened when he remembered the scabbard that hung from his belt. Sheathing the metal, he looked back at the trio of inquisitors and smiled.

"There! I guess that's what I was going to do with it." The smile plastered on his face resembled that of several of the lesser sculptures that decorated the exterior of the rectory: bemused, but not vacuous. "I hope we're not giving you good people any trouble?"

"No," the woman told him confidently, "no trouble at all. It's nice to see you right thinking. A lot less painful, isn't it?"

"It sure is." But even as Simna spoke, his lips seemed to be doing battle with his jawline. Small veins pulsed in his forehead and neck, and perspiration broke out on his forehead even though it was quite cool in the darkened chamber. Everything about his expression and posture indicated a man at war with himself—and losing. One hand trembled visibly as it attempted to clutch the hilt of the now sheathed sword. The fingers would twitch convulsively forward and miss, twitch and miss, as if their owner was afflicted with any one of several neuromuscular infirmities.

It was dispiriting to watch Simna take a step toward the table. One leg worked well enough, but the other hung back, obviously reluctant, as if fastened to the floor by metal bolts.

The paralyzed grin on the swordsman's face hinted at internal mental as well as physical conflict.

"Better," the monk in the middle declared tersely even as he raised the singular device and pointed it in Ehomba's direction. "As your friend can tell you, this won't hurt a bit. A few weekly treatments and your thinking will be right as rain."

"Yes," agreed the man on his left. "Then you can choose freely whether to return to your homeland, or remain here in beautiful Tethspraih, or continue on your way. Whichever you do, it will be as a contemporary, right-thinking person, with none of the irritating emotional and intellectual baggage that so cripples the bulk of humanity."

"I like my intellectual baggage," Ehomba responded. "It is what makes me an individual."

"So do unfortunately inherent human tendencies to commit murder and mayhem." The woman succored him with an angelic smile. "But they do not contribute to the improvement of the person."

Ehomba tried to duck, to twist out of the way, but it was far more difficult to avoid a cloud than a spear thrust. As the pallid vapor enveloped him he tried not to inhale, only to find that it was not necessary to breathe in the powder directly to experience its effects. The delicate fragrance was an ancillary effect of the substance, not an indicator of its efficacy. It sank in through his eyes, his lips, the skin of his exposed arms and ankles and neck, from where it penetrated to the core of his being.

While his feet remained firmly on the floor, he felt his mind beginning to drift, to float. Ahead lay a pillowed rosy cloud, beckoning to him with pastel tendrils while masking his view of the three savants. He was aware that they were continuing to observe him closely. If only he would let himself relax and fully embrace the mist, a great deal of the inner torment and uncertainty that had plagued him throughout his life would vanish, dispersed as painlessly and effectively as vinegar would kill a scorpion's sting.

He fought back. He conjured up stark images of Mirhanja and the children that were faithful down to the smallest detail. He recalled the time he had been fishing in the stream the village used as its source of fresh water, and had stepped on a spiny crawfish. The remembrance of that pain pushed back the insistent vapor, but only for a moment. He recalled the specifics of discussions he had engaged in with the village elders, and arguments he'd had with his wife, and the day they had celebrated his mother's eightieth birthday and it had rained on everyone and everything. He reviewed the minutiae of his journey to this time and place, assigning each an emotion and a day.

He did everything he could think of to keep his thoughts his own—even if they were not "right."

"He's fighting it." Through the brume of befuddlement that threatened to overwhelm him he heard the woman's voice. She still sounded confident, but not quite as confident as previously.

"His channels of thought are more deeply worn and solidly set than those of his companion." This from the monk seated at the other end of the table. "Give him another dose."

"So soon?" The senior of the trio sounded uncertain.

"We don't want to lose him to irresolution." The other man's tone was kindly but firm. "It won't hurt him. He's strong. At worst it may cost him some old memories. A small price to pay for a lifetime of proper thinking."

Benumbed within the fog of right thinking, Ehomba heard what they planned for him, and panicked. What memories might he lose if subjected to another dose of the corrective dust? A day hunting with his father? Favorite stories his aunt Ulanha had told him? Remembrances of swimming with friends in the clear water pool at the base of the little waterfall in the hills behind the village?

Or would his losses be more recent? The number of cattle he was owed from the communal herd? Or perhaps the knowledge of how to treat a leg wound, or bind up a broken bone. Or the wonderful philosophical conversations he had engaged in with Gomo, the old leader of the southern monkey troop.

What if he forgot his name? Or who he was? Or what he was?

The only thing that seemed to fight off the soporific effects of the powder was strong thinking in his accustomed manner. Behind him, Ahlitah had finally roused himself from his slumber. He could hear the big cat growling, but softly and uncertainly. Seeing his friends standing unbound or otherwise unrestrained, freely confronting the three unarmed humans seated behind the table, the cat was not even sure anything was amiss. When it came to the realization that all was not as well as it seemed, it would be too late for it to help. And a burst of thought-corrective powder from the big-mouthed apparatus might render its feline mind incapable of intelligent thought altogether.

No matter how persuasive or compelling the effects, Ehomba had to fight it off—for the sake of his friends as well as himself. The inimical darkness he knew how to combat, but the sweet-smelling pink powder was far more treacherous. It did not threaten death or dismemberment, only a different way of thinking. But the way a man thought determined who and what he was, the herdsman knew. Change that and you forever change the individual behind the thoughts.

Desperately, he struggled to keep rigid, uncompromising images at the forefront of his thinking. Cloying and insistent, the subtle aroma of the powder suffused his nostrils, his lungs, the essence of himself. It ate at his thought processes like acid distilled from orchids.

No! he shouted to himself. *I am Etjole Ehomba, and I think thusly, and not thatly. Leave my mind alone and let my friends and me go!*

"Definitely needs another dose." The woman's expression reflected her compassion and certitude. "Give in to the way of right thinking, traveler! Let yourself relax—don't fight it. From the bottom of my being I promise that you will be a happier and better man for it."

"A happier and better man perhaps." On the other side of the fog that had enveloped him he believed he heard his voice responding. "But I will not be the same man."

The senior of the trio sighed regretfully. "I would rather not do this. I hate to see anyone lose memories, no matter how insignificant."

"It is for the greater good," the savant on his left pointed out. "Society's as well as his."

"I know." After performing a quick check of the small canister attached to the top of the contrivance, the monk raised the metal tube and for a second time aimed it in Ehomba's direction.

The herdsman was frantic. The pink haze was no longer advancing on his thoughts, but neither had it gone away. It hovered before him like a fog bank awaiting a ship being thrust forward by the current, waiting to swallow him up, to reduce his individual way of thinking to the mental equivalent of zero visibility. Reinforced by a second burst from the long-barreled device, its effects would doubtless prove overwhelming.

Ehomba cogitated as hard as he could. Concentrated on bringing to the forefront of his thoughts the most powerful, most convincing images he could call up. Not right-thinking notions, perhaps, but those of which he was most soundly and resolutely convinced. He envisioned Mirhanja, and the village. He contemplated the stark but beautiful countryside of his homeland, the hunting and herding trails that crossed its hills and ravines. He conjured up the faces of his friends and relatives.

Taking careful aim, the well-meaning monk triggered the powder shooter. Thought-paralyzing pinkness blossomed in the herdsman's direction. When it surrounded him he knew he would be the same, but different. Identical in appearance, altered within. He concentrated furiously on the pain of his own birthing, of the lightning strike that had killed an old childhood friend, of the way he and the other men and women of the village had spent all of a night debating how to deal with a visiting hunter who had availed the Naumkib of their hospitality only to be discovered attacking one of the young women. Strong thoughts all, couched in his own unique, individual manner of thinking. From the mouth of the device the salmon-hued haze approached as if in slow motion, like bleached blood.

He thought of the sea.

Behind him, the litah yelped. Another time, the herdsman might have remarked on the unusual sound. He had heard the big cat snarl, and growl, and snore, and even purr in its sleep, but he had never heard it yelp. It would not have mattered if Ahlitah had suddenly burst into traditional village song, so hard was Ehomba fighting to concentrate on his way of thinking. Had he identified it, that which had made the cat yelp would have surprised him even more than the uncharacteristic feline expression itself.

Ahlitah cried out because his feet were suddenly and most unexpectedly standing ankle deep in water. Cold, dark water that smelled powerfully of drifting kelp and strong salts. Nearby, Simna ibn Sind blinked and found himself frowning at something he could not quite put a finger on. Something was not right and, try as he might, he couldn't identify it.

Behind the table, the three savants gaped at the water that had materialized around their feet. Where it was coming from they could not imagine. It seemed to well forth from the solid floor, oozing upward via the cracks between the stones, replacing vanished mortar. Oblivious to what was happening around him, Ehomba continued to concentrate on the oldest, most distinctive entity in his copious store of memories, one he could reproduce with the least amount of effort. He thought of how the sea tasted when sips of it accidentally forced their way past his lips while he was swimming, of the cool, invigorating feel of its liquid self against his bare skin, of the spicy saltiness that tickled his palate and the burning shock whenever any entered his nose. He remembered how its far, flat horizons provided the only real edge to the world, recalled the look of specific creatures that swam sinuously through its depths, saw in his mind's eye the humble magnificence of the abandoned skeletons of creatures large and small that each morning found cast up on its beaches like the wares of a wise old merchant neatly set out for inspection and approval.

And as he remembered, and thought, the sea continued to fill the interrogation chamber, the water level rising with preternatural, impossible speed. It covered him to his knees, reached his hips. Behind him, the agitated litah rumbled and splashed. Having risen from their chairs, the three stunned savants were backing away from the travelers and wading dazedly toward the door. All around Ehomba, pink powder drifted down to the water and was absorbed, dispersing within the rising dark green depths like ground tea leaves in a boiling kettle.

The monks shouted and the door was pulled aside—only to reveal two of the armed servitors slipping and floundering in water up to their waists. The deluge from nowhere was as prominent in the hallway outside the room as it was within, offering neither safety nor dry environs for the fleeing savants.

Half standing, half floating next to Ehomba, Simna ibn Sind shook his head sharply, blinked, and seemed to see his newly saturated surroundings for the first time. Wading with difficulty through water that was now up to his chest, he grabbed the herdsman's arm and pulled violently.

"Etjole! Hoy, bruther, you can turn off the spigot now! Our happy mentors have fled." The swordsman nervously eyed the rising waters. "Best we get away from this stagnant seminary while the awaying's good."

Ehomba seemed not to hear his friend. Cursing under his breath, Simna directed the disoriented Ahlitah to join them. By dint of much hasty pushing and shoving, they managed to position the unresponsive herdsman facedown across the big cat's broad back. In this manner, with their lanky companion wallowing so deep in thought he was unable to rise above his thinking, they walked and waded and swam out of the room.

Emerging from the hallway into the rectory's central inner hall, they kicked their way into a scene of complete chaos. Frantic monks were struggling madly to keep irreplaceable scrolls and tomes above the rising water, which was rapidly climbing toward the second floor. Foaming waves broke against banisters and railings, and thoroughly bewildered fish leaped and flopped in the troughs.

"The main entrance!" Simna shouted as he plunged headlong into the agitated combers and whitecaps. "Swim for the main entrance!"

Though water was able to escape from the few open first-floor windows, these were already submerged and proved themselves unequal to the task of coping with the rising flood. Monks and acolytes bobbed helplessly in the waves. Off to the rear of the hall, above the now sunken master fireplace, a miniature squall was brewing. Looking down into the water, Simna thought he saw something sleek and muscular pass beneath his body. Behind and to the right of him, a flailing servitor, having divested himself of his weapons and armor, suddenly threw both hands in the air. Shrieking, he disappeared beneath the chop, dragged down by something that should not have been living so many hundreds of leagues from the sea, should not have been swimming free and unfettered in the center of the rectory of right thinking.

Following close behind the swordsman, the black litah paddled strongly through the salt-flecked rollers. Turning onto his back while still making for the almost entirely submerged main door, Simna yelled to his limp friend.

"Enough, bruther! You've made your point, whatever it was. Turn it off, make it stop!"

Words drifted back to him, across the water and through the black mane. It was definitely Ehomba's voice, but muted, not as if from sleep but from concentration. Concentration that had led not only to a realization more profound than the herdsman could have envisioned, but to one from which he seemed unable to liberate himself.

"Cannot . . . must think only . . . of the sea. Keep thinking . . . straight. Keep thinking . . . myself."

"No, not anymore!" The swordsman spat out a mouthful of salt water. It tasted exactly like the sea, even down to the tiny fragments of sandy grit that peppered his tongue. "You've done enough!" Around them the residents of the rectory screamed and cried out, kicked and flailed as they fought to keep their heads above water. Not all were good swimmers. At that moment the hall and the rest of the structure were filled not with right thinking or wrong thinking, but only with thoughts of survival.

"Ow! By Gelujan, what . . . ?" Turning in the water, Simna saw that he had bumped his head against the heavy wooden double door that sealed the main entrance to the rectory. Only a small portion of it remained above the rising waters. Opening it was out of the question. Not only would it have to be opened inward, against the tremendous pressure of the water, but the twin iron handles now lay many feet below his rapidly bicycling legs.

Something gripped his shoulder and he let out a small yelp

of his own as he whirled around to confront it. When he saw that it was only Ehomba, awakened at last from his daze, he did not know whether to cry out with relief or deal his revived friend a sharp blow to the face. In any event, the uneasy waters in which they found themselves floating would have made it impossible to take accurate aim.

"What now, humble herdsman? Can you make the water go away?"

"Hardly," Ehomba replied in a voice only slightly louder than his usual soft monotone. "Because I do not know how I made it come here." Treading water, he scanned their surroundings. "We might find a second-story window to swim through, but that would mean spilling out onto the streets below and risking a dangerous drop." He glanced down at his submerged feet. "How long can you hold your breath?"

"Hold my . . . ?" Simna pondered the question and its implications. "You're thinking of diving to the bottom and swimming out one of the first-floor windows?"

The herdsman shook his head. For someone who spent so much of his life tending to land animals, the swordsman mused, Ehomba bobbed in the water as comfortably and effortlessly as a cork.

"No. We might not locate one in time, or we might find ourselves caught up and trapped among the heavy furniture or side passageways below. We must go out the front way." He indicated the upper reaches of the two-story-high main door. "Through this."

"Hoy? How much of your mind did you leave in that little room, bruther? Or are your thoughts still tainted by that virulent pinkness?"

Ehomba did not reply. Instead, he turned in the water to face the methodically paddling feline. "Can you do it?"

The big cat considered briefly, then nodded. With his great mane plastered like black seaweed to his skull and neck, he managed the difficult feat of looking only slightly less lordly even though sopping wet. Wordlessly, he dipped his head and dove, the thick black tuft at the end of his tail pointing the way downward like an arrow aimed in reverse. Ehomba followed, arching his back and spearing beneath the surface like a sounding porpoise. With a last mumbled curse Simna ibn Sind pinched his nose shut and initiated a far less elegant and accomplished descent.

The ocean water itself was clean and unsullied, but since only limited light penetrated the rectory, underwater viewing of any kind was difficult. Visibility was limited to a few feet. Still, while Simna's stinging eyes could not locate Ehomba, they had no trouble picking out the massive, hulking shape of the litah. As he held his position, his cheeks bulging and the pack on his back threatening to float off his shoulders, the big cat sank the massive curving claws on its forefeet into the secondary human-sized entry door that was imbedded in the much larger, formal gateway. Then it did the same with its hind feet—and began to kick and claw.

Though working underwater reduced the litah's purchase and slowed its kicks, shredded wood quickly began to fill the gloom around them, drifting away and up toward the surface. A burst of daylight suddenly pierced the damp gloom, then another, and another. Simna felt unseen suction beginning to pull him forward. Kicking hard and pushing with his hands, he held his submerged position. His heart and lungs pounded against his chest, threatening to burst. He couldn't even try to harangue Ehomba into performing some of the magic the herdsman insisted he had not mastered. If something didn't happen very soon, the swordsman knew his straining, aching lungs were going to force him back to the constricted, wave-tossed surface.

Something did.

Beneath the constant attack of Ahlitah's claws, the water-logged wood of the secondary door not only gave way but collapsed completely. Simna felt himself sucked irresistibly forward. Flailing madly with hands and feet, he tried to maintain some semblance of control over his speedy exodus—to no avail. His right arm struck the doorjamb as he was wrenched through and a dull pain raced up his shoulder.

Then he was coughing and sputtering in bright sunlight as he bobbed to the surface. After making sure that his sword and pack had come through with him, he looked around for his companions.

Ehomba was rising and falling in the current like a long uprooted log. He waved and shouted back to Simna. The swordsman, he noted, was far more agile and confident on land than he was in the water, even though the torrent was slowing as it spread out on the rectory square. Just ahead of him, Ahlitah was already scrabbling for a foothold on the paving stones.

Behind them, seawater continued to gush from the shattered doorway as if from an open faucet. Furniture, pieces of coving ripped from floors, sodden carpets, utensils, and the occasional gasping acolyte broke through the otherwise smooth surface of the flood. Screaming filled the air as stunned, startled citizens scrambled to escape the clutches of the saltwater river. Those who failed to move fast enough found themselves knocked off their feet and ignominiously swept down the street.

Dragging themselves clear of the main flow, the travelers reassembled behind a walled mansion. As Ehomba and Simna checked their packs, they were drenched all over again when the litah chose that moment to shake itself vigorously. After a few choice words from the swordsman, they resumed their inspection.

"Everything I own is soaked." Grousing, he held up a package of dried mutton. "Ruined."

Ehomba was sorting through his own possessions. "We are not in the desert anymore. There will be places to buy food." Rising, he looked around. "We need to find a source of fresh water and rinse everything out. If we do it quickly enough, some of the jerky should survive."

"That's the last time I listen to you where officialdom is concerned." The swordsman's pack squished wetly as he slung it over his shoulders. "Next time we put up a fight instead of going quietly." As they started down the deserted street, he looked back the way they had come. The torrent of salt water continued to gush unabated from the bowels of the rectory. "Sure is a lot of water. When will it stop?"

"I do not know. I thought of the sea to try and keep my thinking to myself, and you see what followed. I do not know how it happened, or why, or how I did what I did." He looked over at his companion. "Not knowing how I started it, I have no idea how to stop it. I am not thinking of the sea now, yet the water still flows." Behind them, cries and the sounds of frantic splashing continued to fill the square around the rectory.

Finding an unsullied public fountain, they removed everything from their packs and rinsed it all in the cool, clear fresh water to remove the salt. That task concluded, they did the same for their weapons to prevent the metal blades from corroding. Few citizens were about, most having locked themselves in their homes or places of business to hide from the intemperate sorcery. Everyone else had run to the rectory square to gawk at the new wonder. Gifted with this temporary solitude and shielded from casual view by Ahlitah's bulk, the two men removed their clothes and washed them as well.

"I feel as if I shall never be dry again." The disgruntled swordsman struggled to drag his newly drenched shirt down over his head and shoulders.

As Ehomba worked with his kilt he squinted up at the sky. "It is a warm day and the sun is still high. If we keep to the open places we should dry quickly enough."

"Hoy, we'll keep to the open places, all right!" Picking up

his sword, Simna slid it carefully back into its sodden sheath. "I'm not setting foot in another building until we're clear of this benighted country. Imagine trying to control not what people think but the way they think. By Gwiswil, it's outrageous!"

"Yes," Ehomba agreed as they started up the deserted street. "It is fortunate that the savants have to confront the unconverted in person. Think how frightful it would be if they had some sorcerous means of placing themselves before many people simultaneously. Of putting themselves into each citizen's home or place of business and talking to many hundreds of subjects at once, and then using their magic to convince them to all think similarly."

Simna nodded somberly. "That would truly be the blackest of the black arts, bruther. We are fortunate to come from countries where such insidious fantasies are not contemplated."

His tall companion indicated agreement. "If the sheepherder's description of the boundaries hereabouts was correct, we should be out of Tethspraih before midnight and thus beyond the reach of the guardians of right thinking."

"Can't be soon enough for me." Simna lengthened his stride. "My way of thinking may be skewed, or conflicted, or sometimes contradictory, but by Ghev, it's *my* way of thinking."

"It is part of what makes you who and what you are." Ehomba strode on, the bottom of his spear click-clacking on the pavement. "Myself, I cannot imagine thinking any differently than I do, than I always have."

"Personally, I think the guardians had the right concept but the wrong specifics."

Both men turned to the litah in surprise. Water continued to drip from the big cat's saturated fur. "What are you saying?" Ehomba asked it.

"The problem is not that men think wrongly. It's that they

think too much. This leads inevitably to too much talking."
Ahlitah left the import of his words hanging in the air.

"Is the big pussy saying that we talk too much?" Simna retorted. "Is that what he's saying? That we just babble on and
on, with no reason and for no particular purpose, to hear ourselves jabber? Is that what he's saying? Hoy, if that's how he
feels, maybe we should just shut up and never speak to him
again. Maybe that's what he'd like, for us not to say another
word and—"

Raising his free hand so that the palm faced the swordsman, Ehomba replied softly as they began to leave the urban
center of Tethspraih behind. "I am not saying that I agree
with him entirely, Simna, but perhaps it would be good if we
measured out our words with a little more care and fore-
thought."

"So most of it is waste? Most of what we say has no meaning, or makes no sense, or is of no use to anyone just because
he thinks so? Our words are just so much noise hanging in
the air, containing no more sense than the songs of the birds
or the buzz of bees? What we speak is—"

"Simna, my friend—be silent. For a little while, anyway."
Ehomba smiled encouragingly at the smaller man.

"Then you do agree with him?" The irascible swordsman
would not let the matter drop. "You think we do talk too
much, about nothing of substance?"

"Sorry, my friend." Smiling apologetically, Ehomba
pointed with his free hand to the side of his head. "My ears
are still full of water, and I cannot hear you properly."

Simna had a ready reply, but decided to set it aside. Was
the cursed cat smiling also? That was absurd. Cats could not
smile. Yawn, snarl, tense—but not smile. Storing his rejoin-
der in an empty corner of his memory, he traipsed on in silence, knowing that he could summon it forth for delivery at
a later time. He never did, of course.

Both Ahlitah and Ehomba were counting on it.

XII

The country ruled over by the enlightened Count Tyrahnar Cresthelmare proved as welcoming and hospitable as Tethspraih had been treacherous. They were passed through the border gate by curious but cheerful guards, who assured the blunt, inquisitive Simna that in Phan not only would no one try to change his way of thinking, no one would give a damn what he thought.

Never absent for very long in the worst of times, the spring returned to the swordsman's step and the glint to his eye as they accepted a ride into Phan City from a farmer with a wagonload of hay. The city itself put even prosperous Tethspraih to shame. Not only were the buildings more impressive and the people more elegantly attired, but there was a definite and distinctive sense of style about the modest metropolis that exceeded anything the wide-eyed Ehomba had ever seen. The more worldly Simna, of course, was less impressed.

"Nice little burg." He was leaning back with his hands behind his head and using Ahlitah's chest for a pillow. Rocked to sleep by the wagon's motion, the big cat did not object.

"Nothing like Creemac Carille, or Boh-yen, or Vloslo-on-the-Drenem, but it does have a certain dash." He inhaled deeply, a contented expression on his face. "First sign of an upscale community, long bruther: The air doesn't stink."

"I wonder if all these little kingdoms the sheepherder told us about are as prosperous as Tethspraih and Phan?" Ehomba was admiring the graceful people of many hues and their fine clothing. Here and there he even spotted an occasional ape, suggesting that the Phanese could boast of more cosmopolitan commercial connections than the more insular inhabitants of Tethspraih. Despite the ornate and even florid local manner of dressing, he was not made self-conscious by his own poor shirt, kilt, and sandals. It would never have occurred to Etjole Ehomba to be embarrassed by such a thing. While the Naumkib admired and even aspired to pleasing attire and personal decoration, not one of them would ever think of judging another person according to his or her appearance.

"Off ye go, boys." The hay farmer called back to them from his bench seat up front. "And be sure and see to it that great toothy black monster gets off with ye!"

Digging his fingers deep into Ahlitah's thick mane, Ehomba shook the cat several times until it blinked sleepy eyes at him. Rumbling deep in his throat, the litah took its own good time stretching, yawning, and stepping down from the back of the wagon. The farmer was not about to rush the operation and, for that matter, neither was the herdsman. No matter how friendly and affectionate when awake, a cat half asleep was always potentially dangerous.

Taking note of the oversized feline, a few stylishly outfitted pedestrians spent time staring in his direction. But no one panicked, or looked down their nose at the tired, sweaty travelers, or whispered snide comments under their breath. Ehomba's excellent hearing told him this was so, and in response to his query, Ahlitah confirmed it.

"This seems to be an unusually cultivated clustering of humans," the big cat commented. "One even remarked on how handsome and imposing was I."

"Evidently all their intelligence has gone into design." Hands on hips, Simna stood in the center of the street surveying their surroundings. A middle-aged man on horseback came trotting past and barely glanced in their direction. While the swordsman admired his flowing green cape, Ehomba noted with interest the schematics of the leather and brass tack, and Ahlitah lowered his gaze and growled deep in his throat at the nearness of so much easy meat. Luckily for the rider's ride, his mount did not meet the big cat's eyes.

"We need to find some sort of general trading house or store where we can replenish our supplies." Reaching around to pat his pack, Simna grinned affably. "One thing about gold: Not much hurts it. Not even seawater."

"I thought your purse was drained." Ehomba eyed his friend uncertainly.

The swordsman was not in the least embarrassed. "I didn't tell you everything, Etjole. I was keeping some in reserve, for myself. But"—he shrugged resignedly—"where I go so goes my belly, and right now it's more empty than my purse. I imagine it's the same with you."

Ehomba gestured diffidently. "I can go a long time without food."

"Hoy, but why should you?" Simna put a comradely arm around the tall man's shoulders. "Take food when and where you can, says I. By the look of this place, whatever we purchase here will be fresh and of good quality. Who knows what the next port of call may bring? To a general store for victuals and then, onward to Hamacassar!"

Ehomba followed his friend across the street. "Why Simna, you sound almost enthusiastic."

The swordsman responded to the observation with a

hearty smile. "It's my way of concealing desperate impatience. But I'm not really worried, because I know that the treasure that lies at the end of this quest will be well worth all the time and effort and hardships."

Ehomba thought of Roileé the witch dog's prediction, which echoed Rael the Beautiful's prediction. "I hope so, friend Simna."

Citizens gave them directions to a high-ceilinged establishment several blocks distant. Immediately upon entering it, Simna knew they had been guided to the right place. Larger goods were stacked in the center of the wooden-plank floor, while on either side shelves and compartments filled with smaller articles rose to a height of nearly two stories. Like bees probing flowers for honey, young boys on rolling ladders slid back and forth along these walls, picking out requested items in response to sharply barked orders from busy attendants below. At the far end of the single long room was a small bar fronting a handful of tables and chairs at which habitual denizens of the store's depths sat chatting, drinking, and smoking.

Polite customers made room for the travelers to pass. Or perhaps they were simply getting out of the litah's way. As it always did in the presence of so many humans, the big cat kept its massive head down and eyes mostly averted. This premeditated posture of specious submission went a long way toward alleviating the concerns of old men, and women with young children in tow.

While Simna shopped, Ehomba pestered the clerks with question after question. So much of what he saw on the shelves was new and wonderful to him. There were small mechanical devices of intricate design, and brightly dyed fabrics and household items. Much of the prepackaged food was outside his experience, and an exasperated Simna was obliged on repeated occasions to explain the nature of foreign imports and exoticisms.

When they had accomplished what they had come for, and finalized their purchases, a dour Simna held the last of the Chlengguu gold in one hand and counted the pieces that remained to them. "I'd thought not to retire on this, but to at least make myself comfortable for a while. Now it seems there won't even be enough to last out our journey."

"Be of good cheer, friend Simna." Ehomba put a comforting hand on his friend's arm. "Gold is only as good as the purpose it serves."

"I can think of a few I'd like to have served." The swordsman exhaled tiredly. "We have enough for a drink or two, anyway." He nodded at the patient Ahlitah. "Even the cat can have a drink."

"A pan of water will suffice, thank you." His fur having finally dried out, the litah had regained his last absent iota of dignity. Content, he made himself regally comfortable in a rear corner, much to the relief of the regular patrons of the limited drinking area.

Taking seats in finely made chairs of wicker and cloth, the two travelers luxuriated in the comfort of drinks with actual ice. This striking and unexpected phenomenon so intrigued Ehomba that he insisted they linger over their refreshment. Those seated in their immediate vicinity proved willing listeners to their tales of travels in far-off lands. Expanding in his element, Simna proceeded to embroider the truth and fill in the gaps with extemporaneous invention. Whenever the swordsman would unload a particularly egregious fiction on the audience of rapt listeners, Ehomba would throw him a disapproving frown. These his loquacious companion would studiously ignore. Meanwhile, snug in his corner, Ahlitah slumbered on.

In this manner, plied with cold drinks by an eager and attentive audience, they passed not only the rest of the afternoon but a good portion of the early evening. Eventually though, it appeared that even Simna ibn Sind's fertile narra-

tive was beginning to pale as their once fervent fans began
to drift away and out of the store in ones and twos, taking
their day's purchases with them.

At last it was pitch dark outside, and their audience had
been reduced to two: a pair of husky, bearded manual labor-
ers of approximately the same age as the travelers themselves. Their manner of departure, however, was as
unforeseen as it was abrupt.

Catching sight of the blackened street just visible through
the distant main entrance, the slightly smaller of the two
rose suddenly. His eyes were wide as he clutched at his still
seated companion's shoulder.

"Nadoun! Look outside!"

The other man's jaw dropped. He whirled to glare at the
man behind the compact bar. That worthy spoke solemnly as
he finished putting up the last of his glassware.

"That's right. Ye lads best get a move on or you'll have to
make your way home—after."

"Why did ye not warn us?" The first man's tone was
strained and accusatory.

This time the proprietor looked up from his work. "Ye be
grown men. I am a tradesman, not a baby-sitter."

Were it not for the terrified expressions on their faces, it
would have been comical to watch the two men fight frantically to don their fine evening jackets and flee the general
store. The shorter of the two flung a handful of money at the
proprietor, not bothering either to count it or wait for his
change.

Smacking his lips, Simna set his goblet down on the table
in front of him and inquired casually of the shopkeeper as he
knelt to pick the scattered coins off the floor, "What was that
all about?"

The heavyset merchant sported a florid black mustache
that curled upwards at the ends. It contrasted starkly with his
gleaming pate, which was as devoid of hair as a ceramic

mixing bowl. Perhaps in compensation, his eyebrows were ferocious.

"You don't know?" Straightening, he let the fruits of his coin gathering tumble into the commodious front pocket of his rough cotton apron. "You really don't, do ye?"

"It would appear not." Ehomba toyed with the rim of his own drinking utensil. "Could you shed some illumination on our ignorance for us?"

Shaking his head in disbelief, the proprietor came out from behind the bar and approached their table. His expression was thoroughly disapproving. As near as Ehomba could tell, they were alone in the establishment with the owner. All other customers and employees had long since departed.

With a thick finger their reluctant host indicated the wooden clock placed high on a small shelf. "D'ye know what that portends?"

Unfamiliar with mechanical clocks, Ehomba kept silent. But Simna nodded once, brusquely. "It 'portends' that it's twenty minutes to midnight. So?"

The merchant looked past them, toward the main entrance, and his tone softened slightly. "Midnight is the witching hour."

"Depends where you happen to be." Kicking back in his chair, the swordsman put his feet up on the table and crossed them at the ankles. "In Vwalta, the capital of Drelestan, it's the drinks-all-around hour. In Poulemata it's the time-for-bed hour."

"Well here," the proprietor observed sharply, "it be the witching hour."

"For a good part of the evening those two men were relaxed and enjoying themselves in our company," Ehomba pointed out. "When they realized the time they became frantic." He turned in his chair to look outside. On the silent, night-shrouded street, nothing moved. "What happens at this witching hour? Do witches suddenly appear?"

"Nothing so straightforward, friend." Quietly annoyed, the owner glanced meaningfully at Simna's sandaled feet where they reposed on the table. The swordsman responded with a good-natured smile and left his feet where they were. "If it were only a matter of the occasional witch, no one would care, and there would be no need for the Covenant."

"What is this Covenant?" An unpleasant, tingling sensation made Ehomba feel that they were going to have to leave their comfortable surroundings in a hurry. He made sure that his pack and weapons were close at hand.

Leaning back against the bar, the proprietor crossed his arms over his lower chest, above his protuberant belly, and regarded them sorrowfully. "Ye have never been to Phan before, have ye, or heard of it in your travelings?"

The herdsman shook his head. "This is our first time in this part of the world." Off in his corner, Ahlitah snored on, blissfully indifferent to the prattlings of men.

Their host sighed deeply. "Long, long ago, the province of Phan was known as the Haunted Land. Though it was, and is, surrounded by fertile countries populated by happy people, Phan itself was shunned except for those daring travelers who passed through it on the river Shornorai, which flows through its northern districts. Even they were not safe from attack."

"From attack?" Simna's eyes were slightly glazed, a consequence of downing all the free drinks that had been contributed by their now vanished audience. "By whom?"

Hirsute brows drawing together, the owner regarded him sternly. "Not by whom, friend. By *what*. It is a well-known fact that Phan has always provided a home to the dregs and rabble of the Otherworlds, to the noisome trash that is too debased and depraved to find asylum in those regions where such creatures normally dwell." He looked down at his arms and apron. "All spirits and entities need a place to abide, even the most wicked and corrupt. Phan was that place.

They congregated here, making this fine land uninhabitable, preying upon and tormenting any daring enough to try and homestead its fruitful plains and lush river valleys."

"Obviously, something happened to change that," Ehomba observed. Simna was listening more closely now, drawn not only to the proprietor's story but to the growing feeling that it just might have something to do with the hysterical egression of their last two listeners.

The owner nodded. "Led by Yaw Cresthelmare the Immutable, distant and greatest ancestor of the present Count Tyrahnar the Enlightened and founder of the dynasty of Phan, a great gathering of opportunists and migrants resolved to test the limits of the befouled occupiers of this land. The momentous battle that ensued raged for years. Many died, but were replaced by hopeful pilgrims from elsewhere. The debased and profane suffered far fewer casualties, for the dead are hard to kill, but neither could they drive the determined Yaw and his followers from Phan. Whenever they wiped out a cluster of pitiful, newly established huts or a wagon full of would-be immigrants, a new squatter's camp would spring up elsewhere."

Ehomba indicated the fine, well-stocked store in which they sat. "Yet here we sit, in the midst of much comfort, and in passing through your land we saw no sign of the kind of devastation to which you allude."

"As I be saying, this all took place long ago." Uncrossing his arms, the owner moved back behind the bar. "Neither side could wholly defeat the other. The degraded had the resources of all the dark crafts at their disposal, but they could not wreak havoc and destruction everywhere at once. The followers of Yaw had on their side numbers and persistence. Eventually, by mutual agreement, an accommodation was reached." He shook his head at the audacity of it. "Yaw Cresthelmare was a great man. Imagine, if you will, sitting down to negotiate with goblins and apparitions and demons so vile they are not even welcome in Hell."

Ehomba looked thoughtful. "And the result, it was this Covenant you speak of?"

"Yes. The Inhuman tried everything to trick Yaw, but it was not for nothing that he was christened the Immutable, and that Phan and its neighbors are called the Thinking Kingdoms. The terms of the Covenant were set solid as the stone that underlies Phan itself, and bolted directly to it. The debased could not breach the terms, nor even bend them."

"These terms . . . ?" A now fully attentive Simna left the question hanging.

Elaboration was not needed. "The day was given to the followers of Yaw, made theirs in which to live and love, to cultivate and populate the land of Phan as they should see fit. In return, the corrupted and disembodied and their ilk were given the deepest part of the night, to roam freely wherever they might choose from midnight 'til dawn, free from insult, attack, or exorcism by the humans who had so forcefully settled among them."

Simna laughed uneasily as he eyed the now suggestive darkness that ruled the street beyond the still unbarred door. "I'd think that would make for some unsettled sleeping."

"Not so." The proprietor smiled thinly. "The impure keep to their compact." He nodded in the direction of the entrance. "If you will look down as you travel through Phan, you will see that the entrance to every building is circumscribed by a strip of pure copper the width of a man's thumb. This the specters of the night will not cross. It is so established in the Covenant. Behind that copper line, in any building, one is safe not only in body but in dreams. Step outside that line between midnight and dawn and . . ." He shuddered slightly, as if a quick, sharp blast of cold air had just passed over his body and through his soul.

A no longer smiling Simna set his goblet aside and

brooded on the import of the proprietor's words. "You're fair game."

"Just so," the owner conceded. "And now ye must be moving along."

"What!" The swordsman did not remove his feet from the table so much as yank them off. "After what you just told us you mean to throw us out into the night?"

"I do." The owner's response was firm. "I accord ye no greater hospitality than I did that pair that left moments ago, and in haste. Now you know the reason for their flight. This is a general store, not an inn." He glanced significantly at the clock, whose soft wooden ticks had grown much louder in the room. "You have time yet. There is a boardinghouse around the corner, only a block distant. It is a modest establishment, but clean and reasonable. The owners are good friends of mine, and not unused to greeting apprehensive patrons caught out celebrating too late to make it back to their homes. A spirited dash of but a few seconds will see you safely there. The street is empty and clear."

"By Gobolloba, let's get out of here!" The swordsman scrambled to slip his arms through the straps of his pack, not forgetting his sword, nor to drain the last drops of liquid gratification from his goblet.

Rising from his chair, Ehomba moved quickly but without panic to rouse Ahlitah from his feline slumber. The big cat was slow to awaken. As Ehomba knelt by its side and spoke softly, Simna fairly danced with impatience in front of their table, his eyes flicking rapidly and repeatedly from his companions to the brooding darkness outside.

"For Gudgeon's sake, will you hurry! Spit in his ear, already! Kick him in the balls. Get him *up*! Unwilling to kick the litah himself, the swordsman had to be content with flailing at the floor.

Rising on all four powerful, attenuated legs, the big cat

stretched and yawned languorously while Simna could only look on and grind his teeth helplessly.

"*If* your hairy majesty would be so kind as to join us in departing," he finally snapped, "it would behoove us to get the hell out of here."

The litah yawned again as he began padding toward the exit. "Ehomba explained things to me."

"Then why aren't you moving faster?" Knowing it would only provoke a delaying confrontation, the swordsman refrained from whacking the cat across its backside with the flat of his blade.

It was Ehomba who responded. "The street appears deserted, and it is not yet midnight, but it is a wise man who checks the ground outside his house before running wildly into the night."

"Hoy, all right. But let's not delay." Simna's sharp eyes were already scanning what he could see of the street to north and south as they approached the doorway.

"You worry needlessly." The proprietor was trailing behind them. A brass ring heavy with keys hung from one hand. "The dead are very punctual."

As they reached the portal, Ehomba looked down. Sure enough, a copper strip gleamed metallically beneath his feet. Inlaid in and bolted to the thick planking, it shone with the light of regular polishing. He stepped over it.

Nothing happened. The night was still and the coolness a relief from the heat of the day. In both directions, neatly shuttered shops looked out on the silent street. Flowers bloomed in window boxes, their blossoms shut against the cold until the next coming of the sun. Someone had washed and swept not only the sidewalks but the road itself. All was orderly, well groomed, and deserted.

Simna and Ahlitah crossed the threshold behind the herdsman. To prove that his words had meaning, the proprietor followed them outside onto the small covered porch that fronted the store. He showed no fear, and Simna allowed himself to relax a little as their erstwhile host pointed.

"Five storefronts that way and ye will find yourselves at the corner. Turn right. The boardinghouse will be the fourth door on your left. Knock firmly lest ye not be heard. And a good night t'ye."

Stepping back inside, he shut the door behind them. Looking through the glass, Ehomba could see him rotating a large brass key in the lock.

"What are we standing here like stupefied goats for? We only have a couple of minutes." Without waiting for his friends, Simna broke into a sprint. Ehomba and Ahlitah followed, running from need but not desperation.

They made it to the corner, but did not turn it.

"What was that?" Ehomba came to an abrupt stop.

"What was what?" Breathing as quietly as possible, Simna halted a few feet in front of the herdsman. "I didn't hear anything. Hoy, what are you looking for?"

Ehomba was peering into the depths of a dark close between two silent, darkened buildings. Simna would not have thought it an activity worth pursuing at the best of times, which the present most emphatically was not. As he looked on in disbelief, the tall southerner stepped into the shadows that were even darker than the surrounding night. With the time beginning to weigh heavily on him and knowing it would not wait or slow its pace for any man, the swordsman moved to place a forceful hand on his companion's arm.

"What do you think you're doing, bruther? I've been late to funerals, and late to appointments, and late to meet with friends on a fine summer's night, but I don't want to be late to the door of this boardinghouse. Come on! Whatever piece of trash has piqued your inexplicable interest will still be there in the morning." Behind them the litah waited quietly, contemplating the abandoned street.

"No," Ehomba replied in his usual soft but unshakable tone, "I do not think that it will."

Within the hidden depths of the close, something moaned. The hackles on the swordsman's neck bristled at the sound. Tight-lipped, he tried to drag his friend back onto the sidewalk. Ehomba resisted.

The moan came again, and while Simna did not relax, some of the fearful tension oozed out of him. It was manifestly a human throat that had produced that muffled lamentation, and not some gibbering perversion set loose from the nether regions of unimaginable perdition.

"Here." The dim outline of the herdsman could be seen picking its way through the rubble. "Over this way."

Muttering under his breath, the swordsman lurched forward, cursing as he stumbled over discarded containers, rotting foodstuffs, and equally pungent but less mentionable offal.

The figure Ehomba was trying to help to its feet was slight to the point of emaciation. It was a man; a very little man indeed, barely four feet tall. It was hard to judge because despite the herdsman's strong supportive arm, the figure's legs seemed to have trouble working. They exhibited a distinct tendency to wander off by themselves, as if possessed of their own individual itineraries. Understandably, this caused some small difficulty to the rest of the attached body.

Once Simna got his arm beneath the man's other shoulder, the two travelers were able to walk the hapless figure out of the close. He weighed very little. Back out on the sidewalk, they set him down, leaning him up against a wall. The swordsman wiped distastefully at his arm. The frail figure was rank as a wallowing boar and the stink attached to him displayed an unwholesome tendency to rub off on anyone making contact with it. Glancing in the humans' direction, Ahlitah wrinkled his nose in disgust.

"Who are you?" Somehow ignoring the stench, Ehomba knelt to place his own face close to that of the barely breathing little man. "We would like to help you. Do you know what time it is?" He nodded toward the dark, empty street. "You cannot stay here, like this."

"Glad to hear you say it, bruther." Apprehensive and impatient, Simna stood nearby, his keen gaze anxiously patrolling the roadway. "Can we go now? Please?"

"Not until we help this poor unfortunate. If necessary, we will bring him with us." The herdsman looked up at his companion. "I will not abandon him to the kind of fate the shopkeeper told us skulks through this city late at night."

"All right, fine! There isn't time to argue. Let's get him back on his feet, then." Simna bent to help the vagrant rise once more, only to draw back just in time as the figure forestalled its incipient deliverance by spewing the contents of his stomach all over the sidewalk.

"By Gieirwall, what a foulness!" Turning his back on the slumping frame, Simna inhaled deeply of fresh night air. Ehomba held his ground, though he was careful to keep out of the line of fire.

Slight as he was, the pitiful fellow had very little left in his stomach to regurgitate. That did not stop him from puking for another minute or so. In counterpoint to his rasping dry heaves, bells rang out solemnly the length and breadth of the city, simultaneously announcing and decrying the arrival of midnight.

"That's torn it," the swordsman muttered. "We've got to get out of here. Now." Bending low but keeping his face turned as much away from the fellow as possible, he spoke in words harsh and distinct. "Did you hear that, whoever you are? It's midnight, and if all we were told is true, the defiled can now freely roam the streets in accordance with your damned Covenant. It is time, friend, to move your bony ass. Why Ehomba wants to save it I don't know. If it was up to me, I'd leave you here, pickings for whatever shambles along."

Rheumy yellow eyes turned to meet the swordsman's. A shaky smile materialized on the bewhiskered, unwholesome face. Pressing one unsteady finger to the side of the tapering, twice-broken nose, the figure replied in a boozy cackle.

"Knucker knows, Knucker does!" Upon delivering himself of this proclamation, he blew yellow-green snot in the direction of the swordsman's sandals.

Simna hopped deftly aside. "Hoy, watch what you're doing, you putrefying little relic! Who the Gwerwhon do you think you are?" To Ehomba he added, "He's stinking rotten drunk. By the look and sound and smell of him, he's been that way for some time."

Bracing his scrawny back against the wall, the man rose to an approximation of a standing position. "Didn't you hear what I said? Don't you know who I am?"

"No," Simna growled as he tried to listen and watch both ends of the stygian street at the same time. "Who are you, you walking pile of fossilized spew?"

Frowning uncertainly, the man drew himself more or less up to his full, unimpressive height. "I am Knucker. Knucker the Knower." The precarious smile essayed a tentative reappearance. "I know everything." He focused on Ehomba. "Ask me a question. Go on, ask me a question. Anything."

"Maybe later." Gently gripping the fluttering leaf of a man by his shoulder, the herdsman managed to get him turned up the street. "My friend is right. We have to go now."

"Sure, why not?" Knucker the Knower was nothing if not agreeable. "Come on, ask me something. Anything."

Irritated and wary in equal measure, Simna kept pace with Ehomba. "What's the name of my maiden aunt on my mother's side?"

"Vherilza," Knucker replied without hesitation. "And her sisters are Prilly and Choxu."

The swordsman blinked, the potential invisible terrors of the night momentarily forgotten. "How?—by Grenrack's beard, that's right. He's right." Gripping the emaciated figure by one skinny arm, the swordsman thrust his face close to that of the sad figure. "How did you know that?"

"Knucker knows." Once more the man pressed his finger to the side of his nose, but when a worried Simna drew back, the tottering drunkard only sniggered anew. "Knucker knows everything. Go on, ask me another." Like a thirsty supplicant in search of rain, he spread shaky arms wide. "I know *everything*!"

Together, Ehomba and Simna half dragged, half carried the lightly built frame around the corner. Up the street they could see a single light burning through the darkness: the identifying, welcoming emblem of the boardinghouse. Simna redoubled his efforts.

"Come on, Mister Know-it-all. Only a little ways farther to go and then you can explain yourself."

"What's to explain?" Head wobbling on his neck as if at any moment it might fall off, Knucker turned to the smaller of his three saviors. "I know everything. Nothing more, nothing less. What part of that don't you understand, you insipid little conscript in the army of the avaricious?"

Gritting his teeth, Simna ignored the insult and concentrated on dragging the feeble corpus up the side street. Trying to keep their charge awake and alert for another couple of moments, Ehomba ventured another question.

"How long before we reach that boardinghouse up the street?"

"I'm not the right one to ask that question."

Simna let out a derisive snort. "I thought you knew everything."

"So I do, but I ain't the one that's going to delay your arriving. Maybe you better ask it."

"Ask him?" Searching both ends of the street, Simna saw nothing. "I don't see anything."

"Not himsh—'it,'" the Knower corrected him, slurring his words.

The swordsman was about to fetch the incoherent drunk a blow to the side of the head when something immensely large and vital appeared directly in their path. Behind him, Ahlitah snarled sharply. The apparition that had materialized to block their path wore no clothes, no shoes—and, more frighteningly, no face.

XIII

Unmoving and silent in the middle of the deserted street, they stared at the phantasm. Despite its lack of a countenance, it conveyed the unmistakable impression of staring back. Ehomba leaned over slightly to whisper to the swaying, shaky enigma who called himself Knucker.

"Okay, you know everything. What is that?"

Lachrymose eyes fought to focus on the forbidding specter. As before, the drunkard did not hesitate. "A vohwn. Having no face of its own, it envies those that do." He tapped the side of his nose with his middle finger. "Be careful: It will try to take yours."

Simna drew his sword. "Well, he can't have this one. I need it." Behind him, Ahlitah tensed and hunted for an opening.

Pulling the sky-metal blade from the scabbard on his back, Ehomba closed ranks with his friend. "And I mine. Mirhanja would still recognize me if I returned home without a face, but how would she look deep into my eyes if they were taken away?" He held his sword out in front of him, the moonlight glinting off the sharply angled etchings in the singular steel.

The vohwn looked at the double display of sharp-edged weaponry, though what it looked with no one could say, and laughed from the vacancy where its mouth might have been had it enjoyed a mouth. It was a sly suspiration, a sound that played beguilingly around the outer ear without ever really intruding, yet they heard it anyway, a laugh that froze only random drops of blood within their veins.

A phantasmal hand, skeletal and blue, reached toward them. Simna ducked. Ehomba held his ground and swung. The sky-metal sword moaned as it cleaved air and wrist. Like an emancipated moth, the severed hand of the vohwn went drifting off into the night, possessed of a life of its own. The specter cried out elegiacally and drew back its arm. As the empty face stared down into the severed wrist, it promptly grew another hand.

The herdsman hissed at the swaying, unsteady Knucker. "How do we get around it?"

"Well," the drunk responded thoughtfully, "you could make a break to your left and cross the street, but then you'd run into the borboressbs."

Glancing in the indicated direction, Ehomba and Simna saw a dark slit of an alley give birth to a dozen or so pony-sized homunculi. They had cloven hooves and walked with a permanent crouch. Bright red skin was subdued somewhat by the feeble moonlight. Goatlike tails switched back and forth and bristle-black hair covered their bodies in isolated, unwholesome patches. Their faces were blunt and plump, distorted by mouths full of sharp snaggle teeth that ran from ear to ear. When they gaped, it looked as if their skulls were split horizontally in half. Each had a single horn of varying length growing from the center of its forehead, and they were armed with curving, scythelike short swords fashioned of metal as bloodred as their exposed flesh.

They had been gabbling in an unknown tongue until they caught sight of the travelers. Now their unfathomable discourse was transmuted into an ominous muttering as they turned toward Ehomba and his companions. The presence of the towering vohwn did nothing to dissuade their advance.

Knucker spat something lumpy and brown onto the street and wiped his mouth with the back of his hand. "Beware the borboressbs. They like to pluck out a man's veins while he's still alive and slurp them down for a snack."

Ehomba tried to count the advancing freaks while keeping a watchful eye on the vohwn. It was still busy regrowing its hand, and had not moved from its position in the middle of the street.

"What about the other way?"

Knucker squinted and struggled to focus. "Well, you might have done that a minute or so ago, but it's too late now." He nodded to no one in particular. "Grenks."

Slithering down the sidewalk came a trio of four-legged blobs that blocked the way from street to structure with a splotchy mass of pulsating pustulance. They looked like animals that had been fashioned from tied-together balloons. Big as buffalo, they loped along on barrellike legs that bounced them lightly off the ground. They had no feet and no hands. Everything about them was rounded and pulpy. Behind them they left triple trails of ichorous lump-filled slime whose stench reached the travelers even from a distance. It lay where it dripped for long moments before evaporating.

The repulsive, malformed heads were all pop eyes and gaping mouths, the latter limned with greasy, saclike lips. They had no teeth, but from the depths of those revolting maws a single tentacle-like tongue writhed and coiled like a snake carefully examining the world from the depths of its lair. Possessed of a sincere single-minded stupidity, they humped forward indifferent to the presence of the advancing borboressbs and the immovable shade of the vohwn.

"Use your magic!" Confronted by so many numerous and disparate horrors, Simna drew as close as possible to his tall friend as he could without compromising the arc of their weapons. "Call down the wind from the stars!"

"You think it is so easy?" Ehomba gripped his blade firmly. "Such things take time and are not always responsive. Drawing a sword is simple; persuading it to do anything besides cut and slice is not." He was already starting to retreat. "I am trying."

"Hoy, you have to try harder. No, try faster."

"Be quiet and let me concentrate!"

Ahlitah leaped forward, his thunderous snarl echoing off the surrounding structures. The size and presence of the big cat caused the borboressbs to begin to spread out so as to encircle the travelers. Perhaps because it had no face with which to look upon the litah, the vohwn was not intimidated. And the comical carnivorous masses of the grenks came sliming on, oblivious to everything before them.

As they retreated, Ehomba grabbed the stuporous Knucker by the shoulder and pulled him along. Either unaware of or indifferent to the danger confronting them, the besotted little wreck of a man tottered unresistingly backwards in the herdsman's firm grasp.

"What should we do?" The tall southerner gave the drunk a good shaking. "Tell us what to do. How do we get away from these foulnesses?"

Turning bleary eyes to the herdsman, Knucker replied in quavering tones. "You can't. The borboressbs are too agile, the vohwn will be wherever you see, and the grenks never give up until they've been sated. Fight one and the others will fall on you from behind. You're outnumbered, stranger. You're dead." He coughed weakly.

"He doesn't know everything," Simna declared grimly. "We're not dead yet."

"You need help," the frail drunk mumbled.

"Hoy, you don't have to be all-knowing to see that. I have a feeling we can't expect much from these happy, civilized

Phanese." Simna scanned the surrounding buildings. A few lights gleamed behind shuttered windows, but none had been flung open to allow the inhabitants to observe what was taking place in the quiet street outside their homes. In the morning, no doubt, a jolly and competent cleaning crew would scrub the pavement clean of any loitering unpleasantness. Children would run hoops and chase each other across bloodstains that would fade with soap and rain and time, and no one would hazard a breach of etiquette by troubling to inquire what had happened.

Its hand regrown, the vohwn moaned and drifted forward. The nearest borboressbs gave it a wide berth. Too ignorant and persistent to recognize a possible danger to themselves and anxious for prey, the grenks oozed closer.

A wisp of cold wind sparked from the tip of the sky-metal blade.

"Hurry up!" Simna eyed the borboressbs nearest him. Four more had already scuttled behind him and were beginning to close in, holding their curved weapons above their loathsome heads like egg teeth extracted from some Ur-snake.

Reaching up and around, Knucker the Knower wrapped fingers sticky with phlegm and puke around the carved figurine that hung from the cord around Ehomba's neck, and yanked. Startled, the herdsman responded angrily.

"Give that back! It will not buy you more than a drink or two."

"Give it back?" Holding it up to his eyes, the little man struggled with difficulty to concentrate on the graven image he had purloined. "Sure, I'll give it back. Here." Drawing back his arm, he somehow managed a shaky throw.

The figurine soared past Ehomba's outstretched fingers to land in front of a pair of borboressbs. It bounced a couple of times before rolling to a halt. One of the cloven-footed abnormalities gave it a passing glance, then stepped on it, grinding it into the pavement. A repellent snaggle-toothed grin split the repulsive face from side to side.

It vanished as the borboressb rose straight up into the air, did a complete head-over-hoof flip, and landed hard on its back. It lay stunned and unmoving.

In place of the carving stood a tall, erect figure limned in pale white flame. Its statuesque shape barely blurred by a coil of tight-fitting crimson and brown fabric, it carried a shield of mastodon hide in one hand and a slim wooden club in the other. The club was thickly studded with the three-sided thorns of the pyre bush. In all his life Ehomba had never seen a pyre bush. It was a part of Naumkib lore, more legend than shrub. But he recognized the thorns instantly, from the tales he had been told as a child. Mirhanja had never seen a pyre bush either, but she could describe one in detail to Daki and Nelecha while reciting bedtime stories. Any Naumkib mother knew what a pyre bush looked like, even if she had never seen one herself.

Momentarily startled, the angry borboressbs turned to confront the intruder in their midst. Two sliced viciously with the scythe-swords they carried. The blows glanced harmlessly off the shield of the new apparition. Swinging the club, it struck the nearest borboressb on one shoulder. Instantly, flames engulfed the horrid creature as fire exploded from its arm. Wailing wildly, it raced away up the street, trailing flame and smoke.

Two more borboressbs jumped the figure. One fell flopping to the pavement, its neck broken by a swinging blow from the edge of the shield. The other caught the tip of the club in its mouth. For a second its eyes grew wide. Then its head exploded in a ball of flame. Gathering themselves, the rest of the enraged aberrations prepared to attack the club-wielding shape simultaneously.

Their coordinated assault was disrupted by the ferocious black mass that landed in their midst. Emitting a ground-shaking roar, Ahlitah sent one borboressb flying with a single swipe of one huge paw. An instant later, it bit off the head of a second.

Seeing their chance, Ehomba and Simna rushed the grenks. Repeated blows from their weapons sliced away huge chunks of quivering, jellylike flesh without halting the creatures' progress. They had no bones and, for all the two furiously flailing men could tell, no blood and no nervous systems. A tentacle-tongue lashed around Simna's sword arm, only to be severed by a downward stroke of the herdsman's blade. The amputated organ lay coiling and writhing on the ground like a worm driven to the surface by a heavy downpour.

Hewing and hacking methodically and without pause, they reduced the trio of obstinate but sluggish grenks to tremulous heaps of coagulated muck that littered the street and sidewalk. Even then, individual lumps of legless tissue tried to hump and slime their way in the travelers' direction.

Having sent the remaining borboressbs fleeing, some with scorched tails and burned limbs and with the raging Ahlitah in literally hot pursuit, the phantasm that had issued from the figurine turned its attention to the looming shade of the vohwn. The incorporeal specter twisted and coiled itself around the new arrival, encircling it with its own ghostly corpus. The faceless perversion began to contract, tightening its own self securely about the figure.

Undaunted, the tall newcomer swung the club lightly but firmly. A pair of pyre thorns made contact with the constricting miasma. An expression of uncertainty, a surprised moan, emanated from the spiraling vohwn. With a soft, empyreal hiss, it saw itself sucked up by the thorns, until only a last wisp of noxious vapor remained to show where it had once writhed. Wetting two fingers by touching them to its lips, the figure reached down and pinched the final bit of vohwn out of existence. A single last, sharp hiss marked its ultimate passing.

Covered in loose lumps of quivering, gelatinous grenk and breathing hard, Ehomba and Simna turned to face the tall, lithe figure that had emerged from the shards of the herdsman's petite carving. Holding firmly to shield and club, it came slowly toward them. Devoid of external assistance and support, Knucker the Knower's legs finally gave out. His bony butt landed hard on the pavement. There he sat, hunched over, rocking back and forth and mumbling to himself, staring down at nothing in particular.

Still edged in pale white flame, the figure halted before the two panting men. And smiled. Ehomba hesitated, uncertain, staring hard, reluctant to trust the interpretation his brain insisted on applying to the information his eyes were conveying.

"Fhastal?"

"Hello, Etjole Ehomba." And the magnificent smile widened.

It *was* Fhastal. But not the wise, wrinkled, hobbling old woman he had known since he was a child. Standing before him was a figure of towering feminine power, unforced sensuality, and burgeoning knowledge. Simna looked on in admiring silence.

"I do not understand," the herdsman said simply.

Placing one end of her shield on the ground, Fhastal leaned the club up against it and rested her folded hands atop both. "The little figure of me was carved not when I was a child or when I was as you know me, Etjole, but when I was like this. So when the seal was broken, I came to you not as I am, but as I was." She chuckled softly. "Was I not something uncommon when I was young?"

"By Gospoed's galloping gonads, I'll vouch for that!" Despite Ehomba's frown of disapproval, the swordsman made not even a veiled attempt to lower his gaze.

Without knowing quite why, the herdsman found himself twitching uncomfortably beneath her white-flamed, uncompromising gaze. Yet it was the same look, only slightly moderated by venerable age, that he had seen in her eyes on the day he had set off from the village. But that was Fhastal: spry, learned, and occasionally coarse, still as fond as anyone of a crude joke or good laugh despite her crippled physique and enfeebled senses.

There was nothing of frailty or failing about the body that stood straight and lithe before him now. But the white flame in which she was circumscribed was growing dimmer even as she spoke.

She glanced briefly down at herself. "Yes, this part of me is withering. From here on I can only be with you in heart and spirit, Etjole Ehomba. A comforting memory at best. Would that it could be otherwise." Raising her arms up and to the sides, she executed a leonine stretch. Observing the swordsman's reaction, Ehomba feared the smaller man's heart would fail him.

"You saved us," he professed simply.

Picking up shield and club, she advanced until she was standing within inches of him. The pale flame that emanated from her body exuded no heat. Her kiss, however, was as full of fire as the pyre thorns.

"Ah, Etjole!" she husked as she stepped back from him. "What a most excellent man you have grown up to be, and what a lucky woman is Mirhanja." Her expression turned serious. "You have a long ways still to travel."

He nodded. "I have been told twice now that if I continue on I will be killed. What can you tell me?"

The exquisite face shifted from side to side. "Nothing, Etjole Ehomba. I can tell you nothing. I am the Fhastal of my youth, and that young woman fought hard to learn what was around her. I had neither the time nor the ability to look ahead. Even now, that is a gift that is denied to me." Turning slightly, she gestured in the direction of the cringing, rocking figure. Having returned from its slaughter, the black litah stood watch over the helpless human shape. "Why not ask him? He knows everything."

Simna made a rude noise. "Knucker the drunker? He knows a lot, I'll give him that much. But everything? Not even the greatest of wizards knows everything. And that disgusting little snot's no wizard."

"No, he isn't," Fhastal the younger agreed. "But I think it barely possible that he may very well know everything, just as he says. The trouble is, knowing everything does not make one perfect. And just as he is no wizard, neither is he perfect." The last vestiges of flickering white flame had nearly vanished from her body, for the first time isolating her supple, graceful form sharply against the frame of night.

Reaching up to his neck, Ehomba grasped the torn strip of cord from which the figurine had hung. It had been with him ever since he had left the land of the Naumkib, a small, cool companion against his bare skin, a familiar weight to remind him of home. Now it was gone.

"I will miss you, Fhastal. Until I return home."

"I hope I'll still be alive by the time you get back. I would like to learn how this turns out for you."

"You should have told me about the carving's power." He spoke in a tone that was chiding but also affectionate.

"I did, Etjole Ehomba, I did!" She was laughing at him now, and for a brief moment the all-encompassing white flame seemed to dance higher, like a live thing summoned fleetingly back to life. "Did I not tell you when last we spoke that you were speaking to the image and that the figurine was the real me? That by your wearing it I would be able to travel with you?"

Now it was his turn to smile as he remembered, fondly. "So you did, Fhastal. I listened to your words but did not hear."

She wagged a finger at him and the simple gesture caused

him to experience a start of recognition. When chiding children and their elders alike, as she did frequently and every day, aged Fhastal, real Fhastal, the chuckling, easygoing old Fhastal of the village, wagged her finger in exactly the same way.

"You see clearly and far, Etjole Ehomba, but there are times when you need to listen better!"

"I will remember," he assured her solemnly, speaking as an unruly child would to a doting parent.

"See that you do."

Simna stepped boldly forward. "Hoy, don't I rate a farewell kiss as well?"

The tall figure gazed speculatively down at the eager swordsman. "I think not, friend of Etjole's. You are too quick with the hands that wield that fine sword and, modest maid that I am, I have only enchantment and fire to protect me." Reaching out, she playfully tousled his hair. "Perhaps in another life." With those words, the last of the ethereal enveloping flame flickered out.

"Fhastal, wait!" Ehomba stepped forward, into the space where she had been. No pale efflorescence, no lingering glow, marked her final passage. There was only a faint warmth in the air, a smell of natural perfume, and the teasing tail end of a dissipating, girlish laugh.

"For us." There in the dark and deserted street far from home he stood and murmured to the sky. "She gave the last of her youth to save us. It was embodied in that figurine that she gave me for protection." Turning, he confronted Simna. The swordsman was still staring at the space the beauteous phantasm had vacated, savoring an already dwindling memory. "She could have enjoyed those moments in the company of old friends back in the village, or among those equal to her in experience and learning. But she gave it to us."

"Hoy, and a wondrous thing to behold it was," Simna readily agreed. "Knowledge and fighting ability and a sense of humor all in one woman. Not to mention those—"

Ehomba cut him off. "Show some respect, Simna."

"I would love to, bruther. Hoy, would I give a month of my life to show that woman some respect!"

"That was a vision of her as a youth. Nowadays she is old, and wrinkled, and bent."

The swordsman nodded somberly. "But still beautiful, I'd wager."

"Yes. Still beautiful." Taking a deep breath, he turned toward Ahlitah and the big cat's mewling, unhealthy charge. "She told us to ask questions of Knucker. We should follow her advice."

"Hoy." Simna walked alongside his friend. "Just so long as we keep in mind that no matter how much he knows, he doesn't know everything." The swordsman sniffed. "I don't care what she said. Nobody knows *everything*. Especially a broken-down ruin of a human being like that."

While a disgusted Simna stood nearby and the litah preened blood and bits of dismembered gut from his fur, Ehomba crouched before the gently swaying form of the man they had rescued from the close. A firm push from one finger would have been enough to knock Knucker over.

"How are you doing, my friend?"

The rocking stopped. Bloodshot eyes looked up and blinked like broken shutters. "Fine, fine! Why shouldn't I be?"

Ehomba glanced up at his companions. Ahlitah was ignoring everything while he concentrated on matters of individual feline hygiene. Simna snorted derisively and turned away. The herdsman looked back at the pathetic figure cowering before him.

"You did not see what happened?"

Knucker made an effort to peer around the kneeling form of the tall southerner. The effort would have caused him to keel over had not Ehomba reached out to steady him.

"Something's happened?" Wispy brows drew together. "Who are you, anyway? And why are you standing out here at night in the middle of the street?" He blinked again. "Why am *I* out here at night in the middle of the street?"

"We found you lying moaning in a close." Ehomba was gentle and patient. "It was after midnight and so we . . ."

Fear snapped Knucker's eyes wide open. "After midnight?" Looking around wildly, he tried to rise and failed, having to rely on Ehomba's strong arm to steady him once again. "We've got to get off the street, find shelter! The—"

"We know, we know." The herdsman shifted his supportive hand from the little man's waist to his upper arm. "I think it will be all right for a while, and there is a boardinghouse close by. Come." Rising, he helped Knucker erect.

"You don't understand," the drunkard was babbling apprehensively. "After midnight, there are things abroad in Phan. Bad things. They come out of the darkness and—"

Ignoring the coating of filth that helped to keep the man warm, Ehomba put a steadying arm around the scrawny back. "But we do understand, friend Knucker. We do understand. Thanks to you."

"To me?" Total confusion washed over the grimy, unshaven face. "What did I do? Who are you people?" As Ehomba gently shepherded him toward the unwinking, welcoming light of the boardinghouse and Ahlitah and Simna fanned out to either side to keep watch for trouble, they made their way up the empty but bloodied avenue. "And what am I doing out at night in the middle of the street?"

Off to Ehomba's right, Simna scanned the shadows for signs of potential trouble. But the side streets and alleyways were as quiet as they were dark, innocent in the light of his patrolling vision. As he strode purposefully forward, he shook his head and chuckled harshly. "Knows everything. Sure he does. Sure. Giliwitil knows he doesn't even know where he is!"

XIV

The sleepy-eyed proprietor of the boardinghouse woke up fast when he got a good look at the supplicants who had come knocking at his door. No ex-mercenary backed by a wall full of weapons, no towering muscular warrior nor even especially bold in his personal life, he was nonetheless a man of some determination and, within the limited bounds of his comparatively commonplace profession, courage.

"Come in, quickly!" Holding the door aside, he hastily scanned the street behind the nocturnal visitants.

Ehomba and his friends piled in, the herdsman and Simna supporting the intermittently driveling Knucker between them. Glancing downward as they stumbled through the portal, the tall southerner took note of the thick band of polished copper that gleamed beneath the doorjamb. Out of sight within the night and hugging the front wall of the boardinghouse, Ahlitah had remained unseen by the proprietor. Now the big cat trotted up the steps in the wake of his companions. The owner's eyes grew wide.

"You"—he gulped as he pressed his back against the wall

to make room for the massive feline to pass—"you can't bring that thing in here!"

Lambent yellow orbs swung around to regard the stubby little man haughtily. "Who are you calling a 'thing'?"

Startled, the landlord ceased trying to sidle desperately sideways up the hall. "It talks."

"Yes," Ahlitah replied dryly, "it talks." Jaws that were capable of crushing furniture hovered a few feet from the terrified owner's perspiring face. The litah's breath was warm on the man's skin. "Don't you have a house cat?"

"N-n-no," the proprietor stammered weakly.

"Well you do now." Turning away, Ahlitah followed his companions deeper into the building. His broad, padded paws made less noise on the thick throw rugs and wooden planking than did his far less weighty human friends.

The owner trailed behind, anxious to query his visitors but fearful of pressing too close to the big cat. At the same time he dared not raise his voice lest he wake sleeping patrons and precipitate a panic. So he compromised by whispering as loudly as he could.

"Is it a room you want, or just a temporary refuge?" An intense desire to be rid of these eccentric vagabonds and the carnivore that accompanied them fought against his inherent good nature. At the same time he tried to place a distinctive and most disagreeable smell that did not, surprisingly, come from the big cat.

Ehomba looked wordlessly at his friend. With a sigh, Simna checked his remaining gold, knowing even as he did so that there was very little left. Still, if any of it was magicked, it might have reproduced while resting in his purse. A quick check revealed that the gold was still plain, ordinary gold. What remained was no more and no less than what he had seen there the last time.

"Hoy," he exclaimed frostily as he let Knucker's fetid arm slide off his shoulder, "we wouldn't have had to go through all that if not for this maundering sot. It's time for him to contribute to his own stinking survival." Taking a deep breath before he did so, the swordsman put his face close to the drunkard's. "Look here, you. Have you got any money?"

Bleary eyes struggled to focus. "What?"

Making a face, Simna momentarily turned away from the blast of liquorish vapors. "Money. Gold, convertibles, currency of the realm, legal tender. Have you got any?" When Knucker did not reply, the swordsman reached down and began going through the man's pockets. Another time, Ehomba might have objected. But their financial condition was parlous, and any group of village elders gathered to pass judgment on the situation would have agreed that the fellow owed them something for saving his life.

Simna's burrowing produced a handful of dirty coins. Recognizing them, the wavering Knucker tried to protest. "No—not my drinking money!" With one hand he made a grab for the metal disks, only to miss them and the swordsman by a wide margin. Unable to focus clearly, he could not properly judge the proximity of objects, even if the most prominent of those objects was one of his reluctant saviors.

Simna confronted the landlord. "It's a room we want. You wouldn't put a man back out on these streets in the middle of the night, would you?"

Hesitantly, the proprietor accepted the money, counting out only enough to pay for a single night's stay. "You'll, um, be gone in the morning?"

The swordsman's reply was brusque. "We're not hanging around to sample the delights of greater Phan, if that's what you mean."

"We are not tourists," Ehomba added, stating the obvious. He continued to support Knucker by himself while Simna dealt with the landlord. The effort did not exhaust the herdsman. He was used to carrying young calves around, and the small man weighed very little.

The landlord sighed and nodded. "Very well. Come with me." Edging around the litah's bulk, he started up a set of wide wooden stairs. Having settled business, Simna moved to assist Ehomba with his limp burden.

"We appreciate you extending your hospitality to us at this late hour." As they climbed, Ehomba admired the wallpaper and the small pictures that decorated the stairwell.

"You should," the landlord grumbled. While leading the way, he sorted through a large iron ring heavy with keys.

"I—I need a drink," Knucker mumbled.

Looking back, the proprietor gave him a disapproving look. "There is no liquor in this house."

Vacant eyes struggled to meet the owner's. "Yes there is. There are two bottles in a secret drawer in the bottom of your desk. One of brandy, another of whiskey. You hide them there from your wife."

As stunned as if he had walked face-first into a lamppost, the landlord stopped on a landing where the stairs took a leftward turn. "How—how did you know that? Are you a wizard?" He gaped at Simna. "Is this sorry specimen of humanity a wizard?"

"Nope." The swordsman nodded at Ehomba. "He's the wizard. This one here, he's just a dipso who knows everything."

"He can't know everything," the proprietor protested.

A line of slightly yellowish drool dribbling from the scabby right corner of his mouth, Knucker cackled softly. "Your wife knows where the drawer is. Why do you think each time you go there that there's always a little less in the bottles than you remember?" The landlord's lower jaw fell farther. "She also knows that you're tumbling the downstairs maid."

A look of tentative satisfaction came over the stocky landlord's face. "Ha! You may be some kind of besotted seer who can see certain things, but you can't see everything! I know my wife. If she knew that, she would have confronted me with it."

Turning away from the men supporting him, Knucker coughed once. "Not in this instance. Because, you see, she is tumbling the downstairs maid also. It's a matter of mutual tumbling, actually."

The proprietor looked stricken. "By all the deities, you may not know everything, but you know too much!" Turning away angrily, he resumed the ascent. "No more, tell me no more!"

As they struggled up the stairs, Simna leaned closer to the man he was helping to support. "So the lady of the house and a servant are having a twiddle, hoy?" An inquisitive leer stole across his face. "If you know that, you must know all the details."

Turning to him, Knucker tried to stand a little straighter as he was half carried, half dragged upward. "I may be many things, sir, but at least I am not degenerate."

"Hoy. There lies the difference between us, bruther. I admit to what I am."

"A drink." The little man licked his lips and smacked his tongue against his palate, sending out the universal signal of need common to all his kind. "I've got to have something to drink."

"We will try to get you some nice tea as soon as we are settled," Ehomba told him reassuringly. A look of horror came over Knucker's face.

The landlord had stopped outside a door. "I have only one room vacant, and it is far too small for your party. But this one here is a spacious chamber and you will be quite comfortable within—if I can persuade the current occupant to move." He put his finger to his lips as he gently inserted the key in the lock and opened the door. "The gentleman is presently within, but I will offer him a discount and a free breakfast, and I think if I explain the situation to him calmly and rationally he may be willing to accept alternate quarters for the night."

As soon as the door was open, Ahlitah pushed past the assembled humans. "I'll explain the situation to him."

"No!" As the proprietor reached out to grab and try to restrain the big cat, a small but loud voice shrieked warningly within his head, "What do you think you are *doing*?" Ordinary common sense immediately overwhelming his stalwart sense of managerial duty, he hastily drew back his hand.

Silently padding across the floor, the black litah approached the large bed and the single sleeping shape within. Reaching up, he rested a forepaw on the figure's shoulder.

"Mmph—wha . . . ?" The sleeper's eyes flickered. Then they opened wide. Real wide.

Ahlitah leaned close and spoke softly. "Go away."

Wide awake, the naked sleeper gathered sheets and blanket around him and flew off the bed in the direction of the door. "I'm gone," he responded. And he was, not even pausing to complain to the landlord. The stubby owner did not try to stop or slow him. He could not have done so in any event.

"I expect I'll find him downstairs, in my office." He sighed again. "He'll probably want a refund." Stepping into the room, he brought out a striker and lit the two oil lamps within, one on the wall by the doorway and another that sat on a small writing table. "There is another, smaller bed in the second sleeping room. Through that door, there." He pointed. "Please try to keep quiet. It's very late, and everyone else in the house is asleep."

Ehomba assured him that they would prepare for slumber as noiselessly as possible. Having curled up next to the unlit fireplace, the litah was already halfway unconscious.

"Come," the tired herdsman directed his friend. "We will put this fellow into the other bed."

"How come he gets a bed?" Simna protested as they

hauled their mumbling cargo toward the other room. "Why not just dump him right here? He doesn't make a very good man. He might make a serviceable doorstop."

Ehomba eyed his companion sternly. "It was his money that paid for these lodgings."

"Hoy, right—but he won't remember that in the morning." He uttered a subdued expletive. "I know, I know. Do what's right. But it pains me, it does."

"There is no need for you to pout," the herdsman chided him. "You may have the large bed. I can tell by the look of it that it is too soft for me." He nodded back the way they had come. "There is a couch, and thick carpets on the floor. I will be fine."

"I wasn't worried about you, long bruther." But the swordsman's tone belied his attempt at callousness.

Together they stripped Knucker of his ragged, profoundly stained clothing. Undressed, he looked even more pitiful than when clothed.

"I wonder when he last ate?" Ehomba murmured as he examined the emaciated torso.

Simna grunted as he tossed short, tattered boots into a corner. "You mean when last he chewed something. This lush has been drinking his meals for some time."

"Perhaps we can get something solid into him in the morning," the herdsman speculated.

Pausing in the process of undressing, Simna looked up curiously. "Why do you care? He's a total stranger and, whether he knows everything or simply less than that, not a particularly admirable one. There are candidates more deserving of your concern."

"No doubt," Ehomba agreed, "but they are not here. He is." He studied the mumbling, self-engrossed figure thoughtfully. "Tell me something, Knucker."

"What?" Looking up, the exhausted little man they had

saved from the demons of the night locked eyes with his rescuer. "Who are you?"

As they laid the drunk down on the clean sheets, Simna ventured a coarse observation on the ingratitude of the inebriated.

When a man stands all day doing nothing but watching cattle and sheep crop grass, he learns patience. "It does not matter," Ehomba told him. Bending over the bed, he murmured, "Knucker, what is the meaning of life?"

Their charge was already half asleep. His lips moved and Ehomba leaned close. He stood like that, inclined over the bed and its single diminutive occupant, a look of intense preoccupation on his long, handsome face. After a moment he nodded, and straightened.

"I thought so." His tone suggested quiet satisfaction.

Simna waited. When nothing further was forthcoming, he blurted sharply, "Well?"

The herdsman looked across the bed at his companion. Knucker was sleeping soundly now and, as far as Ehomba could tell, without difficulty. "Well what?"

"Bruther, don't play the coy with me. What *is* the meaning of life?"

"Someday I will tell you." The herdsman started around the foot of the bed, heading for the main room.

"Someday? What do you mean 'someday'?" Simna followed him, leaving the little man in darkness and silence.

In the main room Ehomba contemplated the couch. After first removing his pack and weapons, he began to arrange himself on the thickly carpeted floor. "When you have grown up." Stretching out flat on his back, he closed his eyes and crossed his hands over his lower chest.

"Grown up? Listen to me, master of mewling lambs, I'm not one to take kindly to a comment like that!"

One eye winked open to regard the irate swordsman. "Take it any way you like, but keep your voice down. If we make too much noise and wake the other tenants, the land-lord is likely to throw us back out into the street."

"Hoy, him? That soft little self-important innkeeper couldn't throw Knucker out in the street, and that with him completely unconscious."

"Then if you won't be silent for his sake, be quiet for mine," Ehomba grumbled irritably. "And get some rest yourself. It is not long until sunrise, and I would prefer to spend as few nights as possible in this country that is proper and civilized only during the day and dreadful and deadly after dark." With that he rolled over, turning his back to the swordsman.

"When I have grown up, is it?" Growling under his breath, Simna divested himself of pack, sword, and raiment and slipped beneath the sheets of the spacious bed. It was still warm from the recent accelerated departure of its for-mer occupant. That did not trouble Simna ibn Sind, who had slept on mattresses swarming with insomniac rats.

He fell asleep still angry, and dreamed of falling into a bottomless well filled with unending buckets of jewels and precious metals. It would have been a good dream, should have been a good dream, except for one pesky vexation.

Ehomba was there also, kneeling at the edge of the well looking down at the swordsman as the latter tossed coins and gems about like colored candy. The herdsman was not laughing derisively, nor was he heaping calumny upon Simna for indulging wholeheartedly in his base desires. All the impassive, compassionate herdsman was doing was smiling.

In his sleep, Simna ibn Sind tossed and muttered, uncon-sciously infuriated without knowing why

Breakfast was served in the room by household staff. Sit-ting up naked in the big bed, the swordsman favored the pretty servant who brought their food with a come-hither grin. Greatly to his chagrin, she ignored him completely. He did not let her rejection prey upon him. He never did. Anyway, it made good sense. Since they were ensconced upstairs, she was most likely not the downstairs maid.

"Not bad," he told his companions as he masticated fresh rolls with jam and butter, aepyornis egg, bacon, and fruit. As was his nature, he had completely forgotten the brief but heated disputation with Ehomba of the night before.

In his corner, Ahlitah chewed fastidiously on a large leg of raw ox that the landlord had managed to scrounge from the kitchen. Ehomba sat on the floor with his back against the couch as he ate. In between bites and conversing with Simna, he cast occasional glances in the direction of the rear bedroom. The maid had delivered food to its occupant, but whether that worthy was even awake, much less dining, he did not know. As soon as he finished his own food, he would look in on the man they had rescued.

"You are right, Simna. Everything is quite good." The herdsman set a nearly empty glass of milk aside. "You should thank Knucker. He paid for this."

"Thank him?" Sitting up in the bed, the swordsman grunted. "We saved his miserable life at the risk of our own. He should be the one thanking us. But of course, he can't do that, because it would take too much of the worthless wretch's liquefied brain to string two words together."

"On the contrary, not only can I string two words together, I can tie them in assorted semantic knots if the need should arise."

Simultaneously, Ehomba and Simna looked toward the back-bedroom door. Only an indifferent Ahlitah did not glance up from his food. What the two men saw there came close to stunning them both into silence.

Knucker the Knower stood in the portal, but it was not the Knucker they knew. How he had bathed using only the pitcher and basin in the tiny inner bathroom they did not know, but bathe he had. Somehow he had even managed to clean up his clothing along with his body. A knife or razor had been used to remove the ugly stubble from his face. For all they knew, it might also have been the tool of choice utilized to dislodge the significant growth of unidentifiable greenish material from his teeth, which gleamed more or less whitely as he smiled at his saviors.

"I remember everything now." Stepping into the room, he staggered slightly before bracing himself with one hand against the doorjamb. A rapidly steadying finger pointed. "You—you're Etjole Ehomba. I heard him"—and he indicated the staring swordsman—"call out your name. And you, you are Slumva—no, Simna. Simna ibn Sind."

Setting aside the last vestiges of his breakfast, the swordsman slid out of the bed and began to dress, slowly and without taking his eyes off the little man for more than a moment. The litah glanced up briefly before returning to the bone he was crunching in order to get at the marrow within. Smashed or sober, to the big cat humans were all largely the same.

Slipping into his shirt, Simna nodded admiringly at the figure standing unaided by the doorway. "Never would have believed it. I've got to hand it to you, little bruther: You've gone and pulled yourself up out of the mire. Not many men could do such a thing in a single night. Especially not men as far gone as you were when we dragged you out of that close."

"I remember that, too. It's all coming clear to me now." Taking careful but increasingly confident steps, he walked up to Ehomba and grasped the herdsman's arms gratefully. "I don't know how to thank you. Once you've fallen as far as I did, you become so dazed and blind you can no longer find the way back up. For that you need help. You two have given me that gift."

"Genden's encomiums on you, Knucker." Having finished dressing, Simna sat down on the edge of the bed and resumed eating. "I take back what I said about you last night. But you probably don't remember much of that."

"On the contrary, I remember all of it. I have an exceedingly good memory—when it's functioning."

"Then you don't mind that we picked your pocket to pay for this room and food?" The unrepentant swordsman bit down into a final muffin.

"Not at all. I'd only have squandered the money on spirituous intoxicants. Far better it be used for sustenance and shelter. I owe you more, much more, than a night's rest."

His words muffled by muffin, Simna gestured at the other man with the crumbly residue. "Hoy, I'll second that!"

"And I would like to repay you further." Knucker smiled apologetically. "Unfortunately, all the money I had in the world was in my pocket. As you can imagine, I have had more than a little difficulty obtaining any kind of paying work lately."

"How did you come by that money, then?" Ehomba asked him.

Their guest lowered his gaze. "I would do anything for a drink, or for a few coins to purchase it. Please don't make me repeat the details. My condition was degrading enough. How far I debased myself to achieve that state of utter wretchedness need not concern you." Determination in his voice, he lifted his eyes. "I will repay you for your kindness by guiding you safely out of Phan by the quickest and easiest route. I do not know where you are headed from here."

"North by northwest," the herdsman told him simply.

Eagerness shining from his freshly scrubbed face, the little man nodded vigorously. "You will first have to pass through Bondressey. I know that country well and can greatly expedite your passage. I have even been to the foot of Mount Scathe, in the Hrugar Mountains, and can guide you at least that far." He looked anxiously from one man to the other. "What say you?"

Simna shrugged and jerked a thumb in the herdsman's direction. "This be the sorcerer's party. I'm just hanging around, kind of like unplanned baggage."

Knucker's eyes widened slightly as he turned to gaze at Ehomba. "Are you really a sorcerer?"

"No," the herdsman replied tersely. He threw a sour look in Simna's direction, but the herdsman had returned his full attention to the remaining ruins of his morning meal. "I am a keeper of cattle and sheep." A sudden thought made him frown. "But you already know what I am. You know everything."

The little man looked baffled. "Me? Know everything? What are you talking about? I know only myself, and the places I have been, and the bits and pieces of a normal life. How would I know whether you are a sorcerer or not?"

Simna was nodding slowly. "Exactly what I've been saying all along."

Ehomba's gaze narrowed as he stared hard at the speaker. If Knucker was, for whatever unknown reasons of his own, playing out a game behind a mask of feigned ignorance, he was performing like a professional. His expression as he returned the herdsman's gaze was all innocence and sincerity.

"What," he asked the other man slowly, "is the meaning of life?"

Struck dumb by this searching profundity, Knucker looked to Simna for assistance or an explanation. Neither was forthcoming. The little man turned back to Ehomba. "Do you expect me to answer that?"

"You did last night. And very well, too."

Knucker could only stand and shake his head in disbelief. "If I did, then I remember nothing of what was said."

"Name my two aunts," Simna challenged him. He was enjoying Ehomba's discomfiture.

This time their guest essayed a tiny, nervous laugh. "How could I do that? I know nothing of your family. I didn't even know you had aunts, or their number. Far less do I know their names." His brow wrinkled. "But I do remember something."

"Ah," Ehomba murmured expectantly. Simna looked uncertain.

"I remember that others have put such questions to me when I was in another of my rare periods of extended sobriety. I could not answer their questions either, and was bewildered that they would ask such things of me. I was amazed to think that they would believe anyone could answer such queries."

"Anyone indeed," Simna exclaimed, once more on top of the proverbial analytical heap.

"I think I understand." The herdsman rose from the couch against which he was sitting. "When you are clean and sober like this, you remember the normal things that go to make up a life. When you are drunk, you forget them—but know everything else. Truly, what a strange and capricious gift."

"If what you say is true, then it is not a gift but a curse," Knucker responded tightly. "Why can I not retain even a little of this knowing when I am rational enough to make use of it?"

"That I do not know." Ehomba began to check his pack. It was time to go. "But this I do know: From what we saw of you last night, you are far, far better off ignorant and sober than intoxicated and all-knowing." He smiled encouragingly. "In consequence of your having raised yourself up, we will allow you to guide us through Bondressey and as far as the Hrugar Mountains. Any help that speeds our journey is most welcome."

"Gryeorg knows that's true." Simna was shoving the last of the breakfast bread into his pack. "The sooner we reach the end, the quicker I'll have my hands on my share of the treasure."

"Treasure?" Once more, the little man looked mystified.

Ehomba pulled his pack up onto his shoulders and set about adjusting the straps. "My good friend Simna is brave and clever, but prone to delusion. In addition to believing that I am some sort of sorcerer, he is convinced that among other things I seek a great treasure. In truth, it exists only in his mind's eye."

"That's me." Simna made the announcement cheerfully as he ambled around the bed while fussing with his pack. Passing Knucker, he leaned close to whisper urgently. "He says I'm clever, and that I am. Clever enough to see through the denials he's forever prattling to me and everyone we meet. Don't you doubt it, bruther—he's a wizard on the trail of treasure. And I aim to get my share." He nudged the little man in his all-too-prominent ribs. "Who knows? If you play your 'predictions' right and can convince him to let you stick with us, you might come in for a share yourself."

"But I can't make any predictions unless I'm moribund drunk, and when I'm that badly under I don't know what I'm saying, much less what I'm hearing." He drew himself up to his full, if unassuming, height. "Besides, I'm through with drinking myself into stupefaction! Better an ordinary man sober than a seer stinking of debasement."

"A wise choice." Ehomba was straightforwardly encouraging. "That decision will make your company as welcome as your experience of the territory that lies ahead of us. It will be good to have a knowledgeable guide along, and not to have to ask one stranger after another which road is the safest to take, which route the easiest."

"I'll do everything I can," the reborn Knucker assured him. Less confidently, he turned to the black litah. Remaining bone snapped explosively beneath the big cat's powerful jaws. "I will even do all that is in my power to help you, most remarkable of all predators."

Languorously indifferent, Ahlitah turned his head to scrutinize the wavering speaker. "I despise you, you know."

"I—I'm sorry, great maned one. What have I done to so offend you?"

"Nothing." The cat returned to the last of its chomping. "I despise the other two as well. I despise all humans. You are weak, and unattractive, and conflicted within. Not only that, the most robust of your males can make love only a few times a day." He sniffed contemptuously through his whiskers. "Whereas the lion in me can—"

"Hoy, hoy," Simna interrupted, "enough! We've heard all that boasting. But can you make a sword, or tie a fishing line?"

Supercilious brows aimed at the swordsman. Thick black lips drew back to reveal gleaming teeth, and claws longer than a man's fingers sprang from their place of concealment within a massive forepaw. Alarmed, the timorous Knucker drew back.

"Here are my swords," the litah growled, "and here my fishing line."

"Stop it, you two." When he wanted to, Ehomba could growl smartly himself. "It is time to go."

"Hoy," the swordsman agreed. "Let's be away from here while my belly's still full and my temperament under control." He started toward the door.

Rising from his corner, Ahlitah padded after him, brushing against the apprehensive Knucker without so much as glancing in the little man's direction. As he passed Ehomba, however, the ebon hulk snarled softly.

"One day I will have to kill that insufferable windbag. Then I will butcher him like a fat young kudu and eat him, starting with his tongue."

"That is between you and Simna." Ehomba was blissfully indifferent. "But mindful of your promise to me, you will not do so until I have finished what I have come all this way to accomplish."

The great maned head turned to face the herdsman. So

close were they that Ehomba could feel the litah's breath on his skin. It was pungent with the bone of dead ox. "You are more fortunate than you know, man, that among cats the code of honor is stronger than it is among humans."

Ehomba nodded his head ever so slightly. "I envy your character as much as your staying power."

The litah grunted its satisfaction. "At least you, Etjole Ehomba, recognize that which is greater than you, and respect that which you yourself cannot achieve."

"Oh, I did not mean that," the tall southerner responded frankly. "By staying power, I meant your determination to remain with me." So saying, he followed the swordsman out the open door.

Ahlitah hesitated, pondering hard on the herdsman's words. Left behind, the little man looked on curiously. He had seen many things, but never before had he seen a cat pondering hard. Then the big carnivore emitted a series of short, pithy yowls, which, if Knucker had not known better, he might well have mistaken for laughter.

XV

The Parable of the Glass Golem

The four strangers paused to watch the ransacking of the house. Several soldiers broke away from their work to report the presence of the large black carnivore among the group of onlookers, but when neither it nor its presumed masters showed any sign of interfering, Proctor Cuween Bisgrath ordered them back to work.

They were an odd bunch, he decided as he studied them from his seat on the back of Rune, his favorite horse. Three men of radically different size, aspect, and color traveling in the company of the biggest and most peculiar-looking feline he had ever seen. Idly, he wondered if they would be worth interrogating, perhaps with an eye toward charging them a "fine" for traveling through Bondressey without a permit. No permits were necessary, but it was very likely they did not know that, and would pay to avoid trouble.

Contrarily, the wealthiest of them looked unconscionably poor, and it might not be worth his time to try to extract from them what few coins they might have in their possession. Furthermore, if the great predator accompanying them proved high-strung, he might lose a man or two in the process of making an arrest, and with little or no gain to hope for in return.

No, better to let the scrutty vagabonds continue on their way, hopefully right out of Bondressey. They were heading northwest. If they kept to that course they would cross the border in a few days, and good riddance. The mere presence on the streets of such uncouth vagrants was an offense to the kingdom's aesthetics.

"You there!" Pushing down on Rune's stirrups, he stood up in the saddle. "Make sure to check thoroughly the attic and any basement, and the walls for hidden compartments! Miscreants such as these often conceal their valuables in such places."

"Yes, Proctor!" came an acknowledging shout from the officer in charge. Sword drawn, he reentered the building. Household goods were already piling up on the front walkway as soldiers ferried them out from within.

Master and mistress of the handsome abode came stumbling out of the imposing entrance. Despite its size, no servants were in evidence. Their absence suggested that the owners took care of all the general maintenance themselves. That insinuated that they were dedicated workers. Bisgrath was gratified. Taking from the poor and the lazy was unprofitable.

"Please, sir, leave us something!" The master of the house looked older than his years, his face and posture reflecting an unpretentious life devoted to hard work. "All that we have has gone into our home!"

Rune stirred slightly and Bisgrath used the reins to steady his mount. "Ungrateful miscreant! Be glad I am leaving you the house. You know the penalty for failure to pay taxes in a timely and responsible manner. Fortunately for you, I am today in a generous and forgiving mood. Otherwise I would order your insignificant lodgings razed to the ground."

The man stepped back, his gaze glazed by hurt. Stumbling blankly about, he could only turn to watch the emptying of his home. After a moment, he fell to his knees, still staring.

Bisgrath magnanimously allowed the woman to clutch at his left leg and continue to plead for clemency. Not because he had any intention of listening to her, or because that was a quality normally ascribed to him, but because he found her pleasant to look upon. After a while, though, her uncontrolled sobbing began to grate on his patience. Putting a booted foot against her chest, he shoved hard and sent her sprawling. Another time he might have stalked her with Rune, using the horse's hooves as threats and making her crawl. But he was too busy directing the plundering of the household. Someone had to make certain that nothing was overlooked and that the spoils were properly loaded onto the waiting wagons. One for the kingdom, and the one with the heavy canvas covers for him. Astute as he was in matters fiscal, he knew better than to rely on official compensation to sustain his status.

For example, this particular family was not actually in arrears in matters of taxation. Only a simple subtle manipulation of certain texts had made it appear so. By choosing his untutored victims at random, he avoided the attention of his superiors, who were anywise gratified by his uncanny ability to root out the disobedient among the kingdom's otherwise virtuous citizens.

Overlooked in the turmoil and confusion was a sandy-haired little girl of seven or eight years. While her parents entreated futilely with Proctor Bisgrath, she walked wide-eyed away from the house proper. Intent on their ransacking, the industrious soldiers ignored her. In the course of her aimless wandering, she found herself confronting an immense black face dominated by huge tawny eyes that seemed to glow from within. Lips parted to reveal canines longer than her hand. A tongue emerged to lick speculatively at her arm. It was rough and raspy as a file and she stepped away sharply.

"Ahhhah!" a man's voice yelled sharply.

The tongue withdrew and the enormous cat looked back and growled irritably. "Just tasting." With a shake of its magnificent mane it resumed its pacing.

The place where the tongue had licked her began to burn slightly. Ignoring the chaos behind her, instinctively shutting out the cries of her mother, she began to cry.

A man was kneeling beside her. While the mild pain produced by the big cat's tongue remained, so strange and fascinating was the face now inclining toward her that her tears stopped. She stared at him, and when he smiled back it instantly made her feel better. Not better enough to smile, but sufficient to put a halt to the crying.

"I cannot tell you not to feel bad," he told her. "Do you understand what I mean by that?" She nodded slowly, wiping at her eyes with the back of one hand as the man looked past her. Her mother and father had always told her not to talk to strangers, but somehow she knew that this oddly dressed man represented no threat.

"My friends and I have a long ways yet to travel, so we cannot stop to help you or your family. And anyway, this is none of our business." He had a leather bag or something on his back. Pulling it around in front of him, he fumbled around inside until he found what he was looking for. "But since they are taking everything, I want to give you something. It is a little dolly. It was given to me by a very wise old lady named Meruba. I know that she would want you to take it."

Opening his fingers, he revealed a tiny doll lying in his

palm. Small enough to fit in her hand, it was carved from a black material that she did not recognize.

"It's very nice. Thank you, sir."

Reaching forward, he used very long fingers to brush hair out of her eyes. "You are welcome, child." He started to rise.

"What's it made of? I've never seen anything like it before."

"It is a kind of glass, but not the glass that is made by people. This kind comes from deep within the earth. Sometimes we find it lying about on the ground where I come from. It takes a good edge and makes fine knives and spearpoints. But your dolly is all smooth and polished. It will not cut you."

One of his companions shouted something to him. They had moved on past the house and were waiting for him to catch up. "I have to go now," he told her. "My friends are calling me." He paused a moment, then added, "Tell your mommy and daddy to go to whoever is in charge of bad things like this. If they will do that, I have a feeling they might be able to get some of their things back."

"Yes sir. I will, sir." The girl clutched the diminutive black doll to her chest. The volcanic glass was slick and cold and slightly waxy-feeling to the touch.

The tall, kindly stranger rejoined his companions and they were soon gone from sight. She concentrated on the doll, cooing and murmuring to it. So she did not see her father rise from his knees to charge Proctor Bisgrath angrily, or see the blood fly from his head as an alert soldier caught him a heavy blow from behind with the solid wooden shaft of his pike. She did not see or hear her screaming mother throw herself atop the crumpled, unconscious form, or hear the soldiers laugh as they roughly pulled her away in the direction of the rosebushes that had been her pride and joy.

Ignoring his minions' harmless frolic, Bisgrath continued to supervise the plundering until even he was convinced

there was nothing more to strip from the dwelling. Content
with the day's work and not a little tired, he ordered the
wagons formed up. Obedient soldiers fell into lines on either
side of the booty, flanking the two carry-alls. At the Proctor's directive, they began to move out. The larger wagon
would be escorted triumphantly back to the city hall. Its
smaller sibling would find itself diverted down a little-used
side street, eventually to come to rest in the impressive enclosed courtyard of the majestic mansion of Cuween Bisgrath, Proctor General of Bondressey.

Tugging on the reins, the Proctor turned to follow the procession. A shimmer of light caught his eye and made him
pause. Curious, he turned back and trotted over to the source
of the gleam. It lay in the open palm of a little girl.

Leaning down from the saddle, he smiled unctuously and
gestured at the object. "What have you there, child?"

She replied without looking up at him. "I'm not talking to
you. You hurt my mommy and daddy."

"Tut now, child. I am only doing my job."

"You're a bad man."

"Perhaps, but I'm good at it. So that makes me a good bad
man." Behind him, the wagons were trundling off in the direction of the central city.

Frowning, she looked up at him. "That doesn't make any
sense."

"Yes it does. You'll understand when you're older. My,
but you're a pretty little thing. Maybe I'll come and visit you
later."

"No!" she responded emphatically.

"You have your father's spirit—but I won't hold that
against you." He leaned a little farther out of the saddle.
"May I see that little toy, please? Where did you get it?"

She turned to point. "A nice man gave it to me. He was
funny-looking."

Bisgrath followed her outstretched arm, but there was no

sign of the untidy foreigners. They had disappeared northward. "An exotic artifact. Perhaps from very far away. How interesting. The carving is very well done. I have quite a collection of art myself, and I have never seen anything exactly like it." He extended his hand. "Let me see it."

"No." Clutching the dolly in both hands, she pulled away from his reaching fingers.

Pouting, he withdrew his hand. "I just want to look at it. If you let me look at it, I'll give you back some of the things the soldiers took."

Hesitantly, she unfolded her fingers and looked long and hard at the carving. Then she reached out and up and handed it to him. He turned it over in his fingers, admiring the exquisite detail and the play of light over the lustrous black surface.

"It's more accomplished than I thought. Thank you, child." Jerking on Rune's reins, he turned to go.

Behind him, the girl started screaming. "Give it back! You promised, you promised!"

"Something else you'll understand when you're older," he called back to her. He slipped the fine carving into a jacket pocket, wishing the girl's mother would take charge of her spawn and shut her up. He disliked screaming. But the mother was in no condition to help her child or anyone else.

He parted with the main body of soldiers after congratulating them on a morning's work well done, and not before slipping a little something extra into the palm of the officer in charge. Leaving them to make their way into the city with the larger of the two booty-laden wagons, he turned to escort the other down a different road entirely.

Capable hands were waiting to unload, as stone-faced servants responded to his return. None smiled at his success, none offered a cheery greeting as he dismounted and climbed the steps that led into the great hall. Those who worked for the Proctor did not smile in his presence lest their expression be misinterpreted. By keeping his staff intimidated, Bisgrath felt he insured their loyalty. It was harder to steal from a master you feared than from one you thought of as harmless.

Lunch awaited and, much to the relief of the kitchen staff and servers, was pronounced satisfactory by the Proctor. As he left the dining room, Bisgrath mentally totaled the profit he would accrue from the morning's exertions. A good day's work all around, he decided.

Entering the library, he pondered a number of possible sites for the exotic carving. There were several empty alcoves that would serve to highlight its luster, and a place on the main reading table already crowded with fine lapidary work. In the end he decided to stand his newest acquisition on the inlaid reading table by his favorite chair, where he could admire it frequently until, as he always did, he grew bored by it and sought a fresh replacement.

Putting on his reading glasses and settling himself into the chair, he selected one of several massive ledgers from a low table nearby and opened it on his lap. Since things had gone so smoothly this morning, he had all afternoon in which to ferret out the next subject for persecution. Or rather, he mused as he smiled inwardly, the next blatant violator of the Kingdom of Bondressey's far too lenient tax laws. Afternoon light pouring through the high, beveled glass windows allowed him to read the fine scrawl without strain.

In this pleasant and relaxed fashion he passed the better part of an hour, using a pen to put a damning mark beside the names of half a dozen potential miscreants. Feeling a slight weight against his right arm, he brushed at it casually—only to have his fingers make contact with something hard and unyielding.

Glancing impassively to his right, he found himself staring down at the diminutive glass figurine. Somehow it had fallen against his arm. He frowned, but only momentarily.

There was no wind in the room, so it must have been placed at an angle on the end table and fallen over against him. His thoughts focused on the ledger, he absently picked it up and set it back down in the middle of the table, and forgot about it.

Until, several minutes later, he again felt the weight against his arm.

Frowning this time, he picked up the carving and placed it, not in the middle, but on the far side of the end table. Mildly irritated with himself, he settled back into the chair and resumed reading. In minutes he had once more forgotten all about the figurine.

In the silence of the library, where no servant would dare to disturb him, a soft tap-tapping caused him to look up from his malevolent perusal. Following the sound to its source, he turned to his right. His eyes widened and air momentarily paused in its passage through his throat.

Blank of eye, black of body, the carving was tottering on slow obsidian feet across the tabletop toward him.

Leaping from the chair, the ledger falling heavily to the floor at his feet, he gaped at the tiny apparition. It promptly changed its direction to a new heading to reflect his rising.

"What manner of foreign necromancy is this?" There was no one in the library to hear him and the figurine, of course, did not reply. Nor did it pause in its advance.

"Preposterous manifestation, what are you?" Tightening his lips, he reached out and grabbed the carving. A chill ran through him as he felt it moving in his hand. Searching the room, he quickly found what he was looking for.

Into the gilt silver box went the ensorcelled figurine. A turn of the key, the click of the latch, and it was secured. Slipping the key into a pocket, a contented Bisgrath returned to his chair. "I'll attend to you later. I count among my acquaintances many knowledgeable practitioners of the arcane arts. They'll investigate the spell that motivates you, and we'll fast put a stop to this unsanctioned meandering."

Satisfied, he resumed his seat and, a bit more intently than usual, continued with his reading. Another hour passed, at which point he decided it was time to call a servant to bring some drink. He rose from the chair.

There seemed to be a weight on his thigh. Looking down, he saw the figurine clinging with tiny but powerful hands to the leg of his pants as it worked its way steadily upwards. And this time, each minute, a perfectly carved eye was glowing a vivid intense yellow.

With a cry he grabbed the carving and wrenched it free of his leg. Without thinking, he drew back his arm and threw the suddenly hideous little manikin as far and as hard as he could. It slammed into one of the tall windows that lined the library's west wall. Even before it did so, he found himself wincing. Fine leaded glass was immoderately expensive.

But the windows were thick and well made, and this one did not crack. Neither did the carving bounce away. As he stared, it adhered to the transparency and, beneath his incredulous gaze, began to diffuse into it, glass melting into glass. The figurine grew smaller and smaller as a black stain spread across the center of the window. It continued to disperse and disseminate until it had disappeared completely.

Realizing that he was breathing hard enough to make his lungs ache, Bisgrath forced himself to calm down. Approaching the window, he reached up to feel gingerly of the place where the carving had struck. There was no sign that anything was amiss. The thick glass was not chipped, and even up close there was no sign of the corrupt foreign blackness that had appeared to diffuse within the material.

Quite astonishing, he thought. He would have to inquire of learned acquaintances as to the meaning of the episode. Meanwhile, there was work to be done. But first, something to drink.

Using a pull cord to summon a servant, he once more returned to his chair and to his malicious scrutiny of the ledger's contents. Finding several more prospective victims helped to relax him and set his mind at ease. When the servant knocked, he barked an irritable "Enter!" without looking up from his work. The choosing of unwitting innocents to savage never failed to raise his spirits.

Entering silently, the servitor approached with tray in hand—only to signal his entrance with an abrupt metallic crash that caused Bisgrath to look up sharply. "What the blazes do—" He halted in mid-accusation. The servant was not looking at him. An expression of utter terror was imprinted on his face. The silver tray lay forgotten at his feet, the contents of the pitcher it had held having spilled out across the immaculate hardwood floor.

Puzzled, Bisgrath turned to follow the man's gaze, whereupon he whipped off the reading glasses and flung them aside, unable to believe the evidence of his own eyes.

Peering out at him from the window and occupying most of its height was an outline of the black glass carving, its eyes burning like oil lamps on a particularly dark and chill night.

With a stuttering scream, the servant fled the room. Rising and backing slowly away from the window, Bisgrath fumbled along the wall for the weapons that were mounted there. Arraigned in a decorative semicircle, they included a great number of killing devices more suitable for use by common infantry than a cultivated gentleman like himself. That did not stop him from wrenching a short, heavy war ax from its holding clips.

Uttering a cry of defiance, he charged the window. The inhuman fiery gaze seemed to follow him as he rushed across the room. It went out when he slammed the ax into the glass, bringing more than half of it down in a shower of crystalline fragments.

Panting heavily, the ax clutched convulsively in both hands, he backed away. Birdsong filtered in from outside and a cool Bondresseyean breeze blew unbidden into the library. The tall black image had vanished. *Help,* he thought fearfully; *I need a magician here to tell me what is going on* He knew several names and would send servitors to summon them immediately—yes, immediately. He turned for the doorway. As he did so, out of the corner of an eye he caught sight of a discrepancy.

The carving had reappeared, its eyes burning as fiercely as ever, in another of the tall library windows. And this time it was not a flat, picturelike image, but a mass formed in glistening, solid relief, its thick arms reaching out, outward into the room. Ten feet tall, the dreadful apparition was composed entirely of black volcanic glass, as if it had drawn strength and substance from the leaded glass of the window itself.

Screaming wildly, Cuween Bisgrath hurled the war ax at the glossy, brutish homunculus that was slowly emerging from the thick pane of the window. It shattered noisily, sending shards both transparent and black flying in all directions. Stumbling from the room, the Proctor General tore up the stairs that led to the second floor and to his private quarters. He was going mad, he decided. None of this was actually happening. He didn't need magicians; he needed a doctor.

He shouted for his servants, but none responded. Having heard from the servitor who had entered the library and subsequently bolted and seen the look on his face, they had one and all fled the mansion. They had found something they were more afraid of than the Proctor's wrath.

Staggering into his bedroom, Bisgrath slammed the door behind him and threw every one of the heavy bolts. Designed to withstand a full-scale assault by a company of armed soldiers or hopeful assassins, its unrelenting solidity helped to reassure him. Breathing a little easier, he made his way to the splendid bathroom. Spacious enough to accommodate six bathers, the marble tub beckoned. He strode purposefully past, knowing that he had to find a physician to diagnose whatever ailment was causing him to experience such profoundly disturbing hallucinations. He would make a cursory attempt to clean himself up and then ride himself to the offices of a particularly well-known practitioner who specialized in unusual afflictions. And when he returned, treated and well, the shrieks of delinquent servants would make themselves heard all the way to the border with Squoy.

Cold, lightly minted water splashed on his face from the magnificent enameled basin refreshed him instantly. Reaching for a cloth, he wiped droplets clear, enjoying the reinvigorating tingle they left on his skin. Raising his gaze to the filigree-edged mirror, he tried to understand what had happened to him, and how.

Bare inches away, incandescent yellow eyes set in an impassive black mask of a face peered menacingly back at him, burning hotter than ever.

Choking on his own fear, he reeled away from the accusing, threatening face in the mirror that belonged not to him but to some emotionless brute. His fumbling fingers contracted spasmodically around the first thing they touched. Drawing back his arm, he tried to throw the iridescent drinking goblet as hard as he could at the silently taunting mirror.

The effort nearly caused him to fall. Looking down at his hand, he saw that the goblet had a hold on his wrist and would not let go. Or rather, the fiend that was emerging from the rainbow-hued glass would not.

Screaming, spinning wildly, he smashed the goblet against the marbled wall. Glass went flying in multicolored splinters, the light from a thousand fragments momentarily illuminating the bathroom with a full spectrum of brilliance and fear. It obliterated the dark demon that had been emerging from the hand-blown glass goblet, but not the one in the mirror. Blood bubbled from a dozen tiny cuts on his hand and face. Ignoring them, he backed out of the bathroom and slammed the door as hard as he could.

Articulating the wordless dirge of the living unhuman, two more hulking representations of the carving were seeping out of the bedroom windows, their jet-black bodies massive and irresistible. Leaping across the bed to the safety of the bedroom door, Proctor Bisgrath frantically drew back one security bolt after another. Before fleeing into the outer hall, he picked up a heavy iron doorstop and threw it at the nearest of the advancing homunculi. The metal struck the figure with a loud crack. Half the face shattered and crumbled away without slowing the inexorable advance of the black glass manikin in the least.

His howls and screams echoing through the empty, great house, Bisgrath flew back down the stairs. For one seeking escape, it was an ill-advised choice. From every window and mirror, from every frosted-glass cabinet and graceful chalice, the indefatigable progeny of the obsidian carving lurched and tottered toward him, heavy arms outstretched, fingers curled like black flesh hooks. In every one of them, pitiless eyes burned soullessly.

There was no way out, he saw. But maybe, just maybe, there was a way in. He had not risen to the position of Proctor General for all the kingdom of Bondressey through dint of slow wit and ponderous thinking. Whirling, he rushed back into the library.

The four monstrous forms that lumbered out of the remaining unbroken windows were each large and heavy enough to crush an entire patrol beneath their bulk. But, relentless as they were, their movements were not the swiftest. Ducking beneath the whooshing sweep of a grasping arm, he darted along the back wall until he reached a bookcase filled with innocuous tomes on the art of gardening. Moaning like a chorus of doom, the four huge figures turned to follow. A menagerie of smaller cousins poured in through the door that led to the great hall.

Pulling out a specific book that was not a book, Bisgrath held his breath as the heavy bookcase that was not a bookcase rotated silently on a concealed pivot. Ducking into the secret room beyond, he leaned hard on a lever set in the wall that was a match to the nonbook outside. The monstrosities were remorseless, but he had seen nothing to suggest that they were in any wise clever.

Since no windows opened onto the secret reading room, he found himself fumbling in the dark. But no windows meant no glass. There were no drinking utensils, no mirrors. He should be safe in the stone-wall chamber, for a little while at least. Feeling along the edge of the reading table, he located the large candlestick standing there. Using tapers stored in a box near the base, he ran his fingers up the length of the candle to the wick. Striking one taper, he lit the cylinder of beeswax and then another on the other side of the table. Warm, safe light suffused the room. Faintly, he could hear the assembling horde keening and moaning horribly on the other side of the bookcase door. Fists of heavy black glass began to pound rhythmically against the barrier, like distant drums. The pivoting gateway held, but for how long it would continue to do so he could not be sure.

Pulling priceless volumes off the wall, he finally found the one he was searching for and carried it to the table. It was bound in fraying old leather and weighed as much as a small saddle. If he could not send word to a magician, then he would make his own magic. He had done so on a limited basis in the past, and he would do so again now. Always more dilettante than pupil, he wished now that he had paid more attention to such studies. But why bother to learn the intricacies of the mystic arts when one could always hire a professional to do the job better?

As the pounding outside increased, he was encouraged by

the continued stability of the doorway. Working the index, which was an entire book unto itself, he finally found the item he was looking for. By the steady, reassuring illumination of the twin candles he flipped through the heavy weight of pages until his fingers stopped them at the appropriate chapter.

There it was: a simple recitation for banishing spirits that might arise up out of statues. Leaning over the open book and squinting in the flickering light, he saw that the spell was deemed effective on sculpture rendered in any medium: stone, metal, wood, bone, shell—and glass.

Turning to the thudding portal, he raised a clenched fist and bellowed defiance. "Pound away, brood of foreign devils! In another moment you'll all be dead and gone, extinguished, like steam off a hot stove! Nothing and no one besieges Cuween Bisgrath in his own house!"

Turning back to the book, he bent low over the relevant paragraphs. Though writ small, they appeared elemental and shorn of unpronounceable terms. To make sure he committed no potentially hazardous errors in the reciting of the formula, he reached automatically for the pair of reading glasses that were always kept safe in the single pull-out drawer beneath the reading table.

And made the mistake of putting them on.

XVI

Hoy, bruther, what did you give to that poor little thing, anyway?"

"Nothing much." Ehomba strode along easily as they climbed into the first foothills. "It was a little doll, a carving that had been given to me by one of the women of the village." He glanced over to where the emancipated Knucker was stopping to inspect every flower they passed, as if seeing and sniffing each one for the first time. "When you are going away on a long journey, people give you peculiar odds and ends, in the hope that this or that frippery might at some time prove useful. I saw no particular use for the carving, and thought that since the girl appeared to be losing everything she owned, she might enjoy the comfort of a doll, however small and hard."

The swordsman took a playful swipe at the tuft on the end of Ahlitah's switching tail. Looking back, the big cat's eyes narrowed. With great dignity, it loped on ahead, effortlessly outdistancing its human companions.

"Maybe you have got kids of your own, bruther, but your

woman must have done the raising. No girl that age is going to cuddle up to a piece of black rock."

"It was not rock." Ehomba stepped carefully over a patch of small, bright blue flowers.

"Whatever." The swordsman shook his head sadly. "You're always the one in such a hurry, Etjole. If you waste time to pause and jabber with children unfortunate in their choice of parents you'll never get to where you're going."

"Yes, I suppose you are right, Simna. There was nothing we could do for her family without making ourselves the targets of those soldiers, and she will probably throw the figurine away at the first opportunity."

"Don't take it to heart, bruther." The swordsman gave his tall friend a condoling slap on the back. "People are always thinking they can make a difference in some stranger's life, and invariably they end up making things worse." Raising his voice, he called out to their new companion.

"Hoy, Knuckerman! There's footpaths all over this place. You're supposed to be guiding us. Stop snorting those stinking weeds and show us the right one."

Bright-eyed and alert, the little man straightened and nodded. "Your animal is still moving forward on the correct line. Keep following him. If he makes a wrong turn I'll let you know. Don't worry."

"Why should I worry?" Simna murmured aloud. "We're following the lead of the man who knows everything. Or used to. I wonder: If we got a drink or two into him—not enough to destabilize him, mind—would he stay sober enough to understand the question and still be able to know the answer?"

As they walked, Ehomba dutifully considered the proposition. "I do not think so. I believe that with Knucker and his knowing it is all one way or all the other. There is no middle ground."

Simna showed his disappointment. "Too bad."

"But he is happier this way. And healthier, with a new outlook on the future. Look at him."

"Hoy, hoy. Clean and sober but useless. A fine trade-off, that." The swordsman strained to see over the next hill. They were entering dense forest, fragrant with towering pine and spruce. "Didn't he say something about an interesting town not far ahead?"

Ehomba nodded. "Netherbrae." The herdsman surveyed the steeply ascending hills. "Two days' journey from here and well outside the borders of Bondressey."

"Good." Simna increased his pace. "I could do with some surroundings that were interesting instead of civilized."

"Cannot a place be both?"

"Hoy, but given a choice, I much prefer the former over the latter. Ow!"

Reaching up, the swordsman felt the back of his head. The source of the slight but sharp pain was immediately apparent: A sizeable pinecone that had fallen from a considerable height was still rolling to a stop near his feet. Ehomba's gentle grin at his friend's discomfort vanished when a similar missile struck him on the shoulder. Together, the two men peered warily up into the trees. As they did, another cone landed several feet away.

Simna took consolation from his tall friend's ignorance. The herdsman had never seen seeds like these before. There were no towering evergreens in the land of the Naumkib.

"Such trees drop their cones all the time," the swordsman explained. "We just happened to be walking in the wrong place at the wrong time." As he finished, another cone struck Ahlitah on his hindquarters. The big cat whirled sharply and smacked the offending seed pod twenty feet before it could roll off his backside and hit the ground. His dignity was more injured than his hip.

"Your location had nothing to do with it." Knucker had rejoined his new friends, but instead of on them his gaze was focused on the interlocking branches overhead. "We're being targeted."

Ehomba's excellent eyesight could discern no movement in the treetops except for the occasional bird or dragonet. One pair of mated azure dragonets was busy enlarging a prospective nesting hole high up in the otherwise solid bole of a giant spruce. Each would inspect the cavity, lean forward and blast it with a tiny, precisely aligned tongue of flame from its open mouth, then sit back and wait for the fire to burn itself out. The pair was already through the bark and into solid wood. Several days of such careful work would leave them with a fire-hardened black cavity in which to raise their young.

The herdsman kept an eye on them as he and his friends continued to make their way through the cool, enclosing woods. Both dragonets were fully occupied with the task of excavating their nesting hole, and neither paid the least attention to the party of three men and one cat tromping through the forest litter. Certainly they did not pause to kick pinecones at the figures far below.

"I do not see anything throwing these cones at us," Ehomba declared. Even as he concluded the observation, two more cones landed close by his feet, just missing him. His eyes instantly darted upward, but there was no sign of movement in any of the branches immediately overhead.

A smiling Knucker tapped the side of his nose with a long finger. This time, nothing came out. "We must be under attack by groats." He scanned the treetops. "Troops of them are common in these woods. They don't like visitors."

As a particularly heavy cone plummeted to strike him a glancing blow on the left foot, Simna loudly offered to trade his blade for a good bow and a quiver full of arrows.

"It wouldn't do you any good," Knucker assured him.

"Why not?" More insulted than injured by the cone, the swordsman spoke without taking his eyes from the branches overhead. "I'm a pretty good hand with a bow. What are these groats, anyway?"

"Small furry creatures that live in the treetops in forests like these." Holding his hands out in front of him, Knucker aligned the open palms about three feet apart. "They have long tails and feet that can grip branches as strongly as hands, in the manner of monkeys, but their faces are like those of insects, hard and with strangely patterned eyes."

Ehomba hopped clear of a falling cone nearly the size of his head that he was fortunate to spot on the way down. It hit the ground with a weighty thump that held the potential for serious injury. As the bombardment continued and the first small cones gave way to far larger woody projectiles, the situation began to deteriorate from merely bothersome to potentially serious.

"I have good eyes and I have been looking for a long time," the herdsman replied, "and still I see nothing like what you describe."

Knucker's expression turned serious. "That's because the fur of the groat is invisible. You have to look for their eyes, which is the only part of them that reflects light."

Searching for three-foot-long furry creatures ambling through the treetops was one thing. Hunting only for isolated eyes was far more difficult. A cone that could have knocked a man unconscious struck Ahlitah squarely on his head, provoking a roar that shook the needles of the surrounding trees. It did not intimidate the unseen groats, who continued to rain cones down on the hapless intruders at an ever-increasing rate.

More cones suggested the presence of more groats. While this made the travelers' situation more perilous, it also improved the opportunities for detecting the elusive creatures. Moments after he executed an elegant if forced little dance that enabled him to dodge half a dozen falling cones, Simna stabbed an arm skyward.

"There! By that big branch thrusting to the east from this tree next to us. There's one!" Reflexively, he fingered the hilt of his sword. The large compound eyes of the otherwise invisible arboreal tormentor glistened in the afternoon light. No accusatory chattering came from the creature or from any of its companions. The barrage of cones was being carried out in complete silence.

Simna was not silent, however. Ill equipped to deal with an attack from above, he was reduced to screaming imprecations at their unseen adversaries. Unsurprisingly, this had no effect on the volume of cones being dropped upon him and his friends.

By this time they had broken into a run. Their progress was made difficult because they had to keep more or less to the trail as located by Knucker while avoiding not only the falling cones but also the dense mass of trees. Straining to pick out eye reflections in the branches overhead, Ehomba struck one smaller tree a glancing blow with his shoulder. While trying to determine the extent of the resultant bruise, he was hit by two smaller cones launched from above. Gritting his teeth, he pulled himself away from the tree trunk and ran on.

"These groats!" he yelled at Knucker, who was having a hard time keeping up with the pace. "What would they do if they killed us? Eat us?"

"Oh no," the wheezing little man assured him. "They'd just make sure we were dead and then go away. They only want their forest back. As I said, they don't like visitors."

"Can't they tell that we're trying to leave as fast as we can?" Raising a hand over his head, the swordsman warded off a cluster of small cones. Despite their moderate size, they still stung when hurled from a considerable height.

"They probably can't." Knucker was gasping for air now. It was clear to Ehomba that their new companion would not be able to keep up for much longer. Something had to be done. But what? How did one fight an opponent beyond reach and impossible to see except for its eyes?

Simna thought he had the solution. "Do something, Etjole! Blast them out of the treetops, turn them into newts, call up a spell that will bring them crashing down from the branches like stones!"

"How many times do I have to tell you, Simna—I am not a sorcerer! I can make some use only of what wiser ones have given to me." Looking up, he dodged to the right just in time to avoid a pinecone as big as a beer tankard, and almost as heavy.

"Hoy, then use the sky-metal sword! Call up the wind from between the stars and blow them clear out of the woods!"

"I do not think that would be wise. The wind that rushes between the stars is not a thing to be trifled with. You do not bring it down to earth every time you have a problem." While running, he waved at the imposing, surrounding trees. "I could try to bring down the wind, but once summoned it cannot be easily controlled. It could bring down every tree in this forest along with the groats. Better to endure a pounding by seed pods than by falling trees."

"In your pack." Simna was tired of running. He wanted to stand and fight, but doubted their assailants would oblige him. Even if they did, it would be hard to do battle with three-foot-long invisibilities. "There's always something in that pack of yours! A magic amulet, or a powder to make smoke to hide us, or another figurine like the one that summoned Fhastal the younger."

"Fhastal's sword would be of no more use to us here than our own." The herdsman looked for a place to halt that offered some concealment from the arboreal barrage. "And I have no magic pills or conjurer's tricks. But I do have an idea."

"Glewen knows I'd rather have an amulet," Simna yelled

back, "but at this point I'll settle for an idea. If it's a right-eous one."

There were no caves in which to hide, no buildings in which to take refuge, but they did find a lightning-scarred tree whose base had been blasted into a V-shaped hollow. In this they all took refuge from the steady rain of spiky projectiles. Glittering eyes gathered in the branches overhead as the peripatetic yet silent groats continued to pelt this temporary sanctuary with cones.

Slipping his pack off his back, Ehomba dug through its depths until he found what he was looking for. Simna crowded uncomfortably close. The tree hollow was barely large enough to accommodate the three men. With the addition of the litah's substantial bulk it was difficult to breathe, much less move about.

Removing his searching hand, the herdsman displayed a slim, irregularly shaped, palm-sized slab that was dull gray metal on one side and highly polished glass on the other. The reflective surface was badly scratched and the metal pitted and dented. It looked like a broken piece of mirror.

"What is it?" The swordsman was openly dubious. "It looks like a mirror."

Ehomba nodded. "A piece of an old mirror. An heirloom from Likulu's family."

"That's all?" Simna stared uncomprehendingly at his tall companion. "Just a mirror? What would you be carrying a mirror around for? I haven't noticed that you've been paying special attention to your appearance." Expectation crept into his voice. "It's more than a mirror, isn't it? It has some kind of unique properties to help you vanquish your enemies?"

"No," Ehomba replied flatly, "it is only a mirror. A device for letting people see themselves as they are."

"Then what good is it?" A large cone slammed into the ground close enough to the swordsman's right foot to cause him to try to jerk it farther back into the hollow. But there was no more room. And the groats, seeing that their quarry was trapped, were growing bolder, descending to lower and lower branches the better to improve their aim. Twinkling compound eyes of bright blue and green began to cluster together. Above and below them, plucked pinecones appeared to float in midair.

"The sun is still high, and very bright." Holding the mirror firmly in one hand, Ehomba prepared to step out from beneath the protection of the tree hollow. "Their eyes are large. If I can bounce the sunlight into them and blind one or two, the others might panic and run." He glanced briefly over at his friend. "This is what I carry it for—to reflect the sun. In my country if one encounters trouble it is the best way to signal for help across long distances."

"I'd rather have bows and arrows." Leaning ever so slightly forward, Simna tried to locate the nearest of their tree-loving tormentors. "But if you think it's worth a try . . ."

The herdsman did not wait for Simna's opinion. Stepping out into the open, he located two pairs of drifting eyes and angled the piece of mirror so that it would shine directly in their faces. Sunlight shafting down between the trees struck the glass and bounced upward, dancing around the groats' heads. It was a difficult and tricky business. The active groats rarely stayed in one place long enough to catch the full glare from the mirror.

What happened next was unexpected. Knucker looked on in fascination, but Simna was not surprised. He had come to expect the unexpected in the herdsman's company.

Catching sight in the mirror not of the reflected sunshine but of themselves, first one, then two, then a dozen of the invisible cone throwers came sliding and climbing down from the branches to gather as if mesmerized around the mirror. Soon the entire troop was clustered before Ehomba, gazing enthralled into the scuffed, reflective glass. It was an unnerving sight: two dozen or more sets of compound eyes adrift above the forest floor. Up close, the travelers saw that the groats' invisible fur did not render them perfectly transparent. Where one of them moved slowly, there was a shimmering in the air that reminded Ehomba of waves of heat rising from the desert floor.

Behind him, Simna was drawing his sword. His tone reflected his homicidal expression. Squeezing out of the hollow in the tree, the black litah was right beside him.

"That's it, bruther. Keep them hypnotized just a moment longer, until I can get in among them." He swung his weapon experimentally. "All I've got to do is aim for the eyes. Packed together like you have them, I'm bound to get a couple with each blow."

"No," Ehomba warned him. "Keep back. For another minute or two, anyway. They are not hypnotized. It is— something else."

The swordsman hesitated. Ahlitah halted also, growling uncertainly deep in his throat. "I don't follow you, bruther. We may not get another chance like this."

He was about to add something more when the groat nearest the mirror suddenly let out a startled, high-pitched squeal, the first sound they had heard one of their invisible assailants utter. Leaping straight up into the air, it promptly turned and fled. Crowding close to fill the space vacated by their rapidly retreating cousin, two more pairs of eyes abruptly sprang backwards. Unseen lips emitted panicked screeches as the entire band scrambled to flee.

It was all over in a matter of moments. One second the groats were there, clustering around the palm-sized fragment of mirror, and the next they were gone, fleeing eye balls escaping in all directions into the safety of the deep woods.

Grateful if bewildered, Simna slowly sheathed his sword. A hesitant Knucker finally emerged from the protection of the scarred tree. Finding a suitable patch of sunlight, Ahlitah began to preen himself.

"By Goroka's coffee, what happened?" He looked to his friend. "You didn't blind them all. I don't think you blinded any of them."

"I do not think so either." A greatly relieved Ehomba turned to face his baffled friends. "The only thing I can think of is that they saw themselves in the mirror—for the first time. Since they are invisible to us, and to the litah, they must always have been invisible to themselves." Slowly, he held up the reflective shard. "A good mirror shows everything as it is. It must have shown them what they looked like under their invisible fur."

Stupefaction gave way to laughter as Simna roared with amusement. "And by Guquot's baggage, they must not have liked what they saw!" Wiping tears from his eyes, the swordsman sauntered over to rejoin his tall friend. "I guess not all mirrors are glazed equal." He reached for the fragment. "Here, let me have a look."

To the swordsman's surprise, Ehomba pulled the mirror out of his reach. "Are you sure, friend Simna?"

The shorter man frowned impatiently. "Sure? Sure about what?"

"That you really want to see yourself as you are." The herdsman's tone was as earnest as ever. But then, Simna reflected, it was usually so. Reaching out quickly, he snatched the scrap of polished glass from his companion's fingers.

"A mirror's just a mirror," he muttered. "Besides, I already know what I look like."

"Then why do you want to look again?" Ehomba asked quietly. But the swordsman seemed not to hear him.

Grinning confidently, Simna turned the mirror in his palm and held it up to his face at arm's length, striking a mockingly noble pose as he did so. It was clear he intended to make light of the enterprise. What resulted was coldly mirthless.

As he stared, the sardonic grin gradually faded from his face. Its place was taken by a sense of solemnity his companions had never before associated with the high-spirited, lighthearted swordsman. It aged him visibly, drawing down the corners of his eyes and setting his mouth into a narrow, tight line devoid of animation or amusement. He seemed to be looking not into the mirror, nor even at his own reflection, but at something much deeper and of far greater import.

What that was none of them knew. Before they could ask, or steal a look at the image in the mirror, Simna lowered it to his side. He had entered a state of deep contemplation that was as shadowed as it was unexpected.

"Simna?" Inclining his head a little closer to his friend, Ehomba tried to peer into the smaller man's downcast eyes. "Simna my friend, are you all right?"

"What?" With an effort, the gravely preoccupied swordsman pulled himself back from the profoundly meditative region into which he had sunk. He raised troubled eyes to his concerned companion. "It's okay, bruther. I am okay."

"What did you see?" Crowding close, Knucker gazed in fascination down at the shard of polished glass and metal dangling from the swordsman's fingers.

"See?" Struggling to resuscitate his affable, easygoing self, he tossed the mirror into the air, watched it tumble end over end a couple of times, and made a nimble catch of the awkward oblong shape with one hand. "I saw myself, of course. What else would you see in a mirror besides yourself?"

"Here, let me have a look." The little man extended eager fingers.

Manifesting an indifference he did not feel, Simna handed

it over. Knucker quickly raised it to his face and peered expectantly into the glass.

Knucker the Knower stared sadly back at him. It was him, to be sure, but not the him that stood on the trail, straight and sure, clear of eye and scrubbed of skin. The face that peered hauntingly out of the mirror was that of the Knucker Ehomba and his companions had found besotted and soiled in a squalid close, lying barely conscious in his own filth. Yellowed phlegm trickled from a corner of the half-open mouth, the face was smeared with accumulated grime and muck, and the disheveled hair was tightly matted enough to repel investigative vermin. It was the face of a man condemned to a short and miserable life of continued drunkenness and destitution.

He resisted the image and everything it said about him, quickly passing the mirror back to the swordsman. "Something's wrong. That isn't me there. That isn't myself as I am. That's a reflection of me as I was." He turned angrily on Ehomba. "Why did you show that to me? Why?"

"I did not show it to you." The herdsman's voice was level and unchanged. "You asked to look into it, and demanded it from Simna. Remember?"

"Well, it's wrong, all wrong." A disgruntled Knucker turned away from both of them.

"It could be," Ehomba admitted. "You would have to ask Likulu about that. Myself, I brought it along to use for signaling, not to serve as an ordinary mirror."

"Hoy, whatever it be, it sure ain't no ordinary mirror, bruther." Simna gripped the rectangle of battered material securely. But he did not look into it again.

Behind him, a loud chuff signified to the presence of the litah. "I'd like to have a look. I've only seen my reflection in still waters."

"Hoy, that's a fine idea!" His characteristic vivacity returning, the swordsman gladly presented the reflective face of the mirror to the big cat, winking at his companions as he did so. He couldn't wait to see what kind of effect it had on the majestic and insufferably arrogant feline.

"There." He strove to position the mirror to ensure that Ahlitah had the best view possible of his own reflection. "Is that all right? Can you see yourself clearly?"

Luminous, tawny eyes narrowed slightly as they gazed into the glass. "Yes, that's fine." The litah nodded slowly. "That is about how it should be."

Simna's expectant "Watch this!" grin soon gave way to a look of uncertainty. Frowning, he directed the hesitant Knucker to come and hold the mirror. As soon as the smaller man had a good grip on the rectangle, the swordsman walked around to stand alongside the big cat, pressing close to the massive, musky mass so that he too could get a good look at the predator's reflection. Because of the slight angle, his view was not as good as the litah's, but it was sufficient to show the likeness in the mirror.

A proud and imperious countenance gleamed back at him, the black litah powerfully reflected in all its mature vigor and resplendent virility. So resplendent, in fact, that the image in the mirror not only sported a pale golden halo, but cast sparks from its extremities, from the tips of its ears and the end of its nose as well as from elsewhere. The black mane had been transformed into a glistening, rippling aurora of ochroid indigo that framed the rest of the regal visage in a magnificent effulgence.

With a soft snort, Ahlitah turned way from the mirror, unimpressed. "Yes, that's about right."

The redness that bloomed on the swordsman's cheeks had nothing to do with a surfeit of sunshine. "It can't be!" Whirling around to confront Ehomba, he shook the fragment of scored, metal-backed glass in the herdsman's face. "Knucker's right! There's something wrong here. This unnatural mirror is possessed by an evil spirit. One that delights in laughing at us."

Ehomba did his best to accommodate his companion's concern. "You may be right, Simna. But do not come to me looking for explanations. I told you: It was a gift, one of many, hastily thrust upon me prior to my leaving the village. To me, it is just a mirror. A piece of polished glass that reflects things as they are—though what other properties it may possess I do not know. To understand more, you would have to—"

"Ask Likcold, or whatever her name is—I know." Frustrated, the swordsman started to return the mirror to its owner—and hesitated. "Hoy, bruther, why don't you have a look?" He gestured behind him. "Everyone else gazed into the glass. Why not you?"

Ehomba smiled amicably. "I already know what I look like, Simna."

"You do, do you?" The smaller man's gaze narrowed, and there was a glint in his eye. "That's what I thought. That's what we all thought." He held the mirror up to his friend's expressionless face. "Go on then, Etjole. Have a look. Or can it be that as a mighty sorcerer, your true reflection might be just a little different from what anyone would expect?"

The herdsman paused a moment before replying. "Oh, give it here. We are wasting time with this." Taking the mirror, he held it beneath his face and peered downward. "What a surprise, Simna. I see me."

"Hoy, but which you?" Stepping over to his friend's side, the shorter man struggled to see the herdsman's reflection. "Here, lower it a bit and let me have a look."

"And me also." An inquisitive Knucker hurried to join them.

Ehomba tilted the mirror slightly downward. Immediately, his two companions let out comparable yelps and looked away, rubbing at their eyes. Wiping with the heel of one hand at the tears that streamed down his face, Simna snapped at his friend.

"Would you mind not including the sun with your reflection?"

"Sorry." Stepping into the shade, the herdsman repositioned the mirror for his curious friends. Pressing close, Simna and Knucker gazed expectantly into the glass. The reflection of Etjole Ehomba smiled halfheartedly back at them.

"Give me that!" Jerking the mirror from the herdsman's fingers, Simna aligned it himself. After adjusting it several times and viewing the resultant reflection from a number of different angles, he finally handed it back to its owner, uncertain whether to be disappointed or relieved.

"Hoy, it's you all right. Nothing but you. Just you."

"What did you expect, Simna?" As he spoke, Ehomba fastidiously returned the mirror to its place in his pack.

"Something else, bruther. Something besides your reflection. Something other than normal." He shrugged. "But it was just you. Might as well have been looking into a mirror in an inn." Sighing deeply, he put his hands on his hips and stared up the narrow trail that wound through the forest. "How much farther to this Neitheray?"

"Netherbrae," Knucker corrected him. "Another day, perhaps two. I know the way, but I have only been there once myself, and that was in passing long ago."

Gathering himself, the swordsman started forward. "Let's get after it, then." He glanced up into the branches. Dragonets could rain fire down on a man, and birds other things, but these he did not mind. It was the groats he had no desire to meet up with again, and where one troop lived, another could follow.

Ehomba and Knucker trailed the swordsman's lead. Rising from his sitting position, Ahlitah brought up the rear. As he padded along in the humans' wake, he focused great yellow eyes on the herdsman's back. He did not say anything, nor did he intend to say anything, about what he had seen. The less he was compelled to converse with men, the better he liked it. But being intelligent, he was curious. For now he would keep that curiosity to himself. Doubtless an explanation would be forthcoming sometime in the future, either by design or by accident.

When the two smaller men had first looked into the mirror held by the man from the south, they had been momentarily blinded by reflected light. Nothing unusual about that.

Except that at the time, the sun had been in front of the herdsman, and not behind him.

XVII

Simna was anticipating a fairly typical isolated mountain village, with pigs and heptodons, chickens and raphusids running loose on rutted, muddy streets, children wailing, laundry hanging from unshuttered windows, and the pervasive stink of waste both human and animal. Given such low expectations, it was not surprising that when it finally came into view through the surrounding trees, the reality of Netherbrae gave a boost to his spirits as well as to his tired legs.

They were all relieved. The previous day had seen them climbing steadily up a trail become increasingly steep. Though it was not mentioned, each of them found the possibility of a night's sleep in a real bed quietly exhilarating.

"What an appealing little place." His fingers locked in the straps of his backpack, Simna ibn Sind's step had become positively jaunty as he gave Knucker a friendly nudge. "I admit I was a bit worried about what we might find, but if anything you understated its charm." He lowered his voice slightly. "I wonder if the local ladies are as attractive as their surroundings?"

As the travelers entered the unfenced, unguarded hamlet,

people looked up from their work to smile and wave. Used to encountering the occasional traveler in their mountain hideaway, they were not wary of the three men and their imposing feline companion. Their unforced greetings were, if anything, effusive.

As Knucker led them deeper into the thoughtfully laid-out community, Ehomba admired the wonderful homes and shops. None rose higher than a single story, though many boasted sharply raked roofs that accommodated spacious lofts. Every exposed beam and post, board and railing had been carved with care and attention. Crossbeams terminated in the beaked heads of forest birds. More animals than the herdsman could count leaped and browsed and slumbered and inclined graceful wooden necks to sip from pools of richly grained carved water.

There were wooden flowers in profusion, gaily painted to approximate their natural tints. The shutters that flanked open, glass-free windows were inscribed with mountain scenes, and the fences that enclosed neat yards and gardens were comprised of pickets of every imaginable style and size. Small stone wells were topped with sheltering roofs of all possible shapes, from round to octagonal.

Each shop or storefront was engraved with scenes that depicted the profession they housed. The entrance to the village cobbler's was lined with oversized wooden shoes in several styles and varieties. A smithy boasted the unique distinction of displaying assorted iron and other metal objects carved in wood. Wooden rolls and muffins, pies and cookies outside the bakery looked fresh enough to eat. Not merely the flowers, but a great many of the other sculptures had been painted with as much skill as they had been carved.

The undersized streets that separated the storybook buildings were hard-packed earth, but the travelers kicked up no dust as they walked. The reason for this became apparent when they encountered a cluster of women bending to pick up any forest debris while pushing heavy horsehair brushes along in front of them.

"I admire their cleanliness." Simna smiled and bowed gallantly as they passed the street sweepers. Several of the women smiled and curtsied in return. "But sweeping the dirt's a bit much."

"I recall another town we passed through that was obsessed with cleanliness." Ehomba's expression was unflappable as ever, but he was keeping a careful watch on the buildings they passed. "Do you remember? We had problems there."

"Hoy, but this is only a little village. I wouldn't expect to find the same kind of trouble here."

The herdsman was unable to relax. "I do not like things that are too perfect."

"Fine." Bending over, Simna spat on the herdsman's foot. "There. Something that's not perfect. Feel better now?"

Glancing down, the tall southerner ignored the trickle of saliva. "I have been drooled on by many animals. Spittle does not make something imperfect."

The swordsman shook his head sadly. "I hope your wife and kids are more spirited than you, Etjole, or it's a dull, dead family life you lead for certain."

Ehomba turned to his friend. "I am told by others that Mirhanja is among the liveliest and most engaging of women. Certainly she seems so to me."

"Or maybe it's just in comparison to you, bruther. In your company, a rock would appear the essence of merrymaking."

"You are not the first to assert that if I have any faults, a sometimes overriding seriousness might be among them."

"Might be?" The herdsman chortled in disbelief. "Hoy, long bruther, and the moon might be far away, the oceans deep, and women fickle. Yes, you might tend to the sedate just a trifle. But that's all right—we don't hold it against you." He looked around at the others. "Do we, friends?"

"Not I," professed Knucker quickly.

"I find you all infantile and silly in the extreme." Ahlitah avowed this with utter seriousness. "Among humans, the most thoughtful strive long and hard to attain the exalted level of perfect twit."

"That's profound," Simna retorted, "coming from one who proclaims the location of his home by pissing all around it."

"Look, there's the inn!" Knucker made the announcement hastily and a bit too loudly. Swordsman and litah glared at one another for a long moment, whereupon the disputation was set aside by mutual unspoken consent, as had been dozens of similar arguments.

Splendid as had been the decorations they had beheld throughout the town, those fronting the inn put all their carved predecessors to shame. It was still only a single-story structure, but the upper loft or attic was proportionately larger in scale, allowing for a number of rooms to be located above the main floor. Not only forest creatures but inanimate inventions of the wood-carvers' fancy stared out from the wide, handsomely milled entrance. There were oaken arabesques and pine flutings, rain clouds of spruce overhanging redwood mountains, and much, much more.

Following Knucker up the steps, they found themselves in an anteroom empty but for a plump, rosy-cheeked woman in her midthirties. She was using a fine-whisked broom to tidy the highly polished hardwood floor. Strain though he might, Ehomba could not see that there was anything to sweep. To his eyes the floor appeared immaculate.

"Welcome, visitors!" She smiled expansively. "Welcome to Netherbrae. I hope that you will fine our rooms comfortable, our linens sweet-smelling, and our food and drink to your liking."

"I'm sure we will," Simna assured her. "I take it you can accommodate four of us?"

"Oh yes, certainly!" Leaning her broom against a wall that was no less spotless than the floor, she clasped her hands together and nodded hospitably, "It is a slow time of year for us and we are glad to have your trade. You should know that there will be a townsparty here tonight. Naturally, as guests, you are invited."

"A party!" The swordsman nodded approvingly. "I don't remember the last time I was at a party." He grinned teasingly at Ehomba. "It certainly wasn't in *your* company." Turning back to their congenial and proper hostess, he added, "We'd be delighted to attend."

Her smile flickered, but only for an instant. "I must have misunderstood. You said that there were four of you? But I see only three."

Turning slightly, Ehomba nodded in the direction of the litah. Having entered late, the big cat had settled down onto its belly, its front legs stretched out in front of it. "Three men, and one feline."

Their hostess's smile did not waver, but a new and unexpectedly biting sternness crept into her voice. "Surely you don't expect that great black thing to join you in your room?"

"Ahlitah is one with us," Ehomba explained. "Why can he not stay? He is intelligent, and can speak as well as any man."

"That is not so." The black cat spoke without lifting his head. "I can speak better."

It required a visible effort, but their hostess managed to maintain her smile. "It is a filthy animal!"

All of a sudden the paint that highlighted the skillful wood carvings outside seemed to dim slightly, the perfectly trimmed rows of flowers to reveal one or two weeds. Seeing the herdsman's jawline tighten uncharacteristically, Simna stepped quickly forward.

"Of course it is, m'dear, and we quite understand. My tall friend here"—he jerked a thumb in Ehomba's direction—"comes from a land far to the south, where shepherds often stay out in the fields with their herds and flocks for days on end. So he's used to being with animals and finds it only natural to sleep in their company. Furthermore, he's unfamiliar with towns. Might I ask, lady, if there is anyplace where our cat could find shelter?"

Much mollified, the proprietress nodded to her right. "There are stables around back. At the moment they're unoccupied, so that monstrous great creature won't have any mounts to disturb. There's water out there, and plenty of straw, and it will keep some of the chill away. It gets cold up here in the Hrugars."

"I'm sure that'll be okay." Grinning tensely, the swordsman turned to look at the nonchalant Ahlitah. "Won't it?"

The big cat's face twitched slightly. It might have been a shrug. "I'd as soon not smell humans."

"And I will stay with him." Ehomba was no longer smiling at their hostess. "I know you have your policies. Please do not concern yourself on my account. I prefer a hard bed to a soft one in any case, as my companions can tell you."

"Fine, good!" Muttering softly, Simna turned away from him. "I suppose you expect me to show solidarity by joining you in sharing the delights of the barn?"

"Not at all," Ehomba told him. "You should enjoy your comforts where you can find them."

"That's good to hear, because that's exactly what I'm going to do." The swordsman was insistent. "After that climb out of Bondressey I want to soak in a hot tub, and lie between clean sheets, and awaken warm and rested."

"As well you should." Ehomba looked past him and in-

quired politely, "Around the back of the inn, you said?"
Arms folded, the hostess nodded sternly.

"Sleep well," Simna told him sarcastically. "Knucker and
me here—we're sure going to. Aren't we, friend?"

"I hope so," the little man ventured uncertainly.

"Right! Come on, then." Putting an arm around the hesitant Knucker, the swordsman started past the proprietress
and up the hall. "If you would show us to our room,
m'dear?"

"Gladly." Favoring Ehomba with a last disapproving
look, she turned and took the lead from the two smaller men.

"Out, back, and around." Pivoting, Ehomba led the way
back out through the entrance. The litah rose and followed.

"You don't have to do this, you know," the big cat told
him as they trooped down the front steps and turned to their
right.

"I know that."

"I'm not asking you to keep me company. I enjoy my solitude."

"I know that also. I meant what I said about town beds
being too soft. Straw will be better for me."

"Suit yourself. It makes no difference to me." Ahlitah was
silent until they reached the stable. It was as sturdy and well
made as every other building they had encountered in the
village—even if it was intended only for the housing of
filthy animals. "What about this 'townsparty' tonight?"

"The woman's sharp reaction to you may have been an
anomaly, but I think it would be better to take no chances. If
these people will not allow filthy animals to stay in their inn,
I have a strong feeling that they will not embrace them at
their social gatherings."

Entering the stables, the litah began to hunt for a suitable
resting place to spend the night. "You are probably right,
Etjole Ehomba. I wonder how they feel about entertaining
filthy humans?"

"From the woman's tone of voice I think she was refer ring only to matters of personal hygiene when she used the word 'filthy.' My fear is that bounded emotions may run deeper and nastier than that."

Poking his head into an empty stall, Ahlitah grunted. "Wouldn't surprise me. I'll stay here and catch up on some sleep." He snorted and shook his head, the great black mane swishing back and forth like a gigantic dust mop. "I have been behind on my sleep ever since we left the veldt." Satisfied, he looked up curiously. "Are you going?"

"I have to. Not because I particularly want to, although in spite of their prejudice this is an interesting place, but because I feel it necessary to keep an eye on Simna. When he is not careful of what he says, his mouth can get him into trouble."

"He and I almost have something in common, then. I like to put trouble in my mouth." He emitted a silky growl. "Here's a good place."

Together, they flopped down on the thick pile of hay. It was a recent threshing, still soft and pliable, with a good view of both the front and back entrances to the stables. There Ehomba would rest until suppertime. After that would come the townsparty, which he, as traveler and guest, would attend. So long as he was there to keep Simna's mouth full of food, he knew, the swordsman was unlikely to cause problems.

Taken in the inn's tavern, the evening meal was excellent, as artistically and competently prepared and presented as the building in which it was served. Nor were the three travelers the only ones eating there. Locals began to trickle in with the setting of the sun, finding their way through Netherbrae's immaculate streets with the aid of small, elegantly repoussed tin lanterns. Soon the tavern was alive with laughter and earnest conversation. Men discussed the opening of a new patch of forest to logging, for the village supplied many wood products to Bondressey and Squoy. Women talked children and household tasks, and both genders indulged in much good-natured gossiping.

As the three travelers sat at one of the long communal benches, they spoke mostly among themselves. But as the evening wore on and the tavern became more crowded, the jocularity more general, and the banter more boisterous, they inevitably found themselves drawn into conversation with the locals. Certainly Simna was. Knucker was a hesitant talker, and Ehomba could be downright noncommunicative.

Leaning out of his chair, the swordsman inquired casually of one burly native seated nearby, "So you cut a lot of trees, do you?"

"Why not?" The man's hands were thick and callused from a lifetime of heavy physical labor. "We have lots of trees, and the Bondresseyeans pay well for our timber. Besides, a two-man cross-cut saw makes awfully quick work of carrots, so we might as well use them to cut trees." His companions roared and Simna deigned to smile graciously at the spirited outpouring of bucolic humor.

"Any lady loggers among you?" He grinned hopefully.

The laughter around him died instantly. Grave expressions took the place of the easy affability that had prevailed. "That would be an abomination. No Netherbraen, man or woman, would stand for it."

"Hoy," murmured Simna contritely, "it was just a question. Remember, my friends and I are strangers here."

"That's true . . . yes, that's so . . ." Gradually the group regained its smiles and humor. "A lady logger—talk like that could get a man condemned."

"Condemned?" Ehomba joined the dialogue. "Condemned by whom?"

"Why, by Tragg, of course." The locals looked at one another and shook their heads in mutual commiseration at the visitors' ignorance. "Tragg is the God of wandering forest paths. Whoever follows His way and His teachings will live a long and happy life here in the Hrugar Mountains. So it has always been for the citizens of Netherbrae."

"This is what your priests tell you?" Subsequent to his initial faux pas, Simna tried to couch his comments in the least offensive manner possible.

"Priests?" The men exchanged a glance and, to the swordsman's relief, burst out laughing once again. "We have no priests!"

"We know the truth of what Tragg tells us," avowed another, "because it has always been the truth. We don't need priests to tell us these things. We are as much a part of the Thinking Kingdoms as Melespra or Urenon the Elegant."

"Yes. The only difference is that we choose to live in simpler surroundings." The villager nearest Simna gestured expansively. "No need here for estates or castles. Our homes we decorate with humble wood, enhanced and beautified by our own hands. All of this Tragg tells us."

"Does he also tell you that animals are filthy creatures?" Ehomba asked the question before Simna could catch the gist of it and stop him.

The swordsman was needlessly concerned. Another of the villagers answered freely and without hesitation. "Of course! Whenever we are unsure about anything, we put our faith in the teachings of Tragg and they tell us what to do."

"And these teachings," Ehomba inquired, "they are never wrong?"

"Never," declared several of the men and two of the women in concert.

"But I thought you said that Netherbrae was as one with the Thinking Kingdoms. If you rely on the teachings of Tragg to tell you what to do, then that means you are not thinking about what to do. You are substituting belief for thought."

Leaning close to his friend, Simna whispered urgently, "I've been around a lot, bruther, and based on my experience and travels, I'm telling you it'd be best to drop this line of conversation right now."

"Why?" Ehomba countered innocently. "These are thinking people, inhabitants of one of the Thinking Kingdoms. People who think are not bothered by questions." Raising his voice, he inquired loudly, "Are you?"

"Not at all, friend, not at all!" declared the villager seated across the table from the herdsman. "Belief does not replace thought. It complements it." Grinning broadly, he added, "We think about what we believe in."

"And we believe what we think." Having had a good deal to drink, the woman who concluded the tenet broke out giggling. Her friend quickly joined in, and once again merriment was general around the table.

Ehomba started to say something else, but this time Simna was in his face before the words had time to emerge. "Hoy, bruther, if you've no concern for your own well-being, then have a care for mine, would you? No more of this. A change of subject to something innocuous is in order."

"I—oh, very well." Observing the strain in the swordsman's expression, Ehomba decided to forgo the questions that were piling up inside him—for now. He replaced his intended words with the contents of the ceramic tumbler that had been set out before him.

Someone was speaking from atop a chair near the rear entrance. Ehomba recognized him as the general manager of the inn. Not the owner—that was a title reserved for the husband of the woman they had first met. The speaker had a prominent belly and cleverly coifed mustache that wrapped around much of his jowly face. A logger he was not.

"Friends, visitors! You've seen it before, watched it and wondered, and now tonight, we once more bring it before you to embellish your enjoyment of the evening and the solidarity of our precious community." Pivoting carefully on the slightly shaky chair, he gestured grandly toward the back door. It was particularly wide and tall, with an interesting arched lintel. A sense of anticipation blanketed the crowd. By mutual silent agreement all conversation was muted.

"I give you," the general manager proclaimed, "the nightmare!"

Cheers and whoops of expectation rose from the crowd, an atavistic howl that rattled the walls of the tavern. By dint of their early arrival and fortuitous seating, Ehomba and his companions had an unobstructed view of the arched doorway. Now they looked on in silence as the doors were flung wide.

Though the cage rolled easily on four thick wheels, it still took the combined exertions of four strong men to pull and push it into the tavern. The spokes of the wheels, the hubs, and the cage itself were decorated with etchings of mystic signs and mysterious figures. Even the bars and the massive padlock were made of wood, lovingly polished to reveal a fine, dark grain. Despite the height of the arched double doorway, the top of the cage barely cleared the twenty-foot-high opening.

Standing inside the cage and gripping two of the bars was a ten-foot-tall something.

It was as massive as it was tall, and Ehomba estimated its weight as equal to that of any three large men. It was hard to tell for sure because the creature was covered entirely in long, thick strands of dark gray hair streaked with black. The skull was more human than simian, and the black eyes that glared out from beneath massive, bony brows were full of rage. The nose was not as flat as an ape's, but not as forwardly pronounced as a human's. Through the waving, gesticulating arms of the crowd the herdsman thought he could make out five fingers on each hand and as many toes on each foot.

Not an ape, then, but not a member of the family of man, either. Something in between, or an offshoot unknown to the people of Naumkib. The more it roared and rattled the tree-sized wooden bars of its rolling cage, the more the crowd jeered and hooted.

Yelling an unimaginative and slightly obscene insult, someone in the throng stood up and threw the remnants of a warm meat pie at the cage. Passing through the bars, it struck the nightmare just above its right eye. Wincing, it turned to roar at its assailant. The laughter this induced caused food to come flying from all directions: pies, half-finished legs of meat, vegetables, gnawed rolls greasy with butter. At first the creature withstood the barrage and continued to bellow defiance at its captors. But gradually its roars and howls died down. Assaulted by food and taunts from every direction, it eventually retreated to the middle of its cage. There it sat, hunched over and no longer trying to deflect the edible missiles, doing its best to ignore the onslaught.

"Make it get up and bellow again!" someone yelled laughingly.

"Somebody get a long stick and poke it!" suggested another.

Ultimately the mob grew bored. Evidently this was not the first time they had amused themselves at the pitiful creature's expense. Ignoring the cage and its lone occupant in their midst, they returned to their banqueting, trading jokes and gossip and casual conversation as if nothing out of the ordinary had transpired. Simna and Knucker slipped back into the easy camaraderie tendered by the citizens of Nether-brae more comfortably than did Ehomba.

"That's a beast and a half." The swordsman tore into a

hunk of fresh, heavily seeded bread. "Where'd you capture it?"

A woman seated across and slightly down the table from him replied. Not because it was her place, but because all the men within range of the swordsman's question had their mouths full of food.

"It was taken in the forest far from here, where the Hrugar Mountains begin to climb toward the sky." She sipped daintily at her tumbler. "Not far from the lowest slopes of Mount Scathe. It took two parties of men to bring it down with ropes, and three to haul it back to Netherbrae on a makeshift sled."

"An impressive feat." Ehomba spoke quietly, as always. "What was it doing?"

She blinked at him, her eyes still lively but her tone momentarily confused. "Doing?"

"When it was captured. Who was it attacking, or threatening?"

The husky man seated next to her cleared his throat and replied before she could respond. "It wasn't attacking or threatening anyone, friend. I know—I was there." He grinned proudly. "I was one of the woodcutters who brought it down. Such strength! It fought us like a mad thing, which of course is what it is. A savage, unclean beast."

Ehomba considered. "But surely the forest is full of animals. Why take this one from where it was living and bring it all the way back to Netherbrae?"

"Because it's not useful." Another man spoke up. "The wapiti and the rabbit, the birds and the rodents, are all useful, all nutritious." With a piece of pork he gestured in the direction of the now silent cage. The slice of meat flapped loosely in his hand. "Just by looking at this thing you can tell it's no good to eat."

The herdsman nodded understandingly. "Then why go to the trouble of bringing it all the way back here?"

Several of the diners exchanged looks of incomprehension. "Why, because its presence was defiling our forest!" another woman declared. Her explanation was seconded by numerous murmurs from those seated nearby.

The oldest man at the table spoke up. "The teachings of Tragg tell us that the forest and everything in it belongs to us, the people of Netherbrae. We have followed those teachings and they have been good to us. Tragg is much pleased. The trees are ours to cut down, the nuts and berries ours to gather, the animals ours to eat. Anything not of use must be given a use, or eliminated." A chorus of exuberant "Aye!"s rose from his fellow citizens.

"You have seen how clean our community is. That is because we are careful to get rid of everything that is not useful."

"Very interesting," Ehomba admitted. "What about us?"

Next to him Simna paused in midbite. Knucker's eyes began to dart and his fingers to fidget. But the silence that enveloped their table lasted barely a second or two before the old man responded.

"Visitors bring stories of other lands, new knowledge, and amusing tales. These things are useful. We look forward to them because we do not travel ourselves." Looking around the table, he grinned and nodded. "Why should we? Who would ever want to leave Netherbrae?"

This time assent was not only general but loud, amounting to cheering more than mere agreement. Ehomba thought some of it might have been a little forced, but in the general melee of good humor it was hard to tell for certain.

"If the beast is of no use, why do you keep him around?"

"Of no use?" Rising from his seat, a slim young man hefted a small bowl of table scraps. "Watch this!" Drawing back his arm, he threw it at the cage. It described a graceful arc before striking the massive, hairy back right between the shoulders and bouncing off. The cowed creature shuffled forward an inch or so, looking neither up nor around.

Sitting down, the young man laughed heartily. His companions at the table laughed with him.

"It amuses us." The words of the woman who had first spoken broke through the general jocularity. "By letting children throw things at it, their fear of the beasts that inhabit the deep forest is lessened. And in this we feel we are truly heeding the word of Tragg, and not straying from the example he long ago set for us Himself."

Someone passed the herdsman a plate full of fat pulled from various meats. "Here, friend. Wouldn't you like to have a go yourself?"

A softly smiling Ehomba declined politely. "Your offer is generous, and in the deep spirit of friendship we have already come to admire here in Netherbrae, but since I am not a true follower of Tragg and am sadly ignorant of so much of his teaching, I feel it would be presumptuous of me to participate in one of his ceremonies. Better not to waste it."

"Who said anything about wasting it?" To the accompaniment of encouraging hoots and hollers, one of the other women seated at the table rose and threw the plate. Her arm was not as strong or her aim as accurate as that of the young man who had preceded her. To much good-natured merriment, the plate fell short and clanged off the floor of the cage. But she was applauded for her effort.

His face an unreadable mask, Ehomba rose from the bench. "We do not know how to thank you enough for this wonderful evening, and for the hospitality all of you have shown us. But we are tired from our long walk today, and must be on our way tomorrow. So I think we will turn in."

"Tired?" Raising his recently refilled tumbler, a gleeful Simna saluted their new friends and surroundings. "Who's tired?"

Glaring down, the herdsman put a hand on his companion's shoulder. A surprisingly heavy hand. "Tomorrow we must start across the Hrugar Mountains. We will need our rest."

"Hoy, bruther, and I'll get mine." The terse-voiced swordsman brusquely shook off the long-fingered hand. "I'm your friend and confidant, Etjole. Not one of your village adolescents."

Next to him, a determined Knucker raised his own drinking utensil. "I'm not tired, either. I can't remember the last night I had such a good time!" Hesitantly, he sipped from his cup. When no one objected, he sipped harder.

"Same here." Simna smiled up at the dour-faced herdsman. "You're so concerned, bruther, use some of your sorceral skills. Sleep for the three of us!"

"Perhaps I will." Disappointed in his companions, Ehomba rose and headed for the entrance to the tavern that led to the inn's outer office and the front door, leaving his friends to their elective dissolution.

Across the table, two men leaned forward, inquisitive uncertainty on their faces. "Is your traveling companion truly a sorcerer?"

Simna took a slug from his tumbler, ignoring the fact that Knucker was once more imbibing steadily. Furthermore, the little man gave no indication of stopping or slowing down. But the swordsman was feeling too content to notice, or to object.

"I'm convinced of it, but if so he's the strangest one imaginable. Insists he's nothing but a herder of cattle and sheep, refuses to use magic even to save his own life. Depends on alchemy he insists arises not from any skills of his own, but from that bequeathed to him by old women and such of his village." The swordsman looked in the direction of the main portal but Ehomba had already disappeared, on his way to rejoin the fourth member of their party in the stables around back.

"I've seen much of the world in my travelings and met many strange folk, but by Giskret's Loom, he's for surely the most peculiar and mysterious of the lot." Silent for a moment after concluding his explanation, he shrugged and downed the contents of his tumbler. Accompanied by smiles and laughter, it was quickly refilled.

"He didn't look like much of a sorcerer to me," declared one of the men.

"You'd far sooner convince me that someone that odd-looking dotes on the droppings of cows!" quipped another. General jollity followed this jest.

Simna knew the not-so-veiled insult to his friend should have bothered him. But he was having too good a time, and the middling attractive woman at the far end of the table was eyeing him with more than casual curiosity. So he thrust the abrasive comment aside and smiled back at her. He'd always been good at ignoring that which distressed him, especially when it came at the ultimate expense of others.

Alongside him, a happy Knucker held out his tumbler to be refilled. Within that sturdy container many things could be drowned—including promises made.

XVIII

Nothing moved in the dark depths of the tavern. The still air stank of stale beer and spilled wine, but it was not silent. Gruntings and snortings that would have been at home in any sty rose from the dozen or so intoxicated bodies that lay sprawled on the floor and, in one case, across a table from which plates and other dinner debris had been solicitously removed. All of the unconscious were male. For a woman to have been left in such circumstances would have gone against the teachings of Tragg. Under the Traggian codex, men and women had clearly defined roles. Public inebriation was not an option available to representatives of the female gender.

When the managers of the inn had finally called a halt to the communal townsparty, the majority of revelers had contentedly tottered or been carried off to their homes. Only the most severe celebrants were left behind to sleep off the aftereffects of the festivities safely. As for the managers themselves, they and their assistants had long since finished cleaning up what they could and had retired to their own rooms.

Amidst the general silence and intermittent snoring, one figure moved. It did not rise from the floor or tables, but instead entered through the front portal. This was not locked and stood open to the outside. No one locked their doors in Netherbrae. There was no need for anyone to do so. The adherents of Traggism had complete faith in one another. They had to; otherwise the entire system would collapse upon the fragility of its own moral underpinnings.

Picking his way among the tables and benches, Ehomba occasionally had to step over or around a somnolent villager. Making less noise than a moth, he approached the motionless cage. It remained where it had been left, in the middle of the tavern, its sole occupant squatting in the center of the caged floor, hunched over and still. Piles of food dimpled the interior and clung stubbornly to the wooden bars.

The herdsman halted a few feet from the rear of the wheeled cage. For several moments he simply stood there, contemplating the massive, hirsute back of the imprisoned creature. Then he said, in a soft but carrying whisper, "Hello."

The nightmare did not move, did not react.

"I am sorry for the way you were treated. It was a saddening display. It is at such times that I feel closer to the apes. There are people whose sense of self-worth is so poor that the only way they can feel better is to degrade and humiliate something else. Preferably something that cannot fight back. I just wanted to tell you that before I left here, so that you would know there are human beings who do not think that way." His encouraging smile was a splash of whiteness in the dim light. "It is too bad you cannot understand what I am saying, but I wanted to say it anyway. I had to say it." His business in Netherbrae concluded, he turned to leave.

A voice, deep and hesitant, halted him in the darkness. "I can understand."

Turning back to the cage, Ehomba walked rapidly but silently around to the other side. From beneath the jutting escarpment of bone that was the creature's brow, dark eyes peered out at the herdsman. One finger traced tiny, idle circles in the pile of slowly decaying food that littered the floor of the cage.

"I had a feeling. I was not sure, but the feeling was there." The herdsman nodded ever so slightly. "It was something in your eyes."

A soft grunt emerged from between the bars. "You not from this place."

"No." Taking a chance, trusting his instincts, Ehomba moved a little closer to the enclosure. "I am from the south. Farther to the south than you can probably imagine."

"I from north. Not so far north."

"We were told how you came to be here." With little else to offer the caged creature, the herdsman proffered another smile. "I did not enjoy the telling of it, just as I do not enjoy seeing anyone being forced to endure such conditions. But there was nothing I could do. My friends and I are strangers here. We are few; the villagers are many."

"Understand." The terse reply was devoid of accusation.

"I am a shepherd of cattle and sheep. My name is Etjole Ehomba."

"I am Hunkapa Aub."

Fresh silence ensued. After several moments of shared contemplation, the herdsman looked up. "Would you like to get out of that cage, Hunkapa Aub?"

Large, sensitive eyes opened a little wider. The hunch in the creature's back straightened slightly. "Hunkapa like." Then the humanoid expression fell once again. "Cage locked."

"Where is the key?"

"No good." The great hairy skull shook slowly from side to side. "Village teacher got."

Ehomba chewed his lower lip as he considered the situation. "It does not matter. I have something with me that I think can open the lock."

The creature that called itself Hunkapa Aub did not dare to show any enthusiasm, but he could not keep it entirely out of his voice. "A tool?" When the herdsman nodded once, the hulking arthropoid rose slightly and approached the bars. "Ehomba go get tool!"

By way of reply the herdsman turned and made his way back out of the tavern as silently as he had entered. In the ensuing interval, the caged creature sat unmoving, its eyes never leaving the doorway through which the visiting human had vanished.

Hope was high beneath all that thick gray hair when Ehomba returned. He was not alone. A muscular jet-black shape was with him, gliding wraithlike across the floor despite its bulk. Together, they approached the rear of the cage. Hunkapa turned to scrutinize the herdsman's companion. Dark eyes met yellow ones. Silent understanding was exchanged.

With a comradely hand Ehomba brushed the bushy black mane. "My tool. Ahlitah, meet Hunkapa Aub."

The big cat's growl was barely audible. "Charmed. Can we get out of here now?"

Extending an arm, the herdsman pointed. "Lock."

Padding forward, the litah contemplated the heavy clasp. It was made of ironwood, umber with black streaks. Opening its massive jaws, the cat bit down hard and chewed. The crunching sound of wood being pulverized resounded through the room. It was not a particularly alarming sound. Nevertheless, Ehomba wished there was less of it.

A few querulous grunts rose from the scattered bodies, but none rose to seek the source of the gnawing. Several moments of concerted feline orthodontic activity resulted in a pile of sawdust and splinters accumulating on the floor. Stepping back, Ahlitah spat out bits and pieces of ironwood. All that was left of the lock was a curved section of latch that Ehomba promptly removed. Lifting the arm that barred the cage door, he retreated to stand alongside the impatient Ahlitah.

Tentatively, Hunkapa Aub reached out with one huge hand and pushed. The barred wooden door swung wide. Lumbering silently forward, he checked first to the right and then to the left, his hands holding on to either side of the opening. Then he stepped down onto the tavern floor. His arms were proportionately longer than his legs, but his knuckles did not quite scrape the ground. How much of him was ape, how much man, and how much something else, Ehomba was not prepared to say. But there was no mistaking the meaning of the tears that welled up in the erstwhile nightmare's eyes.

"No time for that." With a soft snarl, Ahlitah started back toward the entrance. "I'll take him to the stable and we'll wait for you there. You'll be wanting to go upstairs and drag those two worthless humans you insist on calling your friends out of bed."

"I will be quick," Ehomba assured the big cat.

Marking the room numbers as he made his way down the narrow passage, Ehomba halted outside number five. As was customary in Netherbrae, the door was not locked. Lifting the latch as quietly as he could, he pushed open the door and stepped inside. The room was in total darkness, the curtains having been pulled across the window.

A sharp blade nicked his throat and a hand clutched at his left wrist, pulling it back behind him.

"It's too late for maid service and too early for breakfast, so what the Oojorworn are . . . ?" The fingers around his unresisting wrist relaxed and the knife blade was withdrawn. "Etjole?"

Turning in the darkness, Ehomba saw the subdued glint of

moonlight on metal as the swordsman resheathed his knife. "Having trouble sleeping, Simna?"

"I always sleep light, long bruther. Especially in a strange bed. That way I feel more confident about waking up in the morning." Weapon secured, the shorter man stepped away from the wall. "You jested that I might be having trouble sleeping. I might ask you the same question."

"Get your clothes on and your things together. We are leaving."

"What, now? In the middle of the night? After that meal?" To underline his feelings the swordsman belched meaningfully. The sound echoed around the room.

"Yes, now. After that meal. Ahlitah is waiting for us in the stables—with another. His name is Hunkapa Aub."

Grumbling pointedly, Simna began slipping into his clothes. "You pick up companions in the oddest times and places, bruther. Where's this one from?"

"From a cage."

"Hoy, from a—" In the darkness of the room the swordsman's voice came to a halt as sharply as his movements. When he spoke again, it was with a measure of uncertainty as well as disbelief. "You broke that oversized lump of animated fur out of its box?"

"He is more than that. Hunkapa Aub is intelligent. Not very intelligent, perhaps, but no mindless animal, either."

"Bruther, no matter where we go you seem to have this wonderful knack for endearing yourself to the locals. I wish you'd learn to repress it." Darkness blocked the faint light from the single curtained window as the swordsman slipped upraised arms through a shirt. "When they discover their favorite subject for culinary target practice has gone missing they're very likely to connect it to this late-night leave-taking of ours."

"Let them," Ehomba replied curtly. "I have little use for

people like this, who would treat any animal the way they have, much less an intelligent creature like Hunkapa Aub."

Simna stepped into his pants. "Maybe they don't know that he's intelligent."

"He talks." Anger boiled in the herdsman's tone as he looked past his friend. "Where is Knucker?"

"Knucker?" In the dusky predawn Simna quickly assembled his belongings. "You know, bruther, I don't believe the little fella ever came upstairs. Near as I can recall, when I left the townsparty traveling two steps forward, one step back, he was still drinking and carousing with the locals."

"Are you ready yet?"

"Coming, coming!" the swordsman hissed as he struggled to don his pack. "Ghobrone knows you're an impatient man. You'd think it was this Visioness Themaryl who was waiting for you downstairs."

"If only she was." Ehomba's tone turned from curt to wistful. "I could make an end to this, and start back home."

They found Knucker not far from where the three of them had originally been seated, sprawled on the floor with limbs flopped loosely about him. The stench of alcohol rose from his gaping, open mouth and his once clean attire was soiled with food, liquor, and coagulated vomit. His face was thick with grime, as if he had done some serious forehead-first pushing along the floor.

"Giela," Simna muttered. "What a mess!"

Kneeling by the little man's side, Ehomba searched until he found a wooden serving bowl. Tossing out the last of its rapidly hardening contents, he inverted it and placed it beneath Knucker's greasy hair. It was not a soft pillow, but it would have to do. This accomplished, he set about trying to rouse the other man from his stupor.

Simna looked on for a while before disappearing, only to return moments later with a jug three-quarters full. Watering Knucker's face as if it were a particularly parched houseplant, he kept tilting the jug until the contents were entirely gone. The last splashes did the trick, and the little man came around, sputtering slightly.

"What—who's there?" Espying the basics of a friendly face in the darkness, he smiled beatifically. "Oh, it's you, Etjole Ehomba. Welcome back to the party." Frowning abruptly, he tried to sit up and failed. "Why is it so quiet?"

Disgust permeated the herdsman's whispered reply. "You are drunk again, Knucker."

"What, me? No, Ehomba, not me! I had a little to drink, surely. It was a party. But I am not drunk."

The herdsman was implacable. "You told us many times that if we helped you, you would not let this happen to you again."

"Nothing's happened to me. I'm still me."

"Are you?" Staring down at the prostrate, flaccid form, Ehomba chose his next words carefully. "What are the names of my children?"

"Daki and Nelecha." A wan smile creased the grubby face. "I know everything, remember?"

"Only when you are drunk." Rising, the herdsman turned and started past Simna. "Paradox is the fool at the court of Fate."

Simna reached out to restrain him. "Hoy, Etjole, we can't just leave him here like this."

In the dark room, hard green eyes gazed unblinkingly back at the swordsman's. "Everyone chooses what to do with their life, Simna. I chose to honor a dying man's request. You chose to accompany me." He glanced down at the frail figure on the floor. Knucker had begun to sing softly to himself. "He chooses this. It is time to go."

"No, wait. Wait just a second." Bending anxiously over the chanting intoxicant, Simna grabbed one unwashed hand and tugged firmly. "Come on, Knucker. You've got to get up. We're leaving."

Watery eyes tried to focus on the swordsman's. "Your father abandoned your mother when you were nine. You have no sisters or brothers and you have always held this against your mother, who died six years ago. You have one false tooth." Raising his head from the floor, the little man turned to grin at the silent, stolid Ehomba. "There are 1,865,466,345,993,429 grains of sand on the beach directly below your village. That's to the waterline with the tide in. Tomorrow it will be different." Letting go of the dirty hand, Simna straightened slowly.

"The axis of the universe is tilted fourteen point three-seven degrees to the plane of its ecliptic. Matter has twenty-eight basic component parts, which cannot be further subdivided. A horkle is a grank. Three pretty women in a room together suck up more energy than they give off." He began to giggle softly. "Why a bee when it stings? If you mix sugar cane and roses with the right seeds, you get raspberries that smell as good as they taste. King Ephour of Noul-ud-Sheraym will die at eight-twenty in the evening of a moa bone stuck in his throat. I know everything."

A grim-faced Simna was watching Ehomba carefully. Finally the herdsman bent low over the prone body and forestalled the little man's litany of answers with an actual question.

"Tell me one thing, Knucker."

"One thing?" The giggling grew louder, until it turned into a cough. "I'll tell you anything!"

Eyes that could pick out a potential herd predator lurking at a great distance bored into the other man's. "Can you stop drinking whenever you want to?"

Several choking coughs brought up the answer. "Yes. Whenever I want to."

Ehomba straightened. "That is what I needed to know." Without another word, he stepped around the querulous Simna and started for the door. With a last glance down at the giggling, coughing Knucker, the swordsman hurried to catch up to his friend.

"Ahlitah and Hunkapa will be growing anxious. We will pick up my pack and leave this place." As they reached the open entrance to the inn, Ehomba nodded in the direction of the still dusky horizon. "With luck and effort we will put good distance between ourselves and Netherbrae before its citizens connect Hunkapa's disappearance with our departure."

A troubled Simna kept looking back in the direction of the tavern. "But he answered your question! You said yourself that he told you what he needed to know."

"That is so." Exiting the inn, they started down the entryway steps. "You were right all along, Simna ibn Sind. When he is drunk he believes that he knows everything. And it is true that when he is drunk he knows a great deal. Perhaps more than anyone else who has ever lived. But he does not know everything." Exiting the building, they turned rightward and strode briskly toward the stables. "His answer to my question proves that there is at least one thing he does not know."

Anxiously watching the shadows for signs of early-rising Netherbraeans, the swordsman wondered aloud, "What's that, bruther?"

Ehomba's tone never varied. "Himself."

XIX

Simna quickly recovered from the shock of hearing their new companion hold up his end of a conversation, albeit with a severely limited vocabulary. As Ehomba had hoped, they succeeded in putting many miles between themselves and the picture-perfect village of Netherbrae before the sun began to show over the surrounding treetops. Exhausted from what had become a predawn run, they settled down in the shade of a towering gingko tree. Even Ahlitah was tired from having not only to hurry, but also to spend much of the time scrambling uphill.

While his companions rested down and had something to eat, Ehomba stood looking back the way they had come. It was impossible to see very far in the dense deciduous forest, so closely packed were the big trees, but as near as was able to tell, there was no sign of pursuit from Netherbrae. Nor could he hear any rustling of leaf litter or the breaking of more than the occasional branch.

"How's it look, bruther?" Simna ibn Sind glanced up from his unappetizing but nourishing breakfast of dried meat and fruit.

"Nothing. No noise, either. And the forest creatures are chattering and chirping normally. That says to me that nothing is disturbing their morning activities, as would be the case if there was even a small party of pursuers nearby." He turned back to his friends. "Perhaps they do not think Hunkapa worth pursuing."

"Or too dangerous," Simna suggested. "Or maybe there's a convenient proscription in the teachings of Tragg against hunting down and trying to recapture a prisoner who's already escaped." After gulping from his water bag, he splashed a little on his face. In these high mountains, with sparkling streams all around, there was no need to conserve. "There's just one problem."

"What is that?" Ehomba asked patiently.

The swordsman gestured toward the lofty peaks that broke the northern horizon. "Knucker was our guide. How the Garamam are we going to find our way through to this Hamacassar? Without a guide we could wander around in these forests and mountains for years."

Ehomba did not appear to be overly concerned. "Knucker needs to find himself before he goes looking for someplace like Hamacassar. Easier to find a city than oneself." He nodded at the beckoning peaks. "All we have to do is continue on a northward track and eventually we will come out of these mountains. Then we can ask directions of local people to the city."

"That's all well and good, bruther. But scrambling over a couple of snow-capped peaks takes a lot more time than walking along a well-known trail. We could try following a river, but first we have to find one that flows northward instead of south, and then hope it doesn't turn away to west or east, or loop back on itself. A guide would probably cut weeks or months off our walking and save us from having to negotiate some rough country." He stoppered his water bag.

"I've been lost in mountains like these before and, let me tell you, I'd rather take a whipping from a dozen amazons."

"You would rather take a whipping from a dozen amazons even if you were not lost," the herdsman retorted. "All we can do is do our best. Between the two of us I am confident we will not find ourselves wandering about aimlessly for very long."

"Hunkapa see Hamacassar."

"What's that?" Startled, Simna looked up from the last of his dried biscuit. Ehomba too had turned to stare at the newest member of the group. Dozing against a great arching root, the black litah ignored them all.

Ehomba proceeded to question their hulking companion. Seated, Hunkapa Aub was nearly at eye level with the tall southerner. "Hunkapa see Hamacassar," he repeated convincingly.

"You mean you've been in the port city?" Simna didn't know whether to laugh or sneer. Though the shaggy brute was slow, he was not entirely dumb. The swordsman decided to do neither. "How did you find it? Accommodations to your liking?"

"Not visit Hamacassar." Hunkapa Aub spoke slowly and carefully so as to keep both his simple words and even simpler thoughts straight, in his own mind as well as in those of his new friends. "I see." An enormous hairy arm rose and pointed. "From slopes of Scathe Mountain. First mountains go down. Then flat places where men grow foods. Beyond that, way beyond, is river Eynharrmawk—Eynharrowk. On this side Eynharrowk is city Hamacassar." Reaching up, he touched one thick finger to an ear almost entirely obscured by dark gray hair. "See river, go Hamacassar."

Ehomba pondered the creature's words silently. Simna was not as reticent to comment. "Hoy, that were quite a speech, Aub. Why should we believe the least of it?"

"Why would he lie?" Tapping a finger against his lips, Ehomba studied the guileless, open-hearted brute.

"He's not lying." Both men turned to look at the supine Ahlitah. The big cat had rolled over and was lying on its spine with all four feet in the air, scratching itself against the rough-edged woody debris that littered the forest floor.

"How do you know?" Simna's disdain was plain to see.

Concluding its scratching, the litah tumbled contentedly onto its side. "I can smell it. Certain things have strong smells. Females in heat, fresh scat, week-old kills, false promises, and outright lies." He sneezed resoundingly. "The new beast may be slow and ignorant, but he is not a liar. Not in this matter, at least."

Dropping his hand from his lips, Ehomba tried to see into the depths of Hunkapa Aub's being. He was unable to penetrate very far. There was a veil over the creature's soul. Aware that Simna was watching the both of them expectantly, he tried to reassure them all with another question.

"You say that you have seen Hamacassar but have not been there. Have you ever been out of the Hrugar Mountains?"

"No. But been to edge. Stop there." He shook his head and shag went flying in all directions. "Don't like. Humans say and do bad things to Hunkapa Aub."

"But you know the way through the high mountains and down into the foothills on the other side?"

The brute rose sharply to tower over Ehomba. Simna and Ahlitah both tensed—but the hulking creature was only showing his eagerness and enthusiasm. "Hunkapa know! You want Hunkapa take you?"

"We want very much." Ehomba smiled reassuringly.

"Hunkapa not like people cities, but—you save Hunkapa from cage. Hunkapa owe you. So—Start now!" Without another word, their humongous friend turned and headed off in the direction of Mount Scathe, eating up distance with inhumanly long strides.

"Hoy, wait a minute there!" Simna struggled to get his kit together. Ahlitah was already padding off in the brute's wake, with Ehomba not far behind. It took the swordsman some awkward running to catch up to the rest of them.

He hoped they would not run into any free-living, isolated mountain dwellers like old Coubert. Not with Hunkapa Aub and the black litah in the lead. Simna did not want to be responsible for inducing heart failure in some poor, unsuspecting hermit.

Like all high mountain ranges everywhere, the peaks of the Hrugars were loftier than they appeared from a distance. Towering over them all was Mount Scathe, a ragged, soaring complex of crags whose uppermost pinnacle clawed at any cloud passing below sixteen thousand feet. Gashed by deep valleys through which angry, rushing streams commuted to the lowlands, they presented a formidable barrier to anyone advancing from the south.

True to his word, Hunkapa Aub seemed to know exactly where he was going. When Simna complained about having to scramble up a particularly difficult incline, Aub remarked in his own subdued, laconic fashion that the slopes to either side of their ascent were far more difficult. When Ehomba wondered one afternoon why the river valley they were following was curving back southward, their shaggy companion implored him to be patient. Sure enough, by evening the stream and its valley had turned north once again.

They climbed until the air grew thin in their lungs, hardly fit for breathing. In this rarefied clime Ehomba and Simna moved more slowly, and the black litah padded on with head down instead of held high. But their guide was in his element. In the chill, dilute air he seemed to stand taller. His stride became more fluid. His confidence expanded even as his companions began to suffer from second thoughts.

Wearing every piece of clothing he had brought with him and as a consequence looking not unlike one of the unfortunates who haunted the back alleys of Bondressey, Simna kept slapping his hands against his sides to keep warm.

"Are you sure this is the way, o bushy one? We've been walking for many days now."

Hunkapa looked back at the swordsman, who was huffing and puffing to keep up. Actually, Simna welcomed the fast pace. It helped to keep his body temperature elevated. "Right way, Simna. *Only* way." A thick, woolly arm rose to indicate the soaring rock walls that hemmed them in on both sides. "Go up that way, or over there, and you die. Hunkapa okay, but not you, not Etjole." A guileless grin split the bewhiskered face. "You not got hair enough."

"I not got a lot of things," replied the swordsman peevishly. "Right now, patience happens to be one of them."

Though equally as cold and uncomfortable as his shorter companion, Ehomba did not manifest his discomfort as visibly or as vocally. "The mountains lie between where we were and where we are going, Simna. I am as sorry as you that there is no easier way. But we are making good progress." He turned to their pathfinder. "We *are* making good progress, yes?"

"Oh very good, very good!" Back in his beloved mountains, their great, lumbering guide was full of high spirits. His enthusiasm was infectious, and some of it could not help but be imparted to his companions. This lasted for another couple of days.

Then it began to snow.

Only once before had Ehomba seen it snow, during a hunting journey to the far distant mountains that lay to the northeast of his home. It had taken many days to get there, during the coldest time of the year. He remembered marveling at the wet white splotches that fell from the air and melted in his hand, remembered the soft, silent beauty of the sky turning from blue to gray and then to white. It was an experience that had stayed with him all his life.

That snow had melted quickly upon striking the warm ground. This snow remained, to be greeted by that which had preceded it. Instead of melting, it accumulated in piles. In places it reached higher than a man's head, just like drifting sand in the desert. That was what the big, fluffy patches were, he decided. Cold white dunes, rising on the mountain slopes all around them.

Familiar with snow and all its chill, damp manifestations from his homeland and many wanderings, Simna was less than overwhelmed with wonder. What he was, was uncomfortable and increasingly nervous.

"What are you gaping at, Etjole?" Shivering, he did his best to match his stride to that of the tall southerner. "If we don't start down from this place pretty quickly we could freeze to death up here."

"I was just admiring the beauty of it," the herdsman replied. "The land of the Naumkib is all earth colors: yellow and orange, gray and brown. To be surrounded by white is an entirely new sensation for me."

"Is dying a new sensation for you?" Simna indicated their guide, striding along blissfully in front of them. "This is his country. What if he decides to abandon us up here some night, or in the middle of a storm like this? We'd never find our way out. Treasure's no good to a man frozen stiff as an icicle."

"Then think of the treasure, friend Simna. Maybe thinking of it will warm you."

The swordsman's eyes widened slightly. "Then there is a treasure?"

"Oh yes. Greater than any an ordinary king or emperor can dream of. Mountains of gold in all its many manifestations, natural and crystalline, refined and fashioned. Gold as bullion and jewelry, gold that was coined by forgotten ancients, gold so pure you can work it with your bare hands. And the jewels! Such treasures of the earth, in every cut and color imaginable. There is silver too, and platinum in bricks piled high, and precious coral in shades of pink and red and black. More treasure than one man could count in a hundred lifetimes, let alone spend."

Simna eyed his friend reprovingly. "And all this time you've been denying its existence to me. I knew it, I knew it!" One hand clenched into a triumphant fist. "Why tell me now, in this place?"

"As I said. To warm you."

"Well, it's done that." Straightening slightly, the swordsman forcefully kicked his way through the steadily accumulating snow. "Let it blizzard if it wants to! Nothing's going to stop us now. I will not allow it." Tilting back his head, he shouted at the sky. "Do you hear me, clouds? I, Simna ibn Sind, will not permit it!"

By the following morning, with the snow still falling, his energy had flagged. In this the swordsman knew he need not be ashamed, because none of his companions were doing well. Lowlanders all, the unrelenting cold had begun to pick at their remaining reserves of strength, stealing their body heat like vultures biting off mouth-sized bits of flesh from a fresh corpse.

Seated around the morning fire they had managed to build in a snow cave, the two men and one litah huddled as close to the flickering flames as they could without actually catching themselves or their clothing on fire. Seemingly immune to the cold, their good-natured guide had left the cave early to go in search of wood for the blaze. Locating sufficient tinder dry enough to burn had taken him several hours. By the time he had finally returned, it was snowing harder than ever.

"This is not good." Rubbing his long fingers together over the flames, Ehomba spoke solemnly to the hulking form that blocked the entrance hole. Hunkapa Aub was shutting off some of the wind and cold from outside with his own body. "How much farther? How long before we can start down out of the mountains?"

Overhanging brows drew together. "Still several days. Etjole. Hunkapa see this hard for you. I can carry, but only one at a time."

"Our legs are not the problem, Hunkapa." The herdsman fed one of the last dry branches to the little blaze. "It is too cold for us. Our bodies are not used to this kind of weather. And the snow makes it much worse. The wetness freezes our skin when it touches, and blocks out the sun."

"Start down soon." The massive shape shifted its back to seal the entrance to the snow cave more tightly.

"Several days is not soon, Hunkapa. Not in these conditions." Ehomba cast his gaze upward. "If the snow would stop and the sun would come out, then maybe."

Simna shivered beneath his thin clothing. "Bruther, I swear by Gaufremar I'm not sure anymore what you are: sorcerer or steer herder. Maybe both, maybe neither. This cold makes it hard for a man to think straight, so I'm not even sure of what I'm saying right now." He lifted anxious eyes to his friend. "But if ever there was a time for magic, it's come. The rug that walks says it's several days before we can start down? I'm telling you here and now I don't think I can take another morning of this. My skin feels like frozen parchment, my eyes are going blind from staring into this damnable whiteness, and I'm reaching the point where I can't feel my legs anymore. My hips force them forward and when I look down I see that I'm still standing. That's the only way I know that I haven't fallen."

"Simna is right." Everyone turned to look at Ahlitah. The great cat was huddled in a ball alongside the fire. A force of nature, all ebony muscle and fang, even he had exhausted his strength. "Something has to change. We can't go on in this."

It was a momentous moment: the first time since they had begun journeying together that the litah and the swordsman had ever agreed on anything. More than any eloquence or deed it underscored the seriousness of the situation. Both looked to their nominal leader, to the lanky herdsman who sat cross-legged before the inevitably diminishing fire. Ehomba stared into the fading flames for a long time. There was no more wood.

Finally he raised his eyes and looked first at Ahlitah, then at the shivering swordsman. "You know, I am cold too."

Reaching behind him, he dragged his pack to his side. Brushing snow from the flap that Mirhanja had embroidered and beaded herself, he began to search within. Simna leaned forward eagerly, expectantly. Ever since he had joined company with the herdsman, wonderful things had emerged from that pack. Simple things that in Ehomba's skilled, knowing hands had proven to be much more than they first appeared. What would the enigmatic herdsman bring forth this time?

A flute.

Lightly carved of ivory-colored bone, it had eight small holes for fingering and was no bigger around than the herdsman's thumb. Licking his lips to moisten them slightly, Ehomba put the narrow end to his mouth and began to play.

A lilting, sprightly tune, Simna thought as he listened. Foreign but not unfathomable. The herdsman played well, though not skillfully enough to secure a place in the private orchestra of any truly discerning nobleman. Next to him, the litah's tail began to twitch, back and forth, back and forth in time to the music. Hunkapa Aub closed his eyes and rocked slowly from side to side, his immense shoulders rubbing snow from the roof of the temporary shelter.

It went on for some time as the fire died in front of them.

Finally Ehomba lowered the instrument from his lips and smiled thoughtfully. "Well?"

Simna blinked uncertainly. "Well what?"

"Did you like it?"

"Pretty-pretty!" was their guide's enthusiastic comment. Ahlitah let out a snort that was less haughty than usual—a compliment of sorts. But Simna could only stare.

"What do you mean, did I like it? What difference does it make whether I liked it or not?" His voice rose to a shout. "By Gilgolosh, Etjole, we're dying here! I want to see some serious sortilege, not listen to a concert!"

Ehomba did not shed his smile. "Did it make you want to dance?"

The swordsman was so angry he might actually have taken a swing at his friend. What madness was this? That was it, he decided. The terrible, killing cold had manifested itself differently in each of them. With Ehomba, it had finally revealed its insidious self in the form of a hitherto hidden dementia.

"Me dance!" Hunkapa Aub was still rocking slightly from side to side, remembering the music. "Etjole play more!"

"If you like." Bringing the slim flute back to his lips, the herdsman launched into another tune, this one more lively than its predecessor. Simna would have reached out and snatched the accursed instrument from his companion's fingers, but his own hands were too cold.

Rocking to the music, Hunkapa Aub backed out of the opening and into the snow where he could gambol unconfined. Picking up his pack, Ehomba followed him. Ahlitah was not far behind. Muttering to himself, an irate Simna remained in the snow cave until the last vestige of the dissipating campfire vanished in its own smoke. Then he donned his pack and, with great reluctance, crawled outside to rejoin the others.

Halfway out of the cave he stopped, staring. When he finally emerged it was in silence and with eyes wide, gaping at the sky, the ground, and the surrounding mountains. The air was still icy cold, and it was still snowing as hard as ever.

But the snow was dancing.

Not metaphorically, not as the component of some ethereal poetic allusion, but for real.

Across from the entrance to the snow cave two triple helixes of ice crystals were twirling about one another, rippling and weaving as sinuously as a sextet of bleached snakes. The twirling embrace conveyed snow from the sky to the ground in loose, relaxed stripings of white. Nearby, the powdery stuff fell in sheets. That is to say, not heavily, but in actual sheets—layer upon layer of frosty rectangular shapes that sifted down from unseen clouds with alternating layers of clear air between them. As they descended they fluttered from side to side like square birds.

Individual flakes darted in multiple directions, as careful to avoid colliding with one another as a billion choreographed dancers. Miniature snowballs bounced through the air while hundreds of snowflakes combined to form many-pointed flakes hundreds of times larger. The instant they reached some unknown critical mass they fell with a thump into the fresh banks that lined the sides of the icy stream that ran through the narrow valley, leaving behind temporary holes in the snow that assumed the shape of a thousand dissimilar stars.

Snow fell in squares and spheres, in octahedrons and dodecahedrons. Möbius strips of snow turned inward upon themselves and vanished, while shafts of snow winkled their white way through the centers of snowflake toroids. And in between the snow there was light: sunlight pouring down pure and uninterrupted from above. It warmed his face, his hands, his clothes, and sucked the paralyzing chill from his bones.

All of it—shapes and swirls, giant compacted snowballs and individual flakes—danced to the music of the thin bone flute that was being wielded by Etjole Ehomba's skillful hands.

"Come on, then," he exclaimed, looking back to where Simna was standing and staring open-mouthed at the all-engulfing world of white wonder. "Let us make time. I cannot play forever, you know." He smiled, that warm, knowing, ambiguous smile the swordsman had come to know so well. "As you have been so correctly and ceaselessly pointing out for past these many days, it is cold here. If my lips grow numb, I will not be able to play."

As if to underline the seriousness of the herdsman's observation, the minute he had stopped playing the blizzard had settled in once more around them, the falling snow distributed evenly and unremarkably from the sky, and the sun once more wholly obscured.

"You should know better by now than to listen to me, bruther. Keep playing, keep playing!" Simna struggled through the drifts to catch up to his friend.

Turning northward, Ehomba again set mouthpiece to lips and blew. His limber fingers danced atop the flute, rhythmically covering and exposing the holes incised there. The euphony that filled the air anew was light, almost jaunty in expression. It tickled the storm, and the snow responded. As before, a plethora of shapes and suggestions took hold of the weather, buckling and contorting it into a thousand delightful shapes, all of it composed of nothing more animate than frozen water.

As they trekked on, the herdsman continued to sculpt the storm with his music. The shapes it took were endlessly fascinating, full of charm and whimsy and play. But delightful as they were to look upon, Ehomba's companions valued the sun that shafted down between them far more. After a little while Simna found that he was able to remove his outer coverings and hold them up to dry. Ahlitah paced and shook, paced and shook, until even the tips of his mane had regained their optimal fluffiness.

As for Hunkapa Aub, he danced and spun and twirled with as much joy as the snow, his fur-framed expression one of soporific bliss. Even so, he was not so distracted that he failed to notice important turnings in the path. Here, he declared, pointing to an especially large slab of granite protruding from the side of the valley, we turn to the left. And here we leave the river for a while to clamber over a field of talus.

As they marched on in ever-increasing comfort but without being able to truly relax, Simna kept a careful watch over his tall friend. Ehomba's words of warning were never very far from the swordsman's mind. How long *could* he keep tootling on that flute? Hiking and playing each demanded endurance and energy, both of which were in short supply among the members of the little expedition. Ehomba was no exception. Like everyone else, he was cold and tired. A lean, deceptive energy kept him going, but he was no immortal. Without food and rest he too would eventually collapse from exhaustion.

Even as the sun continued to slip-slide down between the pillars and spirals of dancing snow, Simna was keenly aware of the massed, heavy clouds overhead. Shorn of inspiring music, the snow they were dropping would meld once more into a dense, clinging blanket from which there might not be any escape. He willed what strength he could to his tall friend, and tried to remember the melodies of folk songs long forgotten in case the herdsman's musical inspiration began to flag.

Ehomba played on all the rest of the morning and into the afternoon. Conscious of their precarious situation, the travelers did not pause for a midday meal, but instead kept walking. They would rest when the herdsman rested. Until then, it was far more important that they keep moving than eat.

Their bodies screamed for food to turn into heat, but they ignored the demands of their bellies. Time enough later to feed their faces. Time enough later for everything once they were safely out of the mountains.

Ehomba was starting to miss notes, to falter in the middle of alternate tunes, when a gleeful Hunkapa began hopping about with even more ardor than usual.

Simna muttered his reaction to the litah. "I'd say the simpleton has gone mad, except that it would be hard to tell the difference. What's got into him now?"

"Perhaps he is especially inspired by the tune Ehomba is presently fluting," the big cat replied thoughtfully.

"I'm surprised he can hear it." Simna eyed the herdsman worriedly. "For the last hour or so his playing has grown quieter and quieter. I'm afraid our friend may be running out of wind."

The swordsman was right. Ehomba was almost done, his fingers cramped from fingering the holes atop the flute and his lips numb from blowing into the mouthpiece. But Ahlitah was also correct. Their hirsute pathfinder was indeed singularly inspired, but not by the herdsman's playing. As swordsman and cat closed the distance between themselves and their leaping, gyrating guide, they saw for themselves the reason why. Bellowing joyfully into their cold-benumbed ears, Hunkapa Aub confirmed it.

"Go down!" he was hooting. "Go down now; down, down, down!"

Ahead lay more snow-covered slopes. They were no different from the white-clad terrain the travelers had spent the past difficult days traversing, with one notable exception: all inclined visibly downward. Additionally, the stream they had been following intermittently now visibly picked up speed, tumbling and spilling in a series of crystal-clear cataracts toward some far-distant river, as if the water itself could somehow sense the proximity of gentler climes and more accommodating surroundings.

Cloud and fog continued to eddy around them as they picked up the pace. The downgrade enabled them to increase their speed without any additional exertion while simultaneously taking some of the strain off their weary legs. Falling snow sustained its miraculous waltzing, Ehomba's faltering music inspiring ever newer patterns and designs in the air. The only difference was that now the pirouetting snowflakes began to surrender a gradually increasing percentage of the open sky to the unobstructed sun.

By evening they had descended from alpine hardwood forest to slopes thick with dogwood and bottlebrush, oak and elm. The ground was bare of snow, and flowers once more brightened the earth between trees and bracken. As Ehomba finally lowered the flute from his lips, the last dozen snowflakes trickled down from above. Concluding a miniature ballet in twinkling white, they corkscrewed around one another down past the herdsman's face, and paused in the fragile grip of a passing breeze to bow solemnly in his direction. Then, one by one, they struck the warm, rich soil and melted away into oblivion, leaving behind only tiny snowflake ghosts that each took the form of half a second's lingering moisture.

A solicitous Simna promptly came forward to peer into his friend's face. "How are you, bruther? How do you feel?"

"Myph—mimith . . ." Reaching around back, the herdsman took a long, slow draught from his water bag. After wetting his lips, he smacked them together several times before trying one more time to form a reply.

"My mouth is—sore. But otherwise I am all right, Simna. Thank you for inquiring. I am also very hungry."

"We're all hungry." Looking around, the swordsman located the black litah. The big cat was scratching itself against an obliging tree and purring like an old waterwheel.

"Hoy, kitty! What say me and thee go and kill something worth chewing?"

Before Ahlitah could reply, Hunkapa Aub was standing in front of Simna and waving his arms excitedly. "No kill, no hunt!"

"By Gomcpoth, why not? Maybe you're not hungry, fur face, but me and my friends are starving. All that walking and fighting that cold has left us as empty as a triplet of grog buckets on a forty-year-old's first wedding night."

"No need." Taking the protesting swordsman by the arm, their guide dragged him forward. Though the muscular, well-conditioned Simna did his best to resist, it was like trying to brake a runaway mountain.

Hunkapa halted at the edge of an unseen, unsuspected overlook. Once he was exposed to the splendid panorama that was spread out before him, Simna stopped struggling. They were quickly joined by Ehomba and Ahlitah.

Below and beyond the last foothills of the northern Hrugars, lush farmland dotted with numerous towns and small rivers spread out before them. The revealed countryside resembled a landlocked river delta. Hundreds of canals linked the natural waterways, from which the setting sun skipped layers of pink and gold and purple. Several larger communities were big enough to qualify as small cities.

In the far distance, just visible as a sparkling thread of silver below the sky, was the majestic main river into which every canal and stream and waterway between the Hrugars and the horizon flowed. Hunkapa Aub pointed and gesticulated exuberantly.

"See, see! Great river Eynharrowk." His trunk of an arm shifted slightly to the west. "Cannot see from here, but over there, that way, on the great river, is Hamacassar."

"At last." Utterly worn out, Simna sank to the ground as his legs gave way beneath him.

"We are not there yet." Tired as he was, Ehomba chose to

remain standing, perhaps the better to drink in the view that was as full of promise as it was of beauty. "And do not forget that Hamacassar is only a possible waypoint, a place for us to look for a ship with captain and crew brave enough to dare a crossing of the Semordria."

A pleading expression on his grime-flocked face, Simna ibn Sind looked up at his companion. "Please, Etjole—can't we delight in even one moment of pleasure at having lived through this past week? Will you never allow yourself to relax, not even for an instant?"

"When I am again home with my family, friend Simna, then I will relax." He smiled. "Until then, I anoint you in my stead. You are hereby authorized to relax for me."

Nodding understandingly, the swordsman spread both arms wide and fell back flat on the ground. "I accept the responsibility."

Still smiling, Ehomba moved to stand next to the quietly jubilant Hunkapa Aub. "You do not want us to go hunting because you think we can get food more easily in the towns down below."

Their hulking guide nodded vigorously. "Many places, much food. Not see myself, but come here often and spy on flatland people. Hear them talking, learn about flatlands." He eyed the tall southerner questioningly. "We go down now?"

Ehomba considered the sky. Away from the snow and cold, they might have a chance to reach a community before dark. He was not so concerned for himself, but Simna would clearly benefit from a night spent in civilized settings.

"Yes, Hunkapa. Go down now." He put a hand on one massive, shaggy arm. "And Hunkapa—thank you. We could not have made it through these mountains without your guidance."

It was impossible to tell whether the beast was blushing

beneath all that thick hair, but Hunkapa Aub turned away so that Ehomba could not see his face.

"You save me, I help you. Thanks not needed."

Ehomba turned to Simna. "Come on, my friend. We will go down into civilization and find you a bed."

The swordsman groaned piteously. "That means I have to walk again? On these poor feet?"

Their guide immediately moved toward him. "Hunkapa carry."

"No, no, that's not necessary, friend!" The speed with which Simna ascended to his supposedly untenable feet was something to behold.

Together, the four travelers commenced their departure from the lower reaches of the inhospitable Hrugars. As they descended, Ehomba thought to inquire of Hunkapa as to the name of the country they were entering.

"Hunkapa listen to flatlanders talk." He gestured expansively with an imposing arm. "This place all one, called Lifongo. No," he corrected himself quickly, his brows knotting. "Not that." His expression brightened. "Laconda. That it. This place, Laconda."

It was Simna's turn to frown. "Funny. Seems to me I've heard that name mentioned somewhere before, but I can't quite place—" He broke off, staring at Ehomba. The herdsman had stopped in his tracks and was staring, his lips slightly parted, straight ahead. "Hoy, bruther, you all right? You owe someone money here?"

"No, friend Simna. You are correct. You have heard that name before." Turning his head, he met the curious eyes of his companion. "You heard it from me. Laconda is the home of Tarin Beckwith, the noble warrior who died in my arms on the beach below my village." He returned his gaze to the magnificent vista extending before them.

"He cannot ever come home—but now, if fate is willing, perhaps I can return the honor of his memory to his people."

XX

Long before they reached the outskirts of the first town they found themselves in among vast orchards of mango and guava. Planted in even rows and trimmed as neatly as any garden of roses, the trees were heavy with fruit. Eventually the travelers encountered growers and their assistants. Initial cheerful greetings were tempered by fear when the Lacondans caught sight of Hunkapa Aub and the black litah striding along behind the two men, but Ehomba and Simna were quick to reassure the locals that their unusual, and unusually large, friends would do them no harm.

Awed and wide-eyed, the orchardists provided the visitors with instructions on the best way to pass through their country to Laconda North, for it was from there and not Laconda proper that Tarin Beckwith had hailed. Questioning revealed that despite their apparently contented demeanor the people still lived in a permanent state of mourning. Everyone knew the tale of how the perfidious warlock Hymneth the Possessed had come from a far country to steal away the joy of Laconda, the Visioness Themaryl. Of how the finest and most well-born soldiers of both Laconda and Laconda North had sought to effect her return by every means at their disposal, only to return dispirited and defeated, or not to return at all. The warlock Hymneth had taken his prize and vanished, some said across the Semordria itself. A few brave souls from both countries were reputed to have chased him that far. None had ever returned.

"Aren't we going to tell them what you're here for?" Simna kept pace with the tall southerner as they strode along the secondary road of commerce that connected Laconda with its sister state to the north. People on foot, on horse- or antelope-back, or in wagons goggled at the sight of the two men leading the great cat and the hulking beast.

"There is no need." Ehomba kept his attention on the road ahead. It was dusty, but wide and smooth. After struggling through the Hrugars, walking normally felt like flying. "If we stop to speak to these people they will want to know more. Someone will inform the local authorities. Then they will want to hear our story." He glanced over at his friend. "Every day I am away from my home and family is a day I will never have back. When I am old and lie dying I will remember all these moments, all these days that I did not have with them, and regret every one of them. The fates will not give these days back to me." He returned his gaze to the road. "I want as little as possible to regret. We will explain ourselves in Laconda North. That much I owe to the parents of Tarin Beckwith—if they are still alive."

Not only were they alive, but Count Bewaryn Beckwith still sat on the northern throne. This was told to them by the easygoing border guards who manned the station that marked the boundary between the two Lacondas. The armed men marveled at Hunkapa and shied away from Ahlitah, but let them pass through without hesitation. In fact, they were more than happy to see the back of the peculiar quartet.

It was in Laconda North that the travelers encountered the

first fish. Not in the canals or streams that were more numerous in the northern province than in its southern cousin, nor in the many lakes and ponds, but everywhere in the air. They swam through the sky with flicks of their fins and tails, passing with stately grace between trees and buildings. The Lacondans ignored them, paying drifting tuna and trevally, bannerfish and batfish no more mind than they would have stray dogs or cats.

"There's plenty of free-standing water hereabouts in all these canals and ponds, and I feel the humidity in the air," Simna observed as a small school of sardines finned past on their left, "but this is ridiculous!"

"The fish here have learned not only how to breathe air instead of water, but to levitate." Ehomba admired a cluster of moorish idols, black and yellow and white emblems, as they turned off the road to disappear behind a hay barn. "I wonder what they eat?"

His answer was provided by a brace of barracuda that rocketed out from behind a copse of cottonwoods to wreak momentary havoc among a school of rainbow runners. When the silvery torpedoes had finished their work, bits of fish tumbled slowly through the muggy air, sifting to the ground like gray snow. If such occurrences were relatively common, Ehomba knew, the soil hereabouts would be extremely fertile. Having done his turn at tending the village gardens, he knew that nothing was better for fertilizing the soil than fish parts and oil.

Though they did their best, it was impossible to ignore the presence of the airborne fish. The Lacondans they encountered went about their business as if the bizarre phenomenon were a perfectly natural everyday occurrence, as indeed for them it was. Once, they saw a pair of boys laughing and chasing a small school of herring. The boys carried nets of fine, strong mesh attached to long poles. With these they caught not butterflies, but breakfasts.

Ehomba and Simna did not have nets, and Hunkapa Aub was much too slow of hand to grab the darting, agile fish, but they had with them a catching mechanism more effective than any net. With lightning-fast, almost casual swipes of his claws, Ahlitah brought down mackerel and snapper whenever they felt like a meal.

There was no need to look for an inn in which to spend the night. The air of Laconda and Laconda North was warm and moist, allowing them to sleep wherever the terrain took their fancy. This was fortunate, since the swordsman's stock of Chlengguu gold had been exhausted. With food plentiful and freely available, they did not lack for nourishment. It was in this fashion that they made their way, in response to ready directions from farmers and fish-catchers, to the central city. Within a very few days they found themselves standing outside the castle of Count Bewaryn Beckwith, ruler of Laconda North.

It was an impressive sight, a grand palace surrounded by an iron-topped stone wall. Beyond the gate was an expansive, paved parade ground. Elegantly uniformed soldiers stood guard at the gate or trooped past within on fine stallions and unicorns. Beyond lay the palace itself, a three-storied fancy of white limestone and marble. No turrets or battlements were in evidence. The sprawling structure before them served as a home and a seat of governance, not a fortress designed to repel a formal military attack.

"We should announce ourselves." From across the street Simna was conducting a thoughtful appraisal of the layout of the royal residence.

"Yes." Ehomba started forward, the tip of his spear clicking against the paving stones. "The sooner I have done my duty here, the sooner we can move on to Hamacassar."

The guards at the florid wrought-iron gate were dressed in thin coats of blue and gold. They were sleeveless, a sensible adaptation in the warm and humid climate. Long blue pants were tucked into short boots of soft leather, also dyed blue. Each of the four men, two flanking either side of the entrance, was armed with a short sword that hung from a belt of gold leather and a long, ornate pike. They stood at attention, but not immovably so. They became much more active when they saw the unprecedented quartet approaching. To their credit, they kept the pikes erect and made no move to challenge the approaching travelers with weapons poised.

Ehomba walked up to the guard who appeared to be the senior member of the four. The man pushed his gold-trimmed blue cap back on his head and gaped; not at the herdsman, but at the looming mass of Hunkapa Aub.

"Well now, what *do* we have here?"

"A friend from the mountains." Ehomba addressed the man politely but not deferentially. There were only a few individuals in this world whom the herdsman deferred to, and this wide-shouldered gentleman in the blue uniform was not among them.

"The Hrugars, eh?" Another of the guards came forward to join the conversation. He and his colleague exhibited no signs of panic, confident in their position and their weapons. It spoke well of their training, Ehomba decided. "He's dressed for it, anyway. That's a fine heavy coat he's wearing, though I confess I don't recognize the animal it came from."

"It's not—" Ehomba started to say, but Simna stepped in front of his tall companion both physically and vocally.

"And well tailored to him it is, too." Looking back over his shoulder, the swordsman flashed his friend a look that managed to say, wordlessly and all at once, "This is a city, and you're from the country, and I know city folk and their ways better than you ever will." It was enough to prod Ehomba into holding his peace while the enterprising swordsman did the talking.

"We've come a long way to see the Count. Farther than you can imagine."

The guards exchanged a glance. "I don't know," the one who had first spoken opined. "I can imagine quite a distance." Leaning loosely on his pike, he contemplated Simna's semibarbaric attire. "Do you think this is a public hall, where anyone can just walk in and make an appointment?"

"What business have rascals like you with the Count?" Though far from hostile, the second guard was not as amicable as his comrade.

Simna straightened importantly. "We have news of his son, Tarin Beckwith."

It was as if all four guards had been standing on a copper plate suddenly struck by lightning. The two who had said not a word and who did not even appear to have been listening to the conversation whirled and dashed off toward the palace, not even bothering to close the heavy iron gate behind them. As for the pair of casual conversationalists, they no longer gave the appearance of being disinterested in the peculiar quartet of visitors. They gripped their pikes firmly while their expressions indicated that they now held the travelers in an entirely new regard.

"The noble Tarin has not been heard from in many months. How come you lot to know of him?" The senior of the two guards was trying to watch all three of the foreigners simultaneously. For the time being, he ignored the big cat that was snoozing prominently on the pavement.

Simna was forced to defer back to his companion. Noting that his spear was not as long as the sentry's pike, Ehomba once again retold the tale of how he had found Tarin Beckwith and many of his countrymen washed up on the beach below the village of the Naumkib, and of how the young nobleman had expired in his arms. Fully alert now, the guards listened intently, wholly absorbed in the story.

When Ehomba had concluded his tale, the second guard spoke up. "I knew young Beckwith. Not well—I am far below his station—but there were several occasions on which he joined the palace guard on maneuvers. He was a fine person, a true gentleman, who never put on airs and enjoyed a good bawdy joke or a pint of lager. Everyone in Laconda and Laconda North had hoped . . ." The younger man was unable to continue. Evidently the Count's son had been not just liked, but loved, by the populace.

"I am sorry," Ehomba commiserated simply. "There was nothing I could do for him. He was a victim of this warlock who calls himself Hymneth the Possessed."

"Abductor of the fair Themaryl, the Visioness, the greatest glory of the Lacondas." The senior guard sounded wistful. "I never saw her myself, but I've spoken with others who had the privilege. They say that her grace and beauty eclipsed that of the sun itself." His tone darkened. "If what you say is true, then because of this evil magician the Lacondas have lost both her and the noble Tarin." The echo of hastening footsteps made him turn.

A dozen palace sentinels were arriving on the run, led by the two who had formerly been helping to guard the front gate. Badly out of breath, one of these performed an odd salute that the senior among the staff returned with a stiff snap of one hand.

"The Count wishes to see these travelers immediately, without delay!" The messenger gasped for air. "They are to be brought to the main dining chamber, where they will be received by the Count and the Countess themselves!" He looked over at the two men and their odd companions with new respect.

Frowning uncertainly, the senior guard hesitated. "What about the big cat?"

Sucking wind, the messenger nodded sharply. "It is to be

conducted to the dining chamber as well. The palace adviser said clearly to bring all four of them."

"As they wish." Turning back to Ehomba, the senior guard smiled encouragingly. "Don't be intimidated by the palace, or by any representatives of the court you find yourselves introduced to. They're a pretty inoffensive bunch. Laconda North is a very serene country. As for the Count, he's been known to bluster a lot, but not to bully. The fact that he wishes to see you himself is a good sign."

"We're not intimidated by anything." Simna swept grandly past the guard station. "We've fought Corruption and Chlengguu, crossed the Hrugars and the Aboqua, brought down pieces of the sky on our enemies, and made the weather dance to our songs. Mere men we do not fear."

The guard forced himself not to laugh. "Just speak soft and true and you will get along well with the Count. He is not fond of braggarts."

"Hoy," declared Simna as he marched importantly down between the double line of soldiers that had formed up to escort them into the palace, "I don't brag. I only tell the truth. Honest ibn Sind, they call me."

As Ehomba passed the friendly, encouraging sentry, he whispered to him in passing. "Please understand, it is not that my friend is being boastful. He talks like this *all* the time."

The parade ground seemed endless as they crossed it under the watchful eyes of the heavily armed escort, but eventually they reached the shade of the nearest building. From there they were ushered inside and down halls decorated with fine tapestries and paintings. Floating fish were everywhere, their movements constrained by fine netting or transparent glass walls. Exotic tropicals in every color and shape and size were employed in the palace as living decorations. Certainly their iridescent, brilliant colors were as attractive as any of the magnificent but static artworks that dominated the walls.

Eventually they reached a high-ceilinged chamber dominated by a U-shaped table large enough to seat a hundred people. At the far end a dozen anxious figures awaited their arrival. Dazzling tropicals swam freely through the air, unconstrained by netting or other barriers. As the room was devoid of windows, there was no need to place internal restrictions on their movement.

The far end of the table had been set with fine china and silver. Platters had hastily been piled high with the best the palace's kitchens had to offer. Simna's mouth began to water, and Ahlitah licked his lips at the sight of so much meat, even if it had been badly damaged by treatment with fire.

A tall, elegant man with a slightly hooked nose and thinning blond hair that was gray only at the temples rose to greet them, unable to wait for the travelers to make the long walk from the main doorway to the far end of the table. Much to Simna's chagrin, he ignored the swordsman and halted directly in front of Ehomba. His voice was very deep and resonant for one so slim.

"They told me you were dressed like barbarians, but I find your costume in its own way as courtly as my own. As for its imperfections of appearance, and yours, they are excused by the difficulties and distance you have had to deal with in your long journey here." Stepping aside, he gestured expansively at the table. "Welcome! Welcome to Laconda North. Rest, eat, drink—and tell me what you know of my son. My only son."

While the two humans were seated close to the head of the table, room was made for Ahlitah and Hunkapa at the far opposite end. Neither the shaggy mountain dweller nor the big cat felt in the least left out of the ensuing conversation. The litah had no interest in the yapping discourse of humans, and Hunkapa Aub would not have been able to follow it clearly anyway.

The food was wonderfully filling and the wine excellent. Trembling servitors even prevailed upon the cat to try a little of the latter, stammering that it was traditional and to refuse to do so would be to insult the hospitality of the house of Beckwith. Ahlitah magnanimously consented to lap up a bowl of the dark purple fluid. The attendants had less difficulty persuading Hunkapa to do likewise.

At the head of the table Ehomba and Simna displayed a deportment more refined than their attire as they enjoyed the best meal they had partaken of in many a day. Ehomba had always been a relaxed eater, and Simna revealed a surprising knowledge of manners more suited to cultivated surroundings than he had hitherto exhibited in their travels together.

"Not much point in trying to use a napkin when there's none to be had," he explained in response to the herdsman's murmured compliment. "Same goes for utensils. Fingers or forks, I'm equally at home with either of 'em." He sipped wine from a silver chalice with the grace and delicacy of a pit bull crocheting lace.

Seated next to the Count was a woman only slightly younger than himself who had spent much of the meal sobbing softly into a succession of silk handkerchiefs as everyone listened closely to Ehomba's story. When he at last came to the end of the tale of how he had encountered her son, she rose and excused herself from the table.

"My wife," Bewaryn Beckwith explained. "She has done little else these past months save pray for our son's safe return."

"I am sorry I had to be the one to bring you such bad news." Ehomba fingered his nearly empty chalice, gazing at the bas-reliefs on the metal of men pulling fish from the canals and from the sky of Laconda with entirely different kinds of nets. He was suddenly very tired. No doubt the good food and congenial surroundings combined with the exertions expended in crossing the Hrugars were merging within his system to make him sleepy.

"He died as bravely as any man could wish, thinking not of himself or his own wounds but of those being suffered by others. His last words were for the woman."

"The Visioness." Beckwith's long fingers were curled tightly around his own golden drinking container. "To have suffered two such losses in one year is more than any people should be asked to bear. My son"—he swallowed tightly—"my son was as loved by the people of Laconda North as Themaryl was by our cousins to the south. The shock of their disappearance is only now beginning to fade from the body politic."

"I have told you of my intention to try and restore the Visioness to her people in accordance with your son's dying wish. I am sorry there is nothing I can do about him. After his death he was"—the herdsman hesitated, reflecting briefly on how customs differed widely in other lands—"he was given the same treatment my people would have accorded any noble person in his situation." Ehomba rubbed at his eyes. It would be most impolite to fall asleep at so accommodating a table. Someone like the empathetic Beckwith might understand, but they could not count on that.

Still, the need for rest had become overpowering. Looking to his left, he saw that Simna was similarly exhausted. The swordsman was shaking his head and yawning like a man who—well, like a man who had just crossed a goodly portion of the world to get to this point.

As he started to rise preparatory to excusing himself and his companions, Ehomba found that his chair seemed to have acquired the weight and inertia of solid iron. With a determined effort he pushed it back and straightened. Finding himself a little shaky, he put a hand on the table to steady himself.

"I—I am sorry, sir. You must excuse me and my friends. We have been long on the road and have traveled an extreme distance. As a consequence we are very tired." Eyelids like lead threatened to shut down without his approval and he struggled to keep them open. "Is there somewhere we can rest?"

"Hoy, bruther!" Next to him, a sluggish Simna struggled to stand up. Failing, he slumped back in his seat. "There's more at work here than fatigue. Gwoleth knows—Gwoleth knows that . . ." His eyes closed. A second or so later they fluttered open. "Gwoleth be crammed and damned—I should know. As many taverns as I have been in, as many situations . . ." His voice trailed away into incomprehensible mumbling. As Ehomba fought to keep his own eyes focused and alert, the swordsman's head slumped forward on his chest.

Intending to call out to the black litah, he tried to turn, only to find that his body would no longer obey his commands. Tottering in place, he succeeded in resuming his seat. He wanted to apologize to their host, intending to explain further their inexcusable breach of manners, but he found that he was so tired that his mouth and lips no longer worked in concert. An irresistibly lugubrious shade was being drawn down over his eyes, shutting out the light and dragging consciousness down with it. Dimly, he heard someone speaking to the Count.

"That's done it, sir. Fine work. You have them now."

That voice, what remained of Ehomba's cognitive facilities pondered—*where have we heard that voice before?* As awareness slipped painlessly away, he thought he smelled something burning. It too brought back a faint flicker of a memory.

"Murderer!" That accusation was spat in Bewaryn Beckwith's sonorous tone. But whom was he accusing of murder? Someone new who had entered the room?

A hand was on his shoulder, shaking him. In the light, downy haze that had inexorably engulfed him, he hardly felt it. "Murder my son and then brazenly seek my help and hospitality, will you? You'll pay for it, savage. You'll pay for it long and slow and painfully!" As he delivered this pledge the Count's voice was trembling with anger.

Me, Ehomba thought distantly. *He is accusing me of killing his son.* What an absurd, what a grotesque sentiment. If only he could talk, Ehomba would quickly disabuse their host of the feckless fantasy. But his mouth still refused to form words. Where would the Count get such a bizarre notion, anyway?

The other voice came again. It was blunt and the words it rendered terse and to the point.

"Kill them quickly or slowly, sir, it matters not to me. But as we earlier concurred, I claim the sleeping cat for myself and, if you are agreeable, that big ugly brute lying next to it as well."

"Take them if you will." Barely controlled fury now underlay every clipped syllable of the Count's speech. "It is the one who did the actual killing I want. I suppose I'll detain his supporter as well. A man should have company while under torture."

"If you say so, sir. And now, if you'll pardon me, I need to direct the laying of nets on my property."

As the light of wakefulness shrank to a last, intermittent point, Ehomba finally recognized the second voice. It was one he had never expected to hear again, and its presence boded no better for their prospects than did the Count of Laconda North's threatening words.

Haramos bin Grue.

XXI

When consciousness returned it was accompanied by a pounding at the back of the head that would not go away. Wincing, Ehomba fought to keep his eyes open. With every effort his vision grew a little clearer, a little sharper. That did not mean he much liked what he saw.

The dining room with its fine table settings and liveried servants was gone. The travelers had been moved to some kind of reception room, larger but more sparsely furnished. The paintings on the walls were not of reassuring domestic scenes but instead depicted a procession of Lacondan counts and their consorts. There were also landscapes and images of pastoral life, well rendered and patriotically infused. Exquisite tropical fish, those inexplicable living ornaments of Laconda, drifted and swam through the air of the reception hall. Lining the walls, alert and heavily armed blue-clad soldiers stood like silent sculptures.

At one end of the room a double throne of becoming modesty rested on a raised dais. Heavily embroidered banners formed a suitably impressive backdrop to the royal seat while providing some of the opulent trappings of office the chairs themselves lacked. One seat was empty, the other held a brooding Bewaryn Beckwith. Standing next to him was a squat, pug shape from whose thick lips protruding a lightly smoking cigar. No look of triumph scored the merchant's round face. Satisfaction, perhaps. With bin Grue it was only business as usual.

When he noticed the herdsman staring at him, he grunted around the tobacco. "Nobody gets the best of Haramos bin Grue. You should've let me have the cat."

Alongside the herdsman Simna ibn Sind was coming slowly awake. As he returned to the world of cognizance, he became aware of the strong cords binding his arms behind his back.

"Hoy, what's this?" Blinking, he focused not on the pensive nobleman but on the stubby shape standing next to him. "It's the pig-man!" Futilely, he began to fight against his fetters. "Let me free for a minute. No, half a minute! You don't even have to give me a sword!"

While his friend raged, Ehomba saw that a metal net now secured the glowering black litah behind him. A second similar mesh had been used to bind up Hunkapa Aub while he slept. Whatever drug had been slipped into their wine had done its work efficiently and with admirable subtlety. No wonder the Count's servants had insisted that Ahlitah and Hunkapa partake of the specially treated libation.

Their gear lay piled nearby, his pack and weapons atop Simna's. These might as well have been left on the other side of the Hrugars. He was bound so tightly he could barely move his fingers, let alone his arms and legs. No doubt bin Grue had made sure of that. But he was not sorry for himself. He had faced death many times before. His only regret was that he would not be able to tell Mirhanja and the children good-bye, and that they would never know what had happened to him. Also, it was more than a little discouraging to realize that they were going to die for a lie.

If there was anything more depressing than his own situation, it was the pitiful plight of Hunkapa Aub. The big, easygoing beast was sitting hunched over and silent with his head hung down toward his feet, exactly as Ehomba had first seen him penned back in Netherbrae. After all he had been through, and after having his freedom restored, he was once again destined for life in a cage, to be tormented and jeered at by thoughtless, faceless, uncaring humans. Ehomba was glad he could see only the solid, imposing back and not the creature's countenance.

"What have you to say before I pronounce sentence?"

Turning away from his friends and ignoring Simna's unbounded ranting, Ehomba tried to meet Count Bewaryn Beckwith's stare with as much sincere probity as he could muster. "The individual standing next to you does not deserve to share your presence. He is Haramos bin Grue, a false merchant of Lybondai."

"I know who he is," the Count replied curtly. With one hand he brushed aside a dozen amethyst anthias who were swimming across his line of vision. Fins twitching, they skittered silently out of his way. "He came all the way from the far south to warn me of your coming, and to tell me the truth of what happened to my son."

"The truth is he knows only what I told his employee, an old man with no more scruples than himself." Ehomba tried to shift his position and found that he could move his backside and bound legs in concert, but had no chance of standing up. Speaking from a seated position weakened his words, he knew, if only psychologically. "He has twisted and distorted it for his own ends. Every time he opens his mouth, he feeds you bullshit."

"Not only a murderer and a liar, but coarse." Using only his lips, bin Grue manipulated the smoking cigar from one side of his mouth to the other.

"Hear my friend, great Count!" Evincing impressive reserves of energy, Simna continued to fight futilely with the ropes that bound him even as he spoke. "He tells the truth. And if you don't release us, doom will befall you. My friend is a great and powerful wizard!"

A hand slowly massaging one temple, Beckwith regarded the herdsman coldly. "Is that so? He looks like a common assassin to me, one who can do nothing without stealth and a knife to slip into some innocent's back. But I am willing to be convinced." Eyes blazing, he leaned forward on the throne. "Your friend says you are a powerful magician, southerner. Prove his words. Free yourself." Against the walls, a number of the vigilant soldiers shifted uneasily.

"I am no assassin," Ehomba replied. "Hymneth the Possessed is the murderer of your son."

"A wizard." With a blunt, humorless laugh, Beckwith sat back on his throne.

Simna stopped struggling against his bonds long enough to lean to his left and whisper to his companion. "Come on, Etjole. This be no time for reticence. Show them what you can do. Reveal your powers to them!"

The herdsman nodded in the direction of their collected kit. "What small powers I may access lie in the bottom of my pack, Simna, which I cannot reach. I am sorry. Truly I am."

"Well then, remonstrate with this fool! He's so blinded by the loss of his son that he can't think straight. That's when slime like bin Grue can do their work."

"I will try." Redirecting his words to the dais, he spoke clearly and with the confidence of one who speaks the truth. "Think a moment before condemning us, noble Beckwith. If I were truly your son's killer, why would I come all this way and present myself to your court? What possible reason could I have for undertaking such a long and dangerous journey?"

Beckwith replied without hesitation. "To claim the treasure, of course." He glanced to his right. "Now it will go, as it rightfully should, to my new friend here."

For the first time, Haramos bin Grue smiled. And why not? Not only was he going to reclaim the black litah and acquire an additional attraction in the form of the disconsolate Hunkapa Aub, there was apparently a good deal more at stake.

"I knew it!" Simna burst out. He glared murderously at his tall friend. "There was treasure all along! You've been lying to me—but I never believed you, you sanctimonious southern scion of a promiscuous porker!"

Honestly baffled, Ehomba gaped at his friend. "Simna, I do not know what you are talking about." He nodded as best he was able in Beckwith's direction. "I do not know what *he* is talking about."

"But I do know—now! At last I understand. Oh, you were so subtle, you were, so adept at parrying my questions about 'treasure.'" Turning sharply away from the herdsman, Simna ibn Sind gazed expectantly at the throne. "There's a reward, isn't there? For information about your son. That's the treasure!"

A wary Bewaryn Beckwith nodded slowly. "There has been for months. Knowledge of it was spread far and wide in hopes of securing some information as to Tarin's whereabouts. This good merchant earns it by dint of the invaluable information he has brought me. I am only thankful that he arrived in time to tell me the truth of how things really are, and to inform me of your nefarious intentions." His attention shifted back to Ehomba. "It is clear you not only murdered my son, but intended to claim the reward for bringing us the news of his death. Simple man that I am, I cannot conceive of such incredible arrogance."

"Hoy, I can, noble sir!" Not only was an obviously outraged Simna not finished, he appeared to be just warming up. "For weeks I have been attending to this mumbling, stone-faced charlatan, seeing to his needs, waiting upon his desires, helping to protect him from all manner of difficulties and dangers. I did this of my own free will because in my heart I knew he was after treasure. I could smell it in his words, sense it in the way he stared at the far horizons. And, humbly avaricious fellow that I am, I wanted a piece of that treasure for myself. That was all I was interested in: I admit it. Condemn me for my confession if you will, but give me credit at least for my honesty. I am ashamed to admit that it never bothered me that he killed the man who inspired him to come all this way. Your son, noble sir."

Ehomba's jaw dropped in utter disbelief. "Simna!"

The swordsman sneered at him, "'Simna'? What is this use of my name to express outrage? Am I now reduced to nothing more than a surprised expletive? 'Simna' yourself, you fakir, you champion of lies, you user of honest men. You fooled everyone, even the cat, but you can't fool me any longer!" Straining against the ropes that enveloped him, he struggled to bow in the direction of the throne. It required considerable flexibility and effort.

"Sire, Count Beckwith, I abjure this deceptive and conniving villain now and for all time! I was wrong to think the treasure that I knew he sought could be come by honestly, but you must see, you have to see, that I could not have suspected otherwise. He is a master of deviousness, which he cleverly masks with a studied attitude of simple affability. Free me, give me back my life, and I will tell you everything! I see now that there never was any treasure in this for me, fool that I was."

Beckwith stared hard at the bound swordsman, the fingers of one hand tap-tapping against the arm of the throne. "Why should I let you go? You have nothing to give me." He nodded in the merchant's direction. "This good gentleman has already told me everything."

"Impossible, sire! He can only have told you what his an-

cient employee told him. Only I have traveled in this prevaricator's misbegotten company since near the very start of
his journey. Only I have been privy to all of his plans and intentions." He lowered his head and his voice. "Besides the
murderer himself, only I know the most intimate details of
your son's death."

To his credit, bin Grue's expression never changed. "He's
lying," the merchant avowed brusquely.

"Lying?" Bewaryn Beckwith eyed the foreign trader
thoughtfully. "Lying about what? Are you saying that perhaps this stranger was not responsible for the death of my
son?"

"No, sire, of course not. We both know better than that."
Ehomba thought bin Grue might have been starting to sweat
a little, but he could not be sure. Like the rest of Laconda, it
was hot and humid in the reception chamber.

"Then what could he be lying about?" the Count pressed
him. "Not his own participation in my son's murder. You
told me yourself it was carried out by the tall southerner
alone."

"That's true, sire, but—I know a little of this talkative
person, and I know that he is not to be trusted."

"I have no intention of trusting him, but if he knows more
of my son's death than you, he deserves at least to be heard."
Leaning forward, he glared down at the semisupine swordsman. "Speak then, vagrant, and if what you say satisfies me,
I may decide to spare your inconsequential life."

Simna shifted awkwardly on the floor. "Your indulgence,
sire, but the pain in my arms and legs from these ropes is severe, and distracts my thoughts."

Beckwith sat back in his seat and waved indifferently.
"Oh very well—cut him loose."

"Sire," bin Grue protested as two burly soldiers stepped
forward to release the swordsman from his bonds, "I don't
think that's a good idea."

"What, are you afraid of him, Haramos? I thought it was the assassin who claimed to be a sorcerer."

"No, sire, I'm not afraid of him." The merchant was watching the relieved Simna intently. "I just don't trust him. I don't trust any of them."

"You don't have to trust them, my friend. The hairy brute and the giant cat are well and truly shackled, and these troops you see here are my household guard, the pride of Laconda North." He indicated Simna who, freed from the heavy ropes, was gratefully rubbing circulation back into his wrists and legs. "He is but one man, and not a very big one at that. Calm yourself. Why, despite the differences in our ages I think I could take him in a fair fight myself."

"I suspect that you could, sire." The liberated swordsman was eager to please.

"Flattery is for wiping asses, vagrant, and mine is clean. Now—my son's passing? How did happen? Spare no detail, no matter how repellent."

After a glance at the two brawny guards who flanked him on either side, Simna began. It was an elaborate tale, rich with intrigue and deception. Even the pair of sentinels were drawn into the story, though they never let down their guard. Only bin Grue, who knew the real truth, was not taken in. Unable to object more strenuously without bringing suspicion on himself, he could only watch and wonder at the swordsman's exhibition. From the standpoint of pure theater, the tough-minded merchant had to admit, it was quite a performance.

As for Ehomba, he could only sit in silence and wonder at the swordsman's motivations. While he could understand the opportunistic Simna's desire to employ every means at his disposal to try to save himself, the herdsman would have preferred it did not involve digging a deeper grave for the sole local representative of the Naumkib, who were not present to speak in their own defense.

Simna wove more and more detail into his story, one moment gazing imploringly heavenward, the next pointing a trembling arm in Ehomba's direction. Walking up behind the herdsman, he began beating him about the head and shoulders as he spoke, belaboring the bound southerner with insults and accusations as well as solid, unrelenting blows. Beckwith watched expressionlessly while bin Grue gnawed nervously at his cigar and wondered what the swordsman was going to do for a big finish.

It came soon enough. As he returned to stand between the two heavyset guards, Simna's voice rose to a shout, a climax of indignation and outrage. "Look at him, sitting there! Do you see any remorse written on his face? Do you see any hint, any suggestion of apologia for what he's done? No! That's how he always is. Stone-faced, devoid of expression, unchanging whether picking a man's mind or taking his life. He deserves to die! I would kill him myself for what he's done to me, but I am unarmed." Reaching back, he gave the slightly nearer of the two guards a strong shove in the herdsman's direction.

"Go on, get it done, execute him now! I want to see his blood run! I deserve to see it!" When the guard hesitated, Simna pushed the other one forward, shoving insistently. "Show me his head rolling on the floor."

"Simna ibn Sind, you are a faithless and unprincipled man!" Belying the swordsman's accusations, Ehomba's face contorted in a rictus of anger and betrayal. "You will die a lonely and miserable death that fully reflects your worthless life!"

"Probably," the swordsman retorted, "but not just yet." Whereupon he bolted, quick as a cobra, in the opposite direction. Both guards turned and grabbed for him, but having been shoved several steps forward, the wily Simna had put them just out of reach.

Half-somnolent troops instantly scrambled to block the nearest exits. Others rushed to protect the Count. Startled by all the sudden activity, decorative drifting fish darted confusedly to and fro. Another dozen soldiers rushed the agile swordsman. They lowered or drew their own weapons as the frantic Simna scrabbled madly at his and Ehomba's pile of personal belongings. His fingers wrapping around a sword hilt, he pulled it free and threw it not at the grim-faced, oncoming soldiers, but toward his companion.

"Hoy, bruther! Bring down a piece of the sky on this ungrateful place! Conjure forth the wind that rushes between the stars and blow these knaves through their precious walls! Litter the floor with their skeletons as the star wind tears the flesh from their bones!"

Slipping free of the ropes that had restrained him, which Simna's supple fingers had astutely undone in between beating the herdsman madly about the head and body, Ehomba rose in time to catch the tumbling sword by its haft. There was only one problem with the swordsman's bold and bloodthirsty admonitions.

It was the wrong sword.

Instead of the sharp blade fashioned of gray sky metal, in his haste and confusion Simna had snatched up the herdsman's other sword, the one made of bone lined with serrated, triangular sharks' teeth. A fearsome and efficacious weapon to be sure, but not one that could by any stretch of anyone's imagination bring down so much as an errant rain cloud. It was a thing of the sea, not of the sky.

Having taken up his own sword subsequent to flinging the weapon to Ehomba, the rueful swordsman realized his mistake. "Hoy, I'm sorry, bruther." Sword held in both hands, he was backing away from the advancing semicircle of soldiers. A sword was not of much use against pikes, but he was determined to sell his life as dearly as possible. If naught else, at least he would go down with a weapon in his hand and no shackles on his wrists and ankles. They would die like men and not like mad dogs.

"Nothing to be sorry for, friend Simna." Ehomba held the tooth-lined sword high overhead, its sharpened tip pointed at the tense but unconcerned soldiers. "There are fish everywhere in this place, so what better weapon to fight with than one that owes its edge to the sea?"

"Kill them!" It was the curt voice of Haramos bin Grue, declaiming from behind a line of blue-coated troops. "Kill them now, before he . . . !"

Hidden on his throne, Bewaryn Beckwith could be heard responding querulously, and for the first time, with a hint of suspicion in his voice. "Before he—what, Haramos?"

It was a question Simna ibn Sind was asking silently. Nearby, Ahlitah was awake and roaring, adding to the sense of incipient chaos. Emerging from his gloom, Hunkapa Aub had straightened and was shaking the metal mesh of his netting with terrifying violence.

A blue aurora had enveloped the blade of the sea-bone sword. It was dark as the deep ocean, tinged with green, and smelled of salt. At the sight of it the advancing soldiers halted momentarily. From the dais, their liege's voice urged them on.

"What are you waiting for?" Bewaryn Beckwith bellowed. "They are only two and you are many. Take them! Alive if possible—otherwise if not."

One of the two thickly muscled guards who had been duped by Simna stepped forward, holding his heavy sword threateningly out in front of him. His voice was that of reason, not anger.

"This is senseless. Why disgrace yourselves by spilling blood inside the palace? You should meet your fate with dignity." Holding his blade at the ready, he extended his other hand. "Give up your weapons."

"Look!" one of the men behind him shouted. An uncomfortable susurration rippled through the contracting circle of soldiers.

Something was emerging from the point of the herdsman's sword. Gray on top, white on the bottom, it swelled massively as it expanded away from the bone. It looked like a giant bicolored drop of milk oozing out of nothingness parallel to the floor. As it continued to increase in size it began to grow individual features, like a closed flower sprouting petals. And it just kept getting bigger and bigger.

The ornamental floating fish in the reception hall identified it before any of the soldiers. They vanished through open doors as if propelled by lightning and not fins, evaporating streaks of yellow and orange, red and gold. In one case they literally flew through a squad of blue-clad reinforcements hurrying to the chamber. It was as if they had not fled, but vaporized.

The gray-white mass grew fins of its own, and a great, sickle-like tail. A pair of black eyes manifested themselves. They were jet black and without visible pupils. All of these details were ignored by those in the room as they focused on a single predominant feature: the mouth.

It was enormous, capable of swallowing a person in a single swallow. Multiple rows of gleaming white, triangular teeth lined the interior of that imposing cavity. Their edges were serrated on both sides of the sharp point, like steak knives. The largest was more than three inches long. It was a peerless mouth, unlike anything else in all the undersea kingdom. When viewed from straight on, jaws and teeth combined to form a uniquely terrifying smile.

The great white shark broke free of the tip of the bone sword and drifted toward the assembled soldiers. Several broke and ran, but the rest bravely held their ground, their long pikes extended. A second gray-white teardrop shape was beginning to emerge from the weapon. If anything, it promised to be larger than its predecessor.

One of the soldiers thrust his pike at the looming predator. Extending its jaws beyond its lips, the great white ate it.

Left holding a length of useless wood, the soldier sensibly threw it away, turned, and sprinted for the nearest door.

"Hold your ground!" Bewaryn Beckwith commanded from the vicinity of his throne. "Fight back! They are only fish, like the ones you see every day on the streets of the city."

The Count of Laconda North was half right. They were only fish, but they were most assuredly not like the ones the soldiers saw every day. They were not decorative, they were not inoffensive, and they were hungry. And now there were three of them, with a fourth on the way as the fecund sword gave birth yet again.

To their credit, the soldiers responded to the appeal of their liege. They tried to encircle two of the sharks and attack with their long pikes. Several thrusts struck home, and droplets of red shark blood spilled in slow motion to the floor. But the wounds only enraged the sharks. With their great curved tails propelling them explosively through the air, they snapped at whatever happened to come within reach, be it pike, soldier, or unfortunate furniture.

One great white the soldiers probably could have contained. Two and then three forced them into a holding action. When the sixth emerged full grown from Ehomba's sword, the reception hall dissolved into general blood and chaos.

Soldiers broke and fled, pursued by unrelenting carnivorous torpedoes. The fortunate escaped down corridors of panic while their slower, less agile comrades were actively dismembered. It was not long before limbs littered the floor and the fine furnishings and papered walls were splashed with crimson. Convoyed by a close-packed detachment of desperate soldiers, Bewaryn Beckwith, Count of Laconda North, escaped through a secret bolt-hole located behind the throne dais. Many members of his escort were not as lucky.

As for Haramos bin Grue, he attempted to flee along with

the Count, only to find himself shoved roughly back into the bloody pandemonium that had enveloped the hall. As his guard kept them separated, Beckwith had just enough time to shout a passing farewell before ducking to safety.

"Not a sorcerer, Haramos? You lied to me about that. Could it be that you lied also about how my son died?"

"No, sire—believe me, I told the truth!" Despite the fact that he was unarmed save for a pair of small concealed knives, the merchant resisted the soldiers. But it was hard to fight with someone when there was a foot of sharp blade and six feet of wooden shaft between you and your opponent. Such was the advantage of the steel-tipped pike.

"That is the murderer, down there! That uncouth, uncivilized southerner. And he is no sorcerer, by his own word! Though I admit to being fooled by the sorceral devices he carries with him."

"You are right about one thing." Beckwith paused as he crouched to pass beneath the low overhang of the escape portal. His guard fought to keep a curious great white away from their Count. "Someone here is being fooled. I wish I had the time to sort it out." He hurried into the concealed passageway. One by one, his soldiers tried to follow him. Many succeeded. Others lost limbs and, in a couple of cases, their heads to the rampaging shark.

Falling back, bin Grue pressed himself against the wall and began to make his way toward the nearest exit, edging steadily away from the royal dais. Before him was being played out an unparalleled spectacle of remorseless carnage. He had nearly reached the door when he made the mistake of bolting. The rapid movement caught the attention of one of the marauding great whites. When he turned, the merchant did not scream in fear but instead cursed violently. His end, therefore, was in keeping with his nature all his life, a reflection of internal toughness and perpetual ire. It made no difference to the shark, which bit him in half.

Out on the floor of the reception hall there were now eight great whites circling slowly in search of additional prey. The once grand chamber had taken on the aspect of an abattoir, with blood, guts, and body parts scattered everywhere. The last live soldier had fled.

Sloshing through the shallow lake of unwillingly vented bodily fluids, Ehomba advanced on his still imprisoned friends. Simna followed, hugging as close to his tall friend as possible without actually slipping into his clothing. He had seen how fast the floating sharks could move and had no intention of separating himself from their procreator even for an instant. Soulless black eyes tracked his movements, but the sharks did not attack. A number had settled to the floor and were feeding, gulping down whole chunks of soldier, uniform and all.

"You are a very canny man." With a free hand the herdsman rubbed his sore face and shoulders. "As soon as the opportunity presents itself, I intend to pay you back for your canniness."

"Hoy, bruther, I had to make it look real, didn't I? I needed to distract them from what I was doing behind your back. Any sleight of hand needs a good diversion to be effective." He grinned. "I was beginning to wonder if you'd ever pick up on what I was trying to do."

"I admit you had me concerned at first. What finally revealed your true intentions was the degree of your pleading. I think I understand you well enough to know that you would go down fighting before you would grovel."

"Depends on the circumstances," the swordsman replied without hesitation. "If the need arose, I could grovel with the best of them." He nodded in the direction of the throne. "But not because of a lie, and never in front of a fat toad like bin Grue." His tone was harsh. "I saw him go down. He won't be putting anybody in a cage ever again."

Ehomba replied somberly. "Not all the methods a man

perfects to protect himself work all the time. That is one thing about sharks: They cannot be reasoned with, distracted, or bribed. Stay close to me."

The swordsman did not have to be reminded. The presence of twenty tons or so of floating, fast-moving great white rendered the immediate surroundings decidedly inhospitable.

"Let me guess. You're not working any magic whatsoever. You have no idea how this is happening. You're just making use of the enchanted sword fashioned for you by the village smithy Okidoki."

"Otjihanja," Ehomba corrected him patiently. "That is a silly notion, Simna. A smithy works only with metals." He hefted the tooth-lined bone shaft. "This sword was made by old Pembarudu, who is a master of fishing. It took him a long time to gather all the teeth from the shore and mount them together on the bone. It is whalebone, of course. A shark has no bones. It is one of the reasons they make such good eating."

Keeping low, Simna ibn Sind made hushing motions with one hand. "Don't speak of such things, Etjole. One of these finny monsters might overhear and get the wrong idea."

The herdsman smiled. "Simna, are you afraid?"

"By Ghogost's gums, you bet I'm afraid, bruther! Any man confronted by such sights who did say he was not would be a liar of bin Grue's class. I'm afraid whenever you pick up a weapon, and I'm afraid whenever you pull some innocent little article out of that pack of yours. Traveling with you, I have learned many things. When to be afraid is one of them." Still smiling, but grimly, he gazed evenly up at his tall companion. "You're not a man to inspire fear, Etjole, but your baggage—that's another matter."

Ehomba did his best to reassure him. "So long as I hold the sword, I command its progeny. See . . ."

Lowering the weapon, he touched the tip to the metal netting in which Ahlitah was imprisoned. Immediately, the nearest shark turned and swam toward it. Snarling, the black cat backed as far away as it could from jaws that were even more massive and powerful than its own.

With a snap, the great white took a mouthful of mesh. Thrashing its head from side to side, it used its teeth like saws. When it backfinned and drew away, it left behind a hole in the net large enough for the litah to push through.

Under Ehomba's direction, two sharks performed a similar favor for the fourth member of their party. Expanding the resultant gap with one shove of his mighty arms, Hunkapa Aub emerged to stand alongside his friends.

"Big fish, bad bite."

Simna nodded. "I would say, rather: bad fish, big bite—but the end is the same." Looking around, he surveyed their tormented surroundings. The reception hall had been the scene of solemn slaughter. "Let's pick up our gear and get out of here. I've had about enough of Laconda—north, south, or any other direction."

"Soldiers chase?" Hunkapa wondered sensibly as they cautiously exited the room.

"I do not think so." Sea-bone sword held out in front of him, Ehomba led the way. Forming two lines of four each, the great whites fell into place on either side of the travelers.

Their measured departure from the lowlands of Laconda created a stir among the populace that lay the groundwork for stories for decades to come. As was common in such matters, with each retelling the participants expanded in size and ferocity. Ehomba became the malignant warlock of the sea, come to wreak havoc among the gentle floating fishes of Laconda. Simna ibn Sind was his gnomic apprentice, wielding a sword impossibly larger than himself. Hunkapa Aub was a giant with burning eyes and long fangs that dripped olive green ichor, while the black litah was a streak of hell-smoke that burned everything it touched.

As for the escort of flying great whites, they were magnified in the storytellers' imaginations until they had become as big as whales, with teeth like fence posts and the temperaments of demons incarnate—as if the reality were not frightening and impressive enough.

Domestic fish scattered like arrows at the approach of the travelers and their silent escort. Unwarned citizens dove for the nearest cover or hastily shuttered windows and barred doors. More than size or teeth, empty black eyes, or swaying tails, the one thing those who observed the passage of the remarkable procession never forgot were the frightful frozen grins that scored the inhuman faces of the great whites.

No one followed them and, needless to say, no one tried to stop them. By the time they reached the northwestern periphery of Laconda North, the border guards, having been informed of what was making its inexorable way in their direction, had long since decided to take early vacation. Marching across the modest, well-made bridge that delineated the frontier, the travelers found themselves in the jumble of lowland forest known as the Yesnaby Hills.

There Ehomba turned and stood alone, eyes shut tight, the sea-bone sword held vertically before him. As Simna and the others looked on, one by one the great whites swam slowly through the humid air to return whence they had come. The sword sucked them back down as if they were minnows disappearing into a bucket.

When the last tail had finned its way out of existence, Ehomba slipped the sword into the empty scabbard on his back and turned to resume their journey. A strong hand reached out to stop him.

"A moment if you please, long bruther."

Ehomba looked down at his friend. "Is something the matter, Simna?" The herdsman looked back in the direction of the deserted border post and the Laconda lowlands. "You are not worried about the Count sending his soldiers to chase us down?"

"Not hardly," the swordsman replied. "I think they're smarter than that. What I'm beginning to wonder is if I am."

"I do not follow your meaning, my friend." Nearby, Hunkapa Aub and Ahlitah were exploring a small cave.

"When you found out where we were, you decided to inform this Beckwith of his son's fate. The result is that he thinks you killed his heir, and that if he is given another chance, he'll kill you."

"I do not think that is the case. The more time he has to ponder what transpired, the more I believe he will come to question the truth of what bin Grue told him."

"Could be, but after what you did to his court he's still not exactly going to be ready to greet you with open arms if you come back this way. What I'm trying to say, Etjole, is that you don't owe anything to a man who wants you dead. So we can concentrate on finding the real treasure and forget all this nonsense about returning some rarefied blue-blooded doxy to her family."

"Not so," Ehomba insisted. At these words, the swordsman's expression fell. "The Visioness Themaryl, whose safe return home I promised Tarin Beckwith to try my best to effect, is a scion of Laconda. Not Laconda North. She is of a noble family other than the Beckwiths. Therefore, whatever they may think of me, now or in the future, it does not affect my pledge." Smiling apologetically, he turned and resumed course on a northwesterly heading. After uttering a few choice words to no one in particular, Simna moved to join him. The two hirsute members of the group hurried to catch up.

"I guess you're right, bruther. You're no sorcerer. You just have learned friends and relations who give you useful things. So you have those to make use of, and the benefit of remarkable coincidence."

"Coincidence?" Ehomba responded absently. At the moment, his attention was devoted to choosing the best route through the hills ahead.

"Hoy. We find ourselves in a country where the fish swim through the air. Not knowing the properties of your other weapon, when I break free I automatically reach for the magical blade whose attributes I am familiar with: the sky-metal sword. But instead I grab the weapon that, it turns out, can give birth to the most monstrous and terrible fish in the sea." Crowding his friend, he tried hard to make the taller man meet his eyes. "Coincidence."

Ehomba shrugged, more to show that he was listening than to evince any especial interest in what his friend was saying. "I could have made use of the sky-metal sword. Or this." Lifting the walking stick–spear off the ground, he shook it slightly. A distant, primeval roar whispered momentarily through the otherwise still air.

"So you could," Simna agreed. "But would they have been as appropriate? The spear would have summoned a demon too large for the room in which we were imprisoned. The sky-metal sword might have brought down the walls and ceiling on top of us."

Now Ehomba looked over at his companion. "Then why did you want me to use it?"

"Because we would have had a better chance of surviving the smashed rumble of a palace than a certain knife in the neck. Of course, once I threw you the sea-bone sword everything worked out for the best."

"I did not know you were going to fool your guards long enough to grab it and throw it to me," the herdsman responded.

"Didn't you?" Simna stared hard, hard at his tall, enigmatic friend. "I often find myself wondering, Etjole, just how much you do know and if this unbounded insistence on an unnatural fondness for livestock is nothing more than a pose to disguise some other, grander self."

Ehomba shook his head slowly, sadly. "I can see, after all that we have been through together, friend Simna, how such sentiments could trouble your thoughts. Be assured yet again that I am Etjole Ehomba, a humble herdsman of the Naumkib." Raising his free hand, he pointed to a nearby tree heavy with unexpected blossoms. "Look at the colors. I have never seen anything like that before. Is it not more like a giant flower than a tree?"

Hoy, you're a shepherd for sure, mused Simna ibn Sind even as he responded to his friend's timely floral observation. In the course of their long journeying together, Ehomba had talked incessantly of cattle and sheep until on more than one occasion the swordsman had been ready to scream. A shepherd and a—what had the southerner called it?—an eromakasi, an itinerant eater of darkness. The question that would not leave the swordsman's mind, however, was, What else exactly, if anything, *was* Etjole Ehomba?

XXII

When finally they crested the last of the Yesnaby Hills and found themselves gazing, improbably and incredibly, down at the great port city of Hamacassar itself, Simna could hardly believe it. To Hunkapa Aub and Ahlitah it was no cause for especial celebration. Despite its legendary status, to them the city was only another human blight upon the land.

As for Ehomba, there was no falling to knees and giving thanks, or lifting of hands and hosannaing of praises to the heavens. Contemplating the fertile lowlands, the smoke that rose from ten thousand chimneys, and the great shimmering slash of the river Eynharrowk against whose southern shore the city sprawled in three directions, he commented simply, "I thought it would be bigger," and started down the last slope.

Their arrival occasioned considerably less panic than it had in landlocked kingdoms like Bondressey and Tethspraih. Reactions were more akin to the response their presence had engendered in Lybondai. Like Hamacassar, the bustling city on the north shore of the Aboqua Sea was a cosmopolitan trading port whose citizens were used to seeing strange travelers from far lands. At first sight, the only difference between the two was that Hamacassar was much larger and situated on the bank of a river instead of the sea itself.

Also absent were the cooling breezes that rendered Lybondai's climate so salubrious. Like the Lacondas, the river plain on which Hamacassar had been built was hot and humid. A similar system of canals and small tributaries connected different parts of the widespread, low-lying metropolis, supplying its citizens with transportation that was cheap and reliable. The design of the homes and commercial buildings they began to pass with increasing frequency was intriguing but unsurprising. As they made their way through the city's somewhat undisciplined outskirts, they encountered nothing that was startling or unrecognizable. Except for the monoliths.

Spaced half a mile apart, these impressive structures loomed over homes and fields like petrified colossi. Each took the form of an acute triangle that had been rounded off at the top. Twenty feet or so wide at the base, they rapidly narrowed to their smooth crests. Ehomba estimated them to be slightly over forty feet in height. Each structure was penetrated by a hole that mimicked its general shape. Seven or eight feet wide, the hole punched through the monolith not far below its apex.

The mysterious constructs marched across the landscape in a broad, sweeping curve, extending as far to the east and west as the travelers could see. They were not guarded, or fenced off from the public. Their smooth, slightly pitted flanks made them impossible for curious children to climb. Nor were they sited on similar plots of land. One rose from the bank of a wide, sluggish stream while the next all but abutted a hay barn and the third flanked the farm road down which the travelers were presently walking. In the absence of significant hills or mountains, they dominated the flat terrain.

Leaving the road, the travelers took a moment to examine one up close. Beneath their fingers the pitted metal was cool and pebbly to the touch.

"I don't recognize the stuff." Simna dragged his nails along the lightly polished surface. "It's not iron or steel. The color suggests bronze, but there's no green anywhere on it. Standing out in the weather like this you'd expect bronze to green fast."

"It would depend on the mix in the alloy." Ehomba gently rapped the dun-colored surface with a closed fist. As near as he could tell it was solid, not hollow. A lot of foundry work for no immediately discernible purpose, he decided. "If it is not an alloy it is no metal I know."

"Nor I." Leaning back, Simna scrutinized the triangular-shaped hole that pierced the upper portion of the construct.

Hunkapa Aub pushed with all his weight against the front of the structure. It did not move, or even quiver. Whoever had placed it here had set it solidly and immovably in the earth.

"What for?"

Ehomba considered. "It could be for anything, Hunkapa. They might be religious symbols. Or some sort of historic boundary markers showing where the old kingdom of Hamacassar's frontier once ended. Or they might be nothing more than part of an elaborate scheme of municipal art."

"Typical human work. Waste of time." Ahlitah was inspecting the stream bank for edible freshwater shellfish.

"We could ask a local. Surely they would know." Wiping his hands against his kilt, Ehomba started back toward the road.

"Hoy, we could," Simna agreed, "if we could get one to stand still long enough. They don't run from the sight of us, but I've yet to see one that didn't hurry to lock him- or herself away if it looked like we might be heading in their direction." Making a face, he indicated their two outsized companions. "Get the cat and the shag beast to hide themselves in a field and you and I might be able to walk up to a farmhouse without the tenants shutting the door in our faces."

Back up on the road, they once more resumed their trek northward. The nearer they got to the river, the more residents of Hamacassar they encountered. These gave the eccentric quartet a wide and wary, if polite, berth.

"There is no need to unsettle any of the locals." Ehomba's staff stirred up a little puff of dust each time it was planted firmly on the hard-packed surface. "I am sure we will learn the meaning of the monoliths in the course of making contacts throughout the city." He strode along eagerly, setting a much more rapid pace than usual.

"Hoy, long bruther, I'm glad you're in a good mood, but remember that not all of us have your beanpole legs."

"Sorry." Ehomba forced himself to slow down. "I did not realize I was walking so fast."

"Walking? You've been on the verge of breaking into a run ever since we came down out of the hills." The swordsman jerked a thumb over his shoulder. "The brute's legs are longer than yours and the cat has four to our two, but I'm not in either class stride-wise. Have a thought for me, Etjole, if no one else."

"It is just that we are so close, Simna." Uncharacteristic excitement bubbled in the herdsman's voice.

"Close to what?" The swordsman's tone was considerably less ebullient. "To maybe, if we're lucky, finding passage on a ship to cross the Semordria, where we then first have to find this Ehl-Larimar?" He made a rude noise, conducting it with an equally rude gesture.

"Considering how far we have traveled and what difficulties we have overcome, I would think that you could show a little optimism, Simna."

"I'm a realist, Etjole." The swordsman kicked a rock out of his path and into the drainage ditch that ran parallel to the slightly elevated roadbed.

"Realism and optimism are not always mutually exclusive, my friend."

"Hoy, that's like saying a beautiful daughter and her suspicious father aren't mutually exclusive." He watched a wagon piled high with parsnips and carrots pass by, rumbling in the opposite direction. The team of matched toxondons that was pulling it ignored the immigrants, but the two men riding on the wagon's seat never took their eyes off Ehomba and his companions.

They did not pass any more of the monoliths. Apparently these existed only in the single line they had encountered on the outskirts of the city. But there were many other architectural wonders to dazzle the eyes of first-time visitors.

Hamacassar boasted the tallest buildings Ehomba had ever seen. Rising eight and nine stories above the widest commercial streets, these had facades that were decorated with fine sculpture and stonework. Many wagons plied the intricate network of avenues and boulevards while flat-bottomed barges and other cargo craft filled the city canals to capacity. These were in turn spanned by hundreds of graceful yet wholly functional bridges that were themselves ornamented with bas-reliefs and metal grillwork. Though curious about the singular foursome, the locals were too busy to linger and stare. The closer they came to the waterfront, the more pervaded the atmosphere became with the bustle and fervor of commerce.

"A prosperous kingdom." Simna made the comment as they worked their way between carts and wagons piled high with ship's supplies, commodities from all along the length of the great river, foodstuffs and crafts, and all manner of trade goods. "These people have grown rich on trade." Slowing as they passed a small bistro, he inhaled deeply of the delicious aromas that wafted from its cool, inviting interior.

Taking him by the arm, Ehomba drew him firmly away from the scene of temptation. The swordsman did not really resist.

"We have no money for such diversions," Ehomba reminded his friend, "unless your pack holds an overlooked piece of Chlengguu gold."

A downcast Simna looked regretful. "Alas, the only portion of that which remains golden is my memory." By way of emphasis he shifted his pack higher on his back. "Another lunch of jerked meat and dried fruit, I fear." Behind him, crowding close, Hunkapa Aub smiled ingenuously.

"Hunkapa like jerky!"

"You would," the swordsman muttered under his breath. As the sun climbed higher in a simmering, hazy sky, the humidity rose accordingly. But not all was the fault of the climate—they were approaching the riverfront.

Ships of all manner and description crowded the quays as lines of nearly naked, sweating stevedores proceeded with their unloading or provisioning. Shouts and curses mingled with the clanking of heavy tackle, the flap of unfurling canvas, the wet slap of lines against wooden piers and metal cleats. All manner of costume was visible in a blur of styles and hues, from intricately batiked turbans to simple loincloths to no-nonsense sailors' attire sewn in solid colors and material too tough for anything equipped with less dentition than a shark to bite through. It was a choice selection of barely organized chaos and confusion made worse by the presence of frolicking children, gawking sightseers, and strolling gentlefolk.

Ehomba was very hopeful.

It proved all but impossible to convince any of the busy

workers to pause long enough to answer even a few simple questions. Those who at first try appeared willing evaporated into the teeming crowd the instant they caught sight of the black litah, or Hunkapa Aub, or both. Afraid of the trouble his two nonhuman companions might up-stir in his absence, Ehomba was reluctant to accept Simna's suggestion that he and the swordsman temporarily leave them behind.

Exasperated by his tall friend's caution, the swordsman explained that if they could not part company even for a little while, they would have to query the operators of each craft one by one. While Ehomba concurred, he pointed out that they could begin with the largest, most self-evidently seaworthy craft. It was not necessary to inquire of the master of a two-man rowboat, for example, if he would be willing to try to transport them across the vast, dangerous expanse of the Semordria.

They began with the biggest ship in sight, one docked just to the left of where they were standing. Its first mate greeted them at the railing. After listening politely to their request, the wiry, dark-haired sailor shared a good laugh with those members of his crew who were near enough to participate.

"Didja hear that, lads? The long-faced fellow in the skirt wants us to take 'im and 'is circus across the Semordria!" Leaning over the railing, the mate grinned down at them and stroked his neatly coifed beard. "Would you like to make a stopover on the moon, perhaps? 'Tis not far out of the way, and I am told the seas between here and there are more peaceful."

The muscles in Ehomba's face tightened smartly, but he kept his tone respectful. "I take it that your answer is no?"

A vague sensation that he was being mocked transformed the mate's grin into a glower. "You can take it anyway you want, fellow, so long as you don't bring it aboard my boat." As he turned away he was smiling and laughing again.

"Cross the Semordria! Landsmen and foreigners—no matter where a man sails he's never free of 'em."

The response was more or less the same everywhere they tried. Most of the larger, better-equipped vessels plied their trade up and down the great watery swath of the Eynharrowk and its hundreds of navigable tributaries. A whole world of kingdoms and merchants, duchies and dukedoms and independent city-states was tied together by the Eynharrowk and its sibling rivers, Ehomba soon realized. They were the veins and arteries of an immensely extended, living, shifting body whose head lay not at the top, but in the middle. That head was Hamacassar. If they could not secure transportation there, they were unlikely to happen upon it anywhere else.

So they persisted, making their way along the riverfront walk, inquiring even of the owners of boats that seemed too small or too frail to brave the wave-swept reaches of the Semordria. Desperation drove them to thoroughness.

There *were* craft present that from time to time risked the storms and high seas of the ocean, but without exception these clung close to shore whenever they ventured out upon the sea itself, hiding in protected coves and harbors as they plied ancient coastal trade routes. Their crews were brave and their captains resolute, for the profits to be made from ranging so far afield from the Eynharrowk were substantial.

It was at the base of the boarding ramp of one such coastal trader, a smallish but sturdily built vessel, that a third mate supervising the loading of sacks of rice and millet provided their first ray of hope.

"Ayesh, there are ships that cross the Semordria." He spoke around the stem of a scrimshawed pipe that seemed to grow directly from his mouth, like the extended tooth of a narwhal. "More set sail westward than return. But now and again some master mariner reappears laden with wonderful goods and even better stories. Such captains are rare indeed.

They never change ships because their owners keep them content. Their crews adore them and are spoiled for use on other vessels. Having sailed under the best, they refuse to haul a line for anyone not as skilled."

Ehomba listened intently, making sure to let the mate finish before asking any more questions. "Where might we find such a ship, with such a crew?"

Squinting at the sky and focusing on a hovering cloud that might or might not contain a portion of the evening's rain, the mate thought carefully before replying.

"Among those of us who sail the Eynharrowk, the *Warebeth* has passed beyond reverence into legend. It is rumored that she has made twelve complete crossings of the Semordria without losing more than the expected number of seamen. I have never heard of her taking passengers, but then it is not the sort of trip most landsmen would consider. Certainly she's large enough to accommodate guests." As he related this information the mate kept nodding to himself, eyes half closed.

"A three-master, solid of keel and sound of beam. If any ship would take landsmen on such an arduous voyage, ayesh, it would be the *Warebeth*."

"Excellent," declared Ehomba. "Where do we find this craft?"

Removing his pipe, a process that somewhat surprisingly did not require a minor surgical procedure, the mate tapped the bowl gently against the side of a nearby piling. "Sadly, friends, the *Warebeth* left yesterday morning for a two-month journey upriver to the Thalgostian villages. If you're willing to wait for her return, you might have yourselves a ship." He placed the stem of the pipe back between his yellow-brown teeth.

"Two months." Ehomba's expression fell. "Are there no other choices?"

Sea dragonets perched on a nearby piling sang to one another, punctuating their songs with intermittent puffs of smoke. "Ayesh, maybe one." Turning, the mate pointed downriver, his finger tracing the line of the waterfront walk. "Try the out-end of quay thirty-six. If I'm not mistaken, the *Grömsketter* is still there. Captain Stanager Rose on deck, unless there's been a change of command since last I heard of her. She's done the Semordria transit more than once, though how many times I couldn't tell you. Not the wave piercer the *Warebeth* is, but a sound ship nonetheless. Whether she'll take wayfarers or not, much less landsmen, I don't know. But if she's still in port, she's your only other hope."

Ehomba bowed his head and dipped the point of his spear in the mate's direction. "Many thanks to you, sir. We can but try."

"Can but try indeed, bruther." Simna stayed close to the herdsman as they left the pier and began once more to push their way through the dynamic, industrious crowds. Behind them, the broad beam of Hunkapa Aub kept potential pickpockets and busybodies away by sheer force of his hulking presence. Given a space of his own by the crowd, which despite its preoccupations nevertheless kept well clear of the big cat, the black litah amused itself by pausing every so often to inspect pilings and high water for potentially edible harbor dwellers.

It turned out that in his eulogistic description of the *Warebeth* and its accomplishments, the neighborly and helpful mate had underrated the *Grömsketter.* To Ehomba's inexperienced eye it looked like a fine ship, with broad, curving sides and a high helm deck. There was only a single mainmast, but a second smaller foremast looked able to carry a respectable spread of sail between its crest and the bowsprit. Heavy-weather shutters protected the ports, and Simna pointed out that her lines were triple instead of double braided. Even to his eyes, she was rigged for serious weather. Her energetic crew looked competent and healthy.

As he contemplated the craft, the herdsman sought his companion's opinion. "What do you think, Simna?"

"I'm no mariner, Etjole." The swordsman scrutinized the vessel from stem to stern. "Give me something with legs to ride, any day. But I've spent some time on boats, and from what little I know she looks seaworthy enough. Surely no sailor would set out to traverse the Semordria on a craft he wasn't convinced would carry him across and back again."

Ehomba nodded once. Together they walked to the base of the boarding ramp. A few sailors were traveling in both directions along its length, but for the most part the majority of activity was taking place on board.

Putting his free hand alongside his mouth, the herdsman hailed the deck. "Hello! We are travelers seeking to cross the ocean, and were told you might be of service in such a matter!"

A tall, broad-chested seaman stopped coiling the rope he was working with to lean toward them. He was entirely bald except for a topknot of black hair that fell in a single thick braid down his back.

"You want passage across the Semordria?" A tense Ehomba nodded in the affirmative, waiting for the expected laugh of derision.

But the sailor neither laughed nor mocked him. "That's quite a pair you have with you. Are they pets, or tamed for sale?"

The black litah snarled up at the deck. "Come down here, man, and I'll show you who's a pet."

"*Bismalath!*" the man exclaimed. "A talking cat, and one of such a size and shape as I have never seen. And the other beast, it is also new to me." He beckoned to the travelers. "I am Terious Kemarkh, first mate of the *Grömsketter.* Come aboard, and we will see about this request of yours."

As they started up the ramp, a subdued but still obviously eager Ehomba in the lead, he called across to the mate. "Then you are preparing for a crossing of the Semordria?"

"Ayesh, but it's not up to me to decide whether you can, or should, travel with us." Completing the coil he had been working on when they had first arrived, he let it fall heavily to the deck. "That's a decision for the Captain to make."

Once aboard, the travelers saw that everything they had suspected about the *Grömsketter* continued to hold true. She was solid and well maintained, with no rigging lying loose to trip an unwary sailor and her teak worn smooth and clean. Lines were neatly stowed and all hatches not in use firmly secured.

The mate greeted them with hearty handshakes, electing to wave instead of accepting the affable Aub's extended paw. "A seaman has constant need of the use of his fingers," Terious explained in refusing the handshake. "Come with me."

He led them toward the stern and the raised cabin there. Bidding them wait, he vanished through an open hatchway like a mouse into its hole. Several moments passed, during which the travelers were able to observe the crew. For their part, the mariners were equally curious about their unfamiliar visitors. Several tried to feel of the litah's fur, only to be warned off by intimidating coughs.

Hoping that their host would return before the big cat's patience wore thin and it decided to remove an arm or other available extremity from some member of the crew, Ehomba was relieved when Terious popped back out of the hatchway. His expression was encouraging.

"Though in a surly mood, the Captain has agreed to hear you out. I explained as best I could that you were not from the valley of the Eynharrowk and had obviously traveled a great distance to try and effect this transit. I pointed out that with the *Warebeth* having already sailed, and upriver at that, the *Grömsketter* was your last best hope of crossing the ocean." Stepping out on the deck, he waited alongside them.

Both travelers studied the dark opening. "What sort of man is this Stanager Rose?" Simna asked anxiously.

The first mate's expression did not change. "Wait just a moment and you will see for yourself."

A muttered curse rose from below and a figure started to rise toward the light. An open-necked seaman's blouse was pushed into bright red pants with yellow striping, the legs of which were in turn tucked into boots of durable black stingray leather. A tousled mop of shoulder-length red hair was held away from the face by a wide yellow bandanna. A sextant hung from one hand, and a long dagger was slung through a double loop at the waist. Its haft was impressively jeweled.

Ehomba bowed once again. "We thank you for allowing us on board your ship, Captain, and for deigning to consider our request for transportation."

"Right. That's all it is right now, traveler—a request. But I'll give you a hearing." Steel-blue eyes looked the herds-man up and down, speculating openly. "Terious was right: You are a spectacle all by yourself, tall man. Taken to-gether with your companions, you're unnatural enough to claim a marketplace stage and charge admission just to look at you." A sea-weathered hand reached up and out to come down firmly on Ehomba's shoulder.

"Despite what you may have heard, it can get tiresome out in the middle of the ocean. Even on the Semordria. At such times, new entertainment is always welcome."

"We are not entertainers," Ehomba explained simply.

"Didn't say that you were. But you'll have stories to tell. I can see that just by looking at you." A hand gestured expansively downward. "You two come with me and we'll talk. I'm afraid that, garrulous or not, your woolly companions will have to remain on deck, as they'll never fit through this hatchway."

Nodding, Ehomba turned to explain the situation to Ahlitah and Hunkapa Aub. Doing so left Simna alone with the Captain. He was trying to think of something to say before his tall friend returned, but with the first mate standing nearby it was difficult to come up with just the right words, and he sensed he would have to be careful. From first sight, Stanager Rose had struck him as someone not to be trifled with. However much he wanted to.

Because, sea-weathered or not, the Captain of the *Grömsketter* was one of the most beautiful women he had ever seen.

XXIII

After leading them down to the officers' mess and directing them to their seats, she had drink brought by an attentive mess steward. It was some kind of spiced fruit juice neither Ehomba nor Simna recognized, flavorful but only slightly alcoholic.

"What is this?" Ehomba asked politely.

"Sicharouse. From Calex, across the ocean." She smiled proudly. "Sealed in oak casks, it ferments during the return crossing and is almost ready to drink when it arrives here in Hamacassar. Turned a tidy profit on it more than once, we have." Folding her hands on the heavy ship's table, she stared piercingly at Ehomba. "We leave in two days and I've a ship to prepare for departure. You wish passage across the ocean?"

"We do." As Simna ibn Sind appeared to have been suddenly and uncharacteristically struck dumb, Ehomba found that he had to do all the talking. "We journey to a kingdom called Ehl-Larimar."

Eyes widening slightly, Stanager leaned into the embrace of her high-backed chair. The swordsman found himself envying the wood. "Heard of the place, but never been there.

From what I recall, it lies far inland from any seaport. It's certainly not close to Calex." Simna suddenly found his voice: He groaned.

"I understand." Ehomba was unsurprised and unfazed by this information. "Ultimately reaching Ehl-Larimar is our business. But to get there we must first cross the ocean."

She nodded once, curtly. "We have space, and I am willing to take you." Her eyes met Simna's. "Even though it's transparently clear there's not a seaman among you. You and your creatures would have to stay out of the way of my crew. You wouldn't be confined to quarters, mind. I just ask that you be careful where you go, when you go, and what you do when you get there."

"Not long ago we crossed the Aboqua," he told her, "and gave the crew that attended to our needs no cause for complaint."

Turning her head to her left, she spat contemptuously. "The Aboqua! A pond, for children to splash in. I've beaten through storms that were bigger than the Aboqua. But at least you know what saltwater smells like." To Simna's chagrin, she returned her full attention to Ehomba. "What can you pay?"

It was the herdsman's turn to be rendered speechless. In the excitement of searching out and finally finding a ship to carry them, he had completely forgotten that payment for their passage would doubtless be demanded. The oversight was understandable. Among the Naumkib such matters arose but infrequently, when the village received one of its rare visits from a trader making the long trek north from Wallab or Askaskos.

Unable to reply, he turned to his more worldly friend. Simna could only shrug helplessly. "If you're thinking of the Chlengguu gold, it's all gone, bruther. We've spent every last coin. I know what you're thinking, but there's none tucked away in my pack or my shirt. More's the pity. I should have secreted some more away."

Stanager listened silently to the brief byplay. "Do you have anything to trade? Anything of significant value you would be willing to part with?"

The swordsman started to respond, but Ehomba stopped him before the words could leave his mouth. "No! We've risked our lives to save Ahlitah from just such a fate. I will not see him sold to satisfy my own needs."

Simna eyed him sharply. "Not even to get yourself across the Semordria?"

"Not even for that." The herdsman looked back at the Captain. "We have very few possessions, and these we need."

She nodded tersely, her red hair rippling, and started to rise from the table. "Then I wish you good fortune in your difficult endeavors, gentlemen. Now if you will excuse me, I have a long and strenuous voyage ahead of me, and many last-minute preparations to supervise." The audience was at an end.

Ehomba did not panic. It was not an emotion he was heir to. But seeing their best and only hope of crossing the ocean about to walk out the door, he certainly became uncommonly anxious. A sudden thought made him rise halfway from his own chair as he raised his voice.

"Wait! Please, one moment."

An impatient look on her deeply tanned face, Stanager Rose hesitantly resumed her seat. Simna was eyeing his tall friend curiously. The swordsman expected the herdsman to start digging through his pack, but this was not what happened. Instead, Ehomba reached down and fumbled briefly in one of the pockets of his kilt. What he brought out caused Simna's gaze to narrow.

The Captain nodded at the fist-sized cloth sack. "What've you got there, tall man? Gold, silver, trinkets?"

"Pebbles." Ehomba smiled apologetically. "From a beach

near my village. I brought them along to remind me of home, and of the sea. Whenever the longing grew too great, I could always reach into my pocket and rub the pebbles against each other, listen to them scrape and clink." He handed the sack to Stanager. "Once when I was much younger a trader came to the village from far to the south, farther away even than Askaskos. A friend of mine was playing jump-rock outside his house with some pebbles like these. Passing by, the trader happened to see and admire them. He offered my friend's family some fine things in exchange. After receiving approval from Asab, the trade was made." He gestured for the Captain to open the sack.

"If they were valuable to a trader who had come all the way from south of Askaskos, maybe they will have some value to you as well." He hesitated. "Though I would be sorry to have to give up my little memory bag."

Stanager was considerate if not hopeful. Taking pity on the lanky foreigner, she pulled the drawstring that closed the neck of the little cloth bag and turned it upside down. The double handful of pebbles promptly spilled out onto the tabletop. Struck by the light that poured in through the ports, the pebbles sparkled brightly. They were rough and sea-tossed, with most of the edges worn off them.

Simna's eyes opened so wide they threatened to pop right out of his head and roll egglike across the table. Like little else, his reaction did not escape the Captain's notice.

"So, Owl-eyes, you think these pebbles are valuable too?"

Recovering quickly, the swordsman looked away and exhaled indifferently. "Hoy, what? Oh, perhaps a little. I know very little about such things. To me they're nothing remarkable, but I believe my friend is right when he says that they might have some value."

"I see." Her gaze flicked sharply from one man to the other. "*Ayesh,* I am no expert on 'pebbles' either, but my supercargo knows a good deal about stones and their value.

We will soon learn if these are worth anything—or if you are trying to cozen me with stories." Pushing back in her seat, she yelled toward the open doorway. "Terious! Find old Broch and send him down here!"

They waited in silence, the Captain of the *Grömsketter* in all her stern-faced beauty, Ehomba smiling hopefully, and Simna gazing off into the distance with studied indifference.

"What are you gaping at, little man?" an irritated Stanager finally asked the swordsman.

"Hoy, me? Why nothing, Captain, nothing at all. I believe I was momentarily stunned, is all."

She chuckled softly. "The last man who tried to compliment his way into my berth found himself traveling in the bilges until we reached the town of Harynbrogue. By that time he was so ready to get off the *Grömsketter* he didn't much care what I or anyone else look like. You could smell him making his way into town even after he was well off the ship."

Simna adopted an expression so serious Ehomba had to turn away to smother a laugh. "Why Captain, you wrong me deeply! Such a notion would never cross my mind!" Solemnly, he placed one hand over his heart. "Know that I have taken a vow of celibacy until we have successfully concluded our journey, and that every member of this crew, be they male or female, need have no concerns along such lines when in my presence."

Stanager was still smiling. "I think you are one of the more notable liars I have ever hosted on this ship, but since you will in all likelihood be off it in a few moments, your dubious protestations of innocence do not matter." She turned as a figure darkened the doorway. "Broch, come in."

Weatherbeaten as a spar at the end of its useful life, the supercargo entered on bowed legs. He was even shorter than Simna, and considerably thinner. But the wrinkled, leathery brown skin on his arms covered a lean musculature that resembled braided bullwhips. His fulsome beard was gray with a few remaining streaks of black, and his eyes were sharp and alert.

Stanager gestured at the collection of tumbled pebbles spread out on the mess table. "Tell me, what do you think of these?"

The old man looked, and though it seemed impossible, his eyes grew even wider than had the swordsman's. *"Memoch gharzanz!"* he exclaimed in a language neither Ehomba nor Simna recognized. "Where—where did these come from, Captain?"

She gestured at Ehomba. "These gentlemen together with their two, um, nonhuman companions desire to make the Semordria crossing with us. This is what they offer in payment. Is it sufficient?"

Seating himself at the table, the old mariner removed a small magnifying lens from a pants pocket. It was secured to the interior of the pocket, Ehomba noted, by a strong string. Bending low, he examined several of the pebbles, taking them up one at a time and turning them over between his fingers, making sure the light struck them from different angles. After studying half a dozen of the pebbles, he sat back in his chair and repocketed the glass.

"These are the finest diamonds I have ever seen. Half are flawless, and the other half fine enough to grace the best work of a master jeweler."

"That's for the clear ones," Simna agreed even though he was as surprised as anyone else at the table, "but what kind of stones are the others?"

"They are *all* diamonds," Broch explained. "Clear, yellow, blue, red, green, and pink, diamonds all. Mostly three to four carats, some smaller, a couple as large as six." Swallowing, he eyed the tranquil herdsman intently. "Where did you get these, foreigner?"

"There is a beach near my village."

"Ah." The supercargo nodded sagely. "You picked them out of the gravel on this beach."

"No," Ehomba explained quietly. "I just grabbed up a handful or two and dropped them in my little bag." He indicated the scattering of sparklers that decorated the tabletop. "The whole beach is like this. The pebbles are all the same. Except for the different colors, of course." His smile was almost regretful. "I wish I had known that they were so valuable. I would have brought more."

"More." The old man swallowed hard.

Ehomba shrugged. "Sometimes the waves wash away all the pebbles and leave behind only sand. After a big storm the pebbles may lie as deep on the shore as a man's chest. At such times, when the sun comes out, the beach is very pretty."

"Yes," murmured the supercargo. He looked slightly shell-shocked. "Yes, I would imagine it is." Shaking his head, he turned to the expectant Stanager. "They have enough to book passage, Captain—or to buy the ship many times over. Take them. Give them the finest cabin. If they wish, they may have my own and I will sleep belowdecks with the rest of the crew. Give them anything they want."

"Really," an embarrassed Ehomba demurred, "passage will be quite sufficient. Our two large friends can find room in your hold, among your cargo."

"Done." Reaching across the table, Stanager shook the tall southerner's hand. "You really didn't know these stones were diamonds, or that they were valuable?"

"Oh, they have always been valuable to me," Ehomba conceded. "Feeling of them reminds me of home." He glanced over at the supercargo. "Take your payment, please."

"A *fair* payment," Simna interjected in no-nonsense tones. "We've hidden nothing from you, been completely up-front. As the old man says, we could always buy ourselves a ship."

"Ayesh," agreed Stanager, "but it wouldn't be the *Gröms-ketter*, and whatever crew you engaged wouldn't be the *Grömsketter*'s crew. Have no fear, foreigner—this is an honorable vessel crewed by honest seamen." She nodded at her supercargo. "Take the payment, Broch."

Licking his lips, the elderly mariner contemplated the riches strewn so casually before him. Finally, after much deliberation, he settled on the second-largest stone, a perfect deep pink diamond of some six carats.

"This one, I think." Hesitating to see if the owners objected, he then quickly plucked the rough gem from the table. "And a few of the smaller." He smiled. "To give the selection a nice play of color." Having made his choices, he handed them to Stanager.

"Thank you, Broch." She deposited them in her empty drinking mug. "Please wait outside for us."

"Thank you, Captain." He turned to leave.

"Just a second." Simna was smiling knowingly. "What about the one that 'accidentally' got caught under your fingernail? Middle finger of the left hand, I believe?"

"What? Oh, this." Feigning confusion, the old man removed a half-carat stone from beneath the offending nail and placed it back on the table. "Sorry. These small stones, you know, are like sand. They can get caught up in anything."

"Sure they can." Simna was still smiling. "Etjole, pack up the rest of your pebbles."

The herdsman scooped the remaining stones into the little cloth sack. Old Broch watched his every move to see if he might overlook any. When it was clear that the herdsman had not, the supercargo sighed regretfully and left.

"Well then." Planting both palms firmly on the table, Stanager pushed back from the table and stood. "Welcome aboard the *Grömsketter*, gentlemen. I'll have Broch show you to your cabin, and we'll see about getting your oversized companions properly settled below. You have two days to enjoy the sights and delights of Hamacassar. Then we set sail downriver for the Semordria, far Calex, and the unknown."

"Thank you, Captain." Ehomba executed his half bow. "Is there anything else we should know before we depart?"

"Yes." Turning her head to look at an expressionless Simna, she declared sweetly, "If this foreign creature doesn't take his hand off my ass I will have Cook mince and dice him and serve him tomorrow morning for breakfast hash."

"Hoy? Oh, sorry." Simna removed the offending hand, eyeing it as if it possessed a mind and will of its own. "I thought that was the chair cushion."

"Think more carefully next time, foreigner, or I will prevent any further confusion by having the errant portion of your anatomy removed."

"I said I was sorry," he protested.

"Your eyes argue with your words." She led the way out of the mess.

Later, as they followed old Broch through a narrow passage, Ehomba leaned down to whisper to his companion. "Are you mad, Simna? Next time she will have you quartered!"

A dreamy lilt tinted the swordsman's voice. "Her beauty would drive a man mad. A little sunburnt, yes. A little hardened by the weather, to be sure. But to see her at ease on a broad bed, divested of mariner's attire, would be worth a couple of those diamonds to me."

"Then I will give you the diamonds, but keep away from her! We have yet to enter the Semordria, much less cross it. I am a good swimmer, but I do not want to have to exercise that skill in the middle of the ocean."

The swordsman was quietly outraged. "You ask me to deny myself, bruther. To go against the very substance of my being, to refute that which comprises a most basic portion of myself, to abjure my very nature." He deliberated briefly. "How many diamonds?"

By the morning of the third day all was in readiness. Standing tall on the helm deck, the old woman who handled the ship's wheel waiting for orders alongside her, Captain Stanager Rose gave the order to let go the fore and aft lines and cast off. With becoming grace, the *Grömsketter* waltzed clear of the quay and slipped out into the gentle current of the lower Eynharrowk. Adjusting sail and helm, she aimed her bow downstream. With only the mainsail set, she began to make use of the current and pick up speed.

Ehomba and Simna had joined the Captain on the stern while Hunkapa Aub lounged near the bow and the black litah slept curled atop a sun-swathed hatch, his long legs drooping lazily over the sides.

"A fine day for a departure." Stanager alternated her gaze between the busy crew, the set sail, and the shore. Only when she was satisfied with the appearance of all three did she devote whatever attention remained to her passengers. "We'll be through the Narrows by midmorning. From there it's easy sailing to the delta and the mouth of the Eynharrowk." At last she turned to the two men standing next to her, once more focusing on Ehomba to the exclusion of his shorter companion.

"Did you sleep well, herdsman?"

"Very well. I love the water, and the cabin bunks are sturdy enough so that my spine does not feel like it is falling out of my back."

"Good. Later, Cook will begin to amaze you with her invention. We're fortunate to have her. A ship may make do with a poor navigator, feeble sailors, even an indifferent captain, but so long as the food is good there will be few complaints." Her tone darkened. "Enjoy the river while you can, Etjole Ehomba. Where it is smooth the Semordria is wave-tossed, and where it is inoffensive the sea is deadly.

Throughout the crossing each one of us must be eternally vigilant. That includes any passengers."

Simna nodded somberly. "As long as one can see the danger, it can be dealt with. Sometimes even made into an ally."

She frowned at him for a moment, then looked away, returning her attention to the view over the bowsprit. "Your presence here is not required. You may relax in your cabin if you wish."

"Thank you," Ehomba responded courteously, "but after so long afoot it is a pleasure to be able to simply look at and enjoy our surroundings."

She shrugged. "As you wish. If you'll excuse me now, I have work to do."

"Mind if I tag along?" Like a debutante donning her most expensive and elegant gown, Simna had put on his widest and most innocent smile. "I haven't been on that many boats. I might learn something."

Her expression was disapproving. "I doubt it, but you've paid well for the run of the ship." She started forward.

"Now then," the swordsman began, "the first thing I want to know is, what areas of the *Grömsketter* are off limits to us?"

Turning away from them, Ehomba moved to the rail and watched as the outskirts of industrious, hardworking Hamacassar slid past. They were on their way at last. Not on the Semordria itself, not yet—but on their way. How much farther they would have to travel to reach Ehl-Larimar once they landed on the ocean's far shore he did not know. But whatever it was, it too would be crossed. Somewhere, he knew that the shade of Tarin Beckwith was watching, and whispering its approval.

The Narrows were comprised of opposing headlands whose highest point would not have qualified as a proper foothill on either side of the snow-capped Hrugars, but on the otherwise plate-flat floodplain they stood out prominently. Accelerating as it passed through, the vast river's volume was compressed, causing the *Grömsketter* to pick up speed. As they drew near, Ehomba saw that what at first appeared to be trees were in fact more of the extraordinary triangular towers that they had first encountered on the southern outskirts of greater Hamacassar.

With Stanager absent from the helm deck, he wandered over to query the stolid, stocky woman behind the ship's wheel. "Your pardon, Priget, but what are those odd free-standing spires?"

"You don't know?" She had a thick accent that he had been told instantly identified her as coming from far upriver. "They're the time gates. They're what has kept Hamacassar strong and made it the preeminent port of the middle Eynharrowk. Kept it from being attacked and looted for hundreds of years. The Gate Masters' guild watches over them, decides when they are to be used and when kept closed."

Ehomba pondered this as the helmswoman nudged the wheel a quarter degree to port. "What kind of gates did you say they were? Does time gate mean they are very old?"

"No. They are . . . hullo, what's this?" Setting his question aside, she squinted to her left. Moments later Stanager was back on the high stern, Simna trailing behind like an eager puppy.

She ignored both men. "You see the flags, Priget?"

"Yes, Captain. How should we respond?"

Stanager looked conflicted. "The flags are small and still a goodly distance off. Hold your course and we'll see what they do. They may be testing us, or flagging a small boat somewhere close inshore."

"Ayesh, Captain." The helmswoman settled herself firmly behind the wheel.

Sensing that now was not a good time to lay a raft of queries upon the Captain, Ehomba and Simna both held their questions. The *Grömsketter* continued to slip swiftly downriver, using its mainsail more for steering than propulsion in the heightened current.

Following their eyes, Ehomba saw what they were scrutinizing so intently. Near the base of the second triangular monolith on the south bank stood a cluster of reddish buildings dominated by a three-story brick tower. Atop this formidable structure was a mast from which presently flew three large, brightly patterned flags. The designs that were of such evident significance to Captain and helmswoman meant nothing to him, nor to Simna. He also thought he could see several figures waving both arms above their heads.

A hand came down on his shoulder as the swordsman pointed. "See there, Etjole. Something is happening."

Between the towers that stood on opposing headlands a deep blue glow was coalescing. Shot through with thousands of attenuated streaks of bright yellow and white like captured lightning, the effulgence extended from the crests of the towers down to the surface of the river, clearing it by less than half a foot. From the depths of the potent luminescence there emanated a dull roar, like an open ocean wave curling and breaking endlessly back upon itself. The glow flowed swiftly from tower to tower, as far as the eye could see. Remembering what Priget had told him of the structures' purpose, Ehomba imagined that the deep cobalt light must extend to encircle all of greater Hamacassar.

"That's it." Stanager looked resigned. "They're calling us in. Priget, steer for the inspection docks."

"Ayesh, Captain." The helmswoman promptly spun the wheel. Slowing only slightly, the *Grömsketter* began to turn sharply to port.

"What's happening? Why are we heading in?" Relaxed and talkative only moments ago, Simna was suddenly nervous.

"Probably only a random check," the Captain assured him. "The Gate Masters run them on occasion, both to flex their muscles and remind travelers on the river of just who is in charge, and to ascertain the condition of the time gates." She nodded toward the dense blue radiance. "Those, at least, appear to be functioning flawlessly."

"I do not understand." Simna spoke both for himself and his friends. "What are these time gates? What is that banded blue glowing?"

Stanager Rose did not smile. "You really are from far away, aren't you?"

"Captain," the swordsman told her, "all your long and difficult journeys notwithstanding, you have no idea."

She spared him barely a glance before turning back to Ehomba. "The streaked blue glow is Time itself. The ancient Logicians of Hamacassar long suspected that time traveled in a stream, like the Eynharrowk. So they found the Time that follows the great river and channeled it. Here Time flows through a canal, much like the hundreds you have seen crisscrossing the city itself. It runs through the time gates and can be turned on or shut off by a master gate that lies to the northeast of the city. When the master gate is opened, Time is allowed to run in a circular channel all around the border of Hamacassar. Until it is closed and the time stream shut off, no one can enter or leave the city. No criminal may flee, no enemy enter." She nodded forward. "As you can see, it flows as effectively over water as across the land."

"What would happen if you just tried to run it?" Simna was a direct man, and it was a direct question.

By the Captain's reaction, however, not a well-thought-out one. "Why, any vessel attempting to sail through would be caught in the currents of Time and swept away, never to be seen or heard from again. I don't know what that would be like, because no ship or person who has been caught up in the time flow has ever come back out to speak of the experience." She nodded toward the rapidly approaching outpost. "We'll see what they want and then we'll be on our way again. I'm sure it's nothing of significance, and will likely cost us half an hour at most."

Despite the Captain's reassurances, Ehomba was distressed to see a double line of heavily armed soldiers drawn up on the dock. They carried crossbows and battle swords but wore little armor, impractical in the heat and humidity of the Hamacassarian lowlands. They wore uniforms of streaked emerald green and sandals instead of boots, again in keeping with the practicalities imposed by the climate.

Waiting to greet the *Grömsketter* as it bumped up against the dock were half a dozen men and women of varying age. All wore similar colors, but much finer fabrics. The single togalike garments were belted at the waist with yellow-gold braid, and extended only as far as the knee. Sleeves ended at the elbow. Shading their heads were peculiar tricornered hats that mimicked the design of the time gates. None of the assembled were smiling.

Clinging to the mainmast rigging with one hand and leaning out over the water and the dock as the ship pulled in, Terious hailed the gathering. "Good morning to you, virtuous Gate Masters! Do you wish to board?"

A stern-faced, handsome man in his forties replied. "Only if necessary, *Grömsketter*. We won't keep you long. We're looking for someone."

"A fugitive?" Behind the helm deck railing, Stanager was murmuring aloud to herself. "We've hired three new men and one woman for this crossing. I wonder if all were thoroughly checked?" Leaning over the rail, she shouted down at the Gate Master. "Does this person you seek have a name?"

As she spoke, preoccupied faces turned in her direction. Ehomba and Simna stood close by. Suddenly another of the Gate Masters, an older woman, spoke out sharply.

"No name, only an aura—and there he is!" Raising an arm, she pointed sharply.

Straight at Ehomba.

XXIV

On board the *Grömsketter* all eyes turned to the obviously bemused herdsman. When he did not respond, Stanager again addressed the assembled officials. "This man is a passenger on my ship. Though known to me for only a few days, I have found him to be a responsible and worthy individual. What is it you want with him?"

"That is our business," another man shouted upward. "Turn him over and you may proceed on your way. Refuse, and your vessel will be boarded. Those who comply may depart freely. Those who resist will be killed or taken before the Board of Logicians to have their ultimate fates resolved."

Stepping away from the railing, Stanager turned to stare up at her long-faced passenger. "I don't understand any of this. What do the Gate Masters want with you? What have you done?"

"I tell you honestly, Captain: to my knowledge, nothing." Ehomba was aware that the eyes not only of his friends but of the crew were on him, watching and waiting to see what he would do. "But I cannot allow my own circumstances to put you and your people in danger. You have done nothing."

"By Gorquon's Helmet, neither have we, Etjole!" The right hand of Simna ibn Sind rested firmly on the hilt of his sword. "I'll not see you handed over to an unknown fate. Not after all we've been through together!"

The herdsman smiled fondly at his friend. "What is this, Simna? Loyalty? And without a gold piece in sight?"

"Mock me if you will, long bruther. You wouldn't be the first." The swordsman's face was flush with anger. "Dying in combat with some monstrous beast or battling an attacking army is a worthy death for a man. You deserve better than to rot in some cell accused of Gwinbare knows what imaginary crime."

"No one has said anything about dying or rotting in a cell." Ehomba's voice was calm, his manner composed. "They may only want to talk to me."

"Hoy, but for how long?" Simna gestured sharply in the direction of the assembled soldiers and officials. "They said that once they have you, the rest can sail on. That doesn't sound to me like they plan to let you go anytime soon, and you said yourself we shouldn't wait two months for another ship."

"So you should not." Raising his hands, the herdsman placed them on his friend's shoulders. "I hereby charge you, Simna ibn Sind, with completing my task, with fulfilling my promise to the dying Tarin Beckwith. Stay with the *Grömsketter*. See her across the Semordria, and find your way onward from there."

The swordsman tensed. "What madness is this? What are you saying, Etjole?"

Removing his hands, Ehomba turned back to the railing. "I am getting off the ship." He looked to Stanager. "Captain, as soon as I am on the dock and the Narrows are once more cleared to navigation, set your course downriver and sail on."

She eyed him purposefully for a long moment, then nodded once.

A ladder of rope and wood was thrown over the side. Ehomba started toward it, only to be grabbed and held by the swordsman.

"Don't do this, bruther! You have your weapons; I have my sword. There is the black litah and Hunkapa Aub. We can fight them off!" His fingers tightened on the taller man's arm.

Gently, Ehomba disengaged himself from his friend's grasp. "No, Simna. Even if we could, sailors who have no part in this might get hurt, or killed. As could any of us, yourself included. Stay on the ship. Sail on." He smiled warmly. "Think of me as the river carries you to the sea." Turning away, he stepped over the side, straddling the railing preparatory to climbing down the ladder.

"Stop there!" a voice commanded from below. Crossbow bolts were trained on the herdsman. "No weapons. Leave them and the pack on your back on board the ship. You can claim them upon its return."

Removing the sword of sea bone and the sword of sky metal, Ehomba passed them to a stricken Simna. They were joined by the long walking stick–spear. Lastly, the herdsman slipped off his backpack and handed it to a somber-faced Terious. Hunkapa Aub was crying outsized inhuman tears. Ehomba was grateful that the black litah was still asleep. It might not have been possible to restrain the big cat with words. Had it been awake, the spilling of blood might have proven unavoidable.

Descending the ladder, he jumped the last few feet to the dock, landing with a resonant *thump* on his well-worn sandals. Instantly, he was surrounded by soldiers. With an approving nod, one of the Gate Masters turned and gave a signal to someone in the brick tower. Flags flashed in the direction of the opposing headlands, where other flags responded.

How it was done Ehomba could not tell. The time gates that surmounted the headlands were too far away for him to discern the mechanisms involved. But the shimmering, coruscating blue haze that blocked the Eynharrowk abruptly vanished, though it remained in place everywhere else.

Aboard the *Grömsketter* shouts rang loudly. He could make out the brisk, lively syllables of Stanager's commands and the deeper echoes of Terious and the other mates. Deliberately, the sleek ship pulled away from the dock and turned its bow once more toward the Narrows. Along the railing he could see an openly distraught Simna staring back at him. Behind the swordsman the hulking mass of hair that was Hunkapa Aub stood and waved slowly. He continued to follow them with his eyes until a hand shoved him roughly in the middle of his back.

"Move along, then. There are coaches waiting to take us back to the city."

Turning away from the *Grömsketter,* receding rapidly now that it was edging back out into the main current, Ehomba began the long march to the end of the dock. Gate Masters paralleled him on both sides and were in turn flanked by their stalwart, alert soldiers.

"Maybe now you can tell me what this is all about?" he asked the green-clad official on his left. Like his sisters and brothers, the man's hands were locked together in front of him.

"Certainly. We don't act arbitrarily, you know. There is a reason for this. Your arrival was predicted by the Logicians. Taking their measurements from disturbances in the Aether and the flow of Time, they calculated the cognomen of your aura and its probable path. As you have seen, Hamacassar is a big place, where even a distinctive aura can hide. We almost missed you. That would have been tragic."

Ehomba frowned, openly puzzled. "Why is that?"

The Gate Master looked up at him. "Because according to the Logicians' predictions, if you were allowed to proceed on your chosen course unhindered, the flow of Time would have been substantially altered, and perhaps unfavorably."

"Unfavorable to whom?" In the lexicon of the Naumkib, forthrightness invariably took precedent over tact. Ehomba was no exception.

"It does not matter. Not to you," the official informed him importantly. "Having committed no crime, you are not a prisoner. You are a guest, until your friends return. Or if you prefer, you will be allowed to leave in one month's time, once the *Grömsketter* is well out to sea and beyond reach." The man smiled. His expression was, the herdsman decided, at least half genuine.

They were nearing the end of the dock. "What makes you so certain that if I was permitted to continue on my journey Time would react adversely?"

This time it was the woman on his right who replied. "The Logicians have declared it to be so. And the Logicians are never wrong."

"Time may be a river," Ehomba responded, "but logic is not. At least, not the logic that is discussed by the wise men and women of my village."

"His 'village.'" Two of the Gate Masters strolling in front of him exchanged a snickering laugh.

"This is not a village, foreigner," declared the man on the herdsman's left meaningfully. "This is Hamacassar, whose Board of Logicians is comprised of the finest minds the city and its surrounding provinces can provide."

Ehomba was not intimidated. "Even the finest minds are not infallible. Even the most reasonable and logical people can make mistakes."

"Well, according to them, detaining you is not a mistake. Whereas letting you continue on most surely would be."

The tall southerner glanced back down the dock. In the

distance, the sturdy hull of the *Grömsketter* was passing through the Narrows, traveling swiftly westward as the current continued to increase its speed. Turning his attention to the red-brick administration buildings up ahead, he saw several antelope-drawn coaches lined up outside. More soldiers waited there, a mounted escort to convoy him and the Gate Masters back to the city.

"You know," he murmured conversationally, "logic is a funny thing. It can be used to solve many problems, even to predict things that may happen in the future. But it is not so very good at explaining people: who they are, what they are about, why they do the things they do. Sometimes even masters of logic and reason can think too long and too hard about something, until the truth of it becomes lost in a labyrinth of conflicting possibilities."

While the woman on his right pondered his words, the man on his left frowned. "What are you trying to say, foreigner?"

"That anyone, however clever they believe themselves to be, can think too much." Whereupon he lurched heavily to his right, slamming his shoulder into the startled female official and sending her stumbling and crashing into the two soldiers marching close alongside her. In a confusion of weapons and words, all three went toppling together off the end of the dock to land in the shallow water below.

"Stop him! Don't kill him, but stop him!" the senior Gate Master shouted.

With dozens of soldiers in pursuit, Ehomba ran inland. A lifetime of chasing down errant calves and stray lambs allowed him to outdistance all but the most active of his pursuers, not to mention the Gate Masters who trailed huffing and puffing in their wake. Neither group was in any especial hurry. There was nowhere for the herdsman to go. If he entered the water they would quickly chase him down in boats. The headland toward which he was running ended in a low bluff overlooking the river. All other directions were sealed off by the still active time gates, through which the flow of Time continued to ripple and shimmer.

"Stop!" yelled a voice from behind him.

"You can't get away!" shouted another. "There's nowhere to go!"

But there was somewhere to go. Or rather, somewhen.

Taking a deep breath and making an arrow of his clasped hands, Ehomba leaped forward and dove headfirst into the time stream.

Somewhere far around the curve of the world, the most powerful sorcerer alive woke up screaming.

From the hole Ehomba's body made in the channel, Time spewed forth in a gush of unrestrained chronology. Amid shrieks and howls, Gate Masters and soldiers alike were swept up and washed away in the flood of Time, to disappear forever into some otherwhen. The detained deranged foreigner was forgotten in the survivors' haste to close all the time gates and so shut off the flow to the devastating leak.

Once this had finally been accomplished, reluctant soldiers were sent to scour the area where the tall stranger had disappeared. Though not hopeful, the Gate Masters knew they had to try. The Logicians would demand it. As expected, there was no sign or suspicion that the foreigner had ever existed. He was gone forever: vanished, swept away, taken up by the river of Time. With wondering sighs and expressions of regret for those colleagues who had been lost in the short-lived disaster, they set about composing themselves for the journey back into the city. It was an occurrence that occasioned much animated discussion among the survivors.

Caught up by the river of Time, Ehomba kicked and dug hard at the eras that rushed past. Growing up by the sea, he was a naturally strong swimmer. Still, it was hard to tread years, difficult to hold one's breath as wave after wave of eternity broke over one's mind. But to the determined and well conditioned, not impossible.

He swam on, trying to make timefall as close to the point where he had entered the river as possible. The current was strong, but he had expected that and, by his angle of entry, done his best to anticipate it. Caught up in the flow of Time, he was battered and buffeted by astonishing sights. Animals ancient and fantastical rushed past. Great machines the likes of which he had never imagined clanked ponderously forward down unsuspected evolutionary paths, and all manner of men inhabited times immemorial and impossibly distant.

He was almost out of breath when a faint gleam caught his eye. Turning in the Time flow, he kicked hard for it. It was one of the blazing yellow-white streaks he had seen from his own time, viewed now from the inside out. This in itself was a wonderment to him, for he did not know that it was possible to see light from the inside out. The current tore at him, insistent and relentless. He felt himself weakening.

Worse than that, he was running out of Time.

Below the Narrows of Hamacassar the Eynharrowk once more became a broad, placid highway. Smaller boats traveling in the same direction as the *Grömsketter* kept closer to either shore, while those beating their way upstream gave her a wide berth. Small islands dotted with reeds and cattails had begun to appear, the first outposts of the great delta into which the torpid river spread before at last entering the ocean. Fishermen had erected modest homes on the larger islets, and spread their nets from long poles rammed into the shallows.

The *Grömsketter* kept to the main channel. With the widening of the river, the current had dissipated considerably over the past weeks and her speed had slowed accordingly. Crewmen and -women palavered boisterously as they worked the ship, but among her remaining passengers the mood was glum.

Simna was unable to think straight. His friend had charged him with completing the journey begun in the far south, but how was a common mercenary like himself to know how to proceed? Ehomba's mystic weapons remained on board, but the swordsman was more leery than hopeful of figuring out how to make proper use of them. He had no money, the herdsman having carried off the remaining "beach pebbles" in his pocket. His one ally was the imposing but simple-minded Hunkapa Aub. As for the black litah, upon awakening and learning what had transpired, the big cat had promptly announced his intention to leave the ship at the first opportunity. As he explained inexorably to Simna, his allegiance had been to the herdsman personally, not to his cause. With Ehomba gone, the cat considered its obligation at an end.

"Don't you care about what he began?" the swordsman had reproached the litah. "Do you wish all his efforts to go for naught?"

The big cat remained unperturbed. "His efforts are, and were, of no interest to me. It was the person I chose to associate with. I am sorry he is no longer here. For a human, he was a most interesting individual." The moist black tongue emerged to lick and clean around the nostrils. "I always wondered what he would have tasted like."

Simna sneered openly, not caring how the sleek predator might react, finding that he presently cared about so little that it shocked him. "It's all primeval to you, isn't it? Food, sex, sleep. You've acquired nothing in the way of culture from your association with us. Nothing!"

"On the contrary," the litah objected. "I have learned a good deal these past many weeks about humankind. I have learned that its culture is obsessed with food, sex, and sleep. The only difference between us is that you don't do any of it as well."

"By Geenvar's claws, I'll tell you that—"

The discussion was interrupted by a loud cry from the lookout. Posted atop the mainmast, the seaman was pointing and shouting. Fully intending to resume his dialogue with the big cat, Simna glanced curiously in the direction indicated by the mariner. At first he saw nothing. Then the subject of much commotion came into view and he found himself surrounded and carried forward by excited members of the crew. Not that he needed any help.

Etjole Ehomba was standing on the end of a small, handmade pier, waving casually in the *Grömsketter*'s direction. Except for a rip or two in his kilt and shirt, he looked healthy and relaxed.

Unsuspected excitement in her voice, Stanager Rose roared commands. The mainsail was reefed and the sea anchor cast off astern to slow their speed. As she hurriedly explained to Simna, she did not want to risk anchoring and stopping in the event that the soldiers of the Gate Masters were giving chase. This despite the fact that no troops or pursuers of any kind were in evidence. The swordsman did not argue with her. He was of like mind when it came to not taking chances.

One of the ship's lifeboats was quickly put over the side. Commanded by Terious himself, it plucked the waiting Ehomba from the end of the pier and, propelled by six strong oarsmen, returned to the *Grömsketter*. The sea anchor was hauled in, and this time all sails were set.

Ehomba's friends were waiting impatiently to greet him as he climbed back aboard. Attempting to clasp the tall southerner by the arm, Simna was nearly bowled over as Hunkapa Aub rushed past him to envelop the herdsman in an embrace that threatened to suffocate him before he could explain what had happened. From the helm deck, Stanager Rose looked on with pretended disinterest.

When Ehomba finally managed to extricate himself from

Hunkapa's smothering grasp, Simna confronted him with the question that had been bothering him ever since they had first caught sight of the herdsman standing alone on the pier.

"I am half convinced that you are what you claim to be, Etjole: nothing more than a humble herder of cattle and sheep." He gestured back toward the section of river that was falling far behind. "However, the other half of me wonders not only how you escaped the Gate Masters and their minions, but how you managed to appear in the middle of the Eynharrowk *ahead* of us. I know you can play the flute and spew forth heavenly winds and white sharks from your weapons, but I didn't know that you could fly."

"I cannot, friend Simna." With a smile and nod in the Captain's direction, the herdsman began to walk forward, seemingly little the worse for his experience. "No more than a bird without wings. But I can swim."

As had happened to him more times than he cared to remember in the herdsman's presence, Simna ibn Sind did not understand.

"Time is harder to tread than water, my friend, but it can be done. We of the Naumkib are taught how to swim at an early age. It is a necessary thing when one lives so near to the sea, and to other great emptinesses." Reaching into a pocket, he began to roll the remaining beach pebbles in the little cloth sack fondly through his fingers. Whereas before he had never paid any attention to the activity, now, each time he heard them grind together, Simna winced.

"I swam hard, my friend, determined never to give up." Ehomba smiled. "Giving up would have meant renouncing my pledge to Tarin Beckwith, and never seeing my home or family again. I vowed that would not happen. After treading Time for a while I tried to swim back out a little ways from where I had entered the river of Time." A shrug rippled his shoulders.

"But the current was powerful. Time is like that, always moving forward, always flowing strongly. So I did not come out where I wanted to." He looked back over his shoulder. "Emerging several weeks before I entered, I found myself on this little island. I built a small shelter of reeds, and the clumsy pier you saw, and caught fish and mussels and clams. And I waited for you. A month after a few minutes ago, the *Grömsketter* came through the Narrows." Reaching out, he put a comradely arm around the swordsman's shoulders. "And now, here you are."

The explanation did nothing to mitigate the look of utter bewilderment that had commandeered the swordsman's countenance. "Wait now, bruther. We just saw you off the ship and in the surly company of those Gate Masters not more than—"

"A few minutes ago. I know." They were approaching the bow. "But I have been waiting for you nearly a month. Time is a river most strange, my friend. Strange as only those who swim in it can know."

"But if you were there, and now you are here . . ." Simna's brows furrowed so deeply they threatened to pinch off his nose.

"Do not ponder on such things too long," Ehomba advised him. "That was the Logicians' problem. Overthinking can snarl the most elegant logic." Raising a hand, he gestured forward. "Ahead lies the great delta of the Eynharrowk. Soon we will leave behind the land for the Semordria. The eternal ocean that I have fished in, swam in, and played in all my life. If the shore is so amazing, what wonders must lie hidden beneath its outer depths?"

"Some that bite, I've no doubt." Inhaling deeply of the still steamy air, the swordsman leaned against the bow rail and gazed westward.

Feeling something bump him firmly from behind, Ehomba turned to see the black litah standing at his back. Typically, he had neither heard nor sensed the big cat's approach.

"So you're back." The long-legged carnivore yawned, revealing a gape that extended from the herdsman's head to his belly. "Pity. I was looking forward to returning home."

"No one is restraining you," Ehomba reminded him.

"Yes someone is. I am." As he addressed Ehomba, yellow cat eyes glared at the herdsman. "Call it a matter of culture. I am stuck with you lot until the next time you try to die."

"Then I will do my best to avoid that, and make an end to this business as quickly as events allow."

The cat nodded impressively, the freshening breeze from off the bow ruffling the magnificent black mane. "We seek the same thing."

"Hoy, not me," Simna protested quickly. "It's the treasure I'm after!" He eyed the herdsman sharply. "Whether it consists of legendary Damura-sese itself or nothing more than 'beach pebbles.' So don't try to deny it, bruther!"

Ehomba sighed resignedly. "Has it ever done me any good to do so?"

"No," the swordsman replied emphatically.

"Very well. The Visioness Themaryl. Treasure. No denials."

Satisfied, Simna went silent. Its freedom once again postponed, the black litah chose a sun-soaked section of deck, curled up into itself, and went back to sleep. Astern, Hunkapa Aub was watching a handful of sailors at dice while struggling to comprehend the intricacies of the game.

Waiting for the sea, Ehomba watched the river and thought of Mirhanja, and his children, and the way the same ocean they were about to enter lapped at the beach below the village. Soon it would be calving season at home, and he knew he would be missed.

Did ever any among the living drive a man so hard and so far as one dead? he found himself wondering.

About the Author

ALAN DEAN FOSTER is the author of more than eighty books, including sixteen *New York Times* bestsellers. Among his works are *Carnivores of Light and Darkness*, *The Dig*, and the Spellsinger and Flinx series. A world traveler, Mr. Foster lives in Arizona.

THE GRAND
CONCLUSION!

Please turn this page
for a
bonus excerpt
from
the final book in the
Journeys of the Catechist series,

A TRIUMPH OF SOULS

available in hardcover
March 2000.

XXIII

Ehomba met the onrushing eromakadi head-on, without trying to dodge or step clear of their charge. In an instant he was enveloped in black cloud and completely obscured from view. Simna held his breath. Even so, he was less agitated than his companions, who unlike him had not had the benefit of seeing the herdsman deal with eromakadi. But as the minutes passed and nothing happened and Ehomba did not reappear, the swordsman found himself growing more and more uneasy.

Then a soft whistling became audible. It grew louder, until it dominated the room. The vaporous substance of the eromakadi began to twitch, then to jerk violently, and finally to shrink. Moments later everyone could see Ehomba, standing with sword in hand, inhaling and inhaling without seemingly pausing to breathe. Into his open mouth the eromakadi disappeared, sucked down like steam from a kettle traveling in reverse, until the last frantic, faintly mewling black tendril had been swallowed.

Without word or comment of any kind, an Ehomba none the apparent worse for the experience resumed his assault on the dais.

"An eromakasi!" Balling one hand into a fist, a surprised Hymneth raged at the onrushing herdsman. "What have you done with my pets, eromakasi?" Flinging his closed, armored hand forward, the Possessed opened his fingers the instant his arm was fully extended.

Ball lightning flew at Ehomba. It was olive green in hue and crackled with energy. Raising his blade, the herdsman parried the verdant globe. Deafening thunder rattled the reception hall. Simna and the others were momentarily blinded by the shower of green sparks that flew from the sky-metal sword.

Even as Ehomba was opposing this latest assault, the lofty figure seething before the throne of Ehl-Larimar was readying another. Hymneth continued to fling spheres of sickly green energy at his attacker as the herdsman persistently warded them off. In this manner Ehomba, though his approach was slowed by the need to fight off the tall sorcerer's successive attacks, sustained his advance on the throne. As he drew nearer, the ball lightning flew more often. Employing reflexes honed from years of fighting off predators intent on stealing from the Naumkib flocks, he struck down one blazing assault after another. The frenzy of emerald sparks that struck from his untiring blade outshone the far more subdued glow of the chamber's lamps.

Swinging the sword in short, deliberate arcs, he gained the first step, and then the second. If Hymneth the Possessed was growing anxious or uneasy, the evidence of such a condition remained his and his alone. His face remained hidden behind the magnificent helmet. His defense was as unremitting and incessant as Ehomba's advance, and he showed no sign of weakening or abandoning his position before the throne.

Surmounting the last step, Ehomba batted aside a lethal, crackling globe half his size and was swallowed up by the consequent deluge of rabid green sparks and shattered shafts of lightning. Emerging from this cataract of emerald energy, he brought his blade around in a low feint, then swung it up over his head and brought it straight down, edge on, with both hands. Hymneth the Possessed, Lord of Ehl-Larimar, was in the process of throwing another orb of lightning when he saw or sensed what his attacker intended. Quickly raising both mailed arms over his head, he crossed his wrists and caught the descending sword in the Vee they formed.

Green and white sparks erupted from the point of contact and the concussive wave thus generated knocked Peregriff, the Visioness Themaryl, and Simna ibn Sind off their feet. Only the larger and more powerful Ahlitah and Hunkapa Aub were able to remain standing, and even they were staggered by the force of the detonation.

When Simna's vision cleared and he could once again discern the drama being played out in front of the throne, a loss of feeling and belief gripped him the likes of which he had never experienced before, not even when as a child he had been cruelly assaulted by his peers. As receding thunderclaps rolled through the chamber and off into the distance, he saw the remnants of the shattered skymetal sword lying scattered everywhere: on the steps leading up to the dais, on the floor, on the throne itself. Stare at them as he might, they did not slowly revive, did not become dozens or hundreds of new, smaller blades as they had in far Skawpane. They had been smashed into ragged shards and strips of twisted steel, like the vulnerable metal of any common sword.

At the foot of the steps lay a crumpled, motionless figure.

"Etjole!" Heedless of whatever the domineering, armored figure commanding the dais might do, the

swordsman rushed forward. Hunkapa Aub and the black litah were right behind him.

Throwing himself on the prone torso, Simna used both hands to wrench the valiant herdsman over onto his back. Ehomba's eyes were closed and his body limp. There hung about him a sharp, acrid smell, as if he had been singed by something as lethal as it was invisible. The swordsman shook the smooth, lean shoulders; gently at first, then more forcefully.

"Etjole! Bruther!" To his frantic entreaties there was no response. Pressing an ear to the herdsman's chest, Simna's eyes grew wide as he detected no sound from within. Hastily moistening a palm, he held it in front of the herdsman's unmoving lips. Nothing cooled his skin.

"It can't be." He drew back from the motionless body. *"It can't be."*

Dipping his maned head low over the prostrate form, Ahlitah listened and sniffed once, twice. Then yellow eyes rose, flicking first in the direction of Hymneth the Possessed, then meeting those of the stricken swordsman.

"It's over, Simna. He's dead. The herder of cattle is dead."

And he was.

5